ABOUT THE AUTHOR

At home in Surrey, JULIET ASHTON writes all day in her small study while her two dogs stare at her. The rest of her house, which is full of music and books and comfy places to sit, she shares with her thirteen-year-old daughter and her husband, who's a composer (hence the music). She believes wholeheartedly in the power of books to improve lives, increase understanding and while away happy hours.

Praise for Juliet Ashton:

'Funny, original and wise' **Katie Fforde**

'Gloriously and irresistibly romantic . . . It's like *One Day* with all the additional trials and tribulations of female friendship' **Hannah Beckerman**

'Warm, witty and surprising' **Louise Candlish**

'This brilliantly written and captivating story instantly drew us in and refused to let go. Fresh, funny and utterly fabulous, it's the perfect holiday read' *Heat*

'Cecelia Ahern fans will love this poignant yet witty romance' *Sunday Mirror*

'You'll laugh and cry your way through this original and touching love story' *Closer*

Also by Juliet Ashton

The Valentine's Card
These Days of Ours
The Woman at Number 24

THE SUNDAY LUNCH CLUB

JULIET ASHTON

SIMON &
SCHUSTER

London · New York · Sydney · Toronto · New Delhi

A CBS COMPANY

First published in Great Britain by Simon & Schuster UK Ltd, 2018
A CBS COMPANY

Copyright © Juliet Ashton, 2018

3 5 7 9 10 8 6 4

Simon & Schuster UK Ltd
1st Floor
222 Gray's Inn Road
London WC1X 8HB

Simon & Schuster Australia, Sydney
Simon & Schuster India, New Delhi

www.simonandschuster.co.uk
www.simonandschuster.com.au
www.simonandschuster.co.in

A CIP catalogue record for this book
is available from the British Library

Paperback ISBN: 978-1-4711-6838-3
eBook ISBN: 978-1-4711-6839-0

Typeset in Bembo by M Rules
Printed and bound by CPI Group (UK) Ltd, Croydon, CR0 4YY

Simon & Schuster UK Ltd are committed to sourcing paper
that is made from wood grown in sustainable forests and support the Forest
Stewardship Council, the leading international forest certification organisation.
Our books displaying the FSC logo are printed on FSC certified paper.

This book is for Sonia Lopez-Freire
with love and thanks

No hay mejor hermano que
un buen vecino al lado

Prologue

Lunch at Thea's

VOL-AU-VENTS

COD BAKED IN FOIL

STICKY TOFFEE PUDDING

Everything – but everything – had changed.

The cutlery Thea laid out was old and well handled. Mellowed by years of lunches and dinners, it enhanced the flat's eccentric blend of old-fashioned cosiness and hipster style. She picked up a dessert spoon, felt its weight as it balanced on her finger, then set it down again, just so.

The table looked perfect, even if she did say so herself. Not showy, not styled, yet welcoming and beautiful and thought about. She thought deeply about things, this slender woman with the carefully done nails and the well-cut dress in cornflower blue. She bent down to tweak the clean blanket she'd laid over the cat bed, amused at herself for such Mad Housewife attention to detail. This was *not* her usual style.

The doorbell rang.

Thea froze. Had she bitten off more than she could chew? Inside these walls she was safe. When that door opened, the world would flood in, dabbing its fingerprints all over her safe place.

An old fear was exhumed; she could lose everything.

Thea looked at the door to the garden. She could open it, race out, hurdle the low fence, leave the bell ringing and the cod in the fridge and the wine unopened. Each guest was a friend, but what would they make of her? Would they find her odd, exotic, *alien*? Or would they recognise her for what she was?

A quote from a wise old woman popped into her head. 'Your soul never changes,' murmured Thea, taking one last appraising look around as the doorbell repeated itself, churlish this time.

If she'd forgotten anything, it was too late to do a damn thing about it. Thea pushed a strand of hair behind her ear, cleared her throat, gave herself a last searching look in the hall mirror and opened the door.

It was time.

Chapter One

Lunch at Anna's

NIBBLY BITS
ROAST BEEF WITH ALL THE TRIMMINGS/
NUT ROAST
STRAWBERRIES AND CREAM

The Sunday Lunch Club wasn't a proper club.

There were no membership fees, or laminated passes, or rules. It was an ad hoc get-together for the Piper family plus any stray friends or lovers or pets who happened to be kicking around. Sometimes the club sat down together twice a month, sometimes every week; at other times, they forgot about it for weeks on end.

It had started when Anna's parents moved to Florida. There'd been a big send-off, when her mother had served one of 'her' roasts in the conservatory of the family home out in the suburbs. It had been emotional, saying goodbye to the bricks and mortar the four brothers and sisters grew up in. A mass of memories, some good, others bad and one decidedly ugly, had crowded the table alongside the beef and vertiginous yorkies and gravy thick enough to walk across.

They'd realised, as they chewed and drank and argued and laughed, that there'd be no more roasts after Mum left. That was a solemn moment; everybody put down their forks, and in that moment the Sunday Lunch Club was born.

Not that they ate a roast every time. Only Anna could be bothered to undertake the multiple tasks and meticulous time management involved. Anna's roomy conscience put her forward to be keeper of the flame. Sunday lunch had to be perfect, it had to be complete; if there was no horseradish sauce on the table she went to bed in a funk.

Furthermore, there had to be both freshly grated horseradish *and* the supermarket version. Her older brother, who jumped on every passing foodie bandwagon, insisted on the real thing, but her ex-husband said the shop-bought sauce reminded him of his childhood.

There is so much more to roast beef than mere lunch.

Each roast carries echoes of all the roasts that went before. No two gravy recipes are the same. Some families insist on peas; others stage a mutiny if a carrot is involved. A Sunday roast is a comfort blanket made of meat, a link to the past, a reassurance that not everything changes.

Anna understood this, and took everybody's preferences into account. That's why she had to conjure up not only a perfectly cooked joint – rare in the middle, crusty at the edges – but also roast potatoes, mashed potatoes, peas, carrots, Yorkshire puddings both large and small, red wine gravy, gravy from granules, roast parsnips, plus a nut roast.

The kitchen was smallish and imperfectly formed, but there was room for a sofa, and it was improved by the view of Anna's small garden. Mostly paved, the pots loitering around its edge were beginning to wake up. April toyed with them, blowing hot and cold. The sleek lines of the modern garden studio were incongruous among the trellises and benches; it was newly built, a testament to her confidence in Artem Accessories, the business she'd started with Sam. They spent more time in there together than they ever had done during their marriage.

She consulted her spreadsheet. Time to make the batter.

Flour. Eggs. Milk. The comforting, timeless sound of a fork beating plain ingredients in a bowl. Anna decanted the pale sludge into a jug and put it in the fridge. Why, she didn't know; she did it because that was how Dinkie, her grandmother, had always done it.

She turned to the table. Extended, it took up almost the whole of the kitchen floor space. Anna liked to pretend she was indifferent to the style of the table setting, saying loudly that it was the food and the company that mattered. However, the previous lunch, a sumptuous catered affair at her brother's house, was a hard act to follow. Anna felt the pressure, and had splurged on napkin rings.

Then she'd had to buy napkins; her paper ones looked foolish in their new wooden coats. Anna tweaked the flowers, regretting her decision to put them in a glass vase. She hustled them into a jug. Then, no, that didn't look right either, and she shoved them back into the vase. By which time they looked as droopy as she felt.

However often Anna 'entertained', there was always this moment before the first arrival when everything looked wrong. When the battered chairs morphed from shabby chic to plain shabby, and the tablecloth showed its age. It was too late to start again. Too late to re-set the table in her usual slapdash way. Too late to scale back her ambitious menu. Too late to dismantle the updo that now looked overdone and fussy when she checked herself out in the chrome of the built-in oven.

She looked so young in the fuzzy reflection. Her hair looked naturally blonde instead of L'Oréal Sweet Honey, and her eyes glinted greenishly in a pale oval face with not a line to commemorate the hurly-burly of forty years on earth. She'd inherited her mother's tendency to puffy under-eyes; the more truthful hall mirror told a different story. Still,

Anna had long ago made peace with her looks – so-so on a bad day, ramping up to yummy if an effort was made.

Life was a compromise between aspirations and reality. She let go of all her misgivings about the table setting, about the size of the joint, about whether or not the place cards that had seemed so cute when she'd written them were actually pretentious.

Anna took in a deep breath (through the nose? Or the mouth? She could never remember her Pilates teacher's instructions) and let go of all, or almost all, her anxieties. She still cared that her guests had a good time and left feeling nourished; she no longer cared whether or not she impressed them.

Which, she thought, looking at the misspelling on the nearest place card, *is just as well*.

The room filled up. Coats were handed to Anna or dumped on the sagging sofa. Bottles were pressed on her, her cheek was kissed, a gift of champagne truffles was oohed over.

Somebody – probably Neil, the oldest of the four siblings and the one who liked to impress himself on a room – had opened the glass doors to the garden, and the straggly spring sun exposed the neglected pots and an Ikea bookcase she'd dismembered weeks before.

'God, olives, I *love* olives,' whooped her sister. Maeve scooped up a handful and stuffed them all in her mouth, unaware they were artisan olives and their price had made Anna's hair stand on end. 'Did you do me a veggie option?'

'Don't I always?' Even though Maeve's vegetarianism was the shaky sort, easily derailed by the whiff of a bacon sandwich, Anna always made sure to dip into her cookbooks and come up with something that rivalled the mighty roast.

'Somebody,' said Santiago, sidling up to Anna who was pouring Prosecco and worrying whether she'd bought enough, 'has done a poo-poo.'

'Who?' asked Anna and they both laughed. She was grateful to the God of In-Laws for sending her Santiago. Decorative, playful, very very Spanish, his light touch brought out her own inner child. 'I bet,' she said, leaning down to the baby in his arms, 'it was you, wasn't it?'

At three and a half months old, Paloma was all pink and white innocence, blue eyes huge in her chubby face. She was everybody's pet, everybody's favourite, the Piper family's new toy. 'Take her up to my room, Santi,' said Anna. 'There's more space to lay out the changing mat.'

She watched him go.

'I know what you're thinking.' Neil appeared, nudging her. 'You're thinking what a great bum. A ten out of ten, A1, classic of its kind. Santi's bum is more or less why I married him.'

Anna nudged him back. 'Actually, I was thinking what an incredible dad he is. Even though he's so young.'

'Is that a dig at me?' Neil took offence as easily as he took in air. 'I was young once, you know. It's not a skill. Anybody can do it. And Santi's not *that* young. He's twenty-four.'

'Or, to put it another way, two decades younger than you.'

'Don't remind me. In some ways it's lovely having an Adonis beside you in bed every night. But in others . . .' Neil pulled in his tummy and put a hand to his hairline. He whispered, 'It reminds you of what a fat old has-been you are.'

'You're only forty-four!' A mere four years behind her brother, Anna hated it when he lamented his age. She preferred to strenuously believe the magazine articles that told her forty was the new thirty. She'd always felt older than her years; when Anna looked back over her teens they weren't the sunlit beach scenes of other people's youth. With their parents out of the country so much, she'd been a mini-mummy to the younger siblings. Anna and Neil had been born close together. Seven years later, Maeve had come along, then Josh. There'd always been a 'them and us' feel; Anna and Neil still felt vaguely responsible for Maeve and Josh.

'I'm forty-four in *human* years,' said Neil. 'In gay years I'm a thousand and one.' He tutted at the breadstick in his hand. 'Why are your nibbles always so samey?'

'Samey?' Anna was insulted. 'It's tradition, you oaf.'

'Nothing traditional about rocking up to the same old hummus and olives and tzat-bloody-ziki for years on end.'

Neil was extra-arch today. 'And when are we eating? I'm starving.'

'When it's ready.' Anna took off with the tray of Prosecco.

The L-shaped kitchen and family room had been one of the reasons she'd bought the small Victorian semi in a terrace of similarly neat homes near the park, but the open-plan layout was a disadvantage when she hosted the lunch club. There was no escaping the lunchers' endless neediness; they regressed to toddlers as they walked through the door, unable to pour liquid for themselves, all drooling with hunger. *No*, she thought, *not toddlers*. They were baby birds, their beaks open, their squawks filling the air. She imagined herself chucking worms into their open gobs, and Sam heard her giggle.

He was in his chair. Or rather, what used to be his chair when they were married. Six years after the divorce, Sam still colonised the frayed blue velvet cushions whenever he visited, long legs stuck out in a potential trip hazard.

Sitting back, he parroted her giggle. Sam was tall, sturdy, an oak, with low-key colouring stolen from nature – eyes a soft hazel, hair a difficult to describe medley of blond and brown. Like the oak, Sam was calm. Another metaphor Anna favoured was the iceberg; not because Sam was cold – far from it – but because he kept so much of himself hidden. To the world at large, Sam was tranquil, but ten years of marriage had taught Anna how to recognise the giveaways that hinted at inner turmoil. Today he was serene, already a touch tipsy; Sam had no capacity for booze.

A fixture in Anna's life, these days her ex-husband was a cheerleader for her love affairs, such as they were. The latest one had crashed in flames some time ago. Sam had listened to each twist and turn, given advice, consoled her and boosted her confidence. As Anna had said, he'd been almost as good as a woman at all those things.

He seemed to have sworn off relationships. *Perhaps our marriage vaccinated him against romance*, thought Anna, as he took a glass from her tray and said, 'You look nice.'

He said it as if it was unusual. 'Do I?'

'Yeah,' agreed Maeve, snaffling a glass and leaning into Anna's face. 'Your skin's all glowy and your eyes are sparkly. Ooh! You naughty girl! You've been having ess ee ex!'

The boy at Maeve's side, thirteen years old with skin the colour of toffee, winced. 'Mum, for God's sake!'

'That's how Dinkie used to say it. So we wouldn't understand. Ess ee ex!' repeated Maeve, with relish. Their Irish grandmother, often quoted, was an occasional member of the lunch club. 'Who's the lucky guy?'

Anna hurried back to the oven, ignoring their laughter, hoping none of them noticed the blush that crept up her neck. Pretending to check on the beef, she had a vivid flashback.

A utility room. White goods. A Kenwood stand mixer.

Herself up against a fridge–freezer, frenzied, forgetting her own name as a man pounded his body against hers. She'd held out a hand to steady herself and pushed over a litre bottle of fabric conditioner. Neither of them noticed.

Anna stole a look back at the others. Only Sam looked her way. He winked. *He saw the blush all right.* Anna knocked over a salt cellar, righted it again, and was grateful for the chirrup of her mobile.

'Ah,' she said, reading the text. 'Guys! Josh can't make it.'

'What's the excuse this time?' Neil was sardonic.

'He's got something on.' The text had been more precise: *I can't face it, Sis.* As usual, Anna let him off the hook. Although twenty-nine years old, Josh would always be the baby of the family. 'I spoke to him during the week.'

'How'd he sound?' Neil's attempted nonchalance didn't convince. They all worried about Josh.

'Great. He sounded great,' lied Anna.

'Uncle Josh *never* comes.' Storm's mouth turned down.

'Shush, you,' said Maeve gently. There was an unwritten rule not to criticise Josh. Using a family telepathy, they all agreed that he'd been born with thinner skin. He felt knocks more harshly. Took setbacks more personally.

'He promised to come to the next Sunday Lunch Club,' said Anna. Another lie, but one she'd try to convert into a truth.

*

Paloma, whose manners were as exquisite as her face, slept in her carrycot all through the main course, missing the compliments for the beef.

'Even nicer than Dinkie's.' Neil verged on blasphemy.

'My carrots were a bit hard,' said Maeve.

'Yet you bravely managed to eat them all,' Anna pointed out. 'Do you want to let that course go down before I do dessert?'

They all groaned their agreement. Waistbands were discreetly undone. Neil had the look of a man regretting that last roast potato.

'I haven't been this full,' he said, 'since the last time we all got together, at Paloma's Welcome Home lunch.' He was red in the face, as if he'd been doing hard manual labour rather than stuffing his face.

'What was that stew thing we had?' asked Maeve, emptying a bottle into her glass and waggling it at Anna, who understood the code and stood up to fetch another.

'Basque lamb.' Neil closed his eyes in bliss. 'Santi's mum's recipe.'

'That was an *amazeballs* day,' said Storm, who'd barely spoken throughout the meal, his tidy Afro bent over his food.

The last club meeting had been a triumphant finale to Neil and Santiago's efforts to adopt a child. They'd persevered for over two years, tackling every hurdle in their path. At times the process had seemed never-ending. Anna saw first-hand how they perked up with each breakthrough only to wilt when they were knocked back again. Then all the stars had aligned and the impossible had happened.

Or rather, Paloma had happened.

Despite the fact that Neil and Santiago were willing to take a child of any age, they were in the right place at the right time to adopt a newborn. At ten weeks old, Paloma had still been a dot in a nappy. She would never be able to remember her life before she entered the cocoon of care and love that the Pipers wove around her. Anna found that poignant; Paloma aroused a miscellany of emotions and feelings that took her by surprise. She saw something in the baby's round eyes, a question that reverberated through her body.

'Come on, Paloma!' Maeve reached down and plucked the baby out of her opulently dressed crib. The others exchanged glances. Maeve was an impulsive creature who lived in the moment, which often had an adverse effect on the next moment. Inevitably, Paloma woke up and began to squall.

'Aw! Wassamatter?' cooed Maeve, her wild brown hair falling over the baby, her free hand reaching for her glass.

'The matter is the poor kid was fast asleep and now she's not,' said Anna.

'Your Auntie Anna's a gwouch, isn't she?' baby-talked Maeve. 'Yes she is!' she squealed, wine furring the edge of her diction.

'Mum,' said Storm, without looking up from his phone, surreptitiously spirited onto his lap under cover of the table-cloth. 'Don't.'

'We're surrounded by spoilsports, Paloma-woma.' Maeve sank the rest of her drink as Neil harrumphed loudly at this use of an unauthorised nickname for his new daughter. 'Your daddy disapproves of me, and my own son has all the pizzazz of a bank manager.' She reached out to ruffle her boy's hair. 'Where did I go right?'

Ducking away from her, Storm asked, 'What's for afters?'

'Strawberries and cream.' Anna usually resorted to this crowd-pleaser.

'Strawberries are out of season,' complained Maeve.

'So shoot me.' Anna wasn't in the mood for one of Maeve's rants about organic, allergen-free, low-air-miles eating.

'They probably came all the way from Morocco,' sighed Maeve as the big glass dish of ripe red fruit was placed in the middle of the table and everybody leaned in.

'Don't eat them, then,' murmured Neil.

'It'd be wrong to waste them,' said Maeve piously.

Another shared look ran around the Sunday Lunch Club.

'And before you ask,' said Anna, setting down a jug she'd found in a charity shop, 'the cream is from a cow I know personally.'

Maeve looked up, wide-eyed, before bursting into laughter. She believed anything after her third Prosecco.

'Let's make sure Dinkie comes to the next lunch,' said Santiago, holding out his bowl. 'I miss her.' *I mith her.* His English was fluent, but prettified by his accent.

'She seems to be settling in at the home,' said Neil, tossing a strawberry at Storm.

'Don't call it that!' mewled Maeve.

'It's a retirement complex.' Anna quelled Neil with a look. The old habit of talking over the younger siblings' heads died hard.

'It's like battery farming, but with old dears instead of chickens,' said Neil, evidently enjoying the consternation this caused.

'It's a lovely place!' said Maeve, who hadn't set foot in it.

'She's with people her own age,' said Anna uncertainly.

'Exactly. Since when did Dinkie want to be surrounded by *old people*?' said Neil.

'We discussed this.' Anna was quiet, firm. 'She couldn't live on her own any more and—'

'Yeah yeah,' said Neil. 'It's for the best, but ... you know ...'

They did. They knew. They knew that the Sunville communal areas smelled of cabbage. They knew how rabidly proud their minuscule grandmother was.

Sam said, 'It's not easy, but you all did the right thing.'

He sounded so sane that Anna wanted to believe him. That was the voice he'd used back when she'd wake in the night. He'd dry her tears, talk her round, hold her until she dropped off again. Now when she woke up in the night, she was alone with her thoughts. Sometimes they won and Anna had to drag herself out of bed to make the milky drink prescribed at such times.

A strawberry stopped en route to Anna's mouth as something struck her. Would she ever sleep beside a man again? Not for a night or two, but for years on end, with him making a familiar shape in the dark. It wasn't just sex that made a marital bed special; Anna recalled the braided limbs, the snug warmth of it all. The synchronised turnings. The churned pillows. The bed as fortress. *Us against the world.*

She looked at Sam, who was licking cream off his finger. He used to say that. It used to be true. Funny that Anna could miss some ingredients of their marriage so intensely, yet be relieved to have escaped it.

'Storm's started Japanese at school, did I tell you?' Maeve bunched her lips like that when something made her especially happy. Her freckles made a dot-to-dot of joy. 'Don't be embarrassed, sweetie!' She seemed devilishly pleased at seeing her clever son cringe in his Adidas top. 'Only five boys in his year are doing it.'

'*Pantsu*,' said Santi suddenly.

'Eh?' Neil stared at him. 'Steady on, Santi. *I'm* the brains, darling. You're the beauty. You can't speak Japanese!'

17

'That's all I can say,' admitted Santi, dimples deepening. 'I learned it when I was a waiter. It means hello.'

'Err, no it doesn't, Uncle Santi.' Storm pulled a face. 'It means knickers.'

Santi covered his face with his hands, bowing in the face of the laughter. 'I say it to every Japanese person I meet!'

Standing to collect the plates, Anna paused. Her mind skipped back to an earlier topic, worrying at it, trying to shake something loose. 'Um, how long ago was that lunch for Paloma? A month?'

'Four weeks exactly.' Santiago's Moorish dark eyes glittered nostalgically; he was a sentimental soul. 'I'll never forget the day we introduced our *niña* to the family.'

'Hear hear.' Sam's face creased into a smile. 'I got smashed. Remember the cocktail guy?'

'And the chocolate fountain,' said Storm.

'And the amuse-bouche-y things,' said Maeve. 'Actually,' she said, looking into the middle distance, 'that cocktail waiter was bloody gorgeous.'

'I auditioned him myself,' said Neil.

'Don't do that,' said Santiago under his breath.

'Don't do what?' Neil's brows drew together, two peeved beetles.

'Don't be all camp.' Santiago stood up, and crossed to the glass door to the garden. He pulled it closed, and stared out at the darkening afternoon. Nobody had complained of the cold. It was Santiago's way of avoiding a row.

Neil watched him, but changed the subject. 'It *was* a marvellous do. Even though some naughty person spilled fabric conditioner all over the laundry basket and didn't own up.'

The naughty person was otherwise engaged, thought Anna, scraping leftovers into the bin. She wasn't the sort of person who had enthusiastic sex in utility rooms during the cheese course. *Except, apparently, I'm exactly that sort of person*, she thought, not entirely displeased with this version of herself. She set down the stack of plates and said, 'Just popping out, folks. I need to get milk for the coffee.'

The corner shop sold everything. Ketchup. Tissues. Horrible porn. It would certainly have milk, but Anna kept walking.

She was rushing, but not because she was in a hurry to get back. She was on the run from a mounting suspicion. However fast she strode, it kept pace with her. When she pushed at the door of the chemist on the parade, it was right there at her side. Anna bought what she needed, and secreted the package in the bottom of her bag, as if it was contraband.

'There's milk in the fridge!' called Sam as Anna whirled back down her own narrow hallway. He held it up, triumphant.

'Silly me.' Anna pushed past him, tearing off her mac. 'Right. Who's for coffee?'

'I'll have—' started Maeve.

'Your stupid organic whatsit tea, yes I know.' Anna set down a tray with a slam, then banged down cups. Much as she loved her ragbag of visitors, she needed them gone; this laid-back Sunday suddenly had an urgent agenda.

'Whose go is it to cook next?' Sam was saying as he followed her back to the table with the truffles Neil had brought.

'Yours.' The fringes on Maeve's cheesecloth sleeve were damp from trailing in her lunch. 'Don't forget I'm vegetarian.'

'My darling Maeve,' said Neil, 'nobody could ever forget you're a vegetarian.' He had scant patience with his little sister's constant reaffirmation of her various 'ism's. 'You say it once an hour, on the hour.'

'But you love me for it.' Maeve was utterly confident of her place in the world, of the protection of her family, of her welcome everywhere.

'I do,' said Neil, 'but then I bloody have to, don't I, you pest?'

'I can't promise anything as spectacular as Neil and Santiago's "do",' said Sam. He held Anna's gaze for a moment. 'There'll be no fabric conditioner spilled.'

She coughed, looked away, longed to root through her bag and get out her purchase. *Why won't they all go home?*

Neil stood, and hope fluttered in Anna's heart that the others would follow suit.

They didn't.

'Let's break out the Trivial Pursuit,' he said.

All the booze in the house had been drunk. Maeve had scampered to the corner shop for fresh supplies. They'd gravitated to the front room, strewn themselves over the sofas that faced each other, the board game forgotten.

It was Anna's own fault. Her comfortable, untidy house was too welcoming. It invited every stray to make itself at home. Anna's lunches were notorious for carrying on until nightfall; there was always one more cup of coffee to be had, one more strange liqueur from the back of the cupboard, one more scurrilous story. Today she didn't bask in any hostess glory. Instead she cleared up as loudly as she could, slamming drawers as she put away dishes, even starting up the vacuum cleaner.

Nobody budged.

In fact, as she loitered in the hallway, she heard Maeve ask Sam the dreaded question: 'How've you been?'

Anna slumped against the coat stand, letting out a tiny groan.

'Well,' said Sam. 'Funny you should ask. My leg hurts when I do this.'

Evidently, in the sitting room, Sam did whatever 'this' was. They were in for a long sermon; Sam's health was Sam's favourite topic. Like many hypochondriacs, he was absurdly healthy, yet every twinge and cough sent him rushing off to the internet to research his symptoms.

'Then, of course,' he went on to his captive audience, 'there's that rash on my elbow. God knows what that is.'

Anna wanted to shout, *It's a rash!* but she knew from long experience that once Sam found his groove he was impossible to deflect.

Unable to wait any longer, she stole upstairs. Anna needed her fears disproved, her silly imaginings dismissed. The manoeuvre with the tiny plastic paddle wasn't one she'd ever done before; there was a knack to it. She washed her hands and sat and waited, forcing herself to look around the bathroom instead of down at the stick.

The room needed some TLC. There was a cracked tile in the shower. The tap wobbled. She'd get round to it. The house was an endless work in progress, like life. Anna whistled. Then she hummed. Then she tapped her foot. Then she gave in and looked down.

The anonymous plastic wand had big news.

Babies were a closed door for Anna. A no-no. Something that happened to other people. Ten years of marriage had produced no close shave, no near miss. She'd never discussed baby names with Sam, never wondered if their spare room would make a good nursery. Parenthood was a roped-off area.

Like a sleepwalker, Anna plodded down the stairs and headed to the garden, where she drew in deep lungfuls of chilled air.

Wrapping her arms around her body, Anna gave herself a sharp talking-to. This news was too enormous to take in at one bite; she would break it down later, when she was alone. She must hold it together until everybody left.

If they ever did.

Maeve was rustling up more tea in the kitchen, Storm 'helping', if pretending to look for a teapot while staring at his phone could be described that way. 'We're on to Sam's diabetes,' she said cheerfully, her head in the fridge.

'He hasn't got diabetes.' Anna said it so crabbily that Maeve bobbed up over the fridge door to stare at her.

'God, OK,' she said. 'Give him a break.'

Anna didn't want to 'go there' with her sister. One of Maeve's pet theories was that Anna had been crazy to let Sam go. She was all the more emphatic about this when she'd been drinking, saying stuff like, *One day you'll realise and it'll be too late*. 'Sam's the healthiest person I know,' said Anna, taking care to sound less gruff. 'He'll outlive us all.'

'I reckon he misses y—'

'Here, let me.' The sooner Anna made the tea, the sooner they'd all go home.

Anna barely heard the goodbyes, or registered the hugs. Sam was last to leave. When he held her she, clung to him, until he pulled away with a concerned frown.

'Anna?'

'I . . .' She could tell him right now. No messing about. She could say it out loud. Watch his expression. 'Headache.' Anna tapped her forehead.

'Ouch.' Sam looked sympathetic. 'Poor you.'

Poor us, actually. Anna had a stowaway.

The house was quiet again, that special Sunday evening calm. Anna drifted about her home like a ghost.

A baby. The great unmentionable between her and Sam. She'd tidied away the notion, accepted she was different. *I'm not meant to be a mother.* Anna looked down at her body, wondering why it had played such an elaborate practical joke after all those years of doing her bidding.

In bed that night, facing the small hours and still wakeful, Anna's weariness stripped away the jumbled fears and laid bare the real question.

How do I feel about this baby?

Bone-tired, worn out with the effort of predicting the million things that could go wrong, she answered simply, without deliberating.

I love you, she thought.

Chapter Two

Lunch at Sam's

GOAT'S CHEESE TARTLET
BEEF WELLINGTON/
SPINACH AND BLUE CHEESE EN CROUTE
NUTELLA CHEESECAKE

Anna almost backed out of the next Sunday Lunch Club. When she woke that morning, a name she never said out loud was on her lips.

Bonnie.

She rarely dreamed of Bonnie, and what she'd done to her. The pregnancy stirred Anna's brain like a stew, sending all sorts of gristle to the surface. Snatches of the dream tugged at Anna, but as the morning passed, the dream lost its power, so she did something to her hair, dashed a lipstick over her lips, and propelled herself outside into the indecisive May weather.

The modern low-rise block was square and neat, surrounded by clipped gardens and mature trees that made it easy to forget the noisy main road. Sam lived on the ground floor, in the boxy flat he'd bought after the divorce. Even though the split was amicable, the usual resentments had bubbled beneath the surface and it had taken two years for Sam and Anna to speak to each other without conversation turning bitterly to how the CDs had been divided up. Both of them had been relieved to move on from that stage and become what most people agreed they were destined to be; not partners, but best mates.

Meandering up the concrete path, Anna slowed as she neared the door. Trees hung damply over the lawn, and the flats seemed to sink into the mulch. It had rained for three days straight, and the path was pockmarked with dark patches yet to dry.

In the five weeks since the last meeting of the Club, Anna had barely seen Sam. She was accustomed to spending every working day with him in the glorified shed, working hard at Artem Accessories, but he'd been out of the country, visiting their factory in Romania, schmoozing a new client in New York. Their day-long chats had been replaced by snatched minutes on Skype. Time differences meant he was bright-eyed and bushy-tailed as she was inserting herself under her duvet.

Anna wasn't complaining; Sam's globetrotting was a by-product of Artem's success. The company had turned a corner and could finally afford to employ them both full-time. She was doing what she'd dreamed of during her years down the salt mines of a large department store, designing fussy hand-bags for mothers of the bride. Artem was a carefully curated selection of timeless yet modern, fastidiously crafted leather handbags and purses. When Selfridges had placed a big order, she and Sam had got drunker than they'd ever been before, only to find that Bloomingdale's in New York was also keen to stock their deep red, true blue and Arctic white handbags.

Hence Sam's flitting around, and hence Anna's secret still being exactly that – a secret.

Hands in pockets, Anna stared at Sam's windows, barely noticing the crocuses and daffodils nodding a hello from the flower beds. It was time to come clean. Today she'd make a man a father.

Whether he liked it or not.

The doorbell made a tinny noise. A shape grew behind the dimpled glass of the front door. Anna prepared herself to speak as soon as Sam opened up.

'You must be the famous Anna!' The shape wasn't Sam. It was a woman, about Anna's age, her streaked hair loose, her belted dress casual but classy.

'I am I suppose.' Anna took a step back. 'You are ...?'

Sam's face appeared over the stranger's shoulder. He seemed to be lit from within by a thousand-watt bulb. 'She's Isabel.' He kissed the woman's cheek. '*My* Isabel.'

'Oh stop it, you!' laughed *his* Isabel.

'Yeah, stop it, you,' echoed Anna, feeling ambushed as she brandished the mandatory bottle. 'This ...' – she pointed first at one of them, then the other – 'is a surprise.'

Sam threw her a briefly questioning look, as if he'd heard the edge Anna was unable to keep out of her voice.

'We speak every day, you see.' Anna turned to Isabel, who had welded herself to Sam. 'He didn't mention you.' She saw Isabel wince, pull away from Sam, only for him to tug her back into position.

'I could have told you,' said Sam. 'God knows I wanted to, but I decided to keep it to myself for a while. Until I knew Isabel was as keen on me as I am on her.' Sam jiggled the woman's shoulder, mock-fearful. 'You are, aren't you?'

'God yes!'

Sam beamed. 'Just checking.'

The couple's meet-cute was described, but Anna barely heard the tale of them reaching for the same bottle of bleach in the minimart. She was reeling inwardly, and wondering why she was reeling inwardly. This man was not her property. Once she'd had the right to police his private life, but now Sam was allowed to have lady friends.

'That's nice,' she said absently, hanging her jacket up under the stairs. In the six years since the divorce, Sam hadn't been on a single date. He'd always been available, *there*. 'Has Sam taken you to see the lifeboat station at Southwold yet, Isabel?' His geeky love for lifeboats was a standing joke.

'He didn't have to.' Isabel's nose crinkled, and Anna had time to notice how perfect that nose was, and to feel suddenly that her own nose was a mallet made of flesh. 'I'm a member of the Southwold Lifeboat Society.'

'She's been to Southwold more than I have!' Sam seemed ready to burst with joy at this evidence of their 'rightness' for each other.

Anna sat on the burnt-orange sofa. A cat leapt onto her lap, his motorbike purr drowning out the lovebirds clattering pans in the kitchen. 'Caruso – hello, my darling.' She scratched the creature under his chin. Sam got custody of Caruso in the divorce. Stroking his sleek stripes was like going back in time. 'I wanted to tell him about you-know-what,' she whispered into the cat's soft ear. 'Your master always did have terrible timing.'

Anna loved what she still thought of as Sam's 'new' flat. A few minutes' walk from her place, it was manageable, rather bare, pleasingly masculine. The clean lines of the nineteen sixties architecture were complemented by the mid-century furniture. A spindly-legged black coffee table sat by the vinyl sofa, knowingly kitsch artwork hung on the white walls.

After living with Anna's clutter — she left a wake of tissues and make-up and paperbacks wherever she went — Sam kept things minimal.

'A mojito for the lady.' Sam entered with a glass on a tray.

'Mojito?' said Anna. 'You normally have to run out for Blue Nun when you host lunch.'

'Isabel's in charge today.'

'I'll pass, thanks.' Anna was taking the pregnancy guidelines seriously. 'Got any juice?'

'Eh?' Sam looked dumbfounded. 'Jesus, don't tell me you're dieting again.'

'Just trying to cut down.' Anna looked up at her ex-husband in his omnipresent jeans, his hair shaggy, trendy new glasses drop-kicking him into line with fashion at last.

'So, what d'you think of her?' hissed Sam, cocking his head towards the serving hatch. 'Isn't she great?'

'She's lovely,' said Anna, truthfully. Isabel was wholesome, fresh, like a dollop of cream on a slice of apple pie. 'She's not really your type.'

'She's *exactly* my type.' Sam was amused by this nonsense. 'It's as if she was made especially for me.'

Anna had thought that *she* was Sam's type. She felt him wait avidly for her to say something positive. 'She seems very very nice. Lovely hair. And shoes.' Normally a bottomless well of positivity, Anna struggled to be generous. She blamed the pregnancy; the squiggle of cells was a handy scapegoat. 'Isabel's very nice,' she repeated. *But I wish she'd bugger off so we could talk.*

'She's . . .' Lost for words, Sam crouched in front of Anna. 'She's so . . .'

'I get it,' said Anna. 'You like her.'

'It's important that *you* like her.' He was urgent. 'You do, don't you? You like her?'

'I've literally just met the woman.' Anna shoved him playfully so he toppled onto the rug.

The others arrived, in dribs and drabs. Maeve breezed in, shedding faded ethnic layers as she rattled through the pitfalls of the Brighton–London line. 'There was a bus replacement for part of the way. We'd have been quicker coming from Scotland.' She prodded Storm, propelling him towards Anna. 'Kiss your aunt.'

Even though Storm had to be told to do it these days, Anna loved his kisses. He was in a Liverpool trackie; from a distance he was A.N. Other teenage boy, but to Anna he was still the miracle she'd helped into the world thirteen years ago.

The memory of holding Maeve's hand through the birth jolted Anna; in a few months she'd be on that front line herself. Births were messy things. Gory. Painful. Overwhelming. Anna held Storm tightly and he protested. She let him go; *births are joyful too*, she reminded herself.

It required some effort to think of herself as a mother.

After tiptoeing around the idea for so long, Anna had no option but to face it head-on. She felt only the violent glare of Mother Nature's headlights.

'Look who's here!' Maeve shepherded an arrivee into the room, as if he was a guest on a chat show.

'Josh!' Anna could have clapped. 'You made it!'

'Yeah, well . . .' Josh shrugged. He was dark, like Maeve; they both had the Piper gypsy gene. Dark gentle eyes, velvety brown hair that lapped at his collar. 'Sam, mate!'

There was a butch slapping of backs. Sam and Josh had always got on.

Isabel was introduced, looking prettily shy as she nodded and smiled and did the whole New Girlfriend thing. Anna watched her, then felt the prickle of somebody watching *her*. It was Sam, with a question in his gaze that she ignored, turning instead to greet Neil and Santi.

'Who's this goddess?' Neil bent to kiss Isabel's hand, his forehead still slightly pink from his recent hair plugs.

'She's the amazing Isabel,' said Anna, wondering if perhaps baby hormones had seeped into her brain and encouraged her inner bitch.

'*Encantado*,' said Santiago with his exquisite Spanish manners. He introduced Isabel to Paloma, who was in yet another new outfit, kicking happily in her father's arms.

Or one of her fathers. The plan was for the child to call Santi 'Papi' and Neil 'Daddy', but that day was far distant.

Paloma was still a gurgler, taking in her new world with eyes like scraps of sky. She had a level gaze, slightly unsettling in a baby of four and a bit months.

'Are we all here?' asked Neil, restless as ever, already bored by the lovebirds.

'Not quite,' said Sam. 'Guys, you haven't even noticed the table.'

'Whoa! Cutlery?' said Anna, bemused. Nobody expected much from Sam's lunches, punctuated by the ping! of the microwave, and eaten off laps. Anna had once drunk her Pinot Grigio out of a vase, but today an actual table, laid with honest-to-goodness glassware and crockery stood by the window.

'And clean plates,' laughed Santiago, looking around for somewhere to put Paloma as he shed the various bags of baby kit she necessitated. He held her out to Neil, but he was too busy exclaiming over the table.

'This is what happens,' said Neil, 'when you let a woman into the house. Bravo, Isabel.'

'And,' said Sam, squeezing the 'woman', 'the food will be edible.'

'It's only beef Wellington.' Isabel coloured up.

'Only!' squeaked Storm, who'd come out of a vegetarian phase and was now a rampant carnivore.

'But first,' said Sam, with the smugness of a magician about to astonish his audience, 'the starter!'

As the club members gasped at such sophistication, Sam beetled out to the galley kitchen. Anna found him swearing mildly as he burned his fingers on a baking tray of tartlets. She helped him arrange them on a dish she'd never seen before; Isabel was certainly making her mark on the flat. 'Sam,' she began, and her gravity made him stop and look at her.

'What?'

She meant to tell him about the tiny brain currently knitting itself together inside her. Instead, she said, 'How come you never found a moment to tell me about Isabel? I mean, it seems as if you really like her, but, nothing, *nada*, as Santi would say.'

Sam became very still. 'What's this about?'

Puzzled by her question being answered with another question, Anna threw him another. 'What's *what* about?'

'This attitude.' Sam kept his voice low. 'You've been spiky with Isabel since you met her.'

'I have *not*.'

'You know you have.' Sam let out a long breath. 'Look, if you really want to know, I kept Isabel to myself because, well, it's precious, you know? I didn't want everybody chipping in with their opinion. I wanted to get to know her, and work out how I really felt, before going public.'

Smarting at being lumped in with 'everybody', Anna said, 'But I tell you all about my disasters.'

'This feels different,' said Sam. 'Be happy for me, Anna, yeah?'

'Of course I'm happy for you.' She meant it, she was, and yet . . . 'Sam, listen, there's something I need to—'

'About time,' muttered Sam, looking past her.

'I know I'm late, sorry, man.' Tall, golden-haired, with wicked eyes, it was the barman from Neil's big bash. 'Lead me to the drinks and I'll get going.'

'Everybody,' said Sam, ushering him into the small sitting room. 'Remember Dylan?'

'Yes,' said Maeve emphatically, sticking out her chest.

'Dyl?' Neil was delighted to see one of his lame ducks. He met many out-of-work actors and models through his advertising agency, and was always on the lookout for odd jobs to earn them some money. These ducks had one thing in common: they were all gorgeous. 'Are you on bar duty again?'

'Yeah.' Dylan caught Anna's eye and winked. 'Yours, madam, is a G and T, if I remember rightly.'

'A fizzy water, please,' said Anna shyly. The Northern Irish lilt of Dylan's words should have been available on the NHS for drooping female libidos.

The beef Wellington was a triumph. Anna had seconds.

'It's so nice,' whispered Santi in her ear, 'to see Sam with somebody.'

'You old romantic, you.' Anna wanted to agree.

Paloma, struggling on her papi's lap, thumped her little palms onto Santiago's plate and the lunchers all sprang back as gravy rained down on them.

'You can't eat *and* baby-wrangle.' Anna wiped brown goo from her eyebrows. 'Neil! Take your daughter for a minute.'

'I'm busy, darling.' Neil was 'busy' scrolling through snaps of Paloma on his phone for the benefit of Dylan, who, bar duties forgotten, had sat down to eat with the club members.

'S'OK,' said Santi, but Isabel scampered over and scooped Paloma off his lap.

'Let me!' she smiled. 'I love babies.'

Possibly the woman had a handbook somewhere on her person: *Cutesie Things to Say to a New Boyfriend's Chums*. 'We all love babies, surely,' said Anna, aware she'd prompted some odd looks around the table.

'Not me,' said Dylan happily, sitting back. 'Can't stand 'em.'

'I knew you'd say that!' Maeve, changing seats with Storm, plonked herself beside him. 'I'm a bit psychic. I *know* things.'

'She means,' said Neil, holding up a shot of Paloma dressed as a mermaid, 'she's a bit psycho.'

'My big brother's a concrete thinker.' Maeve leaned into Dylan. 'Whereas I'm very open. I feel vibrations. I sense auras.'

'And you drink your own weight in Rioja,' said Neil.

Anna could tell he was riled at Maeve for poaching Dylan, who'd turned in his chair to gaze at her. Anna didn't blame him; her sister was a beauty, with a mesmeric quality to her fine, dark looks despite the tie-dye grunginess. She drew men in, even when her allure was blunted by booze. Anna caught Storm's eye; the youngster had inherited his mother's glamour and then added an austere loveliness of his own. He was sad, Storm; he had been a grave toddler and now he was an introverted teen. She stuck out her tongue and he smiled despite himself; watching his mother flirt was high on his list of unbearable agonies.

Josh, who'd eaten less than anybody else, said mildly, 'We're all a bit psychic. Everybody has intuition, don't we?' All families have sides, and Josh tended to have Maeve's back. No matter how eccentric she was.

'Remember the night Mum and Dad announced they were emigrating?' said Maeve, her face close to Dylan's. 'I knew they were going to say it. Didn't I?' she asked the table at large.

'No,' the table replied.

'What you actually said,' said Sam, amused, pulling Isabel and Paloma closer to him, 'was that your parents were going to announce their divorce.'

'Did I?' Maeve never minded being the butt of the joke. She blew a kiss Paloma's way, which Paloma acknowledged in a queenly manner. 'When is P going to meet her grand-parents? Her English grandparents, I mean.'

Santiago's mother had been on the first flight from Barcelona, bearing frilled dresses and gingham bonnets and a tiny crucifix on a slim gold chain.

'Soon,' said Anna, as Neil said, 'Never, probably.' Their relationship with their parents was subtly different to their little brother and sister's.

Isabel jiggled Paloma as she asked, 'How long did it take to adopt this one?'

'Too long,' said Neil.

'A couple of times we almost came close with other chil-dren – a toddler, then a lovely boy of four, but . . .' Santiago blew out his cheeks. 'It didn't happen.'

The months of interviews and home visits and back-ground checks had taken its toll on the men. Neil had been vocal – as usual – but Santi had absorbed it all, only show-ing emotion on the day they went to collect ten-week-old Paloma. He'd cried and cried and cried. And then he'd cried some more. 'I am bursting,' he'd sobbed, 'with love.'

Now, the inevitable happened. Paloma reacted to Isabel's jiggling by vomiting all down her sugar-candy dress. As her sobs rose, Isabel stood hurriedly and offered her to Neil, but it was Santi who took their daughter and spirited her away with much shushing and kissing and 'there there's.

'What?' Neil felt Anna looking at him. 'Santi's better at

that type of thing.' He turned, addressed Isabel, who'd taken her seat again. 'Adoption isn't for the faint-hearted. We'd have turned back if he, we, didn't want a child so much. Paloma's mother had problems.'

'She was a druggie,' interrupted Storm.

'We don't call her that,' said Neil gently. 'But yes, the poor girl has issues. There was never a question of her keeping the baby.'

'Jesus, poor kid,' said Sam.

Anna shifted on her chair. It was all so close to home. 'Do you think Paloma will ever want to get in touch with her birth mother?'

That was serious stuff for the lunch table, and Neil's expression told her so. 'We're going to be frank with her. I mean, basic biology will tell her that two daddies can't make a baby. We won't hide the facts. What she does with them,' he said, 'is up to her.'

Facts. Those hard-headed, sharp-elbowed busybodies. Anna was full of facts.

'So,' said Isabel brightly, turning to Anna, as if moving on to less personal matters. 'You and Sam were married?'

If anything, this subject was *more* personal. 'Yup,' said Anna, nodding. 'For a long time.' She laughed. 'A l-o-n-g time!'

'Ten years,' said Maeve.

'Ten long years,' laughed Sam.

Isabel asked, 'Why'd you split up?'

Anna stared at Sam and he stared back.

'I don't really know,' said Sam.

'Just, you know . . .' For Anna, the pertinent question was why did they get married. 'It didn't work out.'

'Plus my feet smell,' added Sam.

'Is there afters?' Storm, hunched over the table, was deadly bored with the grown-up chatter.

'Isabel's made a Nutella cheesecake,' said Sam.

'Nutella *and* cheesecake?' burped Maeve. 'Together?'

'They should serve this at world summits,' said Neil, as the dish was brought to the table. 'There'd be no more war.'

'You've found the perfect woman,' said Santi, back now with Paloma in her second outfit of the day. 'What did I miss? Is there custard?'

'He'd never tasted custard before we met,' said Neil. He smiled soppily at his husband. 'We're making a real Brit out of him.'

'No way.' Santi's black brows beetled. 'Chips and curry sauce? *No gracias.* I'll keep my *paella* and my *tortilla.*'

Josh held out his arms. 'I can, you know, take Paloma if you want.'

Surreptitiously, Anna watched her brother with the child. Josh's beauty was outrageous, shimmering, with those bread-knife cheekbones and full mouth, yet he kept himself shut away, always in shadow, as if ashamed. She had seen many people do double takes at Josh; his reticence made him easily ignored, but on closer inspection he was both lush and delicate. A hothouse flower.

Seeing Josh spontaneously reach out for Paloma brought a swell of optimism. Anna kept waiting for Josh to connect; Neil told her she was setting herself up for disappointment. It is what it is, was his take on Josh. Anna wanted to dig down deep, solve the mystery of her brother's isolation. She scolded herself; human beings aren't puzzles to be solved.

'There's loads more cheesecake, if anybody wants seconds.' Isabel's shoulders went to her ears. 'I made two.'

'My darling, I like you more and more,' said Neil, his mouth full.

'I could go another plateful.' Dylan stood up with his plate.

Anna did the same, pushing Maeve back into her chair with a firm 'Sit!' as she passed. In the kitchen, as Dylan hunted out the dessert, Anna's heels squeaked on the floor. He turned at the noise.

'Looking for an action replay?' Dylan lunged, cheesecake forgotten.

'No, God no.' Anna put up her hands, keeping her voice low, and glancing neurotically at the open kitchen door. 'Dylan, something happened.'

'You're telling me!' Dylan was all wicked glee,

manoeuvring her into a corner against a folded ironing board. 'You were awesome, Annabel.'

'*Anna.*' She pushed him away. 'Seriously, Dylan, I don't – stop – get off!' She finally convinced him that their romp had been a one-off and he stepped away, arms by his sides.

'Hell, sorry, I thought . . .'

She felt sorry for him. Dylan looked about seven years old when he hung his head like that. 'Listen, something's happened. I'm—'

'Mad about me?' said Dylan, suddenly goofy.

'You didn't even remember my name,' Anna reminded him. 'I'm . . .' There were plenty of ways to say it. With child. Expecting. Up the duff. Anna went for simplicity. 'Dylan, I'm pregnant and please don't ask; yes, of course it's yours.'

He didn't say a thing. He turned and walked to the front door, let himself out and flattened some daffodils in his haste to be elsewhere.

'What did you say to Dylan?' Maeve appeared, her face accusing.

'Nothing,' said Anna automatically. 'Actually, I did say something.' She took her sister's hand. It was small, the fingernails bitten; Maeve was such a child next to tall, long-limbed Anna. 'Come on. I have an announcement to make.'

In the sitting room, with all faces turned expectantly to her, Anna said, 'I'm nine weeks pregnant.'

There was a pause.

'No you're not,' said Neil.

'I knew it,' said Maeve dreamily. 'I felt it here.' She clutched her chest.

'Congratulations.' Sam rose slowly out of his chair as if fighting gravity. His gaze asked a hundred questions. 'Who's . . .'

It all came out. The assignation in the utility room. The pregnancy test. The departure of the father-to-be as if his hair was on fire.

Maeve stroked Anna's arm as the others gathered round.

'This is brilliant, Sis,' said Josh, his sweet face curved into a massive smile. 'You'll be a brilliant mummy.'

Santi said, 'We'll support you, *querida*. It'll be a cousin for Paloma!'

'Neil?' prompted Anna. His opinion mattered. 'Don't you have anything to say?'

'You're stark staring mad.'

'Oh shut up!' Santi swatted at Neil with Paloma's dimpled hand. 'No more mad than us.'

Storm looked appalled. 'But you're so *old*,' he said.

'Your auntie's in the prime of her life,' scolded Maeve. She said this about all women, no matter what age they were. 'Mind you, Sis, you have *no* idea, believe me, what you're letting yourself in for.'

*

The teasing about utility-room sex would probably never end. Family in-jokes are the most durable; Anna was doomed to go to her grave with 'Don't let her get you near the tumble dryer!' ringing in her ears. As Neil dropped her home in the enormous 4×4 that tiny Paloma somehow made necessary, he kissed her on the cheek and said, 'You owe me a litre of fabric conditioner, you trollop.'

Alone in her house, the evening closing in, Anna flopped on the sofa, still in her coat. Her head teemed; much like her womb.

The quiet Sunday dusk felt like a breathing space, and Anna crawled into it, grateful for the chance to bring some order.

They were all on her side, that teasing, mocking crew of hers. Even Sam, who only had eyes for his shiny new girlfriend, had privately asked how she was, how she really was. She was able to tell him that she was fine. They both stumbled, as if learning a new language; they'd never used words where babies were concerned.

It was true; Anna was fine. She was calm at last, after weeks of swinging from euphoria to despair. That's an exhausting journey to make twice a day. *A baby! How wonderful!* she'd think, only to stuff her fist in her mouth later. *A baby! I can't, I just can't.*

'I can.' That was her mantra today. She could do this and she wanted to do it. No baby should have the responsibility of healing their own mother, but this new Piper would square a circle it didn't even know existed.

At the thought of Dylan, she wilted. She hadn't expected much, but even so ... The baby was a shock, yes, but it had been a shock to Anna as well. It takes two to tango – or bonk on a washing machine – but unlike Dylan, she didn't have the luxury of running away.

That was a new thought. Wherever she went, her chick would go too. Her shadow. Her responsibility.

That sent a current of electricity through Anna. More profound than the orgasm she'd experienced among the white goods, it jolted her forwards in time to the day she'd hold somebody in her arms, somebody she'd made. By accident, admittedly, but the baby was her doing, and she pitied Dylan for not grasping the wonder of it.

Her life was now a No Bad Vibes zone. Neil's disbelief, Sam's concern, the thinly veiled censure she expected from her parents, none of these would be allowed past the front door.

'I'm in charge,' murmured Anna, moving gently around the room, lighting a candle, removing her coat, savouring the sanctuary.

Early to bed allegedly makes a man (and presumably woman) healthy, wealthy and wise, so at ten o'clock Anna was already in a dressing gown, mixing up a milky something in her kitchen.

'Hello?' A ghostly voice wafted through the letter box.

'Who's there?' asked Anna uncertainly.

'Me.' The ghost turned out to be Dylan. His exuberant hair was flat, his smile tentative. 'We should talk.'

Bang went her early night. Anna sat him down in the tiny front room, where he made the furniture look doll-sized.

'I'm sorry about, you know, fleeing.'

'I understand. At first I felt like fleeing myself.'

'It wasn't very manly.' Dylan hung his head.

'Who cares about manly? You're a person first and foremost, Dylan. Do your friends call you Dylan?'

'Yeah.'

'Right.' She knew nothing about this man, other than he was extremely good at impromptu sex. 'I'll call you that, then. Because we should be friends, shouldn't we?'

'Of course,' said Dylan.

'How old are you?' It was rude to ask so abruptly, but this was a unique situation. Anna tensed herself for the answer and almost threw up when he said he was twenty-one.

'How, you know, old . . .'

'I'm forty,' said Anna.

'You're a cougar,' smiled Dylan, instantly regretting it and rebooting his expression. 'Sorry. I didn't . . .'

'How'd you find my address?'

'Your brother.'

'Ah. Yes.'

'Look,' said Dylan, with an emphatic air. This was evidently rehearsed. 'If you want to keep this baby, that's cool. It's your body, you know? But I can't have a kid now. I have to be honest. It's too soon. And you and me . . .'

'We're not love's young dream.'

'Exactly!' Dylan seemed encouraged by her acceptance of the situation. 'It was just a bit of fun. And by the way, it was epic.' Dylan put his head to one side and raised his eyebrows. 'I'm a bit of an idiot, Anna. I'm not really an actor, and I'm not really a barman, I'm still finding myself, you know?'

Anna smiled at his earnestness. She liked him, she realised. That was a relief.

He went on. 'I'm broke. I'm always broke. I kip on people's floors. I smoke weed. Lots of weed. I can't keep a relationship going.'

'Do you want to?'

Now Dylan smiled. 'Not really, no.'

'I don't expect a thing from you, Dylan. Not a thing. I'll bring up this baby, I'll look after it, I'll be a single parent. But it's important to me that you acknowledge it.' Anna swallowed, her composure buckling for the first time since he'd arrived. 'This child must be welcomed.'

'God yeah, sure!' Dylan bounced, energised at being set free. 'I'll be its dad, you know, the fun dad who takes it to Disneyland and teaches it to play the guitar and goes backpacking in Thailand with it!'

A small voice inside Anna said, *This baby is going nowhere near Thailand with this man-child.* 'Be around when you feel like it. There's no need to pretend we're a normal family. I can do the heavy lifting. You show up for birthdays and stuff. Deal?'

'Deal.' Dylan sprang up and wrung her hand. His skin was warm, robust and sent a zip of sexual heat through Anna.

Dousing it speedily, she said, 'We should swap numbers. Bit late, but there you go.'

As they exchanged details, both looking down at their phones, Dylan said, 'Jeez, thank God you're being cool about this, Anna. My mum's gonna kill me.'

It was clear that Dylan was incapable of going more than a couple of sentences without making Anna feel like a geriatric cradle-snatcher. As she saw him to the door – there was an aura of crushed expectation about him, as if he was ready to scamper up to bed with her – she said, 'We know where we stand, Dylan. You're the father, but this baby is *mine*.'

'I can love the little dude, though,' he said, his hair a halo in the porch light.

He'd probably never know how grateful she was to him for that. Dylan might be an idiot – he couldn't open the front gate without her help – but he had heart. And hearts trump brains every time.

'Goodnight, mother of my child,' he sang, hands in

pockets. He half turned back and said, 'Hey, Anna, how'd you get to forty without having a baby?'

'Next time,' said Anna, meaning *Never*, as she closed the front door.

Chapter Three

Lunch at Josh's

STEW
POSSIBLY ICE CREAM

It was an unusual name. Anna rarely heard it. When she did, she jumped.

'So, our next caller,' said the radio presenter as Anna's car idled at the lights, 'is Bonnie from Merton.'

Anna never heard what Bonnie from Merton had to say. She was jolted back to when she said goodbye to the Bonnie in her own life. She'd tried to explain, apologise, but it felt pointless. *I knew what I was doing.*

A horn honked impatiently. Anna raised a hand – *sorry sorry* – and jerked away from the lights.

It came and went, but never quite left her, the feeling of

loss. When she saw an illuminated letter 'B' in a gift shop. Green eyes. The scent of vanilla. The loss was tainted, made darker by guilt.

The car slowed to pull into the car park and she wondered what Storm would make of his auntie if he knew the cruelty she was capable of. He wandered towards her – Storm never hurried – in trackie bottoms and a zip-up jacket, bag slung over his shoulder, attitude intact.

'All right?' he said, climbing in. 'There was no need to come to Clapham Junction. I could have got the tube to yours.'

'It's no bother.' Anna knew that Maeve gave the boy a lot of freedom, but London was a bigger, badder place than Brighton. She wondered how her own child would cope with the alarming levels of protectiveness that came so easily to her. 'Ready to work your ass off?'

Storm fluttered his eyelids. Among his pet hates was adult members of his family swearing or trying to be cool. Anna's comment ticked both boxes. 'Yup,' he said.

Back at the shed, Anna waved him in, telling Sam, 'Behold, our new assistant.'

'First things first,' said Sam sternly. 'Elevenses.'

The day's work experience was part of a new initiative at Storm's school. Anna felt he was a bit young at thirteen to be thinking about a career, but had been chuffed when Storm asked to see how Artem Accessories was run.

Sam had a sadistic urge to wear out the teenager. He set him photocopying, running to the post office, stuffing envelopes, washing mugs, printing labels. They stopped him answering the phone as he could only mumble 'Artem 'cessories', and answered the simplest query with 'I dunno'.

Looking up from the digital mock-up of her latest design, Anna took pity on Storm and motioned for him to come and sit beside her. She walked him through the process of creating a piece. 'This one, the Cassandra, looks simple, but they're the ones that need most work. It's a flat, plain-looking messenger bag, but I'm adding pockets for keys and mobile phones and stuff. No point being pretty if you're not practical.'

The template on the screen dragged Storm in. Soon he was suggesting refinements.

'Actually,' said Anna, 'that's not a bad idea.' She sketched a small rectangle. 'A travel-card holder that's attached by a chain . . . I like it.'

When Storm was proud of himself, he was the image of his father. Another person for Anna to miss; she hadn't seen Alva in over a decade.

When Alva and Maeve got together, it had been love, wild crazy love. With Maeve, it always was. He'd been scrawny then, a wisp of a boy from a strict, chaotic, loving Caribbean family, so different to the ordered home life of the Pipers.

College had been scrapped in favour of a squat in the

pre-hipster East End of London. Anna remembered visiting with her mother and being amazed to find there was no loo; they had to nip next door to the pub when nature called. But the place pulsed with young love. Maeve and Alva were joined at the hip.

Then, at twenty, Maeve had missed a period. She hadn't been sure what to do, had sobbed to Anna about her 'options', but Alva knew exactly what to do. First a job, then a flat. With no qualifications, he fell into IT.

It was a perfect match. Galvanised by upcoming father-hood – Alva wouldn't hear of 'options' – he learned from the bottom up. He was a natural entrepreneur, and by the time Storm was two years old, Alva branched out on his own as a consultant. The squat was swapped for a pristine two-bedder in the suburbs.

Maeve loathed it. Something in her pined for hardship, or at the very least peeling lino. When she left, in the middle of the night with Storm tucked under her arm like a handbag, it was Anna and Sam she'd fled to.

They'd tried to mediate, to stress what a wonderful part-ner and provider she had in Alva, but Maeve had fallen out of love as abruptly as she'd fallen into it. Anna suspected there was somebody else involved, but she kept such dark imaginings to herself.

Alva recovered as best he could, and now supplied scaf-folding to his son's rackety life with Maeve. He paid for his schooling, took care of the rent and some of the bills, provided the iPad and iPhone that are essential kit for any self-respecting modern teenager. He picked him up every other Friday evening and delivered him home on a Sunday, and colluded with Storm's insistence that he be known as 'Stephen' at school.

In short, he was an excellent dad. Anna realised it was Friday. 'Is your dad picking you up from here?'

'Nah.' Storm was a natural spy; he never gave up information willingly, so Anna had to ask why not. 'I haven't been to his for a couple of weeks.' And that was that. No further data. He sloped off at the sound of the doorbell, a two-note warble that Anna recognised as the postman's.

Anna tidied as she waited for that day's bills and junk mail to be brought to her. She constantly battled the mess on her side of the shed. The timber office housed two desks, lots of filing cabinets and shelves, plus a draughtsman's easel where Anna sketched handbags and purses. It was the heart of the Artem empire; Sam baulked at that word, but Anna countered that empires can be small.

Storm returned with a large box.

'Gimme gimme!' Anna was already drooling at the thought of what was inside; not edible goodies but still delicious, these must be the Italian leather samples they'd ordered. Opening up packages full of hides always felt like Christmas. Artem was considering a move from vegetable-tan leather to chrome-tan; Sam focused on cost, whereas Anna was seduced by the feel, the depth of colour, that musky smell of a new skin.

She deferred opening the box until she had a coffee in her hand. As she made her way back to the house, she wondered whether she should look up 'caffeine intake during pregnancy' and decided against it in case the prevailing wisdom was to cut down.

Waiting for the kettle to do its thing, Anna sifted through the envelopes, passing over the brown ones for Sam to deal with, and picked up a handwritten one. This envelope, she noticed, had no stamp; it had been slipped through the door at some point, and Storm had scooped it up with the delivery.

Handwritten notes were the best. She and Josh communicated in this way; she hadn't had one of his quirky drawings for a while. Shaking out the flimsy notepaper, she reached out to scribble 'pressie for Josh' on the chalkboard by the fridge. He was hosting lunch on Sunday; it would be nice to turn up with a little something. Maybe his favourite chocolate, a dark, bitter variety that set Anna's teeth on edge.

The small handwriting marched self-confidently across a folded piece of thin paper. Anna put it down as she cast about for her glasses. She remembered the conversation she'd had with Sam after the last lunch club a fortnight ago.

'So,' he'd said at work the next day in Artem Global HQ/ the shed. 'You don't like Isabel?'

'Eh? Of course I do. She's a lovely girl.'

'She's not a girl, Anna. Isabel's a woman. And that sounded sarcastic to me.' He mimicked her, his mouth turned down, *'She's a lovely girl.'*

'I didn't say it like that. It wasn't meant to be sarcastic.' Anna withstood his sceptical look before saying, 'Oh, all right, maybe a tiny bit. She *was* trying a bit too hard, wasn't she?'

That had been a classic mistake, expecting a lover to have clarity of vision about his beloved. Sam's vision was more rose-tinted than most. Anna had been glad of it when they were first together, when he told her she was the loveliest girl in the world.

'Of course poor Isabel tried hard! She wanted to make a good impression. She's heard so much about you all.' Sam had paused before saying, 'About *you*.'

The kettle danced, and Anna was back in the present. She poured hot water into the cafetière and then, glasses on, leant back against the fridge to enjoy the letter.

She read it twice. She looked at the ceiling. There was no answer there as to why life had stretched out a paw and mauled her. On automatic pilot, she took the tray out to the others, adding a glass of orange juice for Storm. It crossed her mind to show Sam the letter, but that was out of the question.

*

Sunday brought with it a lie-in, but Anna was chased from her warm bed by those small, neat words dancing behind her eyelids. In the shower, Anna watched her outline shimmer in the wet glass surround. As yet, her body was minimally changed by her pregnancy. Accustomed to being long and lean, Anna braced herself for the moment her tummy suddenly popped, but for now the baby was merely a polite swell of flesh.

When, she wondered, *will the boobs arrive?* She planned to make the most of them. Her push-up bras had precious little to push up; as soon as her cup size increased she would buy a strapless maternity dress and enter rooms like a ship in full sail.

Pity there would be nobody to appreciate her new figure when she took off the dress.

As a divorcee and a survivor of numerous scarring flings, Anna was accustomed to thoughts of romance gathering in her peripheral vision. She was always wondering who it would be, the big love, the great man, the defining passion. At forty, she still had the optimism of a schoolgirl; surely everybody has a chance at lasting love? It was virtually a right. As for her age – that was a number from a hall door. It was outlook that mattered.

Now such idealistic daydreams must be parked indefinitely. Surely all her attention, all her capacity for love, must centre on her pregnancy. At times like this, naked and foamy in the shower, the baby seemed more like an idea than a real living being. It couldn't chat to her, or heckle the TV with her, or do any of the dull, wonderful things women expect from their men. Cutting herself off from the big guns of love and sex felt like wilful cruelty, but it was better to do it herself than wait for the time when her body did it for her. Surely a pregnant body is a turn-off for anybody but the prospective father? There can be no more definite way to signal 'Sorry, guys, I'm taken.'

Stepping out of the shower, Anna admitted that she wasn't in the mood for Sunday Lunch Club. The letter demanded her attention, like a bony finger from the past tapping her rudely on the shoulder.

'Say cheese!'

'No.' Neil hated having his photo taken. 'I'm driving, darling. It's dangerous.'

'Shut up and smile, you swine. This is for Josh's project.'

Neil grimaced, then gave in and turned quickly to the lens, flashing his veneers.

'That's better.' Anna's Polaroid camera, a Christmas present from Josh, was one of her favourite playthings. The retro coolness of its bulky design and the playful magic of the picture swimming into focus were nostalgic pleasures.

'What project?' Neil looked over his shoulder at Santi and Paloma in the back seat. They were in a world of their own, a peachy world where Spanish endearments figured highly.

'You know, Josh's thing. He wants me to take a Polaroid every day and he takes one every day and . . .' Anna wasn't sure about the point of all this Polaroiding. 'And then he'll stick them up on a wall or something.'

'Sounds like Josh.' Neil rolled his head and winced as his neck cracked like a pistol shot. 'Arty.'

'He's been texting me all week about what to cook today.' It was rare that the club convened at Josh's. He was a guest, not a host. *Not even a guest*, thought Anna. *More of a ghost.*

'It won't be vegan shit, will it?' Neil was profoundly anti healthy eating; a balanced diet was a biscuit in each hand as far as he was concerned.

'No, it won't be organic, soulful, vegan cuisine,' said Anna repressively. She was every bit as relieved as Neil – she'd met all the tofu she ever needed to – but she supported Josh's obsessions. 'I emailed him an easy recipe for chicken casserole. Should be delicious. Are we nearly there?' Repeating one of Dinkie's Dublin sayings, she said, 'I'm so hungry I could eat a child's arse through a chair.'

'Eating for two,' said Neil. 'Then again, you always did.'

'How many weeks now, *querida*?' asked Santi as they swung round a corner.

'Only eleven.' Putting that 'only' in front of the number made the end game – Anna with her legs in stirrups – manageably far in the future. 'He or she is the size of a grape.'

'Are you drinking lots of water?' Santi was stern. 'Getting lots of rest?'

'Trying to.'

'Morning sickness?'

'Now and then.'

The physical symptoms were manageable. The fear was a different matter. The hormones supplied bouts of euphoria, but these daydreams were popped by self-sabotage. *Can I really bring up a child on my own?* Her close circle, family and as-good-as-family, would support her, but would that be enough?

Sometimes extraordinary things happen in the most ordinary of places. In the car that smelled mildly of Paloma's nappy, and where Santi's bass recitations of Spanish nursery rhymes argued with the satnav's robotic directions, Anna had a premonition.

It popped into being, whole and perfect, a belief based on nothing, yet one that firmed up like a warm loaf baking in the oven.

Love is waiting.

Biding its time. Just when her body was telling her to narrow her focus to the baby, she had a premonition that life was about to open up.

Unlike Maeve, Anna had no delusions about being psychic; yet this romantic optimism felt like gospel truth. Like maths. Or gravity. Despite being pregnant with the child of an itinerant cocktail maker, Anna sensed a big love circling.

'Look at the state of the place.' Neil edged the car into a space right outside the peeling stucco terraced house where Josh lived. They assembled in the once grand stone porch, now home to a cornucopia of kebab wrappers. Torn curtains hung at grimy windows, and marijuana smoke curled from the basement. 'What a palace.'

'Shush.' Anna was curt. Neil sometimes forgot that not everybody had his wealth. 'I can hear Josh.' Feet were bounding down the stairs, jumping the last two, and she smiled, relieved; *He's in an 'up' phase.*

Pushing the letter and its toxic contents from her mind, Anna grinned as the door opened. Her smile froze.

It was the surprise, maybe, of once again a complete stranger answering the door. Or perhaps it was the physical shock of the man who filled the space with such vitality.

'You're not Josh,' said Neil amiably. He, too, had a thing for guys with hair that curled; this man had the rioting hair of a Roman statue.

'Not even slightly.' He stood aside to let them in. 'Josh sent me down to get you. Apparently he's at a critical point with the food.'

Paloma wailed as they climbed the stairs, possibly with dismay at being in such a lowly postcode. The man was Luca, it transpired, and Anna, who had assumed that her pregnancy inoculated her against lust, wished with all her heart she'd worn one of her better bras and not opted for the striped tee and jeans combo that amounted to a uniform for her.

For three flights, each with its own cocktail of smells — dope on the ground floor, cheese on the first, armpits on the second — Anna stared at Luca's bottom. She could find no fault in it. He turned back, interrupting her studies, and nodded at the beribboned bar of chocolate in her hand.

'You've brought a present? Josh has one for you as well.'

'That's sweet of him.'

'I'm not sure you'll like it.'

'Why not?' Josh rarely bought presents; his empty hands at family birthdays were taken as a symptom of introversion rather than stinginess; it would be just Josh's style to suddenly produce a gift when there was no need.

'You'll see.' Luca had dark eyes that sloped slightly. He was warm and lazy-looking, like a hot afternoon in a hammock. Tall, wide, he opened the door to Josh's flat and something small and covered in hair raced through it, bounding up at Luca, at Anna, at Neil who screamed, and at Santi who lifted the baby over his head.

'A dog,' said Anna, holding the little beast by its scrawny paws. 'This isn't . . .' She looked to Luca.

'It is. That's your present.' It was the first collusion between them, a shared recognition of life's absurdity. He held her gaze for a second longer than was strictly necessary. Or so Anna thought.

'Sit!' said Josh to the dog, who jumped and barked and slobbered as they edged into his tiny flat. 'Sit. Please.'

'Sit,' said Anna. The dog miraculously sat. Its tail thumped and he stared greedily at her.

'He likes you,' said Luca.

'He doesn't know her yet,' said Neil. 'Josh, where did this creature come from?' They filled the monastic studio room. A few books. Chairs donated from Dinkie. A standard lamp without a shade. It was as if Josh's 'real' life went on elsewhere.

'I've been volunteering at a dog shelter.' Josh put his hand through his thick dark hair. His hands were constantly in motion around his face, as if to obscure it. 'This fella's been passed over so often.'

'I wonder why,' murmured Neil as the dog scraped its bottom along the carpet tiles.

'He's so full of love,' said Josh, squatting down to have his face roundly licked. 'Nobody understands him, that's all. He needs a good home. So ...' He looked up at Anna. 'I thought of you.'

'But I ...' Anna was at a loss. She'd never hankered after a dog. The timing was way off; surely being pregnant and single was enough? 'I'll take him, of course.' She never could deny Josh. He asked for so little.

After the requisite blow-by-blow retelling of the train journey from Brighton, Maeve sat at the shaky table Josh had somehow fashioned for lunch. Isabel and Sam were together at one corner, with Storm opposite them checking his phone for . . . what? Anna wondered what urgent news stories kept teens glued to their mobiles, so she leaned over and saw a Buzzfeed quiz labelled 'Build a Pizza and We'll Tell You Which Celebrity You'll Marry'.

'Serious stuff,' she whispered to her nephew, who burrowed even further down into the wonky stool Josh had provided.

Circling the lunchers, the dog jumped first at one lap, then another, with no hard feelings when it was shooed away. Ears flopping, tail whirring, it pounced and leapt, its button eyes bright.

'Guess what?' Many of Maeve's stories began this way.

Neil guessed what immediately. 'You have a new bloke.'

'How'd you know?' Maeve's mouth fell open.

'You always have a new bloke, darling.' Neil looked around. 'No napkins, Josh?'

'Um, sorry, no.' Josh looked around too, as if napkins might suddenly jump out of a drawer.

'Shut up, Neil.' Anna kicked him under the table. 'You're not at The Ivy.'

'So is nobody interested in my life?' asked Maeve loudly.

'Tell us, Maeve.' Santi's gaze flicked to Paloma, snoozing behind a dam of cushions on the sofa that would later double as a bed. His expert appraisal told him everything he needed to know about his girl; she was safe/warm/dry. 'Who's the latest *tio bueno*?'

'Latest and last.' Maeve pulled in her chin. 'Honestly, guys, Paul's a keeper. Take that look off your face, Anna, I mean it.'

'That's not a look,' said Neil. 'That's her face.'

'I wasn't aware I had a look on my face,' said Anna.

'You always have a look on your face,' laughed Sam.

A roll-call of Maeve's lovers didn't make pretty reading. She stepped over decent guys to get at the lowlifes. If they were likely to borrow money and then disappear, or sleep with her friends, or lash out with their fists, Maeve would make goo-goo eyes at them.

'This one's different,' she said. 'Yeah, yeah, I know.' Maeve laughingly accepted the comments. 'I've said that before, but this time I mean it. Paul is ... oh, he's ... you tell them, Storm.'

Looking up, horrified, Storm shook his head. His father, calm trustworthy Alva, was the exception to Maeve's rule. 'He's a bloke,' was all that Storm would contribute.

'Oh, you.' Maeve shoved her son. 'I know you all disapprove of me and my quest for love,' she said, 'but this time I've landed on my feet. He's solvent, for a start.'

'Money isn't everything,' said Luca.

Anna, who'd clocked Luca's chunky watch and knew that artfully crumpled shirts like his weren't to be found in

M&S, raised an eyebrow. Luca saw it and raised one back. Something raised inside Anna; something deep inside. She shifted on her seat, startled by her feral physical reaction to a mere eyebrow.

'He's divorced but he's a great dad. He's got an amazing job as a . . .' Maeve frowned. 'Something or other, something *proper*.'

'So he's not a street performer? Good start,' said Anna. Her sister's last beau had juggled fire outside the Brighton branch of TK Maxx. Anna listened patiently to the recital of this 'amazing' man's qualities — 'He's clever, and barely drinks, and he wears actual shoes' — in the knowledge that next month there'd be another contender for The One. Maeve skipped from hopeless bozo to hopeless bozo without ever truly engaging her feelings. Anna wondered sometimes about what effect this revolving-door policy had on Storm. 'Oi, Stormy,' she whispered, and he looked up. 'Soon I'll only be able to recognise you by the top of your head.'

'The main thing is,' Maeve went on, 'he's *normal*.'

'Is he good to you?' Anna asked the only important question.

'He's kind and he cares.'

'Can't wait to meet him.' This white lie pleased Maeve.

The casserole, brought to the table from the abbreviated kitchen that took up a corner of the studio, was brownish, thickish, the 'Ooh!'s it provoked dutiful and a touch scared.

Anna took a huge portion, to show solidarity. Josh bit his lip as the others tasted their lunch.

'Is there paprika in this?' asked Isabel, with polite interest.

'Yes,' said Josh, grateful. He grinned, until Neil said, 'There's a whole packet of paprika in mine.'

'Joshy,' said Maeve, in a cutesy voice. 'Did you make me a meat-free version?'

'Oh shit, Sis!' He'd done the impossible: Josh had forgotten that Maeve was vegetarian.

Luca leapt up. 'No problem.' He put his hands – strong, workman hands that nevertheless had neat nails – on Josh's shoulders. 'Sit, eat. I'll rustle something up.'

The little dog pit-patted after him, parking its bottom to watch him cook.

'How long have you been seeing this new man?' asked Santi, pushing chicken around his plate.

'Since last night,' beamed Maeve.

'Jesus,' muttered Neil.

'*What?*' spat Maeve.

This Sunday Lunch Club was in danger of deteriorating into a badly catered brawl, so Anna turned, glass in hand, to ask Luca if he was really Italian. 'Or did your parents just like the name?'

'I'm the real deal.' Luca let rip with a torrent of fluent Italian.

As far as Anna knew, he could have been asking for

directions to the abattoir, but it sounded super sexy. 'So you were born here?' she asked as Luca located a clean pan and some spaghetti in Josh's barren cupboards.

'No, I was born in Saluzzo, near Turin. When I was a baby, my mother took a teaching job at Oxford. She and my dad loved it here and they never went home again. So. Here I am. Practically an Englishman.' He chopped up a tomato with more verve than any Brit ever could.

'Do you miss home?' Santi's question was low-key, freighted with emotion, and Neil looked at his partner and put one hand over his.

'This is home,' said Luca. He bent over the pan. 'I prefer English TV, English newspapers, English politics.'

'But not food!' said Josh.

'How about women?' Maeve's mind was one-track. 'Surely you prefer a gorgeous Italian *señorita*?'

'That's Spanish,' smiled Santi, as Luca said, almost to himself, 'I prefer English women. I like their pale skin. Their soft eyes.'

He looked directly at Anna. She met his look, sensing the dare in it. She swallowed hard and he turned away, saying, *'Allora! Spaghetti al pomodoro!'*

Maeve pronounced it 'heavenly'. It smelled fresh, with a promise of summer, even using tired old tomatoes. The others watched enviously, and did their best to finish up the stew.

'Guess I'll never be a chef,' said Josh, rounding up the plates and balancing them precariously on the few square inches of worktop. 'Maybe next time I'll do something Russian.'

'Brilliant idea,' said Anna. Sometimes Josh took petty failures hard; today he was different, more energetic.

Sam explained to Isabel. 'Josh is a translator. Russian to English, and vice versa.'

'Wow,' said Isabel.

'Not really,' said Josh. 'I love the language.' He waited a beat, then went on. 'It's not like English at all. It's Slavic, so it's . . . different.'

Like you, thought Anna.

'There's lots of Russian poetry, isn't there?' said Isabel, leaning forward. She was feeling it, Anna could tell, the off-key power that Josh sometimes exerted over people. If they bothered to look closely, and listen carefully.

'Russian is lyrical, beautiful.' Josh wasn't nibbling his nails, or picking at a strand of hair. Plus, Anna noted, his hair had been *washed*. She sensed a Christmas Eve tingle about him, as if something big and glittery was coming up.

Luca, settled again at the table, said, 'I was hoping to meet the famous Dinkie today.'

'She cancelled at the last minute,' said Josh.

'So, Luca,' said Sam, 'how do you and Josh know each other?'

Something passed between Josh and Luca, a tiny frisson. 'Oh, you know,' said Josh, 'around and about.'

'We both enjoy . . .' Luca had evidently taken off before knowing where he'd land. 'Tennis,' he said.

'Tennis?' Maeve gaped. 'Josh? Tennis? Seriously?'

The youngest, devoutly un-sporty Piper had few friends. Or, at least, few he introduced to the clan.

'What is it that you do, Luca?' Neil had given up with the chicken.

'Hey,' said Santi. 'Don't define people by their careers.'

'When I need to hear hippy shit, I'll call the nineteen sixties, thank you, Santiago,' said Neil.

Luca didn't answer the question. Instead – *almost as if deflecting it*, thought Anna – he nodded his head towards Paloma. 'Lovely kid,' he said.

'Do you have children?' Maeve lurched over another boundary.

'Thankfully, no.' Luca shook his head. 'Children annoy me,' he said. 'Their voices. The crying. And I'm not inter-ested in their imaginary friends.'

While the others laughed – and Neil controversially agreed – Anna let a small hope die. Refusing another glass – *I hope you appreciate my sacrifice, baby* – she rose and went to the insultingly small bathroom the developers of Josh's building had shoehorned into a corner.

Through the thin partition wall, Anna heard snatches

70

of conversation. Neil, it seemed, had kick-started a Sunday Lunch Club basic – why didn't Josh try to earn more money. Knees up to her chin on the minuscule loo, she heard Neil say, 'Have you been networking like I suggested?'

The sound of Maeve's snort made Anna grateful to her.

'Josh, network?' spluttered Maeve. 'Neil, not everybody's like you, schmoozing and showing off. Josh can't network.'

There was no toilet roll. Anna improvised.

'Look, Josh, your work is pretty niche.' Neil wouldn't drop it. 'If you want to move up from this dump, you need to start pushing yourself.'

A low rumbling voice which Anna didn't at first recognise proved to be Luca. 'One person's dump,' he said, 'is another person's palace.'

Anna punched the air. Neil didn't 'get' Josh. Four walls, space for his books and access to music was all he needed. *Plus toilet roll*, she reminded herself. She could imagine Josh, eyes sliding away, coughing nervously. 'Neil, leave him alone!' she shouted as she pulled up her pants.

Laughter exploded on the other side of the spit-and-tissue wall. Anna's tendency to mother Josh was a family joke; they should have known she was never off duty, even when in the loo.

The mirror was a relic from her old house; everything in Josh's flat was a donation. The tiny crack on one corner brought her back to when she used to stare at a younger version of this same face when she was married to Sam. He would tell her she was gorgeous most mornings; nobody had said so for a while. Putting a hand to her cheek, she imagined that it felt plumper, softer, as if a halo of flesh was growing around her outline in order to insulate the baby.

Shoulders back. Face sideways on. Hint of a smile. Nope, the terrible lighting in Josh's bathroom refused to let her look one second younger than her years. *I'm supposed to glow*, she thought, washing her hands vigorously.

Anna closed her eyes to the condition of the hand towel. *I must not tidy up*, she said to herself. *I must not wipe.*

It was useless fighting the need for a fix. She'd been tidying Josh's life since he was born, and this bathroom was an affront to all right-thinking people. Swishing around with a damp flannel, she soon had the shelves and mirror sparkling. She stood the toilet brush to attention. She lined up his shampoo and shower gel.

On a shelf to the right of the mirror stood a colourful tube that stood out in this bare bathroom.

Lipstick? Anna had never seen a single speck of femininity in Josh's home. Gingerly she pulled open the cabinet. A facial wash peered back at her. Josh was a soap and water man. More clues dotted the glass shelves. Foundation. By Armani; this mystery woman had taste and bucks. She liked red lipstick and glittery eyeshadow. Anna's heart raced. Her baby brother was taking baby steps. *Maybe not such baby steps* – this girl evidently stayed over often enough to merit leaving toiletries at his place.

Slipping back to her seat, Anna was met by the dog. She thought of him simply as 'The Dog'; naming it would suggest permanence. Beneath the hum of conversation, she bent down and put her nose to his. 'I don't want you, got that?'

The dog's tail hammered the floor.

'He wants *you*.' Luca had bent down so his voice was intimate in the dark space under the table.

When he smiled, Anna had no option but to repay him with interest. His eyes were very dark – like those of The Dog – and could turn on a dime from intent to frisky. That was a good analogy for Luca; a big, strong, healthy dog. 'It's nice,' she whispered, 'to be wanted.'

As they straightened up, carefully casual, Anna realised that nobody had mentioned her pregnancy, no asking after her health, or commenting on her non-bump. Had they sensed the charge in the air between her and Luca? Silently she thanked her circle for their atypical discretion.

'Josh does not ... what's the word?' Santi sometimes fumbled with English. He laid a hand on Neil's arm as if to silence him while he thought. 'Conform!' He clicked his fingers triumphantly. 'Josh likes to live in his own way.'

'All I need,' said Josh, before Neil had a chance to let rip again, 'is to keep things simple. I don't want to accumulate tons of . . .' He held out his palms. '*Stuff*. I like to see everything I own.'

'He's not competitive,' said Maeve, adding a pointed 'unlike you' at Neil.

'Bollocks.' Neil, who imagined multimillion advertising campaigns every day, couldn't stretch to imagining Josh's take on life. 'Nobody lives in a rathole like this by choice.'

'I like this flat,' said Isabel. 'It's cute.'

'Cute!' Neil sat back, a giveaway that he was going to shake this particular bone all night.

Luca stepped in by standing up. 'Hey, you know, we all measure success in different ways. My own definition is that I have enough money left over at the end of the month for a decent bottle of Barolo.'

'Is that wine?' asked Maeve.

'It's the best wine in the world.' Luca went to the loo; soon they heard him singing a loud operatic aria, presumably to cloak whatever else was going on in there.

'Shit,' said Josh for the second time that day. 'Ice cream. I promised ice cream, didn't I?'

'You did,' said Santi slowly. He was very very fond of ice cream, even the pallid English stuff.

'Right. I'd better . . .' Josh pointed at the door. 'You know. Buy some.'

'How does he do it?' said Neil after Josh pulled on his battered Converses and dashed out. 'He always—'

'Nobody always does anything, Neil.' Anna was tired of defending her brother.

'Yeah, let's drop the Josh-bashing,' said Sam genially. He and Anna had often discussed the way genial, unassuming Josh managed to spark conflict in the family.

'Time for *la niña*'s meal.' Like a conjuror, Santi produced a bowl and a spoon and a starched bib out of the lacy sack that went everywhere with him; Anna's own *niño* would inherit top-notch hand-me-downs from its cousin. It was starting to feel right, or at the very least not wrong; Anna felt solid ground beneath her feet.

Unless she happened to glance at Luca. She did that now as he retook his seat, only to find he was looking straight at her. The ground trembled, but she found she wasn't alarmed by the tremors.

Interrupting a monologue from Sam about the strange pain in his side – was it serious, he wondered, or a stitch? – Anna hissed, 'I think Josh has a girlfriend!'

'Rubbish,' said Neil.

'Eh?' said Sam, still feeling his side.

'Oh, I hope so,' said Maeve, leaning down to fondle The Dog. 'We all need love in our lives. Did I tell you that Paul has—'

'It's getting serious. She's left some of her stuff here.' Anna led a search party to the bathroom to show them exhibit 1: lipstick, and exhibit 2: eyeshadow.

'How come he hasn't said anything?' puzzled Neil.

Because you'd shoot him down in flames. Anna turned to Luca. 'Do you know about this woman?'

'Yeah.' Luca radiated unease. 'But . . . it's Josh's business.'

'Which makes it my business.' Anna was a warrior when it came to Josh. 'Have you met her?'

'Yes.' Luca ushered them out of the tiny room. 'Look, I don't—'

'What's her name? You can tell us that surely?' smiled Anna.

'You're a wicked woman. Her name's Thea.' Luca raised his hands, and she saw the satisfyingly correct amount of hair on his forearms – neither werewolf nor virgin. 'That's all you're getting out of me. Josh'll introduce you in his own good time.'

'In that case, just tell me . . . is this Thea a good thing?' Anna couldn't help but imagine a femme fatale with a gun.

'Very.' Luca tipped his head back, and looked down into her eyes. 'Trust me?'

'For some reason, yes.'

Anna was the first to look away. Was the best possible thing happening at the worst possible time?

The ice cream was, alas, not vegetarian, so Maeve smoked through dessert. 'So,' she said, blowing a smoke ring as the others ate their raspberry ripple. 'Thea.'

'Oh God,' whimpered Sam. Beside him, Isabel was agog; the Sunday Lunch Club was a crash course in Piper family dynamics.

'How did you . . .' Josh's face collapsed in bafflement.

'Make-up in the bathroom,' said Luca, biting his words.

'Ah.' Josh laughed. They all breathed out. 'I can't keep anything from you guys.' It was double-edged, that comment; Josh didn't usually 'do' sarcasm. 'There *is* somebody. It's all very new. Bit fragile. Before you ask, Anna, no, I'm not introducing her to the Sunday Lunch Club yet.'

'Charming,' said Neil, pretending to be offended. 'We'll be gentle with her. What's Thea short for? I'm imagining a fey sprite, all floaty fabrics and flowers in her hair.'

Luca laughed, short and sharp, as if to intimate that Neil was in for a surprise, while Josh said, 'See? This is why you can't meet her. You'd tear her apart.'

Standing up abruptly, he went to the bathroom, as Maeve and Anna began to hiss at Neil.

'What did you say that for?'

'You bloody idiot!'

'What did I do?' Neil turned to Santi. 'Back me up, darling. Thea is a silly name, isn't it?'

'It's a charming name,' said Santi, wiping the baby's chin.

'Ssh, he's coming back,' said Isabel, who really was learning fast.

*

Piper goodbyes took ages. Lots of hugging, much running back up the stairs to say one more thing, promises to meet up. Anna stood in the porch, alone, staring out at the half-gentrified street.

Any moment now she'd have to take her leave of Luca. She was surprised he hadn't asked for her number. By forty, women know when men are interested; Luca was interested.

Probably married, she thought. *Or perhaps my radar is unreliable.*

At the top of the stairs, Josh held the door open for the stragglers to leave. Polite. Genteel. But longing to be alone again. Or longing to call Thea?

Anna was tuned into Josh in a way that verged on the unhealthy; many nights she lay awake worrying about his future when she should have been catching up on her beauty sleep. Lately, her little passenger had pushed Josh off the top spot; that was only natural, but she felt guilty about it.

Another concern had barged in, shoving both the baby and Josh out of the way. That damn letter obscured all else. Anna paced on the pavement. She felt a special loneliness descend.

I have to confront this on my own.

If she brought it up with Neil, he'd groan; neither of them wanted to remember the time when the people she loved turned monstrous faces towards her. Her other siblings, the younger two, would look at her in a completely differ-ent light.

Maeve and Josh were in the dark about what their big sister had done: *I intend to keep it that way.*

The letter waited for her, like a bad smell, like a head cold, like a lover who doesn't know when to quit.

As Anna switched on lights, threw down her keys and shook off her jacket, the letter sat where she'd left it on the worktop. She didn't have to pick it up. One reading had set the words in stone.

Dear Anna,

Does the eleventh of November ring any bells? It should do. It was a big day for you, although I know you'd rather forget it. There's one person who can never forget it. That person is me.

Thanks for nothing, Anna Piper.

Carly

A thud. The Dog had bumped into something. Anna had almost got away without him, but Josh had thundered down the stairs with the gormless scrap in his arms. Now the beast was getting to know Anna's kitchen, scattering the fridge magnets and getting stuck in the gap between the washing machine and the dryer. A bowl of water was set down, but the dog had already blundered into it, soaking itself and the floor.

Anna bent down to tickle under the animal's chin; she already knew how much he loved that. 'You're such a mess,' she said. 'You look like a yeti. A very small yeti.' The dog would be handy for distracting her from the letter. A noise in the hall made her straighten up.

And talking of distraction . . .

Luca ambled into the kitchen. He cocked an eyebrow. 'So,' he said. 'When do I take you out? And where do we go?'

'I like . . . eating,' she offered.

'Good start. Me too.' Luca folded his arms, put his head back and studied her. 'Hmm. I'm not sure whether to be obvious and suggest an Italian place.'

'Be as obvious as you like. I love Italian food.'

'Great.' He smiled at her, not moving, enjoying the view.

'Great,' she reiterated, putting her hand to her hair. 'There's something I want to tell you . . .'

'Yes?' Luca closed the space between them. He was near enough to put his arms around her, and he looked as if he wanted to. This close, his eyes were like coal.

Anna let it happen. He was a rockface of linen and warmth. 'The dog's name is Yeti,' she murmured as he kissed her.

Chapter Four

Lunch at Dinkie's

A SMALL SWEET SHERRY
QUICHE, SAUSAGE ROLLS, COLESLAW
DINKIE'S SPECIAL CHOCOLATE CAKE

A lot can happen in a fortnight. For example, you can almost-but-not-quite fall in love.

Two weeks is long enough to penetrate the top layer of another person. Particularly if, like Anna and Luca, you see that person most days. Fourteen days of getting to know each other had revealed a few facts about Luca.

He called when he said he would; his chest-hair game was strong; he was unpretentiously knowledgeable about wine; he was expert at sneaking up noiselessly behind Anna and kissing the back of her neck; he tended to be grumpy if she rang him first thing in the morning. *He's a bear*, she'd think happily, as he growled and tutted. She was unable to like him any less even when he was surly and monosyllabic. *He's a great big Italian bear.*

A fortnight had done nothing to dim the power of the letter. It lay in Anna's bedside drawer, its voltage making the whole house hum. It had raised questions to which Anna had no answer, but by leaving out a return address or even a surname, it gave her no right of reply.

Unusually for such a decisive woman, Anna was stuck. The letter had brought chaos and then freeze-framed it, like a photograph of an erupting volcano.

Given the chance, she might be able to defend herself about the events of the eleventh of November. Carly – the name meant nothing to her – might scoff at the pathetic reasoning, but it was all Anna had to offer. It was all that stood between Anna and self-loathing.

She thought of the trunk in her attic, and how she would add to it again this November. That solemn ritual of creeping up the ladder, offering in hand. It was traditionally the worst day of her year, but now its power had leaked all over the other three hundred and sixty-four.

'Ye-ti!' The two-note call was pointless. The dog was untrainable. Sometimes Anna wondered if she should have his ears tested, but a dog who galloped from the far end of the house whenever the fridge door opened was *not* deaf.

Yeti widdled joyously and generously on carpets and floor-boards and feet. Any shoe left lolling about was chewed up. He had an irrational loathing for the sofa and ambushed it with his needle-sharp puppy teeth. Anna did her best to love him, but it was hard to love a creature who made your house stink and left tidy poos in the bottom of your wardrobe.

'He's a rescue dog,' Luca would remind her. 'He's been neglected.' The tiny dog looked even smaller in Luca's big hands. He built a kennel in the garden, which the dog refused to use. As a surprise, he took Yeti to be groomed, but the result was disappointing.

'He looks worse,' wailed Anna, as the demented furball barked indignantly at his own reflection in the back door.

'You'll learn to love him.' Luca seemed sure of this. 'Soon you'll wonder how you ever managed without him.'

That's you you're talking about, thought Anna, giving in to Luca's arms, his mouth, his greedy need for her. While giving herself, Anna held something back. Allowing him to eat her up as if she was a cream cake, she managed to withhold a little.

It wasn't easy; Anna loved being a cream cake.

Two weeks into the relationship – for that's what it was: Anna had heard Luca describe her as his girlfriend; even at forty these calibrations mattered – and it was time for the next Sunday Lunch Club.

'At last I get to meet the mysterious Dinkie.' Luca was buttoning up his shirt in Anna's bedroom after removing it in a hurry the moment he'd arrived.

'She'll have you wound around her little finger by the time you get your coat off.' Anna scrutinised her wardrobe. Dinkie liked Anna in blue, so blue it was. She slipped on a linen shirt dress and slid her toes into leather flats. Angling her foot, she took pleasure in the stitching of the shoe, and the density of the midnight blue dye. She made a mental note to ask Sam if they could move into shoe production at some point, and picked up her camera.

Luca threw up his arm and stepped back at the lightning flash. 'What the—'

'I take a Polaroid a day, remember? For Josh's project.' Anna fanned the small square, watching Luca materialise. Off guard, his eyes merry, it was a great likeness. She would pin it to her noticeboard in the shed. Already she perceived it as a keepsake. *I'm creating souvenirs for after he's gone.*

Certain truths had to be faced. One such truth was assembling itself in her uterus. The sexy, thoughtful man currently jiggling his car keys and imploring her to get a move on was not the child's father. When Anna put these two truths together, it gave her a reason to hold back.

*

The Germans probably have a word for a place that is both institutional *and* cosy. Sunville's breeze-block blandness was only slightly warmed up by the floral curtains at the double-glazed windows.

The corridor to Dinkie's room was a maze that smelled of talc and onions, dotted with figures hunched over walking frames. Anna hated to overtake them; her vigour high-lighted their feebleness.

In a glass-walled communal dayroom, somebody enthu-siastically played an electric keyboard. Anna peered in as she and Luca passed, waving hello at an elderly man who raised his stick to her. Doors squeaked shut elsewhere in the build-ing. Radios chattered. Plates clattered in a distant dining hall.

A hefty Irish woman in a powder pink Sunville tunic recognised her as they passed. 'You're Mrs Piper's grand-daughter!' Over her shoulder, she shouted, 'Handbags! Divorced! Allergic to coriander!'

Her warmth brought Anna's shoulders down a notch. The internet overflowed with stories of sadistic care home staff; she was grateful for evidence that Dinkie was listened to. She wondered what word described the old people around her. Were they inmates? Patients? She dimly remembered the superintendent referring to 'clients'. Somewhat late, perhaps, she shuddered at the word 'superintendent'.

The client in room 43 – *a ground-floor garden room w. en suite bath/kitchenette/satellite TV* – was holding court in a high-backed chair. Dinkie's name was appropriate; she was the size of a six-year-old, with a doll's face and enamel buttons for eyes. Her soft Irish skin was lined now, and her odd bent little beak of a nose gave her a poignant air. It also made her talk in a slightly snuffly way when she called out 'Anna! Darlin'!' Dinkie's Dublin accent was impervious to the decades she'd spent in London. 'There y'are, hen.'

Anna's appearance was clucked over – her hair was 'lovely', her dress was 'fabluss' – and she was kissed and a chair was found and Anna felt her family lap around her like water. Josh was perched on a stool, Paloma on his lap. Santi and Neil roared together at some joke. Maeve sat at Dinkie's feet like a Labrador, albeit one that smelled of Body Shop musk. Over by the window, Sam and Isabel held hands; Anna made sure to mouth a hello at them.

'And who's this?' Dinkie looked Luca up and down, her tiny blue eyes bright and perceptive.

'That's Anna's boyfriend,' said Maeve from the floor, enjoying herself.

'I'm Luca.' He held out his hand and Dinkie took it imperiously.

'Quare name,' she said under her breath. Using her telephone voice, she said, 'Will you take a small sweet sherry, Luca?'

Luca would, and did. He sat on the arm of Anna's chair and found her hand.

He was, Anna realised, nervous; scrawny Dinkie, with her man-made separates and her stiff white perm, had put this big dark man on his best behaviour.

'Is he Catholic?' asked Dinkie as if Luca wasn't there. She was joking. But only half joking.

'Actually, yes,' laughed Anna. She was thankful to Luca's ancestors for providing him with the correct religion; Dinkie still didn't know about the baby and today was the ideal opportunity to tell her. She foretold carefully concealed disappointment. She foretold her own heart cracking slightly as old-fashioned, devout Dinkie made the best of it.

'Lapsed, though,' said Luca apologetically to his hostess.

'Nobody's perfect,' said Dinkie.

'Seriously, Dinkie,' asked Neil, sherry in hand, paunch arguing with his striped shirt, 'is this really how you want to live?'

'I made me decision,' said Dinkie stoutly. 'Sunville is grand. I'm getting used to it.'

'Are you sure,' asked Maeve, 'you don't regret selling the house?'

The modest terraced Piper homestead was on the corner of a London street that had been dodgy when Dinkie moved in as a newly-wed, but was now slap bang in the middle of trendy territory. The mind-boggling profit would keep Dinkie in Sunville for the rest of her days.

'I never regret a thing,' said Dinkie. 'That's one of me rules.' In the sixty years since she was widowed, Dinkie had kept herself afloat financially and emotionally. Pride was one of the traits she'd passed to her oldest granddaughter.

'The room looks great,' lied Anna. The straight edges of the bland architecture sat uneasily with the big old mahogany bed and the wooden shelves crammed with Dinkie's beloved Catherine Cooksons. The red velvet armchair, its embrace such a part of Anna's childhood, sat beside a radiator instead of a coal fire. The radiator hummed, ignoring the June mildness, and the room was stuffy.

Lunch was a buffet affair of sausage rolls and quiche, eaten on laps. Neil sent Anna a look, one she returned with interest – Dinkie's home-cooking was a thing of the past. It was the end of an era.

And the start of a new one. When you carry the future around inside you, you're duty-bound to be optimistic. Anna loaded her plate: a day that included sausage rolls couldn't be all bad.

'There's something you don't know, Dinkie.' Maeve was coy at her grandmother's feet.

Damn. Anna put down her sausage roll. She'd wanted to tell Dinkie alone, let her grandmother get used to the idea. 'Um, Maeve—'

Maeve bunched her shoulders round her ears. 'I have a new boyfriend, Dinkie. And he's brilliant!'

Sidling up to Anna, Neil whispered, 'Only Maeve could think that trumps a baby.'

'Is he a looker?' Dinkie liked to point out that her husband – the late, sainted, Grandpa – had been dapper.

'Ye-s.' Maeve didn't seem sure. 'Well, he's tall and dark and all that shit. Sorry, Dinkie.' Maeve pulled in her chin, dodging her grandmother's swipe.

'And is *he* Catholic?' asked Dinkie.

'Don't know. Don't care.' Maeve believed in Buddhism on some days, and in Elvis on others.

'As long as he's kind to you, darlin',' said Dinkie, 'this fella's all right by me. But if he touches a hair on your head . . .' She put up two arthritic fists.

'My money's on the little woman!' shouted Neil.

'Less of the little, if you don't mind.' Dinkie beckoned to Isabel, who stepped forward like a deer stepping out onto a motorway. 'This girl,' said Dinkie – everybody under seventy was a girl – 'is a . . . what is it now, darlin'?' She cocked her head at Isabel's prompt. 'She's an environmental engineer!' Dinkie looked amazed as her dentures stumbled over the words. She was from a generation that was amazed if a woman got a degree, even though she herself had worked all her life and raised a son single-handedly.

Anna was surprised too. *I've sat with Sam day in day out and never asked what Isabel does for a living.* She wondered if he'd noticed and decided that of course he had. She watched him as Dinkie continued to sing Isabel's praises. Sam had changed ... was he better looking? His hair was the same. That ribbed jumper was ancient. *It's me who's changed.* Anna was looking at a man who was no longer her property; she was spotting virtues she hadn't bothered to notice for years. *How kind his eyes are ...*

'Hey.' Luca nudged her. Anna turned and he was super-close. Warmth, and a sweet odour that was related to sex, enveloped her. He leaned in, placed his lips against her forehead and her skull rumbled as he said, in his low deep voice, 'Looking forward to when we're alone again?'

'Yes,' said Anna with considerable understatement.

When he crossed the room, summoned by Dinkie to tell her all about his career – 'Therapist! Ooh! And tell me, does that pay well, darlin'?' – Neil skipped to Anna's side again.

'About time you told Luca, young lady.'

'What about?'

'Oh pur-leese. The baby.' Neil mouthed the explosive word.

Neil wasn't to know that she'd told Luca about her pregnancy in the car on the way home from the last Sunday Lunch Club.

They'd been idling at the lights, a few minutes from her door, when he'd said, 'We should have dinner one night.' He turned to her, his smile wolfish in the fading daylight. 'One night soon. Like tomorrow night.'

Instead of yes or no or maybe, Anna had said, 'I'm pregnant.'

He'd taken his hands off the wheel, sat back in surprise. 'Wow! You're super fertile! We haven't even held hands yet.'

They'd howled then, and the car behind had beeped at them to get going.

'You don't look pregnant,' said Luca, parking smoothly, expertly.

'It's new. I'm still getting used to it. It was a bit of a shock.'

'I see. So you're not . . .' Luca pouted as he worked out how to put it. 'You're not with the father?'

'No.'

'So, you're single and I'm single . . .' Luca put his hands behind his head and smiled that expansive smile that seemed to ping on all the street lights along Anna's road. 'And we're talking dinner, not marriage, so let's do it, yeah?'

It was that straightforward. Luca had a way of breaking situations down into bite-size pieces. 'Yeah,' she'd laughed. 'A nice steak. A chip or two. Can't hurt.'

'Thanks for telling me.' Luca leaned forward, closing the gap between them in the car. 'I'm going to kiss you, Anna, and if the kiss goes well I'm going to suggest that I come in for coffee.'

'Jesus, no pressure,' she mumbled, making him laugh so that he sat back again.

'Was that line crap?' he asked. 'It was meant to be smooth.'

'Just kiss me, Luca,' said Anna.

So he had.

'Did he come in for coffee?' asked Neil, underlining the double meaning of the phrase.

Anna jumped at his apparent mind-reading. 'Yes. And sex,' she whispered, with a neurotic look in Dinkie's direction.

'You cheeky girl!' Neil shuddered happily. 'Bet he's a beast.'

'Not telling.' Anna subdued him with a look. She *wanted* to talk about Luca, about his powerful thighs, his muscled back, the way he gasped when he slipped inside her. She wanted to sky-write about the way he'd made love to her in the hallway against the front door, unable to wait, and she wanted to write a one-act play about the love they'd made later, more slowly, in her bed, transforming a John Lewis sale purchase into a tousled temple to Cupid.

'You've gone all pink,' said Neil.

'It's stuffy in here.' Usually Anna needed to warm up to a sexual relationship, to coax herself into undressing in front of a man. Pregnancy should have added even more pressure and self-consciousness. With Luca, clothes were superfluous. Being naked felt right. There'd been no moral qualms, no wondering if it was too soon, no doubts that he'd respect her, or that she'd respect him, if they jumped in too fast.

'Careful,' said Neil, serious now. 'This isn't a good time to fall for somebody.'

'Nobody's falling for anybody,' she assured him as Luca returned to her, swimming through the crowded room.

'Miss me?' he asked hopefully.

'Brazen,' sighed Neil, shaking his head in Dinkie's direction. 'Bloody brazen behaviour.'

'What are you on about?' Anna fed Luca some quiche with her plastic fork. They laughed, in a bubble of their own making. Delicious, erotic, she didn't want it shattered by one of Neil's rants.

'Dinkie. Refusing to even *acknowledge* Paloma.' Neil shut his eyes, turned away.

'Eh?' Anna wondered if he was joking, but the pain on his face was real. 'Dinkie loves Paloma, you idiot.'

Santi had pulled a chair near to Dinkie, and placed Paloma's carrycot by Dinkie's feet, like an offering to a very small, slightly tipsy goddess.

'See?' Anna nudged her brother. 'She smiled down at her.'

'Big deal.' Neil chewed his cheek.

Luca, using a softer version of his usual voice which Anna knew was his therapeutic tone, said, 'There are many people vying for your grandmother's attention, Neil. She's an old lady, she—'

'Excuses,' said Neil in a bitter whisper. 'She doesn't accept Paloma because she's not her granddaughter by blood.'

'That's not true.' Anna frowned; this was hard to hear.

'You know it, Anna, and I know it.'

'It's dangerous,' suggested Luca, 'to tell people what they know.'

'One thing I *do* know about is prejudice. I didn't come out until I was thirty, Luca.' Neil said this as if it might be Luca's fault. 'I was so scared of how my parents and Dinkie would react. Santi there . . .' He waved an arm in his partner's direction. 'He didn't even have to come out!'

Santi, hearing his name, approached them, lugging the carrycot like an oversized handbag.

'Oh do shush, precious, for God's sake,' said Neil at his daughter, who was grizzling and kicking her bootees in the air.

'She wants to be held,' said Santi, who understood every gesture and sound the baby made.

'Dinkie!' called Neil, shame-faced, as if asking a huge favour. 'Paloma's fussing. Would you like to . . .?'

'Later, pet.' Dinkie held up her plate. 'Sure, I'm still eating.'

'Of course,' said Neil. 'I get it. Too busy.'

'Afters!' shouted Maeve, who regressed to toddler manners around Dinkie. 'Is it cake?' she asked lustfully.

'Of course. Chocolate cake. What else?' Dinkie seemed shocked at the idea of a Sunday lunch without its traditional finale.

'*Abuela*,' asked Santi. 'Did you make it yourself?'

Dinkie's cake was famous within the confines of the

family. 'Of course not,' said Sam. 'She couldn't make it here, could she?'

'I could, Sam,' said Dinkie smugly. 'And I did. Press that buzzer for me there, love.'

Sam did as he was told. A statuesque woman who wore the pink Sunville tunic as if it was couture brought in a dark towering cake. Her hair was piled high in dozens of plaits.

'This is Sheba.' Dinkie thanked the care worker, whose face was an introverted mask, her eyes cast down. 'She's from, where is it, love?'

'Lagos,' said Sheba curtly. When she lifted her eyes, they were a soulful brown.

'I love your hair, Sheebs,' said Maeve, who had a habit of awarding perfect strangers instant nicknames. Sheba didn't answer.

The cake was divided, given out, swooned over. It was as moist as it was rich as it was moreish; Anna's carefully applied lipstick was replaced with chocolate icing.

'Stay, Sheba, please,' said Sam as the woman backed out noiselessly. 'Have a piece.'

'Yes, stay,' the others echoed, and Sheba clamped her lips together, which seemed to be her best stab at smiling.

It was typical of Sam to notice her, to include her. Anna saw Isabel study the back of his head as Sam cut a slice of cake for Sheba. Possibly Isabel was also thinking how kind he was, how attentive.

Anna examined the past; had she noticed that about Sam when they were together? *Did I ever comment on it?* Isabel seemed to be doing a better job of being Sam's woman; Anna suffered a twinge of territorial annoyance. She called to him: 'Sam, did you look into that new accounting software Neil mentioned?'

Sam wrinkled his nose. 'Are you the same woman who tells me off for always talking about work? We have all week to discuss software, Anna. *I'm busy.*' He pulled Isabel to him. She squawked, they laughed, Anna tried to do the same.

He was right; she'd often warned him about becoming a mummified old bachelor who lived for his job. It was good – no, *great* – that he had something to distract him. *But the job equals me*, she thought, ashamed once more by her capacity for melodrama. *I'm losing him again* was a thought Anna couldn't fight off, even though she was the one who'd dissolved their marriage.

A whine went up, like a petulant police siren. Paloma had 'gone off', as Storm called it.

Santi, his mouth full of cake, motioned to Neil to take the baby off his knee.

'Sweetie, I'm eating,' said Neil.

'So is Santi,' said Anna.

'He's better at Paloma stuff,' said Neil.

'At changing a baby's nappy? It's hardly a technical challenge.'

'Have you ever changed one?' Neil nodded tartly. 'There you go.'

With Paloma under one arm, Santi hurried out. Anna saw the sideways look Sheba gave to Neil, and seconded it. *She doesn't miss a thing*, thought Anna.

'Come here to me, Anna.' Dinkie regally held out her hand, rubbing Anna's fingers when her granddaughter did as she was told. She lowered her voice, asked in a purring undertone, 'Are you pregnant, love?'

Anna swallowed hard. 'Yes.'

'Ah.' Dinkie held her gaze.

'Thirteen weeks. How did you . . .'

'It's all in your face, pet. You know your granny is an auld witch, don't you?' Dinkie was the seventh daughter of a seventh daughter: she could tell when thunder was on its way, and when one of her brood was lying. 'I knew each time your mammy was carrying one of youse.' She let go of her hand. 'Every baby is a blessing, Anna.'

The straightforward acceptance broke something in Anna. Tears streamed down her face. Sam was first at her side, an arm around her shoulders, asking, 'Hey, hey, what's all this?' like he used to do when they were married.

The others followed suit, apart from Luca, who held back; Anna was grateful for his discretion. Nobody felt it necessary to tell Dinkie how the baby was conceived; Dylan was airbrushed into 'an ex-boyfriend'.

'And does this new fella mind?' Dinkie made a small *hmm* at the modern way of dating. 'Wouldn't have happened in my day.'

'Not all men are like Grandpa.' Maeve was misty-eyed on sentiment.

'That reminds me. Storm, do your special job, lovey,' said Dinkie. She pressed a box of matches into his hands, shooing him towards the shelf over the radiator. Once her great-grandson had lit the tea light in front of Grandpa's photograph, Dinkie sat back, relaxed again as the room let out a satisfied *aw!* 'It's like your grandpa's here with us,' she said.

'Still watching over us.' Anna usually left the soppy stuff to Maeve, but today she was full of gratitude for the family's untidy love.

Lighting Grandpa's candle was a task Storm never whinged about. Silent, they all gave Grandpa a moment in the spotlight, respectfully taking in his clean-cut face, crystallised in the nineteen sixties. Smart, confident – cocky even – he had stayed ebulliently young while his wife shrank into the arms of old age. The jut of his cleft chin gave a hint of power and strength; his charisma had endured long past his life, partly because of endless retellings of the story of how he and Dinkie met.

'Story!' said Storm, who showed zero interest in most adult conversation, but always requested the story.

It didn't take much to set Dinkie off; as a Dubliner, storytelling was in her genes and she beckoned to Luca. 'Come closer, Luca, darlin'. You'll enjoy this.'

The room went quiet. This tale was a cornerstone of Piper mythology, polished to a sheen by constant retelling. Any of them could have recited it alongside her.

'Now then.' Dinkie's voice was sweet and dry, like candied leaves. 'Imagine me, sixteen years old. Hard to imagine me that young, I know. There I was, stepping off the boat from Ireland. I had on me best shoes and they were *killing* me.' She stuck out an ankle as if she could still see the buckled courts on her wide, flat, octogenarian feet. 'A little case in me hand, a St Anthony necklace under me vest and me best hat on.' This hat was infamous; she described it again. 'Jesus, it was gorgeous that hat. Felt. Dark green. Like a beret, but posher. I don't mind saying it – old women are allowed to be vain – but I was lovely. Fresh, with the dew of Ireland still on me silly face.'

'Then,' said Maeve, 'you saw Grandpa.'

'Well, now, let's be honest, Grandpa saw me.'

An *oooh* went up; like a panto, the story had long-established call-and-response set pieces. Luca, catching on, came in late with his *ooh* and everybody laughed.

'The port was big. So many people rushing around, and they looked so hard . . .' Dinkie looked at the ground for a moment, as if the carpet had been replaced with the echoing floors of Holyhead, busy with sharp heels and heavy boots and ground-in dog ends. 'I wanted to turn around, run home, back to me parents, back to our warm kitchen. I felt so small.'

As one, they all said it: 'You are so small, Dinkie.'

'I was jostled all over the place. Nobody had a speck of manners. Some big eejit almost knocked me over and didn't even look back, never mind apologise. Then . . .' she paused, ratcheting up her audience's anticipation, 'this chap steps in front of me and puts out his arm, like this.' Dinkie crooked her arm. 'He says . . .'

They all recited Grandpa's line – 'May I be of any assistance?'

'I'd been warned about you English!' Dinkie waggled a finger at Sam, who put up his hands in defence. 'I was haughty with him. Mother had warned me not to talk to strange men. He persisted, chasing after me as I stumbled off in me hat. He said—'

Again the audience supplied their grandfather's dialogue: 'My name's Charlie Piper. Are you catching the London train, miss?'

'Still I ignored him. Out of the corner of me eye, I could see he looked like a movie star.'

Anna and Josh enjoyed a secret smile; their grandmother was stretching the truth, but they also benefited from her bias. All Dinkie's geese were swans.

'He was guiding me, touching my elbow, and the crowd didn't seem so bad. After a while he says—'

'Where are my manners?' they chanted. 'Let me take your bag.'

This was one of Storm's favourite parts. Cross-legged on the floor, he shouted, 'You thought he was a thief!'

'I said, "Oh no you don't!" and he laughed, and when I heard his laugh I knew that not only had I met a good man, but I'd met *my* man.'

Laying his head on Neil's shoulder, Santi let out a contented sigh.

'Bold as brass, he sat beside me all the way to Euston. "Tell me about yourself, gel," he said.' Dinkie's approximation of her husband's cockney accent was fond and devilish. 'He bought me a cuppa and a bun the size of me head and I chattered about life back in Dublin. Nobody had ever been interested in me before. It was like . . .' Dinkie was lost for a second. 'It was perfect,' she whispered.

'Then,' prompted Storm, '*then*, Dinkie?'

'We had a smoke and a laugh and suddenly we were at Euston station. He saw me to the barrier. Just about to say goodbye. Then he saw the look on me face.'

'You were frightened.' Anna was moved again by this part of the legend.

'London was so much bigger and dirtier than I'd expected.

I was a lost lamb. Then your grandfather turned to me and he said . . .' She paused, let them do it for her.

'You're going to be all right, gel, because I'm going to look after you.'

'And so he did.' Dinkie wrapped up her party piece. 'Afterwards he told me he'd fallen for me on the train, and that was that.'

'They didn't waste much time.' Neil was wry, filling in the newcomers. 'Two months later they were married, and then Dad came along soon after.'

'Whisht you, you cheeky so-and-so.' Dinkie wasn't really annoyed; she had a salty side. 'He worked hard, looked after me and your da, devoted himself to us. Then, when little Alan was six years old . . .'

Maeve said wistfully, 'Grandpa was taken.'

No, he died. Anna disliked euphemisms. She looked at the black-and-white face behind the shimmering candle. The glimmer in Grandpa's eye explained why a God-fearing Irish colleen of sixteen would ignore her mother's warnings.

'One night, Charlie was late home. He was never late and I had this terrible foreboding. I tucked little Alan into bed, slung on me coat, to go out looking. None of these mobile thingies in those days! I opened the front door and wasn't there two policemen coming up the path. Jaysus, the looks on their faces. I felt for them, bringing that news to a family. There'd been an accident at the factory, they said. He was gone.'

Silence fell in the room.

'You had to look after Dad all on your own.' Anna felt the echo keenly.

'Your dad was no trouble,' said Dinkie, lovingly lenient.

The look that travelled between Anna and Neil was so practised and quick that nobody else noticed. As the audience dispersed, as the final slivers of cake were handed out, Luca gravitated back to Anna.

'No trouble?' Neil was surly. 'Remember what Dad said to me when I finally told him I was gay?'

'Of course I do,' said Anna, looking over her shoulder. This seemed neither the time nor the place to dredge that memory out of the murk.

'He told me I got it from Mum's side.' Neil glowered, as insulted now as he had been then. '*It*. As if homosexuality was a disease.'

'Dad is . . . well, he's *Dad*.' Anna and Neil rarely discussed their father. 'He's a man of his generation.'

'So? Those two . . .' Neil jabbed a finger in the direction of Maeve and Josh, currently going through Dinkie's collection of Daniel O'Donnell cassette tapes. 'Those two don't have any concept of what he's really like.'

'They grew up in his house, Neil.' Anna pretended not to know what he was talking about; this hadn't been aired with

Luca yet. 'They put up with his moods, with his opinions being the only ones worth having, with him getting his way. A lot of men his age have to rule the roost.' Sam hadn't been like that; they'd been partners. 'Times have changed, thank God.'

'Not in this family.'

'Mrs Piper . . .' It was the first time Sheba had spoken. Her accent was strong, guttural. 'It's time to—'

Dinkie cut in tersely. 'Thank you, Sheba. You can go.'

'But you must—'

'I said thank you.' That tone was reserved for grave misdemeanours. Anna had winced under it when she'd broken Dinkie's favourite ornament, or missed Mass. As Sheba left the room, Anna's antennae wiggled.

'Don't you like Sheba, Dinkie?'

'She's grand.' Dinkie was short.

'Are you sure? Dinkie, you know I worry about you being in here. Is Sheba, you know, kind to you?' There had been a touch of anger in the set of the woman's shoulders as she left.

Changing the subject, as she always did when she was disinclined to answer a question, Dinkie asked Isabel what she saw in Sam because it surely couldn't be his money or his looks, but Anna didn't join in with the laughter.

'Quick drinkie poos?' Neil's suggestion was met with ardent nods as Dinkie's visitors passed through the sliding doors of Sunville out into the early evening.

'That pub looks ... awful,' laughed Anna, pointing to a dive on the next corner.

'It'll do,' said Sam.

It did do. Sitting round a beer-puddled table, they compared notes on Dinkie's new home.

Josh was inclined to make the best of it. 'It's warm and she's safe,' he said, head dipping, eyes on his drink; he tended to hang back at family get-togethers. 'At least we don't have to worry about her having a fall on her own.'

Anna hadn't realised Josh worried about such things. She hadn't realised he worried much about anything; it seemed to be Josh's destiny to be the one everybody else worried about. She worried now, taking in his thin frame, wondering why he let his hair grow so long, detecting signs of neglect. 'That's true.' She decided to make the best of it; Making the Best of It was one of Dinkie's skills. 'She has all her familiar stuff around her.'

'Grandpa's looking down from the shelf,' said Maeve.

'And from heaven,' said Neil, setting down a tray of drinks. 'Don't forget heaven.'

'What's the matter with you today?' Anna felt Maeve and Josh sit back in their seats; they rarely got involved when big sis and big bro locked horns. 'Why all the bitching?'

'Me? Bitching?' Neil's ruined cherub face looked affronted. 'Santiago, was I being—'

'*Sí*.' Santi was engrossed in arranging Paloma's blanket

105

around her, like a snow cloud. She was a burst of light in the grotty pub.

Neil gave in. 'Sometimes it gets to me, you know? All that stuff about Grandpa. How come Dad's the way he is if Grandpa was so perfect?'

Maeve scowled. 'What's wrong with Dad?' she said indignantly.

'He didn't come to my wedding, for a start.'

'Not that again!' Maeve snorted. 'They live in Florida, Neil. Mum wasn't well.'

'She looked as fit as a bloody fiddle on Skype.' Accustomed to being listened to at his ad agency, Neil expected the same treatment off duty. 'We all know why they didn't come.'

'Can't we move on?' asked Santi, sounding older than Dinkie.

'*His* parents came.' Neil jerked his head at Santi. 'They're Catholics too, so Dad doesn't have the excuse of religion. Dad's bigoted. He's *disappointed*. He doesn't like his son being gay.'

'Bullshit,' said Maeve.

Josh said nothing. But he said it loudly.

'He sent you a present, though.' Anna remembered the size of the cheque. For the first time, that struck her as odd; the last thing Neil needed was money.

'And did you notice Dinkie's behaviour today?' Neil was red with annoyance. His lips thinned as he said, 'Barely *looked* at Paloma.'

Isabel leaned against Luca, her mouth to his ear. Anna heard her whisper, 'You get used to it. All the lunches are like this. It's better than telly.'

'Dinkie loves babies!' Maeve was as miffed as Maeve ever got, which was hardly at all.

'But does she love *this* baby?' Neil pointed at the oblivious Paloma. 'This baby with two dads?'

Luca shifted, looked at the ceiling, his thighs spread. Anna heard him make a small, exasperated noise. She said, 'Neil, you're talking as if we're in the dark ages. None of us think twice about this stuff. We all love Paloma, the way we love you and Santi.'

'I'm not talking about *us*,' said Neil, encompassing them all with a wave of his arms. 'I'm surprised at you, of all people, defending Dad.'

That got everybody's interest.

'What does he mean?' Maeve sat forward.

'Nothing, he means nothing.' Anna opened a bag of crisps and said, surreptitiously, to Neil, 'You can be such a shit.'

They stared each other out. Anna won. She'd been winning staring competitions with Neil since they were tiny. 'He's just stirring,' she said to Maeve and Josh, who, despite the diversion of the crisps, were looking from one to the other in bewilderment. 'Dad and I get on fine, you know that.'

'Don't fight,' said Josh.

Anna crooked her little finger, held it out to Neil. 'Paxies?'

'Paxies.' Neil curled his finger around hers. 'Sorry.' He was chastened. Neil always went too far, and then he always felt terrible about it. As families do, with their elastic love, they forgave him.

Walking to the car, Neil and Anna went ahead, conspiring.

'Did you see how panicked Josh got when he thought we were falling out?' said Anna.

'They think of us as surrogate parents,' said Neil. 'They never minded when Mum and Dad argued.' He eyed her, as if wondering whether to go on. He did go on, of course; Neil rarely held back. 'Does it ever bother you, the way Mum and Dad exploited us? Making us look after Maeve and Josh all the time?'

'It was hardly exploitation. We were babysitting, Neil. And Dinkie was always around to take the strain when they were away.'

'True.' They shared a nostalgic moment. At their grandmother's house, Neil and Anna had been relieved of their duties, allowed to regress, run slightly wild. They'd stayed up late, had ice cream instead of dinner, were never asked to account for Maeve or Josh. Without saying a word against their parents' behaviour, Dinkie showed she understood.

'Sometimes I feel as if we had a totally different childhood to those two.' Neil looked back, checking they were out of earshot. 'We know what Mum and Dad are capable of. And Maeve and Josh . . . *don't.*'

It would have been so easy to tell him about the letter. Neil would . . . *what, exactly?* He'd understand, yes, but nobody could 'solve' the problem it presented. *And he'd be so upset.* She hugged him, so suddenly that he jumped, before hugging her back.

'Maeve and Josh,' she said, into his ear, 'must never know.'

'We agreed that at the time. It's still for the best.'

'Listen,' she said, surfing on their candour. 'You didn't really mean that about Dinkie not loving Paloma?'

'I did.' Neil stopped dead. 'Look at me, Anna.'

'What exactly am I meant to be looking at?'

'How old am I?'

'You're forty-four. Next question.'

'How long have I been out as a gay man?'

'Fourteen years.'

'Which means that for thirty years I pretended to be something I'm not. Now I want to be accepted. Is that too much to ask? Perhaps you think I'm being petty when I complain about Dinkie or whinge about Dad not coming to the wedding.' Through gritted teeth, he said, 'Do you honestly think anything on earth could make me miss Paloma's wedding?'

Anna considered carefully before opening her mouth. He

might explode, but it needed to be said. 'If you'd walk across hot coals to attend Paloma's wedding, what's stopping you changing her nappy now and again?' She took in the way he glared at her, but carried on. 'Santi did everything for Paloma today. You didn't take any of the strain.'

'It's not like that at home,' snapped Neil. 'Oh, and thanks for the support.' Archly, he put an emphatic full stop to their tête-à-tête and stalked back to the others.

Elaborate goodbyes were made. 'I love these Sundays,' said Isabel. 'You're never sure if there'll be way too much food or not enough. There's always some sort of row. Sometimes somebody cries. But they're never ever dull!'

She sounded as if she planned to be around for quite some time. Anna made a point of hugging Isabel, eyeballing Sam over her shoulder with a *See! I'm being nice!* look. There was nothing wrong with Isabel. Perhaps that was the problem. She was a cut-out doll, not what Anna would choose for Sam.

To Maeve, Anna whispered, 'How much did she give you?' She'd spotted the sleight of hand as Dinkie slipped Maeve a bundle of notes. When they were kids, it had been fifty pence, but rates had gone up.

'Just a little something to tide me over,' said Maeve.

Josh lurked. He always skulked at the end of a lunch, needing a lift, too diffident to ask. He was a puppy, hoping for a caress, fearing a slap.

'Hop in, you,' said Luca, unlocking the car.

The bedsit was miles out of their way, but Anna was grateful to Luca for rescuing Josh. The journey gave her a chance to talk to her little brother. Wary of Luca's judgement, she kept the nagging to a minimum, even though she longed to ask if he'd contacted his landlord about the dodgy wiring. She didn't ask about Thea. She asked what she should name the baby.

'We should let babies name themselves,' he said.

If Maeve had said it, Anna would have rolled her eyes until they were sore. From Josh it was cute. 'Oh shut up,' she laughed, slapping him.

He laughed too. Anna felt as if she'd won a prize.

Luca dropped her at her gate, calling her back three times to kiss him, igniting a need that would have to wait until they met again.

Home. The familiar pictures on the wall, the worn carpet on the stairs, the favourite spot in the kitchen where Anna sat herself gratefully down. Yeti bounded into her lap, his paws on her shoulders, licking off her make-up. His breath smelled of shoe.

There was so little evidence of her pregnancy that the fatigue took her by surprise. Sunday Lunch Club had exhausted her. Anna tried to retrace life's steps, to work out when Dinkie had made the transition from somebody to lean on, to somebody she worried about.

It was only fair that Anna look out for her grandmother; it was loving payback. There was no effort required; it was easy. When her parents had moved to Florida, the baton had been passed to Anna; the unspoken assumption being that the oldest, unmarried, childless Piper female would step in.

Sexist, thought Anna. And what's more: *sisterist*. She'd roped Neil in, and they'd found Sunville together after a few dispiriting weeks of nosing around residential care homes. Neil's financial adviser had finessed the house sale; it was the usual modus operandi: Neil paid the bills but didn't get his hands dirty. The anxiety was chiefly Anna's.

There was ironing to do. A bath to be had. Luca to call and talk dirty to.

And the letter to read. Again.

Chapter Five

Lunch at Luca's

ANTIPASTO: PROSCIUTTO, SALAMI, BRUSCHETTA
TORTELLINI IN BRODO
LAMB IN BREADCRUMBS
ZUPPA INGLESE

Anna had morning sickness. She also had midday sickness, afternoon sickness, middle-of-the-night sickness. She wondered who'd named it so misleadingly.

That Sunday morning it was only a vague queasiness, easily forgotten in the splendour of Luca's bedroom. His spacious flat, on the ground floor of a detached period house on a road between a loop of the Thames and Henry VIII's magnificent palace at Hampton Court, was full of books and paintings and *things*. It could have been cluttered, but instead it had a crazy order. Each artwork meant something; he'd read all the books; the furniture had travelled with him through many house moves. She buried herself in its colour and texture, in the changing light that crawled across the rooms throughout the day, completely altering them.

In his bed – a colossal four-poster affair – she tugged the red drapes across, creating a personal night-time. She didn't want it to be Sunday; she wanted to live with Luca in an eternal Saturday night, when love was made and boxed sets were watched and the deep rumble of his laugh made her tingle.

Hampton Court Palace had become one of 'their' places. They picnicked in the grounds and caught the ferry from the riverbank. It was such an unlikely place – a sprawling fantastical castle plonked in a suburb. Gilded dragons and unicorns glowered from its gates yet it was opposite a Pizza Express. It suited their strange romance, which was also caught between two separate realities. There was Anna's, which involved a baby, and Luca's, which did not.

It wasn't that they didn't mention her pregnancy. They did. They never *discussed* it, though. It was a fact, like so many other facts.

Fact: Anna was allergic to coriander.

Fact: Luca snored.

Fact: Anna was pregnant.

Fact: Luca was not.

In the far end of the flat, an oven door slammed. Luca had been up since dawn, and heavenly smells nosed their way through the bed drapes. It had been his idea to host this week's Sunday Lunch Club: 'My way of apologising for keeping you to myself all this time.' Each time Anna had been invited to lunch during the last two months, she'd demurred, preferring her flat or Luca's, just the two of them. The other clubbers had preferred not to meet without her; she'd been both flattered and dismayed. It was a pressure of sorts and she had her fill of that.

The covers moved by her feet. She heard panting. Yeti was waking up.

A bump travelled up the bed, a pointed snout trimmed with impressive whiskers emerged, followed by the rest of Yeti. There was a lot of Yeti; he'd grown into his name and out of his dog basket. Despite Anna's best intentions to train him carefully, he had Access All Areas, shedding hair like a Kardashian spends money.

The latest rule he'd torn up was her most precious one. She'd vowed never to let Yeti on the bed, but the piteous howling got to her and now she and Luca were a threesome. He complained that he was the odd one out, as his girlfriend and her dog cuddled and spooned and shared licky kisses beside him.

The noise of the door easing open and the sound of feet padding across the carpet got Anna wiggling with anticipation, pulling the silk cover up to her chin and enjoying the feel of its rumpled weave against her breasts.

'*Buongiorno, cara!*'

Anna squirmed, corkscrewing herself down among the bedclothes. Luca knew the effect his speaking Italian had on her. She was radioactive with desire around this man; it could be hormones, but she preferred to believe it was chemistry.

The first time they'd made love – a mere five hours after they met, making Anna more or less a slut, and a happy slut at that – could have been awkward, icky. It had taken Anna a while to come to terms with her pregnant body; it had felt 'other', not entirely her own.

In Luca's arms – greedy, lusty, passionate – she'd reclaimed herself. He'd roamed all over her, enjoying the scenery, his mouth on every part of Anna. Their nakedness was so honest she felt clothed in her skin; as if she could wander out and buy a pint of milk without covering up her creamy nudity.

Her body had changed since then. Pregnancy was the gift that keeps on giving – it gave her a new shape every couple of days. Her tum was expanding, her profile rounder, but she was still not obviously pregnant.

That mattered. Anna had a faint fuzzy fear that when her bump rounded out, when it got to the point where strangers gave her their seat on the tube, she would revolt Luca. That moment was some way off, and Anna had trained herself not to think about it. She took each day as it came with Luca; they couldn't, and didn't, make plans.

The breasts, however, *had* arrived, and for that Luca was truly grateful. Anna felt voluptuous, ripe, *powerful*. Undressing in front of him was a joint pleasure; no shucking off her pants and leaping into bed. Two equals enjoying each other.

It was heady stuff.

The bed curtain was drawn back. 'Breakfast!'

'Is there any nicer sight in the world,' said Anna, 'than a great-looking man you've just had superb sex with coming towards you with a tray in his hands?'

'Thank you, madam. We pride ourselves on offering a complete service.'

The flat didn't need much primping to prepare it for the Sunday Lunch Club crew. It looked best in slight disarray, with the sun slanting through the shutters. A spattering of dust only added to the patina, as if a portion of old Italy had been towed across the Mediterranean and moored in Surrey.

As Luca sang and sliced salami among the hanging copper pans in his galley kitchen, Anna vomited discreetly in the en suite.

This was one by-product of pregnancy, unlike the increased cup size and libido, she was keen to keep from

Luca. It would be different if he was the father; *I'd share everything, good* and *bad with him.*

Anna wiped her mouth with a groan, remembering the days when the only times she threw up was when she mixed her drinks on a night out.

The phone trilled. LITTLE SIS read Anna.

'Maeve!'

'I might be a bit late. There's some sort of works on the track or something.'

'No probs.' *Why is she calling to say this?* Maeve was always late.

'Oh, and Paul can't make it.'

'Ah.'

'Don't bloody "ah" me, Anna Piper. I knew you'd do this.'

'Do what? Use a simple two letter word?' Anna cupped her hand, checking her breath.

'You know what you're doing. Making out there's something wrong, that stupid Maeve has cocked up her love life. Well, he has food poisoning. He's lying in his bed, *dying.* Happy now?'

Anna flinched; her dad used to say that to her, with the same ugly inflection. 'I didn't—'

'Sorry to disappoint you, but Paul's ace. I . . . I love him.'

'Then I'm happy for you.' *I'm also wondering why you're so incredibly defensive.* 'You've got me all wrong, Maevey. I just want you to be OK. I want us all to be OK. I want to meet this amazing Paul.' Anna fought to keep the subtext out of her voice; she'd been wondering why Paul hadn't yet been shown off like a show pony.

'He's so keen to meet you lot. I'll have a lunch club down here!'

'Sounds great.' In her mind's eye, Anna saw limp vegetarian pasties and finger-marked glasses.

'Listen, Alva's making trouble.'

'Alva? How?' Surely not the same Alva who covered more than half of the household bills, paid for Storm's schooling and babysat him whenever Maeve had an inkling to 'find herself' at Glastonbury?

'He's saying stuff.'

'What stuff?'

'That maybe Storm should live with him for a while.'

'You mean, literally move in with him and Clare and the kids?'

'Mm-hmm.'

Anna knew that sound; Maeve's lips were pursed to keep in the tears. 'What's the reason? I mean, Storm's happy at home, so . . .' It was hard to tell with the boy. He turned inwards. Perhaps it was his age, but Anna worried he was like his Uncle Josh. That the discontent would linger long past his teens. 'Isn't he?'

'What are you trying to say?'

'Let's talk about it properly when you get here.' Maeve was as prickly as a hedgehog; she only lost her trademark cool when she was deeply troubled. 'We'll sort it out, don't worry.' She'd been making promises like this to Maeve since her sister was a baby. On the whole, she kept them. 'I'm sure Alva isn't planning to take Storm away from you. Perhaps . . .' She trod carefully. 'Perhaps it would be good for both of you, you and Storm, if he went to his dad's for a bit. We all need a breathing space now and then.'

There was no explosion, just a small voice on the other end agreeing that 'you might be right'.

With half an hour to go, Luca was flat out. The oven was on, the hob was crowded with bubbling pots, the girlfriend was banished from the kitchen.

Drifting about in jeans – top button undone beneath a floaty white top – Anna crossed a line. Specifically the line at the door of Luca's consulting room. He hadn't said so, but it was clear that he preferred her to keep out; he was sensitive about client confidentiality. Many times Anna had tried to dig into his professional relationship with Josh, but no matter now subtle the question, Luca warned her off. Gently. But very firmly.

Like an illegal immigrant, Anna flitted across the border

into the dark-walled room. There was, disappointingly, no chaise longue. Between an inviting sofa and a plush office chair, a box of tissues sat ready on a low table.

It was a room of secrets.

Files stood tidily on a shelf. There were no names, just initials. Anna speed-read the labels until she found J.P. Before she could raise her hand to take it down, she heard Luca clear his throat in the doorway.

'Are you trying to get me struck off?'

'No, just . . .'

'Just looking for your brother's file.' Luca stood to one side, indicating she was to leave the room. Now. 'This is my place of work,' he said gravely. His expression, fixed and stern, made him look older, less like 'her' Luca, and Anna was flooded with remorse.

'I know. I shouldn't have. Sorry.'

He smiled, back to himself again. 'Don't make me lock the door, Annie.' She loved it when he called her that; nobody else ever had. 'This has to be private. You understand?'

She understood. She kissed him. He tasted of garlic and tomatoes, and Anna had always liked those ingredients. She could have kissed him for a lot longer, but the doorbell rang and, judging by the sounds of bickering, Neil and Santi and Paloma had arrived.

'Don't look at me!' said Neil instead of hello, flouncing past, leaving Anna with a bottle of good Italian wine and a hand-tied bouquet of white and green and mauve flowers. Her favourite colours; Neil was a genius at gifting.

'We're not talking to each other,' said Santi sniffily, offering Paloma up for adoration.

'From what I could hear, you're talking to each other very loudly.' Anna hugged her brother-in-law, grateful as ever for his presence. He was a radiator, not a fridge; Santi gave out warmth, never hoarding his happiness, always ready to share.

Even when he was miffed.

'What's he done n— oh my God!' Anna stepped back as Neil turned to face her in the narrow hallway. 'Your face!'

'Yes, I've had Botox. Sue me. Crucify me.' Neil's taut face was crimson with emotion. 'I happen to think it takes years off me.'

'It's *your* face,' said Luca, kissing him on both rubbery cheeks. 'You can do what you like with it.' Anna could tell he was hiding his shock. And amusement.

'There was nothing wrong with your face.' Santi spoke low, nostrils inflated, as he whisked past into the sitting room. 'I *like* your face.' He stopped, looking around him, taken aback by the dimensions of the space. 'You've knocked two rooms into one!' He stared about him, delighted. 'Luca, you have taste.'

'I know.' Luca winked at Anna. 'Just look at my bird.'

Slang was so wrong in Luca's mouth; it was strangely thrilling to be called his 'bird'.

Like number fourteen buses, the lunch guests arrived all at once. Maeve and Storm met Josh on the stairs, ahead of Sam and Isabel, who'd brought a pot plant and a strange home-made cake which Isabel kept apologising for.

All were taken aback by the paper plates. Luca was taken aback that they were taken aback. It was, he said, how his mother always served Sunday feasts. 'It's the food that's important, not the washing-up. To Italians, anyway.' He enjoyed a dig now and then at his heathen British friends. 'I go to her place at least once a month and we throw out the plates when it's finished.'

'Why didn't you invite your mum today?' asked Sam.

'It'd be great to meet her,' said Maeve. She turned to Anna. 'What's she like?'

'I, um, wouldn't know,' smiled Anna.

'Mama's a busy woman,' said Luca.

Not too busy to talk to her son daily on the phone, or to meet him in town every week for a cocktail. It seemed like the most natural thing in the world for such a dutiful, fond son to introduce his mother to his 'bird', but so far Luca had never even mentioned it.

'Oh God, this bruschetta,' said Maeve, eyes flickering in bliss, once the obligatory toast to the absent Dinkie had been made.

'And the salami!' Sam spoke with his mouth full, leaning across the lace tablecloth – a strangely feminine choice for a man like Luca, but, apparently, an heirloom – to snaf-fle a bruschetta. He patiently held up his toasted ciabatta topped with an oily tumble of diced tomato so Isabel could Instagram it. Her account was, apparently, 'mainly food and kittens'. Anna knew that the 'old' Sam would have scoffed at that, but the new, smitten Sam looked at Isabel as if she was made of precious china.

'It's so good,' said Santi, putting his hand to his heart, 'to eat food made with real love. And proper seasoning.'

'Are you really enjoying it, Neil?' asked Sam. 'I can't tell from your expression . . .'

'Enough with the Botox jokes.' Neil didn't join in with the laughter. 'Remember that gay years are like dog years – we age quicker than you boring straights.'

'Your daddy speaks such nonsense,' said Santi to Paloma. Once again, she was on his lap. 'We think he's gorgeous, don't we?'

'Youth is currency in my world,' said Neil. 'Which makes me a pauper.'

'I know what you mean,' said Anna. She and Luca were sharing a chair, which was nicely intimate but also hard on her behind. 'Women are up against that, too. We lose value as we age.'

'Not in this house!' said Luca.

'Some women,' said Sam, turning to take in Isabel, 'will improve as the years go past.'

'It's a pressure, though.' Maeve backed Anna up. 'You've got to be thin, you've got to look no older than thirty-five your whole life, you've got to shave your legs, wax your you-know-what. It's a full-time job.' She addressed Paloma. 'Don't get involved, sweetie. Refuse! Be like your Auntie Maeve; my underarms are a jungle!'

Neil tried to scowl. 'Please don't bring your hairy bits to the lunch table, Maeve.'

'So *that's* tortellini in brodo,' said Maeve as Luca put down white bowls. Small pasta shapes swam in a shimmering golden broth. When pressed, Luca explained that he'd simmered beef bones, chicken, onions, carrot and celery for four hours. 'But yours, Maeve,' he added before she could complain, 'is a vegetarian version I made in a separate pot.'

'Four hours?' Anna put an arm around him. 'That's dedication!' she said, with a hint of pride. 'I have a boyfriend who can actually *cook*!'

'That's very sexist, Anna.' Luca tucked his napkin into his collar, *Godfather*-style.

'Nope, it's realistic.' Anna turned to Sam. 'I did all the cooking when we were married, didn't I?'

She regretted it as soon as she said it. Anna often referred to her marriage, but now that Isabel was an SLC regular, perhaps that was inappropriate. She saw Isabel's head droop slightly over her pasta, and said quickly, 'But that was years ago, so ...'

'I managed to knock up a weird casserole thing last week. Remember, Issy?' Sam put his hand to his stomach. 'Maybe that's why I've been having these twinges in my gut.'

Anna tried to share an ironic look with Isabel at this latest evidence of Sam's hypochondria, but Isabel looked away, flustered, as if unsure of engaging with her. *She's wary of me*, thought Anna.

'*More* food?' wailed Maeve as the next wave arrived.

'Jesus, I can't face another morsel, but that lamb looks so-o good.' Neil allowed Luca to pile his plate with slices. 'I half expected to see Thea today.' He raised his double chin, peering down at Josh.

'She's not ready for the spotlight.' Josh helped himself to potatoes.

Santi put his head on one side. Josh touched his soft heart. 'We'll be kind to her,' he promised. 'We don't bite.' He flicked a look at his husband. 'Well, I don't.'

'Whereas,' said Anna, 'Neil is Hannibal Lecter.'

The loudest laugh came from Isabel, who was both trying too hard and sloshed.

'Luca,' said Maeve, 'don't you think it's time we met Thea?'

Nice try, thought Anna, as Luca avoided the question with a shake of his head and a pout of his full lips. Not only did he refuse to be drawn on the nature of Josh's therapy, he was also tight-lipped about Thea's age, nationality, height. Or whether she was as into Josh as he clearly was into her. The only morsel Anna had managed to draw out of Luca was that, yes, Thea was 'good for' Josh.

Now, he said to Maeve, 'Let's respect Josh, and let him decide when we meet Thea.'

All very well, thought Anna, *but it's tricky to respect somebody if you worry about them*. It was, perhaps, a presentiment of motherhood, which meant Anna couldn't share it with Luca. He had no emotional investment in the baby.

'At least,' said Maeve, unable to drop it, 'take a bloody Polaroid of her, Josh. You take a picture of *everything*.' He'd already snapped Storm's new trainers and Anna's ponytail.

Josh pushed back the strand of dark hair that fell over one eye, and didn't answer Maeve, saying instead, 'I'm off to Croatia next week.' He closed his eyes, with make-believe patience, and said, 'Before you ask, Maeve, yes, Thea's coming with me.'

A not so covert look of approval travelled from Piper to Piper. This was progress. Josh had always sloped off abroad when his budget permitted, exploring corners of Europe and Russia and Latin America. Always alone, he sent no postcards, never texted a scenic shot. It was as if a door slammed when he left the country – and his family – behind. Even the inevitable Polaroids he took along the way were devoid of human figures.

'It'll be nice to have company,' said Anna. She was never quite at rest when he was away. She assumed that her brother suffered with depression – it had never been named – and she intuited that these trips were one way of dealing with it. This Croatian trip with Thea sounded like a holiday – a most un-Josh occurrence.

Begging like a professional, Yeti roamed beneath the table. Maeve slipped him cubes of Italian roast potato, freckled with rosemary. Isabel gave him the fat off her lamb. Neil pushed away the damp snout, saying, 'You've spoiled that dog, Anna.'

On cue, Yeti burped. Above the giggles, Anna defended her hairy protégé. 'He wees where he should now!'

'I've had boyfriends who couldn't achieve that level of sophistication,' said Neil.

He was on better form today, not so warlike. Now that Anna wasn't drinking alcohol, she had a hypersensitivity to how much the others drank. And the effect it had.

Neil and Maeve drank too much; *like I used to*. Two hours in and they grew fuzzy around the edges, groping for their words, meandering on when the conversation had changed direction. Sticking to tap water, as ever, Josh was unchanging, calm as a monk. Luca, she noticed, only drank enough to relax, never enough to unravel; at some point, Anna assumed, she would find a fault with her lover, but for now the honeymoon blinkers were still firmly *on*.

Nobody knew what zuppa inglese was. 'It's like trifle,' explained Luca. 'The name translates as English soup.'

Layers of cake – 'He *made* the sponge,' Anna mouthed to an astonished Maeve – were interspersed with pillowy whipped cream and trickled with liqueur.

'None for me, thanks.' Neil's refusal silenced the table. 'What?' he snapped. 'Is there any point me spending a fortune on my face if I let the rest of me get fat?'

'But you're already fat, so ...' Maeve didn't see the problem.

'One bowl of zuppa inglese won't make much difference. You *love* trifle.' Anna hated to see Neil deny himself for the sake of regaining a youth that never really existed; he'd always been tubby. 'Go on, have—'

'Just because you're expanding doesn't mean I have to.'

'Ooh!' Sam made comedy out of Neil's flash of claw, but Anna wondered when her brother had become so brittle. He'd always been arch, a touch camp, but when had that spilled over into irritable edginess and over-the-top put-downs?

Paloma coughed, making a noise like a fairy yodelling, and with a flash of insight Anna pinpointed the moment of change. *The adoption process.*

Conversation turned to politics. Sam had strong opinions about the government. So did Luca. These opinions were polar opposites, and the two men monopolised the table until Maeve, bored, chipped in.

'I had one of my dreams last night.'

'Here we go,' sighed Neil. 'Mystic Meg's back.'

Sam explained to Isabel that Maeve was 'a bit psychic'. He was proud, proprietorial – *even though*, thought Anna, *he pooh-poohs any mention of crystals or mandalas or auras.*

'Ooh, I love that kind of thing.' Isabel sounded credulous, her mouth stained liquorice by the Sicilian wine. Her enthusiasm explained Sam's enthusiasm.

'I saw a letter,' said Maeve.

Anna sat stock-still. The room moved around her, chattering, slurping. Yeti rubbed against her leg.

'Handwritten. It seemed to rise out of the mist.'

'A love letter?' asked Isabel.

'A final demand?' said Neil, nudging Santi, who collapsed against him, laughing.

'It was anonymous.'

Anna felt her interior churn and knew it was nothing to do with the baby, still only the size of a mango. 'And?' she prompted.

'That's it.' Maeve had moved on, her clairvoyant dream forgotten. 'Any coffee going, Luca?'

'Did it seem, you know, *threatening*?' Anna wanted to know.

'Did what seem – oh, the letter. Dunno.' Maeve had lost interest. 'Are you OK?' she asked, peering at her sister.

'I'm tip-top,' said Anna. She stood abruptly. 'I need some air.'

'I'll come with you.' Maeve was at her side, as close as Yeti, as the three of them headed to the wrought-iron balcony.

On the other side of the sheer curtain, with the red geraniums and the snow white hydrangea, Anna composed herself.

'I don't know what to do,' said Maeve.

'About what?'

'I told you.' Maeve was impatient; she'd always assumed that the world ended at the end of her pretty nose. 'Alva!'

'Oh, yeah, sorry.' Anna wrenched her focus away from the supernatural. 'So, fill me in.'

'Like I said, Alva thinks it's time Storm lived with him full-time. Not just weekends and holidays and stuff. You know what Alva's like, banging on about father/son time and a strong male role model and all that bollocks.'

'It's not bollocks, Maeve.' Anna was gentle.

'Storm has *me*.' Maeve beat her chest. 'I'm all the role model he needs. It's not as if he never sees Alva. They're really close.'

'He's a good dad.' Anna emphasised this often; Alva was a good dad despite Maeve's lack of cooperation.

'And I'm a good mum.'

'Keep your hair on. You're as touchy as Neil.' After a brief, irresistible detour to their brother's smooth new face, they stopped cackling and Anna asked the obvious question: 'What does Storm think?'

'He won't say.' Maeve fidgeted, looking out at the rooftops. 'Jesus, I wish Paul hadn't convinced me to give up smoking.'

Storm doesn't want to hurt his mum. 'You've done a great job with Storm.'

Maeve looked startled, as if Anna had spoken in tongues. 'You serious?'

'Of course.' Anna frowned; did she compliment Maeve so rarely?

'It was hard in the beginning . . .' Maeve was lost in the past for a moment.

'You were only, what, nineteen, twenty?' Maeve had grown up alongside her own son. In a way, they'd brought each other up. Anna did a quick calculation: *When my child is Storm's age, I'll be fifty-three.* When Anna got to fifty-three, Storm would be in his thirties. She romped through all the landmark ages: eighteen, twenty-one, forty. *I'll be fifty-eight, sixty-one, eighty.* She gulped. She'd left it late, this baby-making.

'I don't know if I like, if *Storm* likes this idea.' Maeve slipped up; this was as much about her fears as it was about Storm's well-being. 'Will you come with me, to talk to Alva about it? I don't want to go all that way on my own.'

'All that way?' Anna smiled at Maeve's talent for over-statement. 'Hove is one stop on the train.'

'No, Boston.' Maeve was querulous. 'Don't you listen?'

'Yes, I listen to all your guff all the time.' Only sisters

could be that frank. 'You've never mentioned Boston.' Anna shivered. She wasn't going to like this next bit, she could tell.

'Alva's relocated. He's gone into partnership with some big IT company. Or something.' Details never interested Maeve. 'You know how everything falls into Alva's lap.'

That was a perverse take on Alva's hard work, long hours, stamina.

'It all happened really quickly. He and Clare suddenly upped and left and now they're living in one of those massive American houses with a veranda and a pool and ... and ...' Maeve spluttered, groping around for another US stereotype.

'A basketball hoop?' offered Anna.

'Probably. He's found some snotty private school for Storm where everybody goes on to Harvard.' Maeve curled her lip. 'As if that's all that matters.'

'Looks like we're off to Boston then.'

'Thank you.' Maeve almost melted with gratitude. Her eyes swam. 'Will you help me do the right thing?'

I'm the last one to ask about the right thing. The letter proved that. 'You don't need my help, silly.' Anna saw panic flare in Maeve's eyes. 'But I'll be there every step of the way.' She said it and she meant it, but for the rest of the lunch, despite the good food and the better company, Anna was quiet.

I should have been there every step of the way for Bonnie. It was a scar that had almost healed over before the letter ripped the thin skin away, and now it throbbed and bled and threatened to stain everything around her if she didn't get a grip.

They sat around like turkeys fattened for Christmas, nobody energetic enough to make the first move and go home. Except, of course, for Josh, who'd left soon after the last scraped spoonful of zuppa inglese. Luca and he had had a long, intense conversation on the stairs, out of Anna's earshot.

She'd scuttled back to a sofa as Luca's footsteps rang on the stairs. Sam said, 'You're minding your P's and Q's, aren't you?'

'Me? No.'

'You are, my darling,' said Santi, his head on Neil's shoulder, the baby wedged between them, fast asleep. 'No burping. No rudey rudes.' This was Santi's code for farting; he was far too decorous to use such English words.

Eyes closed, Neil murmured, 'I didn't see you scratch your bum once today.'

'Shut *up*,' said Anna firmly as Luca appeared.

'Do you use the loo while Luca's in the bath yet?' Sam seemed to be enjoying himself.

'Shut up,' said Anna, but Luca cottoned on and hooted.

'We're still being very polite about stuff like that,' he

said. Flopping down beside Anna, he laid an arm about her shoulders. 'Aren't we?'

Oh, how she loved that 'we'. Anna held back, fought against slipping down the mudslide of desire. Luca had never repeated his assertion, made at Josh's flat, that he hated children, but it dangled between them. *He's only on loan*, she reminded herself as she settled against his side in the lazy Sunday atmosphere. He was more comfortable than the cushions. *And exciting with it.* 'If you want me to, I can do a rudey rude right now.' She had to subvert her feelings with humour. She had to stop herself blurting out, *Could you love me, Luca?*

Tuning back in, she heard Neil admit, 'I meant to pop over to Dinkie this week, but work . . .'

'You said that last week,' she reminded him.

'Who needs a conscience when you're around?'

'I went to Sunville,' said Santi. When Neil looked taken aback – or as taken aback as a newly Botoxed man can – he said, 'I don't tell you *everything*.'

'Did you bring Paloma?' asked Neil.

'Of course. Did you think I leave her with the servants?' Santi trilled the *r* with Spanish brio as he mixed and matched tenses.

'And . . .?' Neil was anxious.

'And what? We had a nice time.'

'Did she, was she nice to Paloma?'

'Neil, *everybody's* nice to our little Palomita.'

There it was again, that insecurity about Dinkie's feelings for her only great-grandchild. 'Was Sheba there?' asked Anna.

'You noticed it too,' said Sam, looking up from the cat's cradle he and Isabel had made of their fingers as they shared a vast, ageing armchair. 'Something going on there.'

'Yeah.' Anna had hoped she was making it up. 'The way Dinkie talks to her . . .'

'And the way she talks to Dinkie.' Sam was on Anna's wavelength. 'There's something secret between them. Something not good.'

'Oh God.' Neil sat up, perturbed. 'You don't think Sheba . . .' He couldn't find the word, then grimaced at the one he chose. 'You don't think she abuses Dinkie?'

'No, no, no.' Anna tried to convince herself. 'But you read such awful things, about old people in homes.'

'But not Dinkie,' said Maeve. As with all problems, she evidently wanted this swept away as quickly as possible. 'She'd speak up.'

'Yes, she would.' Neil looked at Anna. 'Wouldn't she?'

'Of course she would.' They were all silent. 'I'll ring her this evening.'

'Me too,' said Neil.

'And me,' said Sam.

'She'll be sick of us!' laughed Anna.

*

Sam and Isabel were the last to leave. As his girlfriend sought out her cotton jacket on the spare-room bed, Sam pulled Anna to one side in the hallway. 'Hey,' he said, which was his habitual way of starting a conversation he was unsure about.

'Hey, yourself,' said Anna gently.

Throwing glances at the spare-room door, he said, 'I'm going to ask Isabel to move in with me.'

'Really?' Anna moderated her expression. Sam had winced at her amazement. 'Right. I see.' She tried to gauge what he needed from her; it felt oddly as if he was asking her permission. 'Are you sure? You haven't been together long.'

'When it's right, it's right.'

'Be careful. Don't scare her off. She might freak out.'

He dropped his voice even further. They could both hear Luca and Isabel chatting. 'Yeah, right. Like you'd freak out if Luca asked you? You'd bite his hand off.'

'That's . . .'

'Oh, that's *different*, is it?' Sam ended her sentence when she was unable to. 'Why? Don't I deserve a chance at this? Christ, Anna, you could try and look pleased for me.'

'You seem great together.' Anna scrabbled, trying to make up lost ground. 'I'm not raining on your parade, Sam. She's sensitive and she's—'

'And she loves me,' said Sam. He paused, then took her

hand. The feel of his fingers was a constant throughout her life, at once nostalgic and contemporary. 'Let's not fight, eh? We were never any good at it.'

Before Anna could speak, Isabel bounded out of the spare room. Her effort to look as if she hadn't noticed their entwined hands didn't convince Anna.

'I loved having them here, but I'm glad they're gone.' Luca took the pile of serving dishes out of Anna's hands. 'So I can do this.' He homed in on her, arms about her, mouth on hers. He was warm, solid, and he tasted of lunch.

Washing-up vs Luca was no contest. Lying on the bed, they discovered they were too full of food to make love.

'Sorry,' said Luca.

'Ssh.' Anna was perversely pleased. It felt like a milestone. They were tacitly accepting there would be plenty of other opportunities. Prioritising sleep over sex felt like a couple-y thing to do. *So long as it doesn't happen too often.*

They snoozed, and the light in the room changed from pearly to grey. Stretching, they moved about the flat, setting it to rights, clearing away stray glasses, debating what to watch on Netflix.

Anna yawned. She deserved this delicious Sunday evening, just her and Luca and a romcom. She deserved a night off from the letter.

'Oh, I forgot.' Luca came up behind her at the sink.

'This must have got swept up with my stuff when I was at your place.'

A presentiment warned her as he reached into his leather satchel. She wanted to say 'No!' She wanted him to leave it in the bag until the next morning, but she said nothing and Luca brought out a long narrow envelope.

Chapter Six

Lunch at Maeve's

NIBBLY THINGS
BAKED POTATOES, SURPRISE FILLING,
BEANS À LA HEINZ
ANGEL CAKE AND CUSTARD

Dear Anna,

Contacting you is against the rules, isn't it? But they're not my rules, and as I don't respect you I don't have to respect your rules.

You might wonder why I'm contacting you and I don't have a real answer. I suppose I want to try and finally get my head around your cruelty. You've done your best to forget me but how can I forget you?

I am the victim of your selfishness and I REFUSE to be quiet about it any more.
Yours,
Carly

The worst thing about the letters – and this was a hotly contested competition; everything about them disturbed Anna – was the fact that they were hand-delivered.

This Carly person had stood outside Anna's house, looked at her curtains and the pansies dying in her window boxes and the white-painted brick facade and the glossy red front door. She'd have heard Yeti's berserk barking and the scritch-scratch of his claws on the hall floor the moment the letter box clattered.

Maybe I was in the house at the time.

Pottering. Stirring soup in a pot. Showing swatches of fabric to Sam out in the shed.

The lack of a postmark, or a surname, or return address, took the power out of Anna's hands.

Sam ended his phone conversation – a long, loud, numbingly dull powwow with their Romanian factory manager – and swivelled his chair to face her. He'd suggested a chair race earlier, and when Anna had demurred, he'd agreed that, yeah, maybe she was right, being pregnant and everything.

The baby didn't stop her racing him. She loved beating

him on the course they'd worked out around the desks. It was the letters. They had outgrown their outline, trickling into all the corners of her day. She shoved them into a drawer and attended to him, picking up the conversation interrupted by Romania.

'I know she'll want to Instagram it all.' Sam was planning how to ask Isabel to move in with him. It had to be a 'production', because 'Issy loves that kind of thing'.

'Mm, nice,' nodded Anna, as Sam wondered aloud whether to leave a trail of rose petals through the flat.

'She likes those mini blackboard things,' he said, rubbing his chin. 'What if I chalk it on one of them?'

'Yeah. Could do.'

'Or maybe go to our favourite restaurant – that French place with the courtyard garden – and get the waiter to put a house key in her champagne?'

'Sounds nice.'

'I read about a guy who took half of the food out of his fridge, half the covers off his bed, half the furniture out of his rooms, and led his girlfriend through the house, saying "Without you I'm living half a life." Is that a bit much? Not sure where I'd put the furniture.' Sam sat back, tapping his pen on the desk. He stopped suddenly. 'Are you even listening?'

'Why are you asking me of all people when I've already said I think it's too soon? Isabel strikes me as a woman who spooks easily. All this fuss might make her dart away, like a deer.'

'I'm asking you of all people because I ask you about everything, Anna. Also, because I'm out of practice at being in love, and you're my spy in the land of women. You don't have to support me, but it'd be nice if you at least pretended to be glad that I'm happy again after all these years on my own.'

The dressing-down was deserved. Anna felt ashamed of her inability to lift her eyes from the letters. 'You're right. I'm a moody bitch. Blame the pregnancy. Let's have a break for lunch and we can plan how—'

Already on his feet, Sam gathered documents into the magnificent man-bag of weathered leather Anna had made just for him. 'I'm having lunch with the sales director of Selfridges, remember? Then I've got the afternoon off, so I'll see you Sunday at Maeve's.'

'I didn't mean—'

'I'm going to be late.' Sam fended off Yeti's goodbyes and left.

Anna could have said that he should keep his question simple and to the point; if Isabel was ready, then she was ready, but if not, it would be easier for her to explain why in a normal setting without all the well-meaning razzamatazz.

But I didn't say any of that. Instead, she'd sounded disapproving. Unsupportive. Sam deserved better from her.

Without him, the shed felt lonely. Her ear constantly cocked for the slap of the letter box, Anna was grateful when Yeti laid his long snout on her lap and looked up at her as if he understood.

Sometimes we do things behind our own backs.

There was a valid reason for Anna to pull down the steps to the attic and clamber up in her slippers as Luca slept off a Chinese takeaway in front of a chattering television. Somewhere in a cobwebbed corner sat a family photograph. Maeve would adore it; it would be the perfect offering to bring to lunch the next day.

The picture was easily found, but Anna didn't leave the claustrophobic A-shaped room. She knelt by a sturdy old suitcase gone brittle with age, and unsnapped the clasps. This was a ritual she went through once a year; the rest of the time she pixelated the boxy shape whenever she had to poke around the attic.

Newspapers. A different title every year. The *Sun*; the *Telegraph*; the *Express*; *The Times*; the *Sunday Times*. Even though they spent their life in airless quarantine, the older papers showed their age. No longer white, they were the colour of dead skin.

They crackled at her touch. In 2004, the headline told her, the war in Iraq was in full deadly swing. The newspaper on the bottom of the case, dated 1994, shouted about

Hurricane Gordon, which claimed lives in the Caribbean before heading for the United States. There were murdered toddlers, a suicide bomber, and in 2005 bird flu was everybody's big fear.

A reality star lied about her nose job in 2015, and a tiger cub was born in captivity in 2003. Eleventh of November rolled around every year despite Anna's fear of the memories it dragged up from the dead earth.

She wondered what Carly had in store for her when it rolled around again.

Downstairs again, eyes dried, nose blown, Anna woke Luca as she dropped Peking Gourmet Styrofoam boxes into a bin liner.

'S'leave that. I'll do it later,' he said. He sat forward, muted the television, dipped his head to see her face behind a shroud of hair. 'Annie?'

Luca could hear Anna even when she wasn't talking. She shook her hair out of her eyes and dredged up a smile.

'Do you want to—' he began.

'Talk about it? Nah.' She threw him a prawn cracker. 'You're not a therapist here, Luca. Relax.'

Yeti was especially invited by Maeve, so Anna had to restrain him on her lap all the way to Brighton in Luca's passenger seat. Driving duties generally fell to him and Anna didn't contest it; she preferred to look out of the window and daydream, whereas he relished the changing of gears, the nipping down short cuts. It was an outlet for his Italian brand of masculinity in a world which preferred its men docile.

Growing up in a house governed by her father's moods, Anna had never gravitated towards traditionally butch men. Luca was male, not macho; he didn't expect her to be fluffy or air-headed or to cook his dinner. When it was just the two of them, they found their roles naturally. In the kitchen. In the car. In the bedroom.

Thinking of the bedroom made Anna shift in her seat. It was vulgar to rate partners sexually but Luca demanded it; sex with him was the best she'd ever had. That was partly down to her. It was a team effort. She smiled at that.

'You're thinking about sex,' said Luca, glancing from her to the tarmac of the A320.

'What? Shut up. No.' Anna sank into herself.

'You always smile that naughty smile when you're thinking about us being together.' Luca laid a hand on her leg. 'I'm thinking about it too. The last time. The next time.'

'*Stop*,' said Anna. There was lunch to get through. Meeting Paul. Talking to Storm about Boston. Checking to see if Neil's Botox had relaxed. 'It's hours before we can . . . *be together.*'

'Anticipation,' said Luca, 'makes it all the better.'

*

'Fill up on the nibbly things,' whispered Anna as Luca hovered over the breadsticks and guacamole. 'They're usually the best part of the meal.'

The cottage was minuscule, one of those period properties that make you wonder if England was populated by hobbits in past centuries. The square kitchen at the front, its window giving onto a typical narrow Brighton lane, could only accommodate one person at a time, but it was Maeve's habit to lay out the appetisers on the worktop.

Wedged in together, wolfing grissini, they'd opened the bottle Luca had brought in preference to the cloudy organic brew provided by Maeve.

'What do you think of him?' asked Anna furtively.

'Him who?'

'Paul, of course.' Men could be so slow.

'Seems nice.'

'Yes, he does.' Anna was almost disappointed. She was so accustomed to Maeve choosing creeps that Paul baffled her. 'He's *too* nice,' she said.

'What are you basing that on?'

'Nothing,' confessed Anna. She didn't have a feeling or a suspicion or a hunch. It just couldn't be true that a man like Paul could come along after a conveyor belt of brutes.

They could hear him, talking to Neil and Santi about his property development company.

'He sounds *normal*,' said Anna. 'I can't imagine him

147

talking to Maeve about planning regulations, or equity funding loans.'

'Lovers don't talk all the time,' Luca reminded her, kissing her on the nose.

'He's funny, too.' Anna wasn't used to liking her sister's men. 'Plus he's nice to Maeve. Did you notice how he helped her set the table?' That simple fact had almost moved Anna to tears; she blamed those handy hormones, but it was something that went deeper. It was an acknowledgement of how easily she bruised on behalf of the people around her.

'Mm-hmm.' That noise was an early warning signal that Luca was bored of the conversation, but Anna ignored it.

'You're a therapist. You *know* people. What do you make of him? Is he an axe murderer under that dull exterior?'

'I'm a therapist, not a mind reader.' Luca put a finger to her lips. 'Shush. When you mention my job, it usually means you're about to ask me something about Josh and I can't tell you anything more than you already know. He's not a type or a diagnosis, he's your brother. I can't turn him into a dramatic reveal like you get in the mystery books you read.'

A kerfuffle at the door announced Dinkie. Josh held her arm as she was ushered into the doll's house like a visiting empress.

'I'm grand, leggo of me!' Dinkie waved away her grandson and walked, with a bandy chimpish gait, to the only armchair Maeve owned. It was, like most of her furniture, covered with a crochet blanket. 'Lovely!' breathed Dinkie as she sat.

In full summer plumage, Dinkie wore a cotton dress, and a poppy bobbed hopefully on her squashed straw hat. 'All together again!' she whooped. She liked, she often said, to have all her chicks around her.

One of them was running down the stairs, barefoot, hollering, 'Din-*kie!*' Maeve was tousled; she'd never mastered dressing up. Only one eyebrow was pencilled in and her jumpsuit was not quite done up. Her gypsy glamour didn't need perfection; she was a whirling hub of noise and colour and life. 'I want to sit on your lap,' she cried, 'like I used to!'

'You're too big for that, love, and I'm too old.' Dinkie's spirits were always raised by Maeve's nonsense; there were two bright dots of colour on her pale, papery cheeks. She turned to Anna. Her favourite, according to family lore; Dinkie laughed off any such idea.

But it's true, thought Anna. Somehow her grandmother could make a pet of Anna without hurting the others' feelings.

'Sure, you're barely showing,' said the old woman. 'Your mother was like that. Carried you all at the front.'

Anna nodded, awkward hearing this talk in front of Luca. He'd bent to kiss Dinkie's hand, unfazed. Dinkie was – God help us all – *flirting* with him. 'Oi, Grandmother,' said Anna. 'Hands off my fella.'

'If I was thirty years younger . . .'

'I, unfortunately, wouldn't be born yet,' said Luca.

'Jaysus, you little go-boy,' shrieked Dinkie, delighted. Even more than a compliment, she loved an insult; the Irish are funny that way.

The room had shrunk. That's how it felt to Anna. It had, of course, remained the same size, but with Neil, Santi and Paloma added to it, the sitting room was stretched to capacity.

'It's so sunny,' said Josh. 'Why don't we eat outside?'

'We can't,' said Maeve.

'Why not?' Neil wanted to know, a glass in one hand and the last, fought-over breadstick in the other.

'Rats,' said Maeve, with a *What can you do?* wobble of her head.

'Let's leave it at that.' His youngest sister's unorthodox ways were a mystery to Neil; he tried to keep it that way. *Rats!* He mouthed the word at Paloma and showed his teeth and she screamed happily. The perfect audience for her show-off daddy, she held out her fat arms, bare today in mint green dungarees, and pumped her legs.

'She wants you!' said Anna.

'Put her on the floor, Santi,' said Neil, turning away, embarking on animated 'Hello's and 'How are you's with Luca.

'*This* floor?' Santi frowned at Anna, who shook her head in agreement. Maeve believed hoovering the rug made her a plaything of the patriarchy; Yeti constantly found delicious *amuse-bouches* in the weave.

'Here. I'll have her.' Anna reached out and took Paloma, a warm dumpling, heavy and wriggling, from Santi. He looked depleted. 'Bad night?'

'She's had a growth spurt. She doesn't nap as much, and now she's waking up about four a.m. . . .' Santi's broad shoulders drooped. 'I never thought it could be so exhausting—' He stopped suddenly, brought his tanned hand to his mouth. 'Sorry, sorry. I shouldn't, when you are . . .' He gestured to her body, then did a double take. 'You *are* pregnant, aren't you, *querida*? Where's the bump?'

'It's there, I assure you.' Anna pulled her striped cotton dress tight around her, Paloma on her hip. 'Doesn't your husband take turns getting up at night with the baby?'

'Sweetheart,' said Santi, 'you're his sister. Why do you even ask this? He snores like a *cerdo* all through her cries.' He leaned closer. 'He wears a satin sleep mask.'

They both gave that the snigger it deserved as a foil platter of baked potatoes hit the borrowed table Maeve had somehow squeezed into the room. Turning to Paul, she said, 'Honeybun!' and Storm went into an almost terminal cringe. 'Who're you texting?'

'Making a note,' said Paul, 'to get those rats sorted.'

Maeve unleashed a look of triumph on the others. *See!* it said. 'Eat, eat!' she barked.

'But Sam and Isabel aren't here yet.' Anna sat sideways, refusing to hand back Paloma until Santi had taken a few mouthfuls.

'He texted. Running late, he said, and to start without him.'

'What's the surprise filling?' Josh was noticeably more breezy at Maeve's. Anna supposed the no-rules, no-expectations atmosphere suited him better.

'Ah. Yes.' Maeve was leaning over folk, banging down rusty cutlery. 'It surprised even me, to be honest.' She screwed up her mouth. 'There is no filling. I forgot.'

There was groaning. There was abuse. There was a croaked 'Leave her alone, you maggots!' from Dinkie.

'So it's just baked beans?' asked Neil, one hand protectively over his stomach.

'I love baked beans,' said Paul. He was so crisp and neat he could have come straight out of a box. Anna could smell fabric conditioner and shampoo from across the table. Paul was straighter than straight, and Anna liked him for unbending enough to see the good things in Maeve. To willingly enter a house where no cup was properly washed, where making the beds involved leaving the duvet on the floor. *Perhaps he loves her,* thought Anna.

'I forgot to get baked beans, too.' Maeve was

unapologetic, foraging for salt and pepper in a drawer with no handle.

Sam appeared, in long shorts and a battered hat that Anna had tried to throw out many times when they were married. He was brought up to speed on the food situation, but his sense of humour was slow kicking in. 'Oh. Right,' he said. 'I'll go and freshen up.'

'What's ailing him?' Dinkie bent over her plate, looking down the table at Anna.

'How would I know?' Sometimes Dinkie behaved as if she and Sam were still together.

'Go and look after him.' Nobody was left behind on Dinkie's watch.

Anna glanced at Luca, not for permission, more to pull a face, but he wasn't paying attention, listening instead to Santi tell a joke. Santi was very bad at jokes; it took a long time and he never quite nailed the punchlines.

On the scrap of landing, Anna waited for Sam to emerge from the bathroom. He was in there a very long time, with none of the obvious noises you might expect. When he did come out, he stepped back, surprised to find her on the patch of nylon carpet.

'Sorry,' he said, standing aside. 'Did you want to . . .'

'I've been sent by Dinkie to see what's up.' Anna didn't want to ask, but she had to. 'No Isabel today?'

'No Isabel any day,' said Sam.

'What does that mean?' Anna tailed him down the narrow stairs, even though Sam took them fast enough to convince her he'd rather she didn't.

'It means ...' Sam looked towards the crowded sitting room. Maeve had put on a beloved salsa CD, and he closed his eyes as if the noise hurt his ears. 'Step outside with me a minute.'

The street was weekday-busy; Brighton was a heathen town which didn't believe in keeping Sunday for rest. It was hot too; Anna sweated beneath her stripes. 'So ...' She folded her arms, nudged him with her elbow. 'What's going on?'

'She's gone. Bolted.' Sam threw out his arm. 'Couldn't get away quick enough.'

'What hap—'

'You were right. I freaked her out by baking my front door key into a bread roll then asking her to make me a sandwich. She looked at it and said, "I can't." So you were right. Well done you.'

'I didn't want to be—'

'I need a drink.'

They all noticed how much Sam drank during the meal. He ignored his enormous jacket potato and dragged the bottle of unspeakable plonk towards him possessively.

'Are we allowed to ask why Isabel isn't—'

'No, Neil. None of your business,' said Sam. Heartbreak

stripped away his bonhomie. He was a snarly junkyard dog they all tried to ignore as he drank more and his mood worsened. He didn't even join in with the general joy at dessert.

All of them – except Santi – remembered the lurid yellow, white and pink stripes of angel cake from their childhoods. There was relief that Maeve hadn't made the custard; it was shop-bought, a perfect match for the riot of E-numbers in the sponge.

'I forgot. I brought you something, Maeve.' Anna, squashed up against Luca on one side and Santi on the other, somehow extracted the rectangular package from her bag beneath the table.

'Is it edible?' asked Neil hopefully.

'No, it's *amazing*.' Maeve had already greedily torn off the wrapping paper. She held the old framed photograph on her lap for all to see. 'It's Dinkie and Grandpa's wedding picture!'

'Oh, don't be looking at that auld thing.' Dinkie covered her face with her hands as the others leaned in and devoured all the details.

'You were so cute!' said Santi, holding up the baby. 'Look, Palomita, your great-grandmother.'

'I was sixteen,' said Dinkie, confronting the image sideways, squinting at the child-woman smiling out from the black-and-white church porch. 'Sixteen,' she repeated wonderingly, as if she barely believed it.

'You're not wearing a white dress.' Storm was confused.

'We were poor, my love,' said Dinkie softly.

'I *love* your little tweed suit.' Maeve was effusive. She leaned back, kissed Paul full on the lips, making Anna look automatically at Storm, who pretended not to notice. 'Isn't my Dinkie the most gorgeous bride you ever saw?'

Anna thought that 'gorgeous' wasn't the right word. She was poignant, this newly minted Dinkie with her nipped-in tweed jacket and her posy of wild flowers. 'You were only three years older than Storm, Dinkie!'

'We grew up fast in them days.' Dinkie seemed tired of Memory Lane. She cast about for her handbag.

'So pretty,' said Luca. His tenderness for Dinkie made Anna glow. 'You've hardly changed, Dinkie.'

'Shut up you, y'auld charmer!' Dinkie reached out to slap him. 'I had freckles then. Now I have feckin' age spots.'

'*That*,' said Paul, pointing at Grandpa, 'is a handsome man.'

'Wish I had his hair,' said Neil. He scrutinised the photograph. 'Something looks different about you, Dinkie. Something subtle . . .'

'Like the passage of over sixty years?' Every drop that Sam had drunk was there in his voice. A ripple of disapproval made an invisible lap around the table, but nobody chided him. Sam's pain was palpable.

'I know what Neil means.' Josh traced a circle around his

grandmother's black-and-white face. 'Something about your face has changed . . .'

Anna saw it too, but couldn't pin it down. Her phone cheeped, and she jumped when she saw the caller's name. 'I'd better take this.' Rather than brave the rats in the garden, she stumbled through the maze of chair legs and outstretched feet to stand on the front doorstep. Bending to hold Yeti's collar, she said, 'Hi, Dylan.'

'Oh, hi. Yeah. It's me. So. Um. Thought I'd call. See how things are. With the, um . . .' Dylan took a run at the word and managed to force it out. 'With the baby. And stuff.'

'The baby and stuff are fine.' Anna wasn't sure how much he really wanted to know. He wasn't the person to share her stretch mark fears with. 'Everything healthy and normal and cool. How are you?'

'Oh shit, I'm wrecked,' said Dylan. 'Big night last night. I mean *big*.'

Anna wondered if it had involved intercourse on household goods. 'That's nice,' she said, for the want of anything better to say. *I barely know this man I've made a baby with.* 'It's good to hear from you.'

'Thought I should check in. See if, you know, how, sort of, things are.' Dylan was trepidatious, as if the baby might have faded, like a hangover. 'Is it a boy or a girl?'

'I could have found out at my last scan, but I don't really want to know.' She paused. 'Would *you* like to know?' It was odd, asking somebody else's opinion; so far this pregnancy was a solo effort. 'I could ask if you really want me to.'

'No, God, no, look it's your decision.' Dylan distanced himself hurriedly. He couldn't find the right tone, obviously wary of presuming too much, but anxious not to seem like a heel. 'Has it got all the fingers and arms and that?'

'As far as we can tell.' Anna was often flippant about the baby, but she couldn't bring herself to joke about its health. 'If anything was wrong, I'd let you know.'

'Great. I mean, not great, I mean . . .'

'I know what you mean.' Anna looked down at Yeti. 'I got a dog,' she said.

'Cool! I love dogs.' On safer ground, they chatted for a few moments more. When Anna went back inside, the table had been folded away, and the others were clustered around a large painting. Modern, bold, it took up most of a wall.

'Paul bought that for Maeve.' Sam turned, his wine sloshing out of his glass. 'And she didn't run away! Women are weird.'

'We went to this exhibition,' Maeve was explaining, the chopstick she'd earlier used to open a drawer now stuck in her hair. 'I said I liked it and the next day it was delivered! He spoils me.'

Paul seemed embarrassed; Anna liked him for that. 'What do you think of your Mum's new work of art, Storm?'

'Bit shit,' said Storm.

'Hey!' Neil looked aggrieved. 'Your grandmother doesn't need to hear that language, young man.'

'Manners, Stormy,' said Dinkie, the only one seated.

'He loves it really.' Maeve was blithe, but Anna saw how perturbed Paul was by the boy's reaction.

Sitting, standing, leaning uncomfortably – Maeve was very short on furniture – they all found out more about Paul.

'Two kids. Boys,' he said in answer to Santi's question. 'They keep me busy, I can tell you.'

'You divorced?' Sam's manners were in the same skip as Storm's. He was slurring now. 'What happened? Did you love her too much? Women *hate* that, you know.'

'Yeah, I'm divorced.' Paul smiled at Maeve, mouthed, *It's OK*. 'We split up a few years ago. All very civil. We share the little fellers. We're friends. She's a wonderful person. Like this one, here.' He gave Maeve a playful punch on the arm.

Storm made a gagging noise and ran, heavy-footed, up to his room. They all heard his door slam.

'Ignore him,' said Maeve, placidly. 'He'll come round.'

Tea broke out; Maeve didn't believe in coffee, claiming it stained her chakra.

'I'm not sure I even have a chakra,' murmured Luca.

'I did have one, but my karma ran over it.' Anna and Luca braved the rats, who were nowhere to be seen among the recycling bins and broken chairs that constituted Maeve's garden. 'Not exactly Longleat,' laughed Anna.

When Luca said, 'But it suits Maeve and she loves it like this, so better than Longleat, really,' she felt ashamed.

Luca stretched; the cottage had that effect on a body. So many belongings in such a small space gave Anna what she thought of as a 'Maeve headache'. 'We can make our excuses in a bit, and skedaddle.' She saw how Luca tried valiantly not to look relieved. There is only so much exposure to his girlfriend's family a man can take.

They looked back in through the grimy glass doors. Muted, the family's mouths moved, their hands gesticulated and Sam slumped.

'I don't think Neil's going to get very far with his big idea,' smiled Luca.

'My brother doesn't know when to stop. One of the secrets of his success.' Anna watched Neil loom over Josh, talking passionately, selling his plan.

'Josh is much too independent to take a loan from Neil.'

'It's tempting. No interest. Pay him back whenever. Neil's worried that Josh'll never get on the property ladder.'

'It *is* tempting, but it implies that Josh won't make it on his own.'

'How many siblings offer tens of thousands of pounds, no strings attached?' Generally the first to criticise Neil for his bluff bossiness, Anna was piqued by Luca's analysis. 'Neil wants to make sure everybody's settled. He's kind of the daddy of the family.'

'But the family already has a daddy.'

Anna opened her mouth to answer – evasively, slickly – but Maeve interrupted them, slipping out from the sitting room. 'So hot in there,' she said, lighting up a cigarette.

'I thought you'd given up,' said Anna.

'I did,' said Maeve. 'Then I took it up again. No biggie. Listen. Small favourette to ask.'

'Go on.' Anna kept her face neutral. Maeve had the cheek of the devil when asking favours; she didn't disappoint.

'You know you're coming to Boston with me next week?'

'Yup. Give me your passport number so I can get on and book the flights, by the way.'

'That's the thing.'

'What thing?' asked Anna warily, a lifetime of Maeve's things behind her.

'I can't go.'

'But . . .' Anna didn't understand. 'When *can* you go?'

'I can't. Ever. I . . .' Maeve threw up her arms, as if asking the universe, *What am I like?* 'I don't want to face Alva and see him being all, you know, *American*, with his big house and his barbecue and his sodding *veranda*. So . . .' She plucked at Anna's sleeve. 'You go for me, yeah?'

'No! I'm only accompanying you, it's *you* who has to look around, talk to Storm, make a decision.' Anna frowned. 'What are you scared of, Maeve? I know you're not jealous.'

Alva's success and wealth and domestic happiness had never attracted Maeve.

'You're better at weighing things up and making decisions and sorting shit out.'

'Only because I have to.' This little-girl schtick worked on most people. Not Anna, however. 'This is important. Where Storm lives is something you and Alva have to deal with together.' She softened, hating to put Maeve on the spot, knowing Maeve would do anything for her. *Within reason.* 'Look, Maevey, you liked Alva enough to make a baby with him. That turned out pretty well.' She looked in at Storm, carrying a cup of tea over to Dinkie as carefully as if it was liquid nitrogen. 'Surely you can sit down and work this out like two adults.'

'I'm not going.' Maeve was mulish. She ground out her cigarette beneath her Birkenstock. 'I don't want to,' she admitted. 'Alva does my head in.'

'Not a technical term,' said Luca, making her smile reluctantly.

'He's always *right*. Which makes me . . .'

'Always wrong.' Anna sighed. Partly because her back ached – *Is that you making your presence felt, baby?* – and partly because this scenario had already been written. Of course she would agree. Of course she would go instead of Maeve. 'Don't worry. I'll sort it out.'

'You're the best sis in the world.' Maeve bounced on her heels. 'Hey, why don't you go too, Luca?'

'That had a rather rehearsed ring to it,' said Anna.

'It's about time you two went away together. That's what new couples do. Paul's taking me to Paris while you're in—' She clammed up abruptly.

'I see.' Anna put her hands on her hips. 'Not only am I doing your dirty work with Alva but I'm providing free childcare so you can swan off to the world capital of lurve with your boyfriend!'

'You *could* put it like that.' Maeve winked.

'Luca can't take time off just like that.' Anna clicked her fingers, irritated at how Maeve had put her relationship under the microscope. She, too, had been thinking *Surely it's time for a mini-break by now?*

Luca clicked his fingers. 'It works!' he said. 'Turns out I *can* take time off just like that.' He put his fingers, slightly calloused, around Anna's chin and tipped her face upwards with tender purposefulness. 'Even therapists take holidays, and I've never been to Boston.'

'Great!' Maeve literally applauded.

As Luca's face came closer, Anna hoped her sister would have the good sense to steal away. But no. It took an impatient hand gesture from Anna to get rid of her, so they could kiss in peace.

It started off low-key, but turned dramatic, the way kisses can. Luca pushed her against a wall, the unfriendly pebble-dash grazing her shoulders. 'You and me on the other side of the world,' he said, against her lips.

'No Sunday Lunch Club,' smiled Anna, sensing how badly he wanted to get her alone.

'No nobody. Just us.'

And the baby. Anna concentrated on his mouth, on the way his tongue worked against her own. The baby wasn't something they could share, but ignoring the child suspended happily, innocently inside her felt like a crime. She was a mother – they could never be truly alone. Besides . . . she pulled away. 'Storm's coming too, remember.'

Luca breathed heavily and happily, resetting the kiss to a lower heat, hugging her tight with those thick arms of his. 'I like that kid,' he said. 'We'll have a ball.'

He was a good man. Pity he was the wrong man; pity it wasn't Luca she'd seduced exactly twenty-one weeks ago.

The air had gone out of the party. It was a step away from winding down. Anna had made a tentative attempt to shake Sam awake as he lay on Maeve's bed, entwined around Yeti – who was *anybody's* for a cuddle – but had retreated downstairs again. She picked up abandoned plates, reached over Santi's shoulder for an empty glass, but Maeve snapped, 'Oh leave it, Sis, that makes everybody uncomfortable. I'll do it when you've gone.' She took a swig of wine and threw her leg over Paul, who was crammed onto the sofa with her. 'Or not!'

'Mum, can I . . .' Storm stood up, disentangling himself

from Paloma and handing her to Santi, as the child's other father was engrossed in the *Sunday Times*.

'Yeah, love, off you trot.'

'Where's he going?' Dinkie lifted her chin; she liked to keep tabs on her chicks.

'Off to see his mates,' said Maeve.

'Hmm,' said Dinkie, who had the old lady's traditional dim view of 'mates'.

'Hang on, Storm.' Paul struggled to his feet, escaping Maeve's tendrils. 'I've got something for you.'

'Nah, you're OK.' Storm slipped out as Paul put his hand into his pocket for his wallet.

'He gives Stormy pocket money,' whispered Maeve to the others as her boyfriend followed her son out into the hall. 'Told you. He's perfect.'

Anna yawned, fidgeted. Inside her, her tiny friend fidgeted too, or so it seemed; she'd yet to feel the baby genuinely move. It was a small anxiety, one she smothered by constantly rechecking the guidelines on the internet. *I'll worry when I get to twenty-five weeks.* Surely an alarm would sound in her blood if there was something wrong?

Slipping out to the hall, Anna had one foot on the stairs, determined to wake Sam this time; she and Luca were ferrying him home and she didn't want to hang about any longer. Storm's voice from the kitchen, a tone she recognised as an inch away from tears, made her stop and listen.

'You can't buy me. You're not my dad.'

'You have a dad, a perfectly good dad.' Paul's voice had a smile in it. Anna wondered if he would attempt a manly hand on Storm's shoulder and hoped not. 'I have boys of my own. But we can be mates, can't we?'

There was a mutter from Storm. It didn't sound remotely like a 'yes'.

'Look, Storm, I don't want to steal your mum. I want to take care of her. I happen to think she's a lovely lady who deserves some love and attention. She does everything for you, and now and again she should be spoiled, yeah?'

More rumbling from Storm.

'If everything was fine before I came along, why was your mum so glad to meet me? If she likes me, shouldn't you give me a chance?'

Be nice, Storm, urged Anna, her hand on the bannister. Paul was what any sane doctor would order for Maeve; what was good for Maeve was ultimately good for Storm, even if he did hate sharing his mum.

Whatever Storm said, it didn't please Paul. She could hear his gritted teeth. 'I'm going to keep trying, Storm. Because your mum loves you.'

Storm clomped out on schoolboy feet that had grown faster than the rest of him. Anna held out her arms; she could see, appropriately enough, a storm gathering on his pretty features, but he ignored his aunt and let himself out into the street.

It took a while to rouse Sam, to remind him where he was, to help him to the bathroom. Standing waiting for him, Anna couldn't recall the last time she'd seen him so drunk. *Possibly during the divorce.* Isabel's exit had evidently stirred up painful memories.

Anna thought of the letters, waiting at home in a drawer, conspiring against her, poisoning the well of her happiness. *Memories are powerful beasts.*

'You nearly finished?' she shouted just as he emerged, tousled and bloodshot, his mouth turned down. *Oh God.* 'You're not going to be sick, are you?'

'No. I'm just sick of life.' Sam half walked, half fell down the stairs. 'She won't answer a text.' He pronounced it *tesht.* 'Not picking up when I call. I thought she loved me.'

'She did. Does.' Anna didn't really know that; *I barely know her.* The most important thing now was to get Sam home and into bed where he could sleep this off. They could talk about it at Artem during the week. And talk. And talk. *I owe him that.*

Lurching into the sitting room, Sam almost collided with Luca, who straightened him up with a questioning glance at Anna, who shrugged.

'Soon get you home, Sam,' said Luca, gripping him round the shoulders.

'You are a good good dear good friend.' Sam was close to tears.

There was the usual circle of helpful relatives around Dinkie as she pulled herself to her feet. Santi held her gigantic handbag, Neil had a grip on her upper arm, Maeve was settling Dinkie's collar.

She wasn't that creaky until she went into the home, thought Anna. Like all loving granddaughters, Anna wished Nature would grant Dinkie immunity from old age. She hated all the signs – the stooped posture, the crabbed fingers, the sparse hair showing pink scalp where once there'd been thick curls.

'Soon get you home, Dinkie,' said Josh. He was her chauffeur today, in charge of driving the staid Ford Focus his grandmother kept at Sunville.

'It's not home,' said Dinkie abruptly, plonking back down into the chair like a broken doll. 'That place isn't my home.' She began to cry.

For a moment nobody moved. Dinkie never cried. Not a single tear throughout all the bereavements and disappointments of a long life.

A whisky was poured. Dinkie's cheek was kissed. Her hand was held. And still she sobbed, her puckered apple of a face pink with distress.

'I hate it there,' she moaned.

'Do they ... are they ...' Anna remembered the complicated tension between Dinkie and Sheba. 'Do they mistreat you, Dinkie?'

'I just don't want to live there. I want me own house and

me kitchen and me bed!' wailed the tiny woman, rocking to let out the woe.

Paloma began to fret at the sound of such unhappiness, and Maeve sobbed as hard as Dinkie.

'You don't have to go back!' She hugged her grandmother almost violently. 'You're never going back.'

'Is it your room that's the problem?' Neil knelt in front of the old lady. 'I'll have a word, Dinkie, I'll fix it.'

'She misses home,' said Santi, verging on anger. 'It's not about the size of her room, for God's sake.'

'I miss me old life,' said Dinkie, sniffling now, calmer but no less miserable. 'The peace and quiet. Toddlin' off to the shops.'

'We discussed all this,' said Neil. He was still sweet, still her doting grandson, but he was also pragmatic. 'You had every opportunity to back out.'

'Neil!' Maeve was shocked. 'If she doesn't want to live there, she doesn't have to.'

'Neil's right,' said Dinkie, conjuring up a handkerchief – a proper, ironed one – from the sleeve of her cardigan. 'I'm sorry, loves. I'm getting soft in me dotage.'

'Rubbish,' said Anna. She agreed with Neil, and she agreed with Maeve. Two conflicting facts were true: it was far too late for Dinkie to decide she didn't want to live at Sunville; Dinkie could do whatever she pleased. *We can't let our Dinkie be unhappy.* They owed her so much.

*

Emails flew back and forth all Sunday evening. With Yeti on her lap, and Luca in her orbit, Anna was deep in Piper to-and-fro, where they soon forget the niceties like 'Hello' at the top of the emails, or signing off at the end.

Josh was bombarded with *'How was she when you dropped her back at Sunville?'*, *'Did she cry in the car?'*, *'How did that Sheba seem?'*

'Dinkie was her usual cheerful self,' he told them all. *'She said not to listen to her, she's just a silly old fool. But in a very Irish accent.'*

'She has to leave sunvil!!!' declared Maeve with characteristic poor spelling and extravagant use of exclamation marks. *'NOW!!!!'*

They agreed she couldn't stay at Sunville. Santi was all for staging a midnight raid. *'Let's go and get her straight away. I do not want her to stay there one minute longer than she has to.'*

Touched by Santi's attachment to his grandmother-in-law, Anna nevertheless counselled reason. *'We have to do this properly. Calmly. The next move that Dinkie makes will be permanent.'*

They all knew that Anna had almost typed *'her last'*.

After all the emotion, the outbursts, the proclamations of undying love for Dinkie, came the big question.

Neil was brave enough to type it. *'Where's she going to live?'*

There was internet silence. Anna's fingers were in the air, ready, but she couldn't seem to make them type the words *'with me'*. She looked around the quiet, lamplit room, at her quiet, lamplit boyfriend, and her sleeping, twitching dog. This was a bubble that would burst in December, it was precious; she wanted to preserve it as long as possible. This made her, Anna thought, officially a horrible person. Dinkie deserved her love and care. '*I'll*,' she typed, just as an email broke the silence.

'*I'll happily live with Dinkie,*' wrote Josh.

'*No need darling!!! Dont be silly!!!!*' Maeve was first out of the blocks.

'*Josh, you are a young man you should live your life,*' was Santi's take, echoed by Neil, who added, '*Remember your rabbit? Remember it died under your bed trying to eat wallpaper? Stick to translating Russian, Josh. You're very sweet, but NO.*'

'*I miss Isabel.*' Sam had woken up, apparently. '*How did I get home?*'

'*Go to bed, Sam,*' typed Anna. '*We have a conference call with New York in the morning.*' He'd howled about Isabel for the whole journey home. '*Josh,*' she wrote, '*that's an incredible gesture, but you like to travel at the drop of a hat. You have your whole life ahead of you.*' She pondered for a moment: that sounded as if Anna didn't. '*Let us take care of this.*'

'*But I want to help.*'

'*You can, Josh, but not right now,*' wrote Neil.

Josh added no more to the debate.

'*I can't have Dinkie!!*' Maeve got that in speedily. '*Not with Storm and the rats and everything.*'

'*Everything?*' Anna was archly curious. '*What, pray, is this everything you speak of? Could it possibly be the same as everybody's everything? There's nobody in the world ready to take in an elderly relative with zero notice!*'

'*I've got no money and a new boyfriend and what do old ladies eat anyway?!!!*'

'*Don't worry, you're safe,*' typed Neil. '*Dinkie would be scandalised by what goes on in your bedroom.*'

'*Jealus!!!*'

'*Me and Neil will take in Dinkie to our hearts and our casa.*' Santi was clear. '*It will be no trouble. She is my most special lady.*'

'*Oh that's so good of you! Bless you, Santi. I'll help all I can.*' There was no time for Anna to press send before Neil's email stomped all over his husband's.

'*It's obvious Dinkie can't live with us. Our lifestyle would make her uncomfortable.*'

Before Anna could take him to task for his paranoia, Neil went on:

'*Plus there's Paloma to think of. Anna – you're the obvious person for Dinkie to live with. For one thing, you're her favourite, and for another thing, you're a woman, and surely an old lady like Dinkie would prefer to live in a feminine home?*'

Anna stared at the screen of her iPad for a long time before her fingers flew over the virtual keyboard. '*So I'm the "obvious" one to take in Dinkie because I'm a woman? Because if it comes down to a choice between you and me then it has to be me, because caring work, loving work, basic keeping-people-you-love-alive-and-well work is always down to the woman? Or maybe it's because my house is so much smaller than yours; at last count, you had three spare bedrooms, Neil. Plus a cleaner, and a gardener, and a partner. As a pregnant woman of forty with no spare room, I am, you're right, the obvious choice.'*

Delete delete delete.

Instead, Anna wrote two short lines.

'I'd love to have Dinkie here with me and the baby. It'll be an honour to pay her back for all the love over the years. A xxx'

She logged out before she could be thanked.

She and Luca did not make love that night. He was pre-occupied, his head in a book, frowning through the black-rimmed glasses that he only wore at night and which made him look, to Anna, like a glamorous nerd.

The room grew dark, then light around the two figures in the bed, as they began the night spooning and gradually moved apart, only to find each other in the thin dawn. Anna didn't sleep.

She was greedy for sleep, hoarding it against the days when she'd have a mini-me and, according to the doom-mongers of internet forums, she would sleep like a sentry, snatching an hour here and an hour there, one eye open. That night, sleep didn't play ball. Anna watched the light change on the ceiling to the music of Luca's snores and grunts and lip-smacking. This symphony changed throughout the night, with an impressive variety of notes and tunes.

If she'd liked him a little less, *fancied* him a little less, the night-time concert might have made her retreat from Luca, but she liked him a lot – *Let's not use that other, more explosive L word* – so all it did was make her smile.

Concerns of the day grow fangs in the middle of the night. All their colours are darker, they smell far worse, and they revel in their power. Anna was in the grip of the near future and the distant past.

It was cruel of her to add Dinkie to her list of problems. The woman was the true matriarch of the Piper family – *Sorry, Mum, but it's a fact* – and she had every right to expect a home with Anna.

She moved closer to Luca. They both lay on top of the bedclothes, naked and gently luminous in the half-light.

She wanted a last hurrah with this man. A few weeks of giddy lovemaking and daft jokes and deep conversation. An imminent baby was passion killer enough, but add an eighty-two-year-old to the mix and she might as well pull on her big knickers and concede defeat.

A clock ticked. The house creaked. Somewhere on the street, a fox whined. Then the letters pounced; they knew her defences were down. She wondered if the writer, Carly No-Surname, was also lying awake. *I doubt it.* The letter had probably purged Carly, got the hatred and resentment down on the page and out of her house.

And into my house.

She turned, sparred with her pillow, but no part of her felt comfortable. She said it again, out loud this time. Sometimes she whispered it; she'd shouted it once at the sea; most days it simply said itself inside her mind.

'I'm sorry, Bonnie.'

Then, in the darkest dip of the night, the baby inside Anna moved. A silvery ripple travelled right through her. Like being tickled. Like being loved, by something not yet able to know what the concept meant.

Thank you, thought Anna, and fell asleep.

Chapter Seven

Lunch at Alva's

MARGARITAS ON TAP
SMOKED BABY BACK RIBS/TEX-MEX BURGERS
BARBECUE CHICKEN/CORN IN THE HUSK/
SLAW/BOSTON BAKED BEANS/GRILLED SHRIMP
HOME-STYLE PEACH ICE CREAM/CHERRY PIE

Anna missed Yeti. *Why?* she wondered. To miss a creature that ate your discarded tissues and wet itself during thunderstorms made no sense. But she missed him, and his hairy enthusiasm and his licky kisses and his insane conviction that she was the best human in the entire world.

Luca was a vague shadow behind the frosted glass that divided the bathroom from the hotel bedroom. 'All yours.' He emerged naked. He was wet, his hair a jagged slick. He stood with his back to her, putting on his wristwatch. 'Are you looking at my bum, woman?'

'It's one of my favourite hobbies.'

Luca wiggled his buttocks, and Anna snorted. She bounced off the bed, padding past him in the towelling robe provided by the hotel.

'Hey . . .' Luca reached out, unwound her from it. 'Leave this off. Looking at you is one of my fave hobbies, too.'

'No, I . . .' Anna held the robe to her, backed into the shower. 'Won't be long!'

'Yes, you will.'

A reliable shower – her own was moody – was such a bonus that Anna lingered under the hot water, head back, letting it flow down her body.

A body that didn't quite belong to her any more. Her tummy had finally gone *pop!* It curved from below her breasts, and banished her waist. T-shirts, dresses, all her clothes looked different; some were impossible to wear. She still didn't look unquestionably pregnant; when this thought occurred to her, Anna winced. *Why do I keep saying that to myself?* Her pregnancy was a fact, not something that could be denied as long as she fitted into her jeans. It had become a joy for her, a defining event of her life – but so had Luca.

Yes, she held back. Yes, he was only on loan. That didn't stop her recognising what they had as something to be cherished. She ached to share the baby's landmarks with him, but since the first kick as she lay in bed beside him, she'd kept them to herself.

'Fancy lobster?' he called.

'For a change,' she shouted back, and was rewarded by his laugh. Lobster was on every menu in Boston, coming as standard with the breezy friendliness of the people and the taut perfect blue of the sky.

Water, consistently hot and flowing from a shower head she didn't have to clean, rained down on Anna, and she turned under it, enjoying it. In the shower she felt clothed by the water, and could appreciate the changes in her body as beautiful. There was a purpose in the push of her stomach, a reason why her hips bloomed.

She turned off the shower and shook her hair, droplets of water banging on the glass tiles like bullets. It was time to own her new shape, and share it. Luca wasn't the father, that was true, but he was her lover, and this growing, thriving form was her new reality.

Nonchalant, shaking a little, she wandered past Luca as he pushed a comb through his hair. He saw her in the mirror and stared. He stared at every inch of her and then he turned.

'It's like Christmas every couple of weeks,' he said. 'I get a whole new girlfriend to play with, but she's still *you*.'

*

The post-coital glow didn't last long. In fact, it had disappeared by the time they pulled on shorts and tees and called the lift.

'You did ask, Annie.'

'Yeah, but . . .' Anna's shoulders went up to her ears. 'I didn't expect you to *tell* me.'

The 'How many lovers have you had?' question is always loaded, no matter how casually it's dropped into conversation. With Luca's arms around her, the sheets tangled by their lovemaking, Anna had heard the names of each of his partners.

It wasn't the *number* of women he'd slept with, it was the fondness with which he said their names. The way he was ready with charming memories. Anna had found herself saying, 'I don't know why you ever split up with them if you like them that much.'

Luca had been amused, but now, as they took their seats at a gingham tablecloth and said 'Lobster' in unison to the waiter, he was cheesed off. 'Isn't it a plus that I'm on good terms with my exes?'

'Yes, whatever.' Anna's hair was still wet and she bullied it up into a bun.

They tackled the lobster in silence. There was frosty politeness about pouring water.

Going away together promises to be a smorgasbord of wild lovemaking and three-course dinners, but it also trains a cold spotlight on any fractures in the relationship. Anna had discovered that she and Luca didn't feel the same about chatting on aeroplanes, that he hated room service, that he found the way she spoke to waiting staff – sugary, please-like-me – silly.

Worst of all was the way he'd shouted, 'Come on, Sleepyhead! Can't lie in bed all day,' on their first morning. It was accusatory, Anna felt, as she hugged her pillow, grateful to have neither Yeti nor Artem Accessories urging her to get up.

These things piled up. Anna knew he was irritated by the time she took getting dressed; *but then I do have a bump to disguise!* She could tell he would rather not have long conversations with people behind them in queues, or sitting at the next table in cafés, or waiting for the lift, but Anna couldn't help responding to Bostonians' chatty friendliness. She knew she was driving him mad with her desire to tick off all the local sights; 'We're not on a school trip, Annie.'

Perhaps this was the beginning of the end. The slow turn away from each other. Anna was unaccustomed to the harmony she'd found with Luca; these glitches upset her in a way they wouldn't with any other man. Once perfection is sullied, can it ever look the same again? If something is imperfect to begin with, nobody minds a few scuffs or scrapes.

Luca banged on the table. 'That's it,' he said. 'That's the

end of the daft row.' He leaned over, cupped her face and swiftly kissed her. 'Back to normal, please, for me and my Annie. Yeah?'

'Yeah.' It *was* perfect again; their version of perfect, which somehow could encompass her pregnancy.

Luca was in favour of catching a cab to Alva's for Sunday lunch, but – tick! – Anna wanted to follow the Freedom Trail, a two-mile trek through the centre of Boston that visited all the American Revolution sites.

Cobbles were hard on Anna's new shoes. Actors in eighteenth-century costume shouting 'Hear ye! Hear ye!' were hard on Luca's nerves. A café table beckoned and they gave in, ordering iced water.

'Have you called Dinkie today, Anna?'

'Yup. She's doing an exercise class. She was joking about wearing a sparkly leotard.' Anna now called her grand-mother daily.

'Did she sound . . .?'

'She sounded happy, merry, her usual self.'

'Then, don't worry.' Luca reached out and pushed a strand of sweaty hair out of Anna's eyes; the touch was tender and she held his wrist to keep his hand there a while, leaning into it.

'I do worry, though.'

Dinkie had backed down. Anna had visited Sunville the

day after their last Sunday Lunch Club to find Dinkie in her room, doing a crossword with the aid of a large magnifying glass. The eye turned on Anna through the glass was a childish blue, clear and canny and free of tears.

'I'm turning the spare room into *your* room, Dinkie.' Anna had waited until Sheba was out of the room; the carer hung around, straightening cushions, fussing at Dinkie, until Anna asked for a tray of tea. 'You can move in right away.' The baby would have to bunk with its mother. 'We can repaint if you like.' Anna had rehearsed and rehearsed until any hint of obligation had been rinsed from her voice.

'Sure, now, lookit.' Dinkie had been using this phrase since Anna could remember. 'Don't go taking me seriously, Anna, love. It was the heat. And the excitement. And the . . .' Dinkie had cast around for something else to blame. 'And me arthritis.'

'We've made the arrangements now,' smiled Anna.

'Then you can unmake them.'

'No, we've all decided—'

'Have you now?' Dinkie had looked wry. 'Isn't it my decision, Anna Catherine Theresa Piper?'

You're pulling out my full name? Dinkie meant business. 'But it was you who said you don't want to live here.' Anna glanced at the door, paranoid that Sheba might be listening at the keyhole. 'Is there something going on, Dinkie? Is anybody being mean to you?'

'No,' said Dinkie shortly. 'Haven't I a mouth in me head to speak up if anybody tries taking liberties?'

Anna agreed, yes, Dinkie did have a mouth in her head, but added, 'This is suspicious, Dinkie. One minute you're in tears. The next everything's hunky-dory.'

'What I said,' said Dinkie, 'was I wanted to go home. But I've accepted that home is gone, me house is sold, and this is where I live now.'

'I want you to have a home,' whispered Anna. 'With *me*.'

'You have a life to live, darlin'. A baby on the way, a business to run. Not to mention that big slab of a man.' Dinkie laughed. 'Ah, would you look at her, blushing! My Anna, you have a heart the size of the sun, but I don't need you to rescue me. I just let some sadness out, that's all, and you'll have to trust me when I tell you that things are fine at Sunville.'

In Boston now with Luca, savouring the freezing water, Anna said, 'I don't want Dinkie's life to be *fine*. I want her to be happy.'

'She does have the final say.'

'You're so bloody reasonable and calm and sane.' Anna shoved him in the arm and Luca pretended to be mortally wounded. 'The tables turn when the people you love grow old. You start to worry about them.'

'Dinkie's in her eighties, but that doesn't mean you stop taking her seriously. If she says she wants to stay at Sunville, you have to honour that. Keep an eye on her, but respect her wishes. If we do discover that there's some sort of abuse going on, then we steam in and helicopter her out of there. Until then . . .'

'Yeah. Respect her wishes.' Anna shook out her folded tourist map, registering Luca's infinitesimal sigh as she did so. 'You know what.' She crammed the map back into her bag. 'Sod the Freedom Trail. Let's sit here a while and chill.'

Luca beamed at her. 'If that's what you want,' he said, taking her hand under the table, 'I'll respect your wishes.'

'This house,' said Luca, as Alva brought them the coldest of cold drinks – *how do Americans get their drinks so very cold?* – 'is out of this world.'

'Thank you.' Alva folded his arms, modestly happy with the compliment. He was tall; Anna had forgotten how he towered above her. His skin was a deep dark colour, with a shine to it, as if polished every morning. His bald head gleamed, and behind his glasses Alva's eyes were a sultry coffee colour. His presence was reassuring; a man of few words, he thought before he spoke. 'It's a bit different to where we lived in Hove.'

'That was gorgeous too,' Anna reminded him. Alva had left the squat far behind. 'But this . . . an actual veranda!'

It was the classic American Dream home, with gables and

white-painted cladding. It shone in the Boston sunshine, its soundtrack one of gleeful shouts and splashing from the inevitable pool.

Storm had barely acknowledged them, too busy running from 'his' room down to the pool, in new dayglo trunks and with the family dog at his heels.

'He's fitting right in,' mused Anna, rocking gently to and fro on the canopied swing seat she shared with Luca.

'He's like a different kid,' said Alva. 'He's barely looked at his phone. Too busy in the pool or on his bike or going off to the beach.'

Everything was set up for Storm to slip smoothly into this new life. Monogrammed towels with a gold 'S' in his own shower room. A bike in the yard. A desk at the distinguished school.

Luca said, 'It's a big decision for a kid his age.'

'We're hoping,' said Alva, 'that the decision will make itself. That he'll follow his gut.'

'If he decides to go home,' said Luca, 'how will you feel?' Typically, he cut to the heart of the matter.

Alva looked surprised by the question, and Anna realised that he fully expected Storm to stay, that all the sunny benefits of Boston must surely sway his son. 'I'll . . . I guess I'll have to deal with it,' he said.

'This isn't easy for any of you,' said Anna.

'How's Maeve?' Alva was wary, as if talking about

something illegal. However he approached the mother of his oldest child, it always ended with an argument. 'She thinks I'm selfish, right?'

Anna nodded. No need to pretend with Alva. 'But she wants the best for Storm.'

'Yeah.' Alva didn't seem convinced, but he moved away before Anna could comment, clapping his hands and saying, 'Barbecue time! I'd better make a start.'

'Is Maeve prepared for living on her own?' asked Luca.

'She says she'll manage, but . . .' Anna wished her sister would be frank. 'It's hard to get past the *anger*. She's mad at Alva for some reason, when it was her who left him. He's not one of those absentee dads who pay the bills, he's a proper solid father to Strom, but she seems to resent that. As if Storm belongs to her, and nobody else.'

'Nobody belongs to anybody,' said Luca.

Anna wasn't keen on that sentiment. 'No, no,' she shook her head. 'We all belong to one another, my clever clogs therapist friend.'

Luca laughed. 'I prefer your theory.'

A text announced itself on Anna's phone. She squinted at the screen. 'Sam,' she said.

London calling! Where U file design specs for
Amberley bag/matching purse?

Lamenting Sam's half-hearted approach to TXTSPK, she replied:

> Strangely enough, in the file marked 'DESIGN SPECS' under 'AMBERLEY BAG/MATCHING PURSE'. What are you doing in the office on a Sunday?

Alternative is sitting at home thinking about Isabel.

> Have you called her today?

NO. I told U. I'm a good boy now.

> Have you texted her?

Might have done.

Anna and Luca sighed in unison.

> How many times?

Maybe 10.

> How many?

OK. 14. Nothing heavy. Just telling her she's the love of my life.

That's as heavy as it gets, you idiot!

But I do love her.

Sam, please stop bombarding her. Give Isabel some space. Let her miss you.

Is this real advice, Anna?

???

Don't U prefer it w/out Isabel? U never really welcomed her.

That's not true.

She was scared of U. I told her U were my closest friend & she wanted to make big impression. U blew hot & cold. You know U did!!

Anna prevaricated for a long time over her response.

Anna, U still there?

> Yes. I didn't realise I made
> her uncomfortable.

Ur pants R on fire. U knew.

Anna tilted her shoulder so Luca couldn't read the screen.

> I wish I could make amends.

Bit late for that! But U R rite. No more txts
declaring undying.

Alva's family suited their house. His wife, Clare, was long-limbed in white shorts. Margot, only three, was both cute and smart, with knees so chubby they had dimples. Eight-year-old Damian followed his half-brother everywhere, aping his loping walk and the way his shoulders bowed.

'We cycled to a cove this morning,' said Alva, poking things on an enormous barbecue. 'Did some surfing.'

'Of course you did.' Anna sat back, laughing. 'You're the most annoyingly healthy and wholesome family in the world.'

'We're not always goody-goody.' Clare set down huge

bowls of crispy lettuce and bursting ripe tomatoes. 'We have wine with dinner.'

'You devils.'

'He lies in on a Saturday.' Clare nodded at Alva. 'The outdoors is so gorgeous here, the weather is so perfect, it's a shame to waste it.'

Some mornings in London, Anna had to steel herself to make the journey from her back door to the shed. The luminous sky and the baby-breath air of Boston melted her bones.

'So,' said Clare, setting out napkins and glasses and all the paraphernalia of lunch. 'This Luca. Hot!'

Anna hadn't spent much time with Alva's wife, but Clare talked as if they were besties. Anna liked such social chutz-pah, and answered, 'I know, I know.' Both women watched him patiently lift little Margot onto the steps of the slide, then wait for her to zoom down in her ruffled swimsuit, and do it all over again.

'Hot, *and* good with kids.' Clare stuck a spoon in the coleslaw like a flag. 'Hang on to him, babes.' She waved a napkin in the general direction of Anna's stomach. 'He's not ... is he?'

'No, the father is ...' How to describe her situation with Dylan? 'He's not going to be around.'

'Luca's father material.'

'Perhaps. But to somebody else's child?' It was safer

discussing this with a woman she saw a couple of times a year than broaching it with her closest kin. 'That's a big ask.'

'Some men like a big ask.' Clare smiled at the back of Alva's domed bald head as he tried to get the better of the barbecue. 'If Luca's ready, this could be great timing for both of you.'

It was easy to agree with Clare's optimism on a breezy warm day, surrounded by the accoutrements of the good life. Anna tried to see Luca in that light, to change the focus; maybe he would stick around after the birth?

Certainly, he was charmed by Margot, and the feeling was mutual. Anna was fluent in Luca's body language, and could tell he was getting a kick out of the simple game with the giggly child.

What's said can't be unsaid, however: before Luca knew she was pregnant, before they were a 'thing', he'd said blithely that children annoyed him. He was a man of strong likes and dislikes; Anna luxuriated in his approval, but she knew the important little person inside her did not.

'Have I told you about this school I've picked out for Storm?' Alva turned with a gigantic sausage on a fork.

Alva's fondness for such topics was one of the reasons Maeve kept away from him. He was earnest yin to her kooky yang.

'It's good for languages, you said.'

'He gets such good grades in French and Spanish, I

thought we should encourage him. There's a state-of-the-art science lab at this place, plus it's a shoo-in for Harvard. And—'

'Babes.' Clare broke in gently; obviously a skill she'd honed through marriage to Alva. 'Perhaps we should eat now?' She winked at Anna.

'Sorry.' Alva shouted, 'Rea-dy!' and feet came running from all over the plot to sit at the long table.

'They're *shrimp*?' Anna had seen smaller cats.

'You *have* to try Dad's baby back ribs.' Damian had that feverish look children get around food.

'They're not actual babies,' whispered Margot, in case Anna was worried.

Dripping with sauce, the ribs were obscenely moreish. Luca licked his fingers, and blew Anna a sticky kiss. Gulls cackled. Out in the bay a horn sounded. Storm looked as if he'd finally undone a tight jacket.

Alva stood up. 'I forgot. The Sunday Lunch Club hook-up.'

An arrangement had been made for Maeve to host lunch back in Brighton, and for them all to eat together via the white magic of Skype. With a laptop at the end of the table, keys were tapped, and a cheer went up when a toothy smile filled the screen.

'Hiya!' shrieked Maeve, waving so fast her hand was out of focus. 'Cheers, loveys!' She raised a can of something.

'Move the lens so we can see everyone,' said Alva, in that overloud voice everyone uses for Skype.

'Well, first there's me.' Maeve pulled at her computer and her room swam before Yeti materialised. His tail was thumping and he was eating something directly off the sofa cushions.

'Oh, it's Yeti!' said Anna involuntarily, and the dog stared at the screen. He began to whine.

'He misses you,' gushed Maeve.

'Aw, Yeti . . .' Anna felt a tug at her heart, despite the dog's many bad habits.

'Keep the camera panning. I want to say hi to Dinkie.' Alva was another conquest for the old lady; he'd visited her at Sunville to say au revoir.

'That's it, I'm afraid.' Maeve was cross-legged, still in her pyjamas. 'I cancelled. Soz.'

'Why?' asked Storm, special sauce on his nose.

'No reason. Not in the mood.' Maeve pulled a silly face.

Alva looked to Anna, who frowned.

'It's raining here,' said Maeve. The shadows under her eyes were visible despite the sketchy reception. Anna recognised the hunched posture of a hangover. 'Couldn't be arsed to cook, so . . .'

Anna moved her plate of ribs and *Jurassic Park* shrimp out of shot. She saw an overturned Pot Noodle on Maeve's coffee table. 'Isn't Paul coming over?'

'Nah.'

'Everything OK in that department?'

'What department?' Maeve was sharp. 'The Maeve's Crap Boyfriends department? He has a terrible cold and he doesn't want me to catch it. We're cool. Stop jinxing us.'

'I'm not, I—' Anna felt Clare shift uncomfortably. This dirty laundry could be washed another time. 'We miss you,' she said, meaning it. Wishing she could sling an arm around her sister's narrow shoulders. 'Don't we, Storm?'

'Yeah,' said Storm non-committally. He looked everywhere but at the screen. He'd stopped eating, Anna noticed. As if he didn't want to show off his dad's cornucopia of health and wealth to Maeve. 'I've been kitesurfing, Mum.'

'Call me Maeve, sweetheart,' said Maeve, then, 'Kitesurfing? Brilliant! God knows what it is, but brilliant.'

Over-cheerful, Alva said, 'Storm's already making friends in the neighbourhood.'

'Really?' Maeve's surprise was understandable; Storm took a while to warm up to strangers.

'Good-looking boy like him,' laughed Clare, tweaking Storm's nose, 'makes friends wherever he goes.'

There was a flicker in Maeve's eyes as Clare touched Storm so affectionately, so unselfconsciously. Anna saw it; side-eyeing Luca, she could tell he saw it too. 'But we'll soon be home,' she said brightly. 'We'll bring you back a lobster.'

'Actually ...' Alva folded his napkin neurotically into a

tiny square. 'I've been thinking, Maeve. If Storm wants, he can stay on. You can send his stuff, and we can enrol him at school and he can join my gym and, you know, he could settle in right at the start of this school year.'

Maeve was so still, Anna thought the screen was frozen. But no, Yeti was biting his paw, so it was Maeve who was frozen. 'Sure,' she said. 'Sure sure sure. I can pack up his room, ship it over. No problem.'

'When are you coming over?' asked Clare. 'We have a guest cabin all ready for you.'

'Oh, I'm busy, you know, with this and that.'

There was silence; possibly while everybody wondered what Maeve, who never rose before noon, could be busy with.

'Mum,' said Storm, his voice creaking in that way of teenage boys whose vocals lurch between little girl and elderly cabby. 'It *is* nice here. You'd love it.'

'You obviously do,' said Maeve tenderly.

So tenderly that Anna felt as if she was eavesdropping.

'Yeti,' said Maeve, suddenly and unconvincingly bouncy. 'Talk to your mummy!' She grabbed the dog, who almost obscured her, and waved his paws at the screen.

'Um, hello,' said Anna, kicking Luca for laughing. 'I hope you're being good for your, er, Auntie Maeve.' Anna's shoulders went up to her ears; she'd never subscribed to the 'furry babies' school of thought. As she soldiered on – 'Try not to wee on her bed!' – the others peeled away from the table, lured by the promise of home-churned ice cream in the enormous air-conditioned kitchen.

When there was only Anna left, Maeve put Yeti down, her shoulders heaving.

'I knew you were crying,' whispered Anna. 'Don't, Maeve.'

'Don't say don't!' snapped Maeve. 'Wouldn't you cry? If your child was being taken away? He loves it there, Anna. He likes it better than here.' *Than me.* Maeve didn't have to say it for Anna to hear it.

'Nonsense.' Anna put her face nearer the laptop; Yeti recoiled slightly. 'Storm's still the same boy. He's still *your* boy. Just because he doesn't admit it doesn't mean he doesn't miss you, silly. And yes, this place is amazeballs, but he hasn't decided yet.'

'I used to think about how free I'd feel if I didn't have Storm.' Maeve was red-nosed, defiant. 'Yes, bad-mother alert. But I did. When I was stuck indoors for nights on end, reading him stories and playing fucking Lego, I used to fantasise about being able to do what I wanted *when* I wanted. But now he's not here and I don't know what to do without him . . .' Maeve toppled sideways onto Yeti and bawled.

Yeti let her. He was good that way.

'Listen.' Anna cobbled together some wisdom; there was usually some lying around. 'Whatever happens, I'll be beside you. One hundred per cent. You have me. You have Paul.

You're going to be all right because you're strong, Maeve. You're made of pure steel under all that cheesecloth. Do you hear me?'

'Yes,' sniffled Maeve. She'd gone small, voice and all. 'Storm's a *bit* like me, isn't he?'

'His nose is yours, and so is his heart. Both a touch too big.'

London was eight hours of recycled air and dreadful food away. As Anna unbuckled her seat belt, she did a mental inventory of what would be waiting for her: a hungry Yeti; a pile of Artem tasks; the letters. She'd managed to downsize them while she was on another continent; this Carly didn't seem to be asking anything of her. Perhaps she wouldn't hear from her again.

As the plane effortlessly hoovered up miles, Anna felt in her bones that Carly wasn't done with her. There would be a pile of letters on the mat; one of them, she felt sure, would be handwritten, brutal.

'I can never get properly comfy on an aeroplane seat.' She fidgeted and twisted, pulling at the neck cushion she'd bought in Departures and now hated.

'Especially now you're pregnant, I guess.'

It was one of the few times Luca had directly referenced the baby. Anna didn't respond. He didn't add anything. Eventually, she said, 'Thanks for my perfume.'

They'd dallied in duty-free. 'I was surprised you chose that one.'

'Don't you like it?' Anna took a self-conscious sniff of her wrist.

'I love it. But it's very vanilla-y. I thought you'd go for something more floral.'

'Vanilla has meaning for me.'

'Reminds you of cakes?'

'Well, that too, but . . . I'll tell you another time.' Anna pivoted. 'God, by the time we left I felt like asking if *I* could live with Clare and Alva.'

'They're good people.' Luca took the neck cushion from Anna and said, 'Consider this an intervention,' and tossed it under his seat.

'Alva could never have built that life with Maeve. She gets itchy around status symbols. She's a Romany at heart.'

'It's quite stark, their dynamic.' Luca explained when Anna made a face. 'Alva's the adult and Maeve's another child. He never complains or refuses – possibly because he's scared she'd restrict access to Storm.'

'She wouldn't.' Anna sounded more sure than she was. *Would she?* 'I had a good chat with Alva after Sunday lunch.'

'I noticed. I left the two of you alone. I taught Margot how to jump into the swimming pool.'

Says the man who doesn't like children. 'He told me he knew all about the affair she had, the one that finally broke them up. Yet he's never brought it up with her. Maeve thinks she got away with that.'

'See? He's indulgent. She's naughty. That's their pattern. Thank God they didn't stay together.'

Anna lacked the courage to ask about their own pattern. *Perhaps we won't be together long enough to establish one.* At the moment, though, it was colourful, pleasing to the eye. 'I couldn't put up with infidelity.'

'These days, there's so much opportunity . . .'

'Are you saying you understand people who stray?'

'I'm saying exactly that. It's my job, Anna! I'm not condoning it.' Luca laughed.

Anna didn't. She preferred him in romantic mode to worldly mode. 'I hope Storm doesn't regret his decision.'

'Storm knows his own mind.' Luca took Anna's hand. His fingers were tight, warm, male, around her own. 'You OK?' he asked.

'Me OK,' said Anna.

And she was. *For now.*

Chapter Eight

Lunch at Neil and Santiago's

HOME-MADE MEZE: CHARGRILLED AUBERGINES/
HUMMUS/TARAMASALATA
STUFFED PEPPERS/ARTICHOKES/LABNEH/
PERSIAN RICE SALAD/SLOW-COOKED LAMB/
SPATCHCOCKED GARLIC CHICKEN
BAKED FETA
TIRAMISU/BAKLAVA

'Anna?'

'Neil! Hi, what can I—'

'You've got to get over here.'

'Eh? I'm in my dressing gown, Neil. What's the rush?'

'I'm expecting the whole Sunday bloody Lunch sodding Club in two hours and Santiago's gone missing.'

'Missing? Like, abducted?'

'No! I mean he's ... not here. He's not answering his phone. How can he do this to me? It was *his* idea to ditch the caterers and do the food ourselves this time!'

'He was right – it's more personal when you go to the trouble to do it yourself.'

'Will you keep to the point! I'm going crazy here. The food's not even half done. Paloma is, well, she's being Paloma. How can I cope with an eight-month-old child and prepare the house and the food and me? Oh God, she's crying. Shush, shush, my darling, yes, Daddy's here. Oh God, Anna, she won't stop. Is she ill?'

'Probably hungry. Or wants to play.'

'Play! Are you mad, woman? There are peppers to stuff.'

'Sod the peppers. Roll on the floor with your daughter instead.'

'With *my* back? Anna, I beg you, come over and save me.'

'From what?'

'From Paloma!'

When Anna put down the phone, she turned to Santiago. 'What do you see in him?'

They laughed. For quite a long time.

'I feel bad now,' said Santiago, as the laughter ended in a long, happy sigh.

'No you don't.'

'Actually, I don't.' Santi's eyes were so dark they

seemed black, and now they creased with cheerful wickedness. 'It's about time Neil got to know his own daughter.' He sat up, excited suddenly. 'Do we have time to visit Dinkie?'

They did. As she hurried through the pastel hallways of Sunville, trying to keep up with Santi, Anna wondered if all Spanish men were so soppy about the elderly. She hoped he was typical, but so much about Santi was a one-off. His ability to stand back and let Neil shine without ever competing, his nonchalance about his looks, his rock-solid reliability.

After scolding them for turning up before she had a chance to make herself 'decent', Dinkie extracted every last syllable of gossip from them. She wanted to know how Maeve was; 'She hasn't called me in a while. All that business with Storm . . .' She cheered up when she heard the latest about Neil. 'You mean to tell me he's looking after the baby all on his own?' Dinkie put her hands to her face. 'Jaysus, I don't know which of them to feel more sorry for.'

From the outside, the enormous white cube of a house flanked by neon emerald lawns was serene. Inside, Paloma's wails bounced off the artwork and the porcelain floor tiles. She'd already colonised the glacial spaces of the house Neil had spent years planning and building: a playpen sat beneath the limited edition Warhol prints; a potty had rolled under the white grand piano. Now Paloma was overriding the built-in sound system with her sobs.

'What?' Neil was desperate. On his hands and knees, he was ape-like on her rainbow rug, looming over her as she sat, disconsolate, noisy. 'You're not hungry. You don't want to wee-wee. You've made it very clear how you feel about Teddy.' Teddy had been crammed into her play oven. 'Is it Papi? Do you want Papi?'

'Papi,' said Paloma through her tears. It was her one word, used for most things, like her feet, or her stuffed elephant, but mostly for Santi whenever he came near her.

'Yes, darling, yes,' said Neil in the shushy-wooshy voice he used for the baby, adding darkly in his normal tones, 'I want Papi too. So I can wring Papi's neck.'

How could Santi do this to me? was all Neil could think as he jiggled Paloma in one arm and attempted to chargrill aubergines with the other. Even without the bother of Paloma, he'd had doubts about getting it all done in time.

She'd stopped crying. He stared at her, surprised. 'Thank you, darling,' he said.

'Garsmuz,' said Paloma. Or that's what it sounded like. She giggled at him.

Neil giggled back. Then shook himself. This was all very well, but it wouldn't spatchcock the chicken.

*

'Don't feel you have to hang around, Sheba,' said Anna. It hadn't escaped her notice that the woman lurked after bringing tea and non-home-made cake.

Sheba made a movement, then stopped, as if unsure of the wisdom of what she was doing, before leaving the room on silent feet.

'She doesn't say much,' said Anna. Probing. Dinkie was constrained around the carer; Dinkie was constrained around very few people.

'When we're on our own, Sheba's a regular chatterbox.'

That sounded double-edged to Anna. 'We can ask for somebody else to look after you if—'

'Will you whisht?' Dinkie's sharp eyes didn't meet Anna's. 'So that's what this visit is about.' She rubbed her arm, a nervous tic. 'You're checking up on me.'

'Sí,' nodded Santi. 'We worry about you, *abuela*.'

'That makes me sad,' said Dinkie. 'You don't want to make me sad, do you, chicks?'

Being one of Dinkie's chicks was membership of a very special club.

'I don't buy this change of heart,' said Anna. 'One minute you're crying, the next you're saying, "Oh I didn't mean it."'

'You can leave right now,' said Santi, energised, forceful. 'You can come back to our spare room. I will make *empanadas* for you.'

'Hear that, Dinkie?' Anna laid her hand on her grandmother's; the skin lay over the bones like freckled rice-paper. 'Just say the word.' Santi's generosity was moving; evidently it was Neil who'd insisted that Dinkie be Anna's responsibility. 'Or you can live with me. From right now. This second.'

The door opened. Without knocking or greeting them, Sheba was there. 'Time for aquacise,' she said, her voice a honeyed African mumble, her face disconcertingly blank.

'Tell them, Sheba,' said Dinkie, from her Dralon throne. 'I'm happy here, aren't I? I'm grand.'

'She is grand,' said Sheba robotically.

'We'd better make a move.' Anna rose reluctantly.

'Take care.' Santi bent to kiss Dinkie on her forehead. She swooned slightly into him.

Anna's feet took her sluggishly over to the photo of Grandpa. So many pulls on her heart. She didn't want to leave Dinkie, but she had to rescue Neil. And Luca would be waiting for her. And Maeve had been in a strange mood since the Boston trip. And nobody knew if Josh was even attending the lunch. And Sam – well, Sam was a ball of unhappiness, his misery visible, like a personal fog. 'Don't get up, Dinkie,' she smiled. The photograph was on its side; she righted it, tenderly.

'I'll get up if I like,' said Dinkie defiantly, swaying

slightly. '"Don't get up," she says, and me saying goodbye to visitors.' She squinted at Anna in the doorway. 'Are you sure you're pregnant, chicken? Where's the bump?'

Anna pulled her silk blouse tight around her. 'If I wear a really loose dress, the baby could pass as a heavy lunch,' she smiled. 'If I wear a tight dress, there's no doubt that I'm preggers. Today I'm kind of ambiguous.' Anna stroked the frame of her grandfather's photograph. 'I'm glad you've got Grandpa here.' Emotion crept into her voice. 'He'll make sure you're all right.' She took the photograph over to Dinkie, and closed the old lady's fingers over it.

Sheba lingered. The door closed behind Anna and Santi, and they hurried towards the automatic doors and the outside world.

In the dim room, the blinds half drawn, Dinkie and Sheba didn't speak, until Sheba said, low and bitterly, 'Did you tell them, old lady? Did you?'

The aubergines were ashes. The arctic kitchen was blemished with the corpses of dishes left to burn or spoil. A red wine ring stained the marble; *That'll never come out*, thought Neil as he changed Paloma's nappy on the butcher's block.

A chubby foot knocked a bottle of extra virgin olive oil that Neil had brought back from Capri in hand luggage. It glugged expensively over the floor. Neil was not the sort of man who knows where the dustpan and brush is kept, so he simply threw a towel over the whole mess, reaching over and keeping one hand on Paloma's tummy so she didn't roll off as well.

A flower arrangement delivered earlier sat in its box, blooming invisibly. The witty place cards were blank. The ice, delivered earlier, was now a bag of water. The CD of middle-brow background music had been swapped for nursery rhymes. The host was still in his dressing gown.

'You can't be just one baby,' he muttered, as he inserted Paloma's arms into the sleeves of her third dress of the day. Dress one was splattered with sick. Dress two was huffily rejected. 'You have to be twins to cause this much fuss.'

'Papi,' said Paloma. She clapped. 'Papi Papi Papi!'

Neil sat on the floor, a pile of broken glass on one side of him, Paloma wriggling on her alphabet mat on the other. He wanted to dive into a vat of wine and stay there until Santi came home and the baby was clean with her hair brushed and her skin smelling of talc.

'How,' he said aloud, 'does Santi do this so effortlessly?' Santi was never to be found on the floor, surrounded by chaos. His partner floated through the days, broad shoulders taking everything the baby could fling at him, laughing off every spill or tantrum.

As Santi wasn't there, Neil found himself asking the question Santi always posed: *Why do you call me your partner when*

I'm your husband? Santi would brandish his wedding ring, Spanish eyes flashing.

'Why do I do that, darling?'

Paloma had no answer, but she held Neil's gaze. He felt emboldened by her attention, and answered his own question. 'I never thought I'd have a husband. I had to pretend to be straight at school. And at home. My dad's old-fashioned. My mum . . .' Neil realised he didn't know his mother's views on sexuality. 'Well, your grandmother stands shoulder to shoulder with your grandfather on everything, so . . .' Neil took Paloma onto his lap. She was soft with tiredness, her limbs as floppy as her teddy's. Stroking the dark question mark of hair that lay flat over her forehead, he said, 'There was no gay marriage when I was a boy. Gay men didn't have children. They made a different life. They were discreet. Or else they were woofters, wearing tight trousers and making double entendres on Saturday-night telly. I didn't recognise myself in any of those people. I wanted to be in love.'

Paloma was warm and heavy. Neil cradled her close and spoke in a soft, lullaby voice. 'I didn't dare look for love, though. Instead, I had lovers; it's not always the same, darling. I was born out of place in my family, in my culture. I didn't want to be a poofter; I wanted to be a man. I wanted to be me. But I wasn't me, I was this ridiculous guy who drifted through nightclubs and came home on his own. Until I met your dad. Your papi.'

Santiago Cortes had been literally head and shoulders above the other waiters at the tapas bar where Neil took his dates. The reaction Neil had to him the first time he saw him happened afresh each time Santi showed him to his table; eventually Neil recognised it as something more than lust. Lust isn't endlessly renewable.

'So, one night, I took the plunge and asked him out for a drink. Do you know what he said?'

Paloma sucked the belt of his dressing gown.

'He said, "*No gracias.*" Well, I don't ask twice so I ignored him after that. The sod didn't notice. So, one night, when I'd had a couple of sangrias . . .' No need to tell Paloma he meant a couple of jugs. 'I asked him why he'd said no. After all, I spent a fortune in that place, so he must have known I'd show him a good time. He said he didn't want to be one of many. But he winked, Paloma. Papi winked. So I said, what if I promised not to see anybody else, would he consider dinner? He accepted before I got to the end of my sentence.'

They had dinner. Santi more or less moved in after dessert. They were naked for three days, and recovering for three more. Neil kept his word: Santi was his one, his only.

Neil was jolted back to the present by Paloma sticking her finger in his eye. This was one of her main hobbies.

'Ow!' He held her hand, kissed its palm, said, 'I have one

hour to slow-cook a lamb. Is there a patron saint of Frazzled Dads I can pray to?'

Dinkie looked out of the window.

'Hey, Missy Piper!' Sheba clicked her fingers. 'I'm talking to you!'

Dinkie remained silent. A tear trickled through the ridges of her cheeks and dropped onto Grandpa's sepia face. 'Please,' she whispered. 'Leave me alone.'

Sheba sat heavily, crossed her legs.

Dinkie bowed her head.

Anna dozed on and off, her head lolling, as Santi stopped and started the car in the Sunday traffic jams. 'Where are they all going?' she asked sleepily. Anna was glad to be out of her house. Working from home meant that she was never far from the letter box. Never far from its distinctive *clang* when a leaflet or a circular fell through it.

Or a letter.

Waiting for number three – if there *was* a number three – kept Anna on edge. The necessity of keeping her anxiety from Luca and Sam only added to the stress.

Worse, however, was the thought that there would be no more letters. That Carly would recede. The two women were locked into something. Carly had set in motion a set of cogs and wheels that must grind on to a conclusion.

Anna felt an oil-and-water mix of terror and relief at such a denouement. Everyone would know. But she could stop pretending. She could own what she'd done. And what had been done to her.

Carly had shown Anna that she saw her clearly. That she knew her better than her nearest, her dearest. *But to what end?* Anna was too ensnared in the whole sorry story to discern what Carly wanted. What Carly was capable of doing.

The car jerked forward. Anna sat up straight. It's not advisable to doze when bad dreams are circling.

'Sam!' Anna trotted to catch up with him. The bulk around her middle was beginning to slow her down. 'Wait up.'

Turning on the path to Neil's house, Sam showed her and Santi a face so pale that it was as if somebody had drawn the real Sam badly and forgotten to colour him in.

'Christ, Sam, did you just get out of bed?'

'Yes.'

Santi took Sam's face in his hands. 'My friend, you drank a lot last night, no?'

'I drank a lot last night, yes.' Sam batted away Santi's long brown fingers.

Anna wanted to put her arm through his, pull him close, but Sam had retreated from her. In the shed, as they toiled at the coalface of Artem Accessories, they spoke only about the work in hand. She'd stopped asking him if he was OK when he stared into the middle distance; the answer was always, 'Yes, leave me alone.'

Ironic that I worried Isabel might spoil my friendship with Sam. Anna could now face the truth of that; she'd given Isabel a cool reception because of her own lingering possessiveness about her ex. In the rear-view mirror it was clear. And shameful.

'Where's Luca?' asked Sam. He had developed a dependency on the man. Perhaps it was because Luca was a professional therapist; Sam tended to drag him into corners and bleat at him.

'Coming later.'

'I might shoot off early,' said Sam.

'No, not allowed.' Santi put his key in the door, and shouted, 'Hi, honey, I'm home!'

A trail of wet wipes and baby clothes led them through the hall to the large main room, where Neil lay on a white leather and chrome recliner, fast asleep, with Paloma snoring on the soft cushion of his tummy.

Dinkie stared down at the face of her dead husband, as Sheba prowled the room. She lifted her hand and threw the frame overarm with surprising force across the room.

'Hey, now.' Sheba bent immediately to gather the pieces. 'Not this again. Now I'll have to buy *another* frame before your family visit. Ouch!' Sheba sucked her finger, the blood oozing where she'd cut it on the broken glass. 'What did you tell your granddaughter?' Sheba seemed knotted up with anxiety. 'When will you tell them the truth?' Her accent pulled the words into emphatic syllables. 'Tell them you hate it here. Tell them you want to go home. That kind lady Anna will give you her spare room. You are lucky. *Lucky*, I tell you, to have family so close.'

'Oh, Sheba . . .' Dinkie seemed to sense what was coming next and held out her hand.

Sheba turned away, wiping furiously at her face, before turning back. 'I would give *blood*, I tell you, to be close to my dear mother.'

'I know, I know,' said Dinkie soothingly. 'I do my best to take her place.'

'I know, old woman,' said Sheba, her smile pushing her eyes into dark commas. 'You do, you do. But—' Sheba looked fierce again, 'do *not* ever make me lie to your family again. If they ask me next time, I am telling the truth. I will say your grandmother cries at night. I will say your grand-mother doesn't eat some days. I will say your grandmother refuses to move from her chair for hours at a time.' Sheba mellowed, shook herself. 'Right. Aquacise!'

'Yes,' said Dinkie, struggling to stand. 'I know, I know: Aqua-feckin'-cise.'

*

'Kentucky Fried Chicken.' Neil put his head in his hands. 'You're desecrating my kitchen. This was hand-built. The marble's from Italy. And you fiends eat KFC in it.'

'It was that or burnt aubergine,' said Anna. She leaned happily on Luca, who was on the next high stool along at the kitchen island, making noises of bliss.

Luca had been reluctant to pitch into the plastic cartons, but now he was a convert. 'It really *is* finger-lickin' good,' he admitted.

'The champagne,' said Neil, 'makes it bearable.' He hadn't the energy to be angry with Santi over his prank. Over and over, Neil had apologised for the state of the house but nobody had listened. They'd been too busy ordering fast food and blowing raspberries on Paloma's tummy. Maeve had cast off her vegetarian beliefs for the time being. Sam was dipping Hot Wings in his wine.

'Hey,' said Anna, as she sat Neil down with a rustling paper bag full of delicious saturated fats. 'You did great. Look at your daughter! She's clean, she's fed, and she's happy. As Dinkie's not here, I can say this: fuck the fancy food and the oh-so-witty table setting. We're together and that's the main thing.'

'Is it?' Neil wasn't quite convinced.

'Yes, Grinch-knickers, it is.' Anna, developing another Piper inside her like one of Josh's Polaroids, saw the Sunday Lunch Club swim into focus in much the same way. 'It's you we've come to see, not your cutting-edge kitchen or the chair designed by somebody I've never heard of.' She hesitated, before kissing him swiftly on the cheek. 'You do your best for us, Neil.' It needed saying. Behind the pomposity, and the belief that his wallet could cure all ills, her brother, consciously or not, did his best to step into the shoes their father had relinquished.

He fled. As if she'd slapped him, Neil bolted to the utility room.

Josh arrived. Anna sensed the Mexican wave of relief travel through the room. All of them lived with the expectation that one day they'd get a phone call about Josh. The sort nobody wants. But for now he was here, and healthy. Pale, of course, shy, obviously, but her little brother was in the fold, being bear-hugged by Luca and led to the nuggets by Maeve.

Time to tend to her other brother.

The utility room held memories. *Last time I was here*, she told her child, *I did something enormously enjoyable that set you in motion*. It was an innocent room once more, devoid of sexual connotations, and smelling pleasantly of washing powder

'Hey,' she said, her voice gentle. It was the voice she used when Yeti trembled during a storm.

'Don't look at me.' Neil was hunched over the tiled worktop, sobbing.

215

'What's this about?' Anna moved closer, careful not to touch him.

'All right, if you're so keen on looking at me, look at this!' Neil wheeled around and pointed to the front of his patterned shirt. 'Look!' The buttons strained, gamely doing their best to reach across his paunch. 'And look at this!' He pulled back his fringe, revealing the angry red dots where his hair plugs hadn't quite settled down. 'And how about this?' He pointed to his left eyebrow, which was now higher than his right, thanks to a clumsy Botox injection. 'The tan, my dear, is fake. The teeth are veneers. All this effort and I still look like a . . . a . . . fat forty-four-year-old with receding hair.'

'Yes, but you're *my* fat forty-four-year-old with receding hair.'

She'd judged it perfectly; an appeal to Neil's funny bone usually worked. He snorted, wiped his eyes. 'Jesus, I'm a drama queen,' he sighed.

'I'd normally agree, but this sounds like something that had to come out.'

Neil folded his arms, leaned against the fridge. He contemplated his sister's concerned face and seemed to make a decision. Breathing out, he said, 'What does Santiago see in me? Really?'

'He sees his husband.' Anna was blindsided: Neil having a crisis of confidence? 'You're, well, you're you.' He was singular. He took charge. *Except where Paloma's concerned.* That puzzled her.

'I can't help feeling that Santi wouldn't have chosen me if . . .'

'If what?'

'If I wasn't rich. There. I said it.' Neil threw up his hands.

'Santi would live in a tent with you.'

'A Dolce and Gabbana tent, maybe.'

'He loves you.' Anna was miffed on her brother-in-law's behalf. 'You remember love, don't you?' Unwilling to indulge Neil in this fantasy about Santi being a gold-digger, she said, 'One good way of showing you love somebody is by doing your share of the childcare.'

'I pay the bills, don't I?' spluttered Neil.

'You sound like an archetypal straight macho male,' said Anna. 'You know, the ones you poke fun at.'

'Not the same thing.' Neil was adamant. 'Not the same thing at all.'

'Deep down, you're *straight*.' Anna enjoyed his horror as she left the room to rejoin the others. She didn't see him slump, nor hear what he whispered to himself.

'But I didn't want all this. I didn't want domesticity and parenthood. I wanted Santi.' A riot of emotion – the kind that follows a long-buried truth – overwhelmed him.

In the kitchen, Luca raised a nugget at Anna. Behind him, she saw a woman come in, uncertain, looking for an eye to catch. She was over-groomed for the Sunday Lunch Club, in full WAG armour of bandage dress and absurd heels.

'Um, the door was, like, open?' said the stranger.

'Tilly!' Santi welcomed her enthusiastically. Anna discerned something beneath the surface. As if he was acting. 'Come, *querida*. We have ...' He waved an apologetic hand at the buffet.

Refreshed, hair combed, Neil dashed to the newcomer's side. 'Tilly, darling, say hello to everybody. Tilly,' he explained, 'is new at my agency.' He named everybody, and they all raised a hand or glass in welcome. Except Sam, who half turned his back, staring morosely out at the garden through the glass expanse at the back of the house.

'Sam! Somebody here I want you to meet!'

A penny dropped. Anna closed her eyes briefly. Neil was getting this very very wrong. This Tilly was a sacrificial lamb, about to be burned on the altar. *You won't help Sam get over losing Isabel like this.* Sam preferred quality to quantity; his grief for Isabel paid respect to the feelings he'd had for her.

It panned out as she expected. Sam gave Tilly the merest of welcomes; he didn't notice the freshly washed hair, the hopefully applied make-up. He talked to her as much as he talked to anybody else; hardly at all.

To make up for it, Anna took Tilly in hand. Asking her about herself. Complimenting her earrings. Guiding her to the choicest chicken wings. The woman was polite enough not to comment on the unusual menu, and to ignore the slag heap of ruined and abandoned ingredients. Anna guessed Neil had built up her hopes – 'I've got the perfect guy for you!' – and she tried to make the landing as Tilly came down to earth as soft as possible.

'Storm loves KFC,' said Maeve, pushing coleslaw around her plate. 'Although he reckons his dad's barbecue is better.'

'I can vouch for that,' said Anna. 'I looked up the weather for Boston the other day, when the rain was drumming a heavy metal song on the shed roof.' September had turned its back on the summer, sending the UK scurrying for macs and umbrellas and stiff upper lips. 'It was seventy degrees.' She remembered the kiss of summer like a mourned lover. *Was it the only summer Luca and I will have together?*

Avoiding poignant thoughts such as that was a full-time job; occasionally one slipped through. As a pregnant woman, Anna was contractually obliged to look forward; her very shape signalled hope and optimism. She rallied. 'September always makes me think of going back to school.' She looked at Maeve. 'Remember Mum taking us round WHSmith's, buying up calculators and set squares and pencil cases?'

'At the same time?' Maeve liked to underline the seven-year age difference, as if Anna had been brought up in Victorian times. 'The autumn term's already started in Boston. Or should that be fall term? Storm would know.' She raised her voice. 'St-*orm*!'

He trailed in from the den, where he'd been sprawled in front of the home cinema screen. 'Oh,' said Storm when he saw the spread. 'Proper food! Ace.' He grazed, answering his mother's question about fall term with a disinterested 'Dunno'.

Luca effortlessly picked him up and turned him upside down. For no reason. Because, Anna assumed, boys are like that. Luca's relationship with Storm had been transformed, deepened, by the trip to the States. They had an easy camaraderie, nothing like the wary distance Storm kept from Josh, or the 'bored nephew' pose he maintained with Neil and Santi.

It gave her hope. *Well, not exactly hope.* Because, Anna hastily reminded herself, she didn't need hope. This was not a love affair with legs. Luca's attitude towards children was irrelevant in the long run: *this baby isn't his.*

It felt as if the baby was hers and hers alone most of the time. There was the odd call from Dylan; she'd sent him copies of the scans. Anna had always had respect for single mothers, and it would be untrue to say she would have planned for her life to pan out this way, but her growing outline brought with it a growing acceptance. She sensed her child's limbs firming up, its wrinkly skin firming out as it grew bonny inside her; *I'm firming up, too.* She felt strength flow both ways; this baby would be the making of Anna, not the breaking of her.

Even if the baby chased Luca away simply by existing.

'Stormy,' said Maeve, pulling him to her, planting a sloppy kiss on his cheek. 'Give your mummy a hug!'

This behaviour, forbidden in the small print of every teenager's invisible contract with their parents, chased him out of the room again.

Josh said, as he nibbled a fry, 'He hates mushy stuff, Maeve. Give him space.'

'I can't help it,' laughed Maeve. She lunged for Josh and threw her arms tight about him, despite the difference in their heights. 'I'll have to get mushy with you instead!'

Bundling him onto the white expanse of modern/ uncomfortable sofa – *Why*, thought Anna, *doesn't it have arms?* – Maeve subjected Josh to a comprehensive tickling that had him howling.

'It's not always like this, Tilly,' said Neil.

'Yes it is,' said Luca. He winked at Anna. She marvelled at the effect a wink can have; her heart beat faster, her skin tingled, she felt faint. Being in love is like a cardiac arrest. *But more fun*, she conceded.

Luca ambled over to her, bumped shoulders. 'Do you think Storm made the right decision, coming home with us?'

'Yes.' Anna thought. 'And no. Maybe it's a question that doesn't have a right or wrong answer. Most questions are like that.'

'So if I ask you if you'd like to spend the night at mine, there's no right—'

'Yes,' said Anna.

'Good. That's something to look forward to.' Luca slipped his hand over her bottom, gently, as if reading a message there in Braille. 'After Mama.'

Anna winced, as if he'd trailed his fingers over a bruise. Luca and his mother were close; *why doesn't he introduce us?* He'd met all Anna's VIPs. 'Did you believe Storm's reasons for coming back with us?' she asked.

'No.'

Luca's chin was stubbly, Anna noticed. She imagined it grazing her face and almost didn't listen when he carried on.

'He said he'd miss Maeve, and that's true, any thirteen-year-old would miss his mum, but Storm came alive in Boston. He loved it.'

Anna wrenched her mind from his lips. 'He flowers around Alva. The structure and the boundaries help.'

'Storm didn't come home for Storm.'

'He came home for Maeve.'

The boy hadn't said so – there'd been much waffle about being settled at school and not wanting to miss watching Brighton and Hove Albion play – but Anna sensed his motives. With Storm around, Maeve *had* to stick to the (almost) straight and narrow. Standards had to be kept up.

There had to be food in the fridge. She had to get out of bed on time. She couldn't party too much.

'Storm will grow up into an amazing man.' Anna valued compassion more than exams; *probably he'll ace those too.* 'No Paul, I notice.'

'Not all boyfriends are as obedient as me.' Luca pulled at her nose. 'Stop thinking bad thoughts! Let your sister make her own choices.'

'I'll try.' It didn't come easy to Anna.

Tilly was despatched in an Uber, with a bottle of champagne as consolation prize, and lunch was done for another Sunday. The afternoon was on its last legs, the evening sidling in across the lawn.

Anna helped Sam into his jacket. He wouldn't accept a hug, she knew, so this was the closest she could manage. 'See you tomorrow.'

'Did I behave badly? With that what's her name?'

'Tilly? Not really. Neil shouldn't have tried to set you up so soon after . . .' She didn't know how to describe Isabel's sudden abdication. 'You're still smarting.'

'That doesn't give me permission to be an arse.'

'Like you said, you're not used to heartbreak.' They didn't reference their own heartache. She could hear him not mentioning it; she knew he could hear her doing the same. 'I promise you, you'll survive.'

'You shouldn't make promises you can't keep.' Sam smiled. 'I'll be slightly less of a sod this week. *That* I can promise.'

'I'd rather you promised you'd drink a bit less.'

He stepped away. The barrier clanged down again. 'Christ, a few months of enforced sobriety and you're the high priestess of AA.'

Anna needed to get back to Yeti. *Did I really just think that?* The dog was useless: he was scared of thunder; he hid her shoes when she was about to leave the house; he burrowed between her and Luca at night. Responsibility had bred something else; not love, surely, for the monster shaggy animal that got in her way and shed hair on her furniture.

She watched the others make their elaborate farewells. Storm stood sulkily by the door, looking at the enormous watch his dad had given him. Josh withstood kisses and hugs and concerned looks. Everybody in turn told him to 'take care of yourself, yeah?' with a special emphasis to show that they meant it. They looked him in the eye. They shook him slightly by the shoulders. Anna wondered if years and years of being the family lame duck made his lame duckery worse ... it had never occurred to her before. Fretting about Josh, expecting a phone call one day saying something tragic had happened, was second nature to her. *Quite a prophecy to lay on a young man.*

Around her, lights came on. The house was wired to

react to the shifting moods of the day. The interior glowed, its white edges blurred. Clouds gathered beyond the glass. The garden was moody in comparison to the warm room.

The front door closed. She heard Neil say a hearty 'Well, thank God *they're* gone,' which she knew was for her benefit. As Santi took Paloma up the winding blond wood stairway – he was back in charge – Neil scuttled over to his sister.

'This is the point where we used to break out the brandy and have a good bitch about them all,' he said. 'But thanks to *you*,' he bent to address her tum, 'poor Mummy's stone-cold sober.'

'Where's Luca?' Anna looked around, as if she'd mislaid a glove.

'Last seen heading for the powder room. Listen.' Neil lowered his voice, moved nearer. 'I want to say something.'

'Go on.'

'I'm sorry.'

'What for? Not the KFC? I told you—'

'No, you daft cow. About Dinkie. About forcing you to have her. In theory.'

'Oh, *that*. I was the obvious choice.' Perhaps it was years of habit that made Anna let him off so lightly. Secretly she believed he'd been sexist.

'I was sexist,' said Neil, making her jump with his telepathy.

'You explained. I understood.' Now that Dinkie was content to stay on at Sunville, Anna could afford to be magnanimous. 'You worried about Dinkie being uncomfortable living here. That she might be old-fashioned about gay marriage.'

'That's not really true. I'd say it's the opposite of the truth.'

Somewhere in the cavernous house a loo flushed. Neil sped up. 'I wasn't protecting Dinkie from my lifestyle. I was protecting my lifestyle from Dinkie. I couldn't cope if she tutted at me and Santi living together, bringing up Paloma.'

'She wouldn't, Neil!'

'Oh wouldn't she?' Neil looked at his feet. 'You don't want to believe that she's ignoring Paloma, Anna. But she is.'

'She is *not*.'

Luca appeared, rubbing his hands together, making *let's go* noises. This wasn't the time to discuss Neil's paranoia. She thanked him for lunch, for saying sorry, for being an idiot. He laughed, and she and Luca were out on the drive, alone again.

'At last,' said Luca.

'Oh no, you were bored?' Anna looked stricken.

'No, I wanted you to myself.' He put an arm around her. She snuggled into him. The arm seemed to be made of cosy titanium. 'D'you want to come to my mum's with me?'

'Her house isn't on the Thames, Luca, it's in the Thames.'

The turreted, Edwardian mansion was on a suburban

towpath, its windows reflecting the dark water of the ancient river. 'Mama lives at the top.' Luca pointed to wide flat expanses of glass. 'In the converted attic. The views are incredible.'

'Hang on.' As they climbed the stairs towards Mama's eyrie, Anna patted her hair and, for some reason, patted her blouse, as if that would achieve anything. If she'd had three wishes, number one would have been a comb. 'Do you think she'll like me?'

'She'll love you.' Luca was blithe. 'I like you, so . . .'

They both noticed the last-minute switcheroo of verb.

'Luca!' Mama was waiting at the top of the stairs, marching on the spot, egging him on. '*Mi angelo!*' About the same age as Anna's own mother, this lady had embraced her age with open arms. Her shapeless trousers and wider fit shoes were in stark contrast to the bikinis that featured heavily in Mama Piper's Facebook updates. Whereas Anna's mum was Canute, holding back the tide with stringent diets and artful haircuts, Luca's mother was a typical Italian widow. Black clothes. White hair. Chubby be-ringed hands. A smile that split her face at the sight of her son running the last flight to throw his arms around her.

'English, Mama,' he said, as he kissed the top of her head. 'We have a visitor.'

Mama looked around the bulk of her son. The smile remained. It didn't have such conviction, however.

'Welcome, welcome.' She shot a look at Luca that Anna needed no knowledge of Italian to translate: *You could have warned me, son!*

Anna reminded herself she was forty not fourteen as she sat nervously on a sofa awaiting Mama's return from the tiny kitchenette. She was alone in a knick-knack-filled sitting room, where photographs of dark-haired people who seemed to share a chin jostled on every surface. The furniture was ornate, old, cared for.

She wanted to make a good impression. She rearranged her collar. Checked her nails. Hated herself for being so obvious. Mothers didn't get to vet their sons' girlfriends when the said sons were adults. *But he loves his mama . . .* Ergo, Mama had to be impressed.

The sofa was opposite the large window. The flat itself was tiny, carved out of the servants' quarters, but the view of the river was mind-expanding, the water stippled with the colours of dusk.

'I hope you like cake.' Mama set down plates and forks and napkins.

Luca set down a rather flat and modest yellow cake. There was nothing modest about the taste. The recipe was a family one.

'I use polenta, not flour,' explained Mama, hands in her lap, watching Anna eat. 'The lemons are only English, but . . .' She waggled her head as if to say that English lemons would *do*. 'Call me Elena,' she said, the accent on the first 'e'. 'I wish Luca had told me he was seeing somebody. Why,' she said, turning to him, 'would you keep a lovely girl like this secret?'

'Because you're nosy, Mama.'

Enjoying being thought of as a girl, Anna relaxed. She told Elena about Artem, about her house, her family, the information charmed out of her on a tide of cake and softly whipped cream.

'When is he gonna get married?' Elena asked suddenly, throwing up her napkin in despair. 'Eh, Anna? Don't you think it's strange that a man his age has never married?'

'Well . . .' Anna didn't dare catch Luca's eye. She bit her lip. Went for it. 'Yes, actually.' She nodded earnestly. 'He really should be settled down by now. All this enjoying himself – it's not natural.'

Out of the corner of her vision, she saw Luca's shoulders shake silently.

Elena took her at her word. 'Exactly!' she roared. 'When is he gonna make me a grandmother, eh?'

'Mama.' Luca stopped laughing. 'You go too far. *Fai la brava ragazza!*'

'He tells me to be a good girl.' Elena leaned towards Anna, colluding, two girls together. 'If he is naughty, you tell me, yes? I bash him good for you.'

Before they went, Anna excused herself and slipped into the bathroom. It had all the expected elements – crocheted poodle toilet-roll cover, potpourri, tumble-twist rug. It was a reassuring room in a reassuring flat; Elena was having a good old age.

'*Allora*,' said Elena as Anna emerged. She was looking down at Anna's body.

'Whoops.' Anna had bundled up her silky shirt, caught it on her waistband. Her stomach, proudly convex, was visible. Not only visible, it was hard to ignore.

'A baby,' whispered Elena, her hand to her mouth. She looked to Luca. 'Why would you keep this from me?'

'No, it's . . .' began Anna.

'Mama, the . . .' began Luca.

In unison, they ran out of steam.

'I'm not the father of Anna's child, Mama.' Luca pushed out the words. It was the first time Anna had seen him truly uncomfortable since they'd met.

'I don't understand.' Elena was twitchy. 'Why are you together?' She turned to Anna. 'Where is this child's father? Did he abandon you?'

'Nothing as dramatic as that.' Anna tried to keep it light.

'Be careful, Luca,' said Elena, her tone midnight-dark. A volley of Italian. A wagged finger.

'Can we . . .' Anna made for the door.

'Yes. Let's get out of here. Mama,' said Luca, as Anna hurried ahead of him to the stairs. 'That was rude.'

'I'm sorry!' called the elderly lady as Anna's shoes clattered down through the house.

'She was warning you,' said Anna. A breeze from the river laid a clammy hand on her cheek.

'Yes. You might trap me. That was the gist of it.' Luca slumped. 'I'm so sorry you had to—'

'Shush.' Anna had forgiven Elena already. 'She's traditional. I understand.' She did. She understood perfectly. But it hurt. Elena had underlined Anna's isolation. Her apartness from Luca. The baby didn't unite them; the baby would divide them.

They were quiet on the drive back to Anna's. Luca kept flicking his eyes towards Anna. She knew he was taking her emotional temperature, but lacked the energy to reassure him.

They stopped on her street. 'Would you mind if we didn't?' she said.

'If that's what you want.' Luca watched her get out, then leaned across to say out of the open door, 'Are you sure?'

'Yeah.'

'Is something up?' He was treading carefully.

'I'm tired.' She read the question between the lines: *Are we OK?* 'But that's all. Everything's fine.' She laid a hand on his arm. Felt its strength. 'Don't give your lovely mama a hard time.'

The gate made its familiar *chink* as Luca drove away. Anna hoped she'd been telling the truth. *Are we OK?*

From the double-glazed porch on the house next door emerged an energetic middle-aged woman. 'Glad I caught you!'

No, please, no, said Anna inwardly, as her mouth smiled and said, 'Hi, Geraldine!' Her neighbour was a mistress of minutiae, a woman who could spin a simple comment about the weather into an hour-long monologue. 'In a bit of a hurry, so . . .'

'I can't talk. I've got a chicken on,' said Geraldine. 'But I said to Leonard, I said, I must pop out and catch lovely Anna from forty-three. He said, Oh yes, do, love. So here I am.' She brandished an envelope. 'This was put through our door by mistake.'

The third letter. The usual handwriting, but posted this time. Anna took it over the sickly privet. 'Thank you,' she said automatically.

'What do you make of that new couple on the end?' Geraldine narrowed her eyes. 'Bit stuck-up, if you ask me.'

'Geraldine,' said Anna. 'Your chicken?'

'Ooh, the chicken! What am I like?' Geraldine dashed indoors.

Yeti was throwing himself against Anna's front door. She let him lick her face as she stared at the envelope.

'Later, Yeti. Off, boy.' Anna groped for her phone in her bag. 'Luca? Could you come back? There's something I need to tell you.'

Chapter Nine

Lunch at Anna's

NIBBLY BITS
ROAST BEEF WITH ALL THE TRIMMINGS/
NUT ROAST
ICE CREAM, STRAWBERRIES

Dear Anna,

Me again, like a bad penny.

The pathetic note you wrote years ago holds no power over me. You have no right to tell me how to feel about you. I'm not just the evidence of a mistake you made, I'm a real person.

I EXIST!

Carly

The menu was the same as every other Sunday Lunch Club she hosted. It was expected of Anna. She hadn't eaten much of the beef; after spending all morning tending to its needs she was sick of the sight of it. The kitchen was hot. Her forehead was hot. She reached into the fridge for a carton of cream and lingered there, grateful for the chill.

Yeti almost tripped her up. The sucky sound of the fridge door opening was the most enchanting noise in his universe, and he always raced to the scene, hopeful.

'Shoo!' Yeti hadn't stopped growing. *Perhaps he never will*, thought Anna as she searched out a jug. He already looked like a man dressed up as a dog; he'd take up more space than the baby.

'Oof.' She'd heard her mother make that exact noise when pregnant with the younger ones. Now she knew it was an involuntary expression, one forced out of an expanding woman who still can't quite believe what's happening to her.

Anna had expanded since the last lunch, just seven days ago. Luca was entranced by the tautness of her bump, like a drum. With over three months still to go, she was slowing down. She found herself guarding her energy, much as she imagined Dinkie had to do.

She glanced at Dinkie, content to see her in her rightful place at the head of the table. Somehow that tiny woman had managed to fill the gap her parents had left. Dinkie had never admonished her son and her daughter-in-law;

perhaps, like Anna, she sensed that they didn't realise what they were doing.

At Dinkie's right hand sat Sheba. Silent. Watchful. Giving nothing away. A thread was pulled tight between Sheba and Dinkie. Something covert, that made Dinkie twitch. There was no way to probe; Sheba stuck to Dinkie like Yeti did to Anna. *I used to enjoy helping Dinkie make her stately progress upstairs to the loo.* That was Sheba's job, now.

As Anna set out the strawberries on the table – 'Yes, Maeve, they're imported, shut up' – the baby began to rumba.

The Sunday Lunchers queued impatiently for a feel. *I'm public property*, thought Anna, amused.

Glued together, Maeve and Paul put out their hands in unison. Paul seemed moved, which in turn moved Anna.

Sam, his personal raincloud almost visible above his head, reached out and frowned. 'Blimey,' he said. It was the most he'd said all afternoon. Anna had caught him checking his phone, had wanted to scream, *She's not coming back!*

Sheba declined, eyes down, expression inscrutable.

Neil, predictably, didn't want to touch Anna's tum. 'God, no, it's like that scene in *Alien*,' he shuddered, and went back to sipping the dessert wine he'd brought and eyeballing Dinkie. Anna knew he was on the lookout for signs of anti-Paloma bias. She'd warned him that if he looked that hard, and with that much animosity, he would find evidence.

'May we?' Santi held out Paloma's hand. 'Gentle, gentle, Palomita,' he murmured. 'This is your new cousin.'

Everybody laughed when the baby, with admirable nine-month-old eloquence, shouted 'Lub you!' at Anna's jumper. Paloma bobbed, revelling in the attention, and shouted again. 'Lub you, Papi!'

'Still not saying "Daddy"?' queried Anna.

Santi closed her down with a look. Evidently that was a sore subject.

'Let the poor girl sit down,' said Dinkie.

'I'm fine,' said Anna. She had started to enjoy the fussing. Being public property had its upside. 'Josh? Want to feel your niece or nephew kick?'

Long, poet's fingers splayed over her stomach, Josh said, 'Hello in there, whoever you are!' His eyes met Anna's. *He understands*, she thought. Josh saw the magic in the biology. She almost – *almost* – blurted out, 'Bring Thea next time!' She held back; Josh took things slowly. That was wise. He had no obligation to speed up, so Anna could relax about him. Furthermore, this Thea was just a woman. Anna couldn't expect her to 'fix' Josh.

'My go.' Luca put both strong palms on her bump. He grinned; he and the bump had a great relationship; it always made him smile. 'I think it's a girl, Annie,' he said, low and rumbling so only she could hear. 'She's like you.'

'Poor sod,' said Neil, who *had* heard.

'Takes two to make a baby,' said Maeve. She was looking at Paul provocatively, and Anna felt an *Oh no!* form in her mind.

'True,' she said, even though her baby felt like a miraculous conception. She'd called Dylan last night but he'd yawned throughout the conversation. Newly back from Ibiza, he explained. He'd gone overland, in a jeep, with 'the gang'. When Anna put the phone down, she'd felt a hundred years old.

'You can stop now,' she smiled, and Luca removed his hands.

'I like the kicks. They're like Morse code,' he said, holding out his arm as he sat so that she sank into it.

'Probably saying, "Let me out!"' said Paul.

Maeve laughed very very hard.

Storm almost went inside out with disgust. 'You don't know what it's saying.'

Anna said, 'But I do.' The baby and she spoke the same language. No words. Just love and dependency and expectation. It was a pagan dialect. Raw. Glorious.

Josh twinkled at her from across the table. He was fully engaged today, 'getting' the conversation instead of sitting back and letting it flow past.

It was Anna's turn to sit back. To pop a strawberry into her mouth and draw a parallel between herself and her mother. *She carried me inside her all those months.* Anna knew now the intensity of the long, slow journey towards birth. She knew that each kick spilled open a new hidden casket of love. *Yet Mum distanced herself from me.* From all of them. Anna eyed her siblings around her table. They'd all grown up with good schools and new shoes and weekends on the boat, but their parents had been aloof. More committed to their marriage than their children.

Anna didn't want to play the 'Poor me' card, but her mother had let her down more than the others. *She pushed me into a mistake that could have been avoided, all because of a man.* It didn't make it any simpler that the man was Anna's own father.

She pushed into Luca's side. He reciprocated with a wiggle. They were in tune. This was good. He was a bonus; other men might have fled when she'd laid her ugly truth at their feet. But Luca had stayed.

They'd sat in the dark, only the moonlight saving the room from bleakness. Anna had pulled a cardigan around her as she talked. Luca had sat forward, head down, hands clasped between his knees. Listening. Listening with every cell of his body.

It had been a stop-start tale. Never aired before, Anna didn't know where to begin with. With the third letter on her lap, and fresh tears on her face, she said, 'This letter is from my daughter.'

He didn't recoil.

She carried on. 'She hates me. She signs herself Carly. But to me she's Bonnie. I named her Bonnie, you see, secretly.' She touched her chest, where her heart was. 'Here.' Anna was glad of Yeti's bulk beside her as she said, 'I was sixteen. She had green eyes. Sorry, I'm not making much sense. I was ashamed and excited. I didn't dare do a pregnancy test. Mum took me straight to the doctor and he confirmed it.'

She'd been in school uniform when she heard she was going to be a mother.

'Mum cried, I mean *wept*. She kept saying she didn't know what would happen when my dad found out. But she did know. We both knew.'

Her father had erupted. The younger children bundled off to a neighbour, Neil already living on his own, there was no need for Anna's dad to hold back.

'He told me I disgusted him. That I brought shame on the family. As if we were royalty or something. Nobody mentioned abortion – we were too Catholic for that. But nobody mentioned a future with the baby, either. It was a problem to solve. I had no say.'

Anna's voice stretched to nothing. The memory of her powerlessness swarmed through her. She'd been mute, ignored. A thing, not a girl.

'Dad calmed down and he wasn't quite so hellfire about it. I could tell he wanted to reach out to me.'

Anna paused. Was that true? Or had she retrofitted that detail in order to make the memory bearable?

'They talked to me endlessly about it. Always in hushed voices, behind closed doors, so Maeve and Josh wouldn't find out.'

So that I wouldn't infect my little brother and sister.

'Over and over they said it was the right thing to do. Adoption. The only way. Best for me. Best for the child. But . . .' Anna gritted her teeth. The anger had arrived, red-hot and taking no prisoners. 'But, Luca, what they meant was it was the best thing for them!'

That, she knew, was why they'd pressurised her. Softly. Harshly. With words of love. With reason. Until she'd stood her ground.

'I said I wanted to keep the baby. I was optimistic, the way you are at sixteen. I was so naive about what it would entail. I mean, I couldn't even keep my room tidy. But I said Dinkie would help and Dad shouted that his mother must never ever hear about this or it would kill her.'

A small sigh, heavy with empathy, escaped Luca.

'It felt that nobody loved me any more. The real me. They would only love the version of me who wasn't pregnant, who hadn't had ess ee ex. The baby was a complication to be tidied away. Dad took over. I signed papers, but he had to sign them too, as my guardian.'

She didn't describe the birth. She never thought about

it. She'd efficiently locked it away. But she remembered how proud she'd been of herself for coming through it, and pushing out a perfect human. With green eyes.

'Bonnie arrived on November eleventh. I had her for a week. In a nursing home nice and far away. Maeve and Josh thought I was on a school trip.' She paused, said again, 'I had her for a week.'

'That's a very short time,' said Luca, in a heavy voice. 'And a very long time too.'

'Yes!' Being understood almost made Anna cry again. 'I knew every inch of her. I could draw you a map of her tiny pink body. The way she cried . . .' Anna heard it echoed sometimes in birdsong. 'She knew I was her mother, Luca. She *knew* me. And they took her.'

That memory was one she'd have loved to lock away along with the birth, but it was too bright, too vile.

'They had to physically pull her away from me. I would have killed them all if I'd had a weapon. She was crying.' Anna put her hands to her face. 'Oh God, Luca, she was crying so hard.'

Luca let her sob. Anna was grateful to him for not leaving his post to sit beside her. She needed his calm demeanour to get through it.

'I dressed her in a romper thing I'd saved up for. I brushed her hair. I'd washed it, silly little fluff that it was, with this baby shampoo the nursing home supplied. She smelt so wonderful.'

'Of vanilla?'

'Yes.' Anna smiled, sad, wan. 'That's why ... the perfume ... Anyway. I'd told Dad I wanted to give Bonnie a note for her to read when she was older. He told me that was irresponsible, selfish. The baby – he never used her name – needed a fresh start. He forbade it. But I wrote it anyway.'

The glow of triumph still burned. A small but very important victory had been won when she tucked the handwritten page into the embroidered pocket on the front of Bonnie's outfit.

'I wrote ...' Anna leaned back, closed her eyes. '*Dear Bonnie, I want you to know that you are loved, and you'll be loved as long as I live. I'll think of you every day and never stop hoping that you are appreciated and happy and growing up just fine. You are special. You are beautiful. You are my one and only Bonnie. We must live apart. But we'll be OK, won't we? Because we love each other. Your first mummy, Anna Piper.*'

None of that had ever been said out loud. 'I regretted for years and years that I didn't put our address. A clue. To find me, you know? But I didn't feel I had the right to expect that. My head was all over the place. And now, Luca, she *has* come back.' Anna leaned forward, handed him the letters. 'And she hates me.'

*

Paul insisted on washing up.

'Innee great?' cheeped Maeve, leaning against Anna, almost toppling her.

'He is.' Anna itched to take the plates away from him and put them in the dishwasher. The clue to its job was in its title. She turned away rather than watch Paul put things away in the wrong places. She appreciated any and all help, but Paul's good deed was a performance of sorts.

From the untidy, post-lunch table, Storm watched Paul too. Anna put her arms around Storm from behind, laid her cheek on the top of his head. 'I know you're thinking about everything you gave up for your mum,' she whispered, breathing in that familiar Storm smell of hair goo, pencils, boy. 'You don't have to like Paul. That's OK.'

'I know.'

'He's good to Maeve.' Anna forgave the showing off when she balanced it against the affection, the security, the honesty. This guy was going to be around for a long while; it was her auntly duty to help Storm come to terms with the situation.

'You're strangling me.' Storm shook her off, turning from sweet Jekyll to hormonal Hyde.

Unwilling to fall apart, the party moved to the small sitting room. Dinkie walked through on Luca's arm like a duchess, Sheba her shadow as ever. The others dribbled through, taking glasses and cups, chatting, arguing. Paloma crawled after Yeti; the dog was terrified of the baby.

Sam peeled off, made for his coat hanging in the hall.

'You off?' Anna was disappointed.

'Yeah. Not in the mood.'

'Don't you feel any better?'

'You make Isabel sound like a cold I've got to get over.'

There truly was no way for Anna to mention Isabel that Sam would accept.

'I only meant—'

'Can we not?' Sam kept his gaze pinned on the front door as he wound a scarf around his neck. He took absurd care of himself; the slightest breeze sent him into arctic clothing.

'OK, but . . . when can we be normal again?' That was rushed, garbled. When Anna rehearsed, it had sounded smooth, sane, warm.

'We *are* normal,' huffed Sam, and he was gone.

Yeti skidded to a stop at Anna's legs as she watched Sam's shape fade beyond the leaded lights of the front door. 'I know, I know.' She tickled his ears. 'Paloma is scary, isn't she?'

The full-length hall mirror showed Anna herself and Yeti. No doubts about the condition of the woman in the navy dress and the flat pumps. She was in full sail. And still Luca stuck around.

She was beginning to hope.

Luca been the perfect person to talk to about Bonnie. *Carly*, she corrected herself.

'Your daughter doesn't hate you,' he'd said. Clearly. Firmly. Luca had reached out to take both her hands as they sat on opposite sofas. 'She's confused. Hurt. But she's come looking for you.'

'No, she hasn't suggested a meeting. There's no address, no phone number. Only accusations.'

'Somehow,' said Luca, 'your lovely note seems to have done more harm than good.'

'It's as if she thinks I was mocking her.' Anna had almost retched at that. 'All I wanted was to ... to ...'

'I can hear pain in Carly's letters. Not hate.'

Anna couldn't quite believe that. But it had sounded wonderful to her ears. Then Luca had said, very grave, 'Please don't call this a confession. There's nothing to confess. You were young and powerless. You're a victim of this terrible situation.'

'I don't like being a victim.'

'Nobody does. It's just a word.' Luca had taken her fingers, kissed them. 'Maybe Carly's handing you a second chance.'

So far, this second chance hadn't come about. Telling Luca had changed nothing.

Except it brought us closer together. Anna hugged herself as Neil hurtled out of the room, holding Paloma.

Over his shoulder, he shouted, 'I'm doing it, aren't I?' Taking in Anna, he narrowed his eyes. 'Honestly, I thought *he* was keeping an eye on her.' Paloma had tea all over her white dress. 'How do I . . .' He held the baby out.

Anna refused the cue. 'It'll come out with cold water. I'm sure you've got an alternative couture ensemble in one of the four bags you brought with you.' She leaned into the sitting room, whistled at Maeve. 'Want to look at those clothes I'm chucking?'

'Ooh yes!' Maeve hopped over outstretched feet. She loved a rummage through Anna's jumble sale bags.

Upstairs in the bedroom, Anna gratefully stretched out on the bed as Maeve critiqued her cast-offs.

'Hmm. No. Naff. Too big for me. Too big for me.' Jumpers, jeans, camisoles flew over her shoulder. 'Hang on. That's nice.' She stood up, held a short tartan dress against her in the mirror. 'Maybe . . .'

Anna closed her eyes. This was like when she and Maeve had shared a room, back home. A seventeen- and a ten-year-old is an uneasy mix, but many nights she'd fallen asleep to Maeve's chatter. It was relaxing.

The conversation with Luca was near the surface of her mind. She'd cried. She'd shared her darkest thoughts.

'Did Carly have a terrible childhood? Were they cruel to her? Is she living in squalor? Maybe she's a drug addict.'

'You're joining dots that aren't there,' Luca had said. 'You'll drive yourself nuts if you carry on like this.'

'I've been like this ever since I gave up Bonnie.' It wasn't

247

heartburn that kept Anna awake at night. The feelings came and went, but never stayed away for long. The little baby with the note tucked in her clothes was always in her sight line.

She'd even shown him the newspapers. Luca had followed her to the attic, stood beside her as she opened the trunk. 'I don't want to put another paper in this year.' Anna had turned, slammed herself against Luca's chest, knowing his arms would close around her. 'I want to find her,' she'd whispered.

That had galvanised Luca. 'No, not a good idea.' He'd held her at arm's length so he could look into her eyes. 'Proceed carefully. Let Carly be in charge. Go slow.'

'If I went slow,' she'd said, stroking his face, 'we wouldn't be together.'

'So,' Maeve was saying, 'I'll take this black dress, the tartan one and the shorts. Paul loves me in black.'

'How long have you been going out with him now?' asked Anna idly, straightening the bed.

'Three months.' Anna was eyeing her in the mirror on the wardrobe.

'*Hmm.*' Anna made a non-committal noise; she wasn't concentrating. The small of her back hurt. She kicked the discarded clothes into a pile.

'What does that mean?' Maeve was bullish. Her pointy chin stuck out. '*Hmm* that's not long or *hmm* it'll never last?'

'It's neither, you idiot.' Anna's smile evaporated as she turned and saw Maeve was mad at her.

'I know what you're thinking, Anna.'

'No you don't.'

'You're thinking that I've gone off at the deep end again. Made a fool of myself. But Paul's different.'

'Hey, hey! I know that. Anybody with eyes to see—'

'You can't disapprove of me forever.' Maeve's eyes were wet. Her voice was cracked around the edges. 'At some point you'll have to say, "Well done, Maeve." I'd even settle for "You tried your best".' She lashed out at the hug Anna offered. 'Get off me. I see you and Neil and your little looks.' She affected a hoity-toity voice. *'What's Maeve gone and done now, eh?'* Her face crumpled with the effort not to cry. 'It's not easy, Anna.' She thumped the bed. 'It's not *easy*! You don't know what it's like to have a baby.'

I do! Anna could have replied with equal heat. She could have yelled, *You don't know what it's like to give one away!* She could tell Maeve the truth. Spill her secret. Maybe it would help.

The moment passed. She couldn't admit it. She couldn't offer pressure from Mum and Dad as an excuse because she didn't believe it *was* an excuse.

'I'm on my own, trying to bring up Storm, and I get it all wrong most of the time, and you all think I don't care, but I do bloody care!' Maeve was bawling now, fists in her eyes. 'It's so lonely, Anna. It's so so lonely. That's why I grab at love. You'll do it too.' Maeve shocked herself out of her tantrum. 'Oh God, I don't mean you and Luca will split up! He's great. You're great together.'

'Yes, everything's great,' laughed Anna, taking advantage of Maeve's change in demeanour to lighten the mood. 'Come here, you fool.' She folded her up. Chased away the demons. Like she had when they shared a room and Maeve had illicitly watched a Hammer film.

'Come here.' This time it was Luca saying it. They were alone again, unless you counted Yeti and the small Piper coming together inside Anna. 'Oi!' He laughed good-naturedly as she ignored him, leaning on the sink, staring out at the garden.

'Sorry, sorry.' Anna turned around. Her head hurt. She rubbed her temples. 'I was thinking about Storm. He gave me an extra-hard cuddle when he left. Whispered "sorry". Because he snapped at me earlier.'

'He's a good kid,' said Luca, only half listening as he took up the *Sunday Times* magazine from the morass of newsprint on the table.

So there is *such a thing as a good kid.* The vehemence of her inner voice startled Anna. She often recalled that comment Luca had made before they got together – 'Children annoy me' – but never with such venom.

She looked at him. All the usual Luca bits and pieces were present and correct. His strong forearms. His adamant chin. His long lashes. The bump on his nose that she adored. And yet irritation prickled on her skin.

You have no idea, she found herself thinking. There he was, happy and relaxed, looking forward to an evening of telly and then an hour of naughtiness in bed before falling asleep secure in the knowledge that she'd be up before him and have his porridge ready just the way he liked it.

And there Anna was, tired, overheated, beset by her past, unsure of the future, growing an inch a day, trying not to be 'too pregnant' in case he fled.

Somewhere, a small voice reminded Anna that none of this was his fault. That Luca was relaxed about her pregnancy. She strained to hear that voice, and said, flopping down on the opposite sofa, 'Maeve let rip at me earlier.'

'Yeah?' Still not really listening.

Anna carried on. As if she was laying a trap for him. Why a woman would lay a trap for the man she loved wasn't quite clear. But nothing was clear. Her head was fuzzy. Her judgement had gone for a post-lunch lie-down. Hormones rampaged through her body, holding everything to ransom. 'She said I look down on her. I don't, do I?' She threw the sports section at him. 'Luca! I'm talking to you.'

'Sorry, darling. I'm a bit ...' He held up his brimming wine glass. 'No, you don't look down on Maeve.'

'Good.'

'Although ...' Luca closed the magazine, looked at the ceiling. 'You do this big sister number on her.'

'Well, I *am* her big sister.'

'It's a bit ... what's the word ...'

Anna waited for the word.

'A bit condescending.' Luca nodded, pleased with the word.

'Rubbish!'

'No, you are,' laughed Luca. He didn't see the trap. Didn't realise that whatever he said would annoy her. 'You talk down to her. Especially about men. But then ...'

'But then?'

'You do the same with Josh.'

Anna goggled at him. 'Thanks,' she snapped.

'You know you do.'

'I protect him. I worry about him.'

'He's a grown-ass man, Anna.'

'I think I know him better than you do.'

Luca stared at her. He sobered up slightly. 'OK, I take it back.'

'Good.' Anna was disappointed. That small voice still shouted, *Beware!* but her hormones shouted, *Tell him to shit or get off the pot!*

'Are you ...' Luca paused. Perhaps he saw the mouth of the trap after all. 'Are you OK, Anna?'

'Depends.'

'On . . .?'

'Doesn't matter.'

'When women say that it—'

'Not only women say it.'

'If you're going to bite my head off, I won't bother talking.' Luca went back to the magazine. One brown eye regarded her over a cover picture of a Hollywood actress half Anna's age and half her current dress size. 'Is it safe to come out yet?'

'Did you mean it when you said you didn't like children?' Anna blurted it out. She felt as surprised as Luca looked.

'When did I say that? *Did* I say that?' He looked perplexed.

'The very first time we met. You haven't said it since.' Anna looked wry. 'For obvious reasons.'

Luca looked at her. A long moment passed. His face was set, all his playfulness drained away. 'What is this?' he said eventually.

'We're having a row,' said Anna. 'You should be good at it. You being a therapist.'

'I'm hopeless at them,' said Luca.

Was that a warning? He'd certainly become very sombre very quickly. 'What do you want, Luca?'

'That's a big question.'

'And that's an evasive answer.' Anna was tired with the nebulous nature of their future. *Was he in or out?* 'You do realise I'll have a baby in my arms by the end of December.'

'Well, I knew it wasn't wind,' said Luca. His face had closed down. His arms were folded. His shoulders raised.

'You said you didn't like children, Luca.'

'Are you noting down everything I say? Are you the secret police? Jesus, Anna, why are you asking me what I want from life at half past six on a Sunday? I'm working it out, like everybody else.'

'What do you want from *me*?' From *us*. Anna would soon be a Buy One, Get One Free offer.

'I want this.' Luca raised his arms, looked around. 'You. Me. The dog. The papers. Nothing fancy.'

He didn't mention the baby. Luca was too intelligent to leave out the B-word by mistake. 'And if that's not what I want?' Anna swallowed the words even as she said them. They didn't illustrate how she felt; too late she remembered that bitter sentences coined mid-argument rarely do.

'That's up to you.' Luca was curt. Clipped.

They were on a precipice. Anna didn't dare look down. 'I have something for you,' she said, turning away from the brink.

'Is it a punch in the face?' asked Luca. He'd lightened up, recognised the change of tone.

Anna brought him a small package, wrapped up in palest pink tissue stamped with *Artem*. 'For you.' She was sorry. She'd let daylight in on magic. She didn't want to lose him, to lose this, the scene he'd described. Her. Him. The dog.

The papers. 'It's time you had an Artem Accessories wallet, don't you think?'

It was deep blue leather, sensually pliable. 'It's so cleverly designed,' said Luca, exploring the pockets and slits. 'I wonder who did that?' He wanted peace, too; when she sat beside him, he put his arm around her, kissed her. 'I don't know what happened there,' he whispered. 'Maybe it's your—'

Don't say hormones!

'Hormones.'

'I'm not a walking womb, Luca. Maybe I was genuinely upset about something.' Anna heard herself, heard her tone, felt Luca shrink away. She put her hands up. 'Let's pretend I didn't say that. Let's get on with enjoying our evening.'

'If there's something you need to talk about . . .' Luca didn't sound keen.

'It'll keep.' She slapped her lap. 'Let's fill your new wallet. I put a tenner in it already. For luck.' Dinkie had taught her that superstition; it was bad luck to give somebody a purse without money in it. 'So you'll never be poor.'

'You loony,' said Luca affectionately. He pulled out his old wallet, opened it like a fan. Notes, coins, debit cards rained onto the coffee table. Along with a Polaroid.

She saw his face change. Saw panic scamper across it. 'What's that?' she said, her hand reaching it before his.

The snap was clear, colourful. It was a happy picture of a happy couple. They posed on a chichi street – west London, probably – relaxed, leaning into each other. The woman wore a floppy hat. Luca had a protective arm around the woman's shoulders, their faces grinning cheesily, their heads inclined towards each other.

'An old girlfriend. Nothing.' Luca put out his hand, but again Anna was faster. She held it to her chest.

'You're wearing the shirt I bought for you.' Anna paused. She didn't want to be the one to strike the killer blow but he'd given her no choice. 'Two weeks ago.'

Luca chewed his lips. He held her gaze. 'Give it back, please,' he said.

There was a handwritten message on the white rectangle beneath the image. Anna read it out. 'For Luca, you made me the woman I am.' She read out each X. 'Kiss. Kiss. Kiss. Kiss. Kiss.'

Luca made no attempt to downplay it. The wording could be explained away – possibly – but he didn't try. He put his hands over his face. 'Don't do this,' he said.

'Do what? Ask you who you're fucking as well as me?'

'Anna . . .' Luca put his head back, closed his eyes.

As if, she thought furiously, *I'm the problem!* 'I remember the day you wore that shirt and those linen trousers. You came from her to *me!*'

Luca jumped up. He was mute, as if his lips had been sewn

shut. He searched out his wine, downed it in one. He was seething, as if holding back a great flood of anger.

'Say something!' roared Anna, waving the Polaroid. 'Are you still seeing her?'

'Thank you so much,' said Luca, 'for the benefit of the doubt. I'm allowed to have friends, Anna.'

'That's not a friendly pose. That's not a friendly comment. Those kisses aren't friendly.'

'She and I are close, yes, but—'

'You said this was an old picture, an ex-girlfriend. If it's innocent, why lie?'

'This isn't a courtroom.' Luca's eyes blazed. 'I refuse to be cross-examined.'

'And I refuse to be made a fool of!' Anna couldn't sit down. She couldn't stand up. She crossed to the kitchen window, pressed her fists against her forehead. 'What is this? Am I one of many? Are you kinky for pregnant women or something?'

'Kinky?' Luca took a step back. As if repulsed. 'How can you say that to me?'

Anna held the photo aloft, like a flag. 'How can I say this to you? What's going on? I suppose you needed somebody lined up for after the birth.'

'I didn't realise you had a cut-off point. Thanks for telling me.'

'Stop thanking me, Luca. You sound like a sarcastic schoolgirl.'

'And you sound like a madwoman.'

'Men always say women are crazy when in fact the woman is *furious!*' The volume of that last word startled them both.

'Look,' said Luca, into the silence that followed. 'I've been taking this as it comes. Building one day on top of another.'

'With me and this woman?' spat Anna.

He ignored her. 'My patients talk to me every day about their lives. It's easy to go wrong. So easy. Pain falls like rain. I don't make assumptions. I don't even make plans. And I can't be around chaos, Anna. I live in the moment.'

'I don't believe you.' Anna said it defiantly. 'You do make plans. You planned to two-time me.'

Luca looked at the floor. 'Anything else you'd like to accuse me of, while we're at it?'

'Defend yourself, then.' Anna wanted him to. More than anything, she wanted to see Luca half-smile, and explain it all away.

He didn't do that. He said quietly, still not looking at her, 'Where do we go from here?'

'Let me help you with that,' said Anna. 'We don't go anywhere. I'm in a completely different place to you, Luca. I should have never let you in.'

Luca's head snapped up. 'You're not the only one who let somebody in!' He added, through gritted teeth, 'And then regretted it.'

They were in a cul-de-sac. It wasn't just that Anna wasn't

prepared to share Luca; she didn't want him any more. He was a cheat. He was a liar. She'd idolised his strength of character, congratulated herself on finding a decent man.

They snorted, like horses after a race. Both of them blinked, astonished to find themselves at this place. It wasn't a kiss-and-make-up moment. Anna couldn't kiss a man who kissed another woman the moment her back was turned.

'Look,' she said, dragging the words up from the bottom of her. 'Let's not do this. No explanations. No excuses. No blah blah blah. We made a mistake. It's done. Goodbye.'

Anna didn't know how Luca took that, because by the time she'd finished, she'd turned away, closing her eyes and letting tears roll from under her lashes.

'You really are something else, Anna Piper.'

She heard a door slam.

Chapter Ten

Lunch at Sam's

TWIGLETS

QUORN SPAG BOL

AFTER EIGHTS

Anna's premonition that a big love was heading her way turned out to be right after all, just not in the way she'd expected.

The big love was her baby.

Luca had written himself out of her life story. Presumably he had sloped back to the other woman. *Or was I the other woman?* Whatever: the floppy-hat tart was welcome to him.

Yeti knew better. He crept to her when she cried on the sofa in front of a movie, laying his long snout on her lap.

He joined her on the bed when she woke up in the middle of the night. The dog knew that Anna had made a terrible discovery.

I held nothing back. The plan to withhold the last portion of her heart had failed. Like Napoleon, Luca had conquered all he saw.

Now, four weeks later, the tears scarcely dry on her face, it was another Sunday Lunch Club.

Dinkie looked confused. 'Aren't you meant to be at Sam's today, darlin'?'

'You're on my way.'

'No I'm not.'

'No, you're not,' admitted Anna. 'There's something I want to ask you, Dinkie.' She turned to face Sheba. 'Something private.'

'I—' Sheba opened her mouth. Her expression was fierce. It lasted only a second before she decided against speaking and backed out of the door of Dinkie's room.

'She's *peculiar*,' said Anna.

'Never mind Sheba. Sit.'

Anna did as she was told, pulling a low upholstered chair over to Dinkie's side.

Tranquilly knitting, Dinkie's voice was sharp as she said, 'So? What's up, young lady?'

'Dinkie,' said Anna. The word hung there. She couldn't

find a way in. Her grandmother let the silence swell, broken only by the clacking of knitting needles. 'Dinkie, did you know about . . .' Anna's mouth dried up.

'Your first baby?'

Anna felt her vision swim. 'Oh,' was her underpowered, overwhelmed response.

'I wanted to have her live with me. I wanted to bring her up.'

Anna struggled to process this alternative reality.

'Your father wouldn't hear of it. Didn't want her to be part of the family.' Dinkie stopped, cleared her throat. 'I wondered when you'd come and ask me about this. Has the pregnancy stirred it all up?'

'Yeah.' Anna was scooped clean. She was glad that Dinkie wanted to talk because she was unable to say anything.

'I told your father that you'd never forgive him for giving away that poor little chick. I told him he was cutting a scar into the family. I never forgave him either.' Dinkie patted Anna's hand. 'I know what it's like having a child when you're not much more than a child yourself. I knew you couldn't manage on your own, but you could have managed with our help. I said, "Sure, isn't that what we're for? To look after each other?" But, well, you know better than I do how your dad felt.'

'Would you really have brought up Bonnie?'

'Is that what you called her? Aw, now, isn't that a grand

name. Yes, chick, of course I would. She was the image of you, you know.'

'Was she?' Anna felt absurdly happy with that paltry nugget.

'Why ask now, musha? Why today?'

'I'll tell you another time.' No need to burden Dinkie. 'You had a baby at sixteen, didn't you?'

'Indeed I did. But my situation was different.'

'You had a husband.' Anna rallied. 'Thank heavens for Grandpa, eh?' She crossed to the photograph, looked at it, and said sadly, 'Grandpa wouldn't have made me give up my—'

'Oh whisht, Anna!' said Dinkie passionately. 'That man was a pig!' She put her hands to her face. 'God forgive me, I tried to bring your father up differently, but no, like father like son.'

'Dinkie? I don't . . .'

'That train journey,' said Dinkie, a pleading look on her face. 'The one I always tell youse about? That Storm loves so much?'

'Yes, yes.' Anna sank to the floor in front of her grandmother.

'He forced himself on me.' Dinkie looked up at the ceiling. Anna felt sick. 'Grandpa?'

'All the charm was for one reason only. He liked fear, you see. I wasn't just a virgin, Anna. There's no word for how naive I was. My ma never taught me about *ess ee ex*. All I knew was that it was a sin.'

'No, it wasn't,' said Anna, yearning to comfort Dinkie.

'I didn't even tell anybody. I was too ashamed. He kept sniffing round me. I even went for a bit of lunch with him now and then, but I was never alone with him. It was like he was a snake and I was a mouse.' Dinkie balled her tiny fists in her lap. 'I wish I could get a hold of me younger self and tell me to kick him in his you-know-whats.'

'Don't be angry with yourself,' said Anna. 'Be angry with *him*.'

'I didn't even realise I was pregnant. That's how green I was. Me bump was out here before I cottoned on. So I wrote to me da and he came over on the first boat and he sought out your grandpa and he told him to marry me.'

'What? Why would your own father want you to marry . . .' She couldn't say the word 'rapist' in front of her grandmother. No longer a cherished widow, Dinkie was a survivor.

'That's how it was then, chick. Da thought he was doing right by me. He sobbed all through the service. Don't judge him, darlin'. Religion had Ireland by the throat back then. Appearances meant everything. Ma . . . Ma just wanted me home, in her warm kitchen, safe again. But women didn't have voices then the way they do now. The way *you* do. Always use that voice of yours, Anna. Never be quiet because a man says so.'

'Not my style, Dinkie,' smiled Anna. 'Was Grandpa a good husband?' The question was ridiculous.

'He beat seven shades of shite out of me, pardon my French.' Dinkie pointed to her face. 'I wasn't born with this queer nose, Anna. That was a punch for not having his breakfast on the table.'

That was why Dinkie had looked subtly different in her wedding photograph. Anna wanted to crawl back through time and save her grandmother.

'He never stopped resenting me for getting *meself* pregnant, as he put it. Some days he wouldn't use me name. Called me Peasant. Thought he'd married beneath him, but truth be told, there was nobody beneath him. Souls never change, Anna. He was as bad a father as he was a husband. The only favour that man did me was dyin'.'

'The stories . . .'

'I made them up. Because I wanted to nourish you all. I wanted my little boy to be proud of where he came from.' Dinkie frowned, as if yearning to get this point across. 'When your grandpa died, it was as if God had given me a break at last. He'd taken away this horrible role model. There was a chance for little Alan. He didn't have to grow up tough and hard and arrogant. So I made up an alternative father for him. One who was kind and showed love.' Dinkie bowed her head suddenly. 'I kind of fell for him meself, to be honest with ya.'

'Oh, Dinkie.' Anna said it again. 'Oh, Dinkie Dinkie Dinkie.' There weren't any words to do the situation justice. Well, maybe just three. 'I love you.'

'I know you do, darlin'. I love you right back. Don't go feeling sorry for me!' She was fierce; Dinkie in warrior mode. 'I've made a grand life out of what I was given. Sure, don't I have you?' She reached out and stroked the curve of Anna's cheek.

'You'll always have me.'

'Sometimes I wonder if your father is the way he is because of Grandpa's genes.'

'The way he is . . .?' Anna had never heard Dinkie openly criticise Dad before.

'Domineering. Hard. Always in the right. He silenced your voice, didn't he, when he cut Bonnie adrift.' Dinkie's small face puckered. 'Jesus, I hope that scrap knows how much she was wanted. I hope her new people were good to her.'

'Me too.' Anna couldn't tell Dinkie about Bonnie's bitterness. Couldn't even tell her Bonnie was now called Carly.

As Dinkie waved Anna off, having insisted on coming to the front entrance on Sheba's arm, she called out, 'Only five weeks to the eleventh of November! I'll light a candle at St Jude's as usual.'

All that love bottled up for Bonnie – surely it had to mean something?

'Is it possible,' said Sam, taking the bottle from Anna, kissing her cheek, 'that you've expanded since the day before yesterday?'

'I think it might be quintuplets.' Anna was wearing maternity jeans with an expandable insert at the front. They were the exact opposite of sexy. 'You look odd.' She stood back, not easy in Sam's boxy hallway. 'Haircut!' She followed him into the sitting room. 'New jumper!'

'It's time,' said Sam with a sigh as he threw knives and forks in the general direction of the table Isabel had made him buy. 'I have to face facts. Rejoin the human race. She's not coming back.'

He'd stopped texting Isabel. Stopped drunk-dialling her at two a.m.

'Whatever happens, it's nice to see you looking after yourself again.'

'I've been a bit . . .' Sam looked ashamed. 'I was mean to you, wasn't I?'

'Nothing I didn't deserve.' Anna had confronted her own behaviour about Isabel.

'Look at the pair of us.' Sam plonked a kitchen roll on the table; *Fancy*, thought Anna. 'Sad singletons again. But . . .' He smiled. A poignant, last waltz of a smile. 'I still have you.'

'You'll always have me.' That was the second such promise Anna had made that day. She looked down at her tum. 'I'm going to need you soon.'

'What will the baby call me? I'm not an uncle. There's no official title for the man who used to be married to your mother.'

'You're an uncle, and that's that.' The baby needed as many uncles and aunts as it could muster. Anna gravitated towards the sofa; soft furnishings had begun to exert an irresistible pull. Caruso leapt onto her lap with a happy yowl. Raking through her sadness for a silver lining to Luca's defection, she had realised that she could now act as 'pregnant' as she wanted to. *I can let out a loud 'Oof!' when I sit down. I can wear slippers all day. I can nod off in the middle of sentences.*

'We're in the right place, now, I think.' Unaccustomed to talking about emotions, Sam felt his way along. 'Friends, I mean. We're good at that.' He looked at her for the longest time before saying, 'You're essential to me, Anna.'

Happy crying was another pregnancy side effect Anna could give in to.

With Paul in charge, Maeve was bang on time, with no tale of train woe. She showed off a new necklace – a looped rose gold affair – and instructed Storm to walk up and down in his new trainers. Storm refused, and took to the sofa with his phone.

'No, no.' Paul shushed Maeve. 'Let him, darling.'

'He didn't even say thank you properly,' said Maeve, who rarely used those important words herself. She raised her voice so Storm could hear. 'He's being very childish. His dad won't be impressed.'

'Your hair . . .' wondered Anna, as Paul and Sam had one

of those conversations about motorway traffic that seem to turn men on.

'Do you like it?' Maeve did a twirl.

'It's very neat,' said Anna. *No, I don't like it.* Maeve had never before succumbed to a hairdryer. 'New dress?'

'I've gone all posh!' laughed Maeve.

She'd been tamed by a navy wool sheath. 'You look like somebody playing you in a movie.'

'Paul treated me to a few bits and pieces.' Maeve stuck out a glossy court shoe.

'She looks horrible,' said Storm.

Maeve groaned, but Anna saw the sadness in Paul's eyes as he took in his girlfriend's immovable son.

All the other guests arrived at once. A job lot of Neil, Santi, Paloma and Josh. In the hubbub of hellos, Anna hung back, beside Maeve. 'One of the benefits of being an older mother,' she said, 'is that by the time this kid is Storm's age I'll be too doolally to care about it being rude to me.'

Maeve didn't laugh. Instead, she looked savage. 'An older mum? Shut the fuck up, Sis. There's no such thing. There's just mums.' She prodded Anna in the arm. 'Every baby comes in its own time. There are no rules, so don't go looking at any of those crappy websites. Every mother is the best mother for their baby.'

'O . . . kay,' said Anna slowly. Maeve didn't usually give (or take) advice.

'You hear me? You're going to be an amazing mummy.'

Touched, inspired even, Anna hugged Maeve, who was still going.

'Sexist shit – don't let it into your head!'

Neil led the charge in from the hallway. 'Come on, what have you done with my little sister,' he demanded. 'This woman is obviously a politician's wife.' He held Maeve at arm's length. 'You're *clean*,' he said, disbelievingly.

Santi struggled along behind him. Teething, red in the face, Paloma bounced in his arms like a bad-tempered grasshopper. 'Ladies, *hola*,' he said as politely as he was able while setting Paloma down on her playmat.

She sped off immediately. Neil dodged out of her way as Santi scampered after her on all fours.

'That'll be you this time next year,' said Neil to Anna. 'You won't know what's hit you. We managed three hours' sleep last night.'

'Don't scare her,' said Santi, Paloma now tucked under his arm. 'It's all worth it, my love.'

'But she'll be doing it on her own,' said Neil, accepting a Twiglet from Sam.

Families don't sugar-coat the truth. Anna took a Twiglet, and watched Paloma crawl under the table. Her niece's fate had given Anna hope about Bonnie's adoption. *Carly*, she corrected herself. That was before the letters had told her the real story. That her daughter was resentful, angry, manipulative. *No wonder I hate it when Neil expresses ambivalence about adopting Paloma.*

'Where's Luca?' asked Santi, as Paloma repeated, 'Papi Papi Papi' in his arms. 'Coming later?'

'Um, no.' Anna kept it brief. When they broke into mews of sympathy, she put her hand up like a traffic cop. 'Don't be nice. I'll cry.'

'He'll come crawling back,' said Neil.

The photograph wasn't mentioned. 'We had a row,' was as far as Anna was prepared to go. 'You knew, I suppose,' she murmured to Josh.

'Yeah. He didn't say much. He seemed pretty cut up.'

This both pleased and dismayed Anna. She chided herself for caring: Luca had cheated on her.

'I'm not taking sides,' said Josh, 'but are you OK? Luca didn't go into detail but I said, "My sister's perfect, Luca, so you must have done something really bad for her to give up on you."'

Anna leaned against Josh's narrow chest. She forgot that he was tall; he was an eternal seven-year-old to her. 'That's sweet,' she whispered, glad of him and his characteristic smell of books and gum.

A memory darted past like an eel. 'Josh, did I see a floppy hat at your flat?'

'Yeah. It belongs to Thea.' Josh smiled; the thought of her made him happy, it would seem. 'She's a sucker for floaty scarves and daft hats and accessories in general. Bit like Maeve. Or the old Maeve, at any rate.'

Anna didn't listen. Her thoughts raced round a rut. *Luca is seeing Thea behind Josh's back.* He'd managed to betray a brother and a sister at the same time. 'Eh? What?' she said, when Josh shook her.

'I said I'm worried you won't like Thea.' Josh was deadly serious, as if Anna not liking his girlfriend would be the end of the world.

'I'll like anybody who treats you the way you deserve to be treated.'

'Like a piece of crystal, you mean?' Josh's tone was still mild, but the words had sharp edges. 'Or like a human being?'

'Get the door someone!' yelled Sam from upstairs.

Glad of the opportunity to walk away, Anna took a moment to herself; today was simply *too much*. The letters. Dinkie's revelations. Missing Luca, and hating him for a new abomination. *And now my brother is scolding me for loving him!*

Her hand on the latch, Anna knew who was on the other side of the front door. Somebody she'd last seen six days ago in a cocktail bar carved out of a Soho basement.

Walking into the glittering cube, Anna had seen herself reflected in the mirrors that lined every surface. A woman in pregnancy jeans and flats. Red in the face. Flat of hair.

She'd held her bag before her like a shield as she spotted her guest at the bar.

There had been no air-kissing from Isabel. 'I don't have long. I'm meeting a date in an hour.'

That could have been bravado, but Anna met it head-on as she negotiated the bar stool. 'Cancel it. Go back to Sam. Whoever this new guy is, he couldn't love you half as much as Sam still does.' She'd puffed, then, slightly out of breath, but safe on the seat and with all her cards on the table.

Isabel's sullen mask slipped. 'How is he?'

Good sign, thought Anna. 'Calm at last. He's finally stopped self-medicating with Jack Daniels. He said he's stopped texting you at all hours.'

A curt nod.

'I told him the messages were probably freaking you out.'

'Did you? Did you tell him that, Anna?' Isabel was arch.

I deserve that. It was time to put things right. With only eleven weeks before her baby arrived, Anna needed to tie up loose ends. She had no control over the loose end she'd been living with since she was sixteen, but maybe she could help Sam and Isabel. Like her plan to paint the spare room white for the baby, it was a fresh start. Honest. Immaculate. 'Isabel, listen, I encouraged you to think that Sam, well, *belongs* to me, that I had first dibs on him. The truth is, he belongs to himself. And he wants you. Do you love him?'

'Why should I answer that?'

'No reason at all. You don't owe me a thing.' She waited. And eventually it came.

'Of course I love Sam,' said Isabel in a tiny voice. She shook her hair, defiant. 'But there's unfinished business between you and him. Your marriage loomed over us, and nothing grows in the shade, Anna. I've been second best before and it's humiliating. We all have deal-breakers and that's mine.'

'If you talk to him about it, he'll—'

'You should hear the way Sam talks about you.' Isabel rattled the ice in her glass. 'As if you're the perfect woman.'

'He does? When we're in the shed, he ridicules my every move. Tells me I'm too old for Topshop.'

'Your opinion is the only one that matters to Sam. Before I met you, he built it up as if he was introducing me to the queen. I was so nervous . . .'

'Of me?' *Why would anybody be nervous of this hot mess, an accidental mother twice over?*

'Then I met you and your face . . . You looked horrified.'

Anna remembered. 'Let me explain. I'd geared myself up to announce the baby. I was in a terrible state. And Sam didn't prepare me. He hadn't said a word about you and he tells—'

'—you everything. Yes. We know. We get it.'

Anna had to slap down her instinct to fight back. 'I was threatened by you.' Telling the truth gets easier the more you do it; once Anna had that morsel out in the open she sped up. 'Not because I'm in love with Sam, but because he's part of my daily life. He's always been there, unchanging. He's been so single for so long that I've stopped thinking of him as a sensual man. But it's obvious, isn't it? Sam needs love as much as the rest of us do.' Anna paused, eyeing Isabel to see how this was going down. *Impossible to tell.* 'I really was glad that Sam found you. That somebody appreciated his kindness, his honesty, his sense of humour and fancied the pants off him. Honestly, I liked you, Isabel, but that was buried under layers of rubble.' She might as well use the right word. 'I was jealous.'

It wasn't easy owning up to that. It made Anna feel vulnerable, as if she'd just bared her throat to a knife.

Isabel had no intention of using a knife. She softened. 'I'm so confused. I mean, you two don't even know why you divorced!'

'What does that tell you? Grand passions blow apart. Sam and I wound down until our relationship consisted of rows about the gas bill.' She took a deep breath to prepare for full(ish) disclosure. 'Even on our wedding day, I knew I wasn't the love of Sam's life. There are things you may not know about me, Isabel. I'd been through a lot and Sam, well, he took care of me because that's what he's like. He was dutiful, helping me escape my demons. That's not enough to sustain a marriage. I always knew Sam was special, but I also knew he wasn't mine.'

Isabel stared. 'I don't know what to do,' she said, miserably.

'Can I be bossy for a moment? Give Sam a chance. It might be true love. It might not. But for God's sake don't pass up a chance like this because of me!'

They'd parted without any promises from Isabel, but now, as Anna opened the front door, she saw her on Sam's step. Anna put a finger to her own lips as Sam emerged from the upstairs bathroom, and crept back to the Sunday Lunch Club, leaving them to it.

Paloma stood on her Uncle Josh's lap. Her fingers were in his eyes and up his nose. 'Ooh, ow,' he said. 'She's very – ouch – lively today.'

Easing open the sticky sliding door to Sam's neglected patio, Anna put her phone to her ear. Watching the tableau inside, she heard Luca say a cautious 'Hello'.

'One question. Is that Thea in the photograph with you?'

'Are you serious? I don't hear from you for a month and then you—'

'Is it Thea?'

'Yes. Yes it is. There. Satisfied? Oh, and I strangle kittens as well.'

The line went dead. Anna watched Josh. He was loose, happy. Confident enough to reprimand his older sister. *I can't tell him. Not yet. Not today.*

All the worst jobs seemed to land in Anna's lap.

In the sitting room, Isabel's arrival was going down well.

'Thank God you're back!' said Neil. 'Sam's been bloody unbearable without you.'

'We missed you,' said Josh.

'It's so *so* lovely to be here.' Isabel had tears in her eyes.

'I've promised to take things slowly,' said Sam, who fidgeted beside her, as if he wanted to burst out of his skin with joy. 'No more wild talk of moving in together. Let's see where it goes.'

The afternoon had been dusted with glitter. The sparkle of a new beginning. Anna, in the twilight of her relationship's aftermath, wished them well. She was still processing what had happened with Luca. A month, she knew, was a drop in the ocean of 'getting over' something. She was suspicious of the concept: she'd never 'got over' giving Bonnie away.

I'll process it. Nice and slow. She'd already accepted it; she had no choice. *I can't take back a cheater.* Processing the knowledge that Luca had looked into her eyes, made love to her, while seeing somebody else was like trying to swallow a brick.

She pulled Isabel to one side. 'Were you really off on a date that night?'

Isabel winked. 'I was meeting my mum.' She put her hand over her mouth. 'It gets worse. She took me to bingo.'

*

Anna had been eating Sam's spag bol for years. It had yet to taste of anything. The conversation was raucous; she was glad of it, after her time spent navel-gazing. She leaned into Storm, and said, under cover of the noise around them, 'Cheer up, Stormy. Your mum looks happy. Surely that's a good thing?'

'Won't last. Never does.'

'You're too young to be that cynical.'

'I've heard her screaming and crying at blokes. They turn up drunk and she's drunk too and they have a big row. Or they don't turn up and she's drunk. She calls and calls them until she throws her phone across the room. It's not romantic like in films. It's more like a war.'

Anna looked across at Maeve, who was happily arguing with Neil about what David Bowie's real name had been. Maeve believed she kept her dramas away from Storm, but that cottage they shared was too small for Storm to be oblivious, and here was the proof. 'That's why you came back from Boston. To keep an eye on her.'

'Nah. Boston was boring.'

Anna remembered Storm regressing to kid-hood, tearing around on a bike as the sun bounced off the sea. 'Yeah. So boring.' Suspicious suddenly, Anna said, 'Paul doesn't do any of those things, though?'

'Paul's perfect,' said Storm wearily. A weary teenager is the weariest thing in the world. 'It's all, like, posh restaurants and presents and new clothes.'

'He makes her feel secure, Storm. When you're older you'll understand why that's so vital.'

'I hate him,' said Storm. 'I really really hate him.'

The After Eights went down so well with the Sunday Lunch Club that Anna wondered why she ever bothered whipping up fancy desserts.

'We all have secrets,' Isabel was saying, after being gently ridiculed for a childhood obsession with Cliff Richard.

'Amen to that,' said Anna, who felt stuffed full of them.

'You especially,' said Sam, pointing his After Eight at her.

'What? No.' Anna frowned. He was tipsy. 'Don't—'

'She thinks I don't know,' said Sam, 'but I've seen her. Putting scarves on Yeti.'

'He likes it!' Relieved, Anna defended herself as the others laughed.

'Storm's secret,' said Paul, 'is that underneath all that silence he's a great kid.'

'True!' said Neil.

'He won't tell you, but I will.' Paul was boasting as if Storm was his own child. 'He's been chosen to represent the school at a languages symposium at Oxford University.'

'My little genius,' said Maeve, whose hairdo was unravelling.

'Shut up,' pleaded Storm.

'He hates praise, but he'll have to get used to it,' said Paul.

A squeal and Paloma pushed over Santi's glass. 'Take her, Neil,' he said, as hands reached out to mop up.

Anna was glad that Neil took the baby without demur, even if he did hold her awkwardly. Some progress had been made since she and Santi had pranked him into babysitting a few Sunday Lunch Clubs ago.

Paul said, his arm around Maeve, 'It's not often you meet an amazing woman, and it's even rarer to find she has an equally amazing son.'

'Aw,' said Isabel and Sam together. Then they laughed because they'd said it together. Then they laughed again because they laughed together.

'If my two little lads,' said Paul, 'grow up anything like Storm, I'll feel their mother and I have done a good job.'

Maeve rubbed the back of her neck, a gesture she'd been making since childhood. Anna deciphered it: *She doesn't like him mentioning the ex.* It was healthy, in Anna's opinion, for Paul to be so straightforward; *relationships break up, but parents remain parents for the rest of their lives.*

Inevitably, she thought of Dylan, her own co-parent. The urge to roll her eyes was strong, but unfair. When she'd called him after her latest hospital appointment, he'd been full of his new girlfriend, a model. He'd texted Anna twenty-three pictures of this girl in a bikini. *Which is not what you want when you've spotted your first varicose vein.*

'Hey, Palomita,' said Josh, borrowing Santi's pet name

for the baby. 'You're getting After Eight all over your daddy's shirt.'

'Oh *no*,' whined Neil, pulling a face. At his side, Santi used his freedom to wolf down his wine, and finish off the pasta he'd barely touched; he knew he was on borrowed time – Neil never held Paloma for long.

'She's got chocolate all over her face,' laughed Anna. Paloma, always ready to enjoy herself, chuckled, setting them all off.

Slapping the table, Josh guffawed. Anna noticed how ready he was to laugh these days; she noticed everything about him, from the tips of his long pale fingers to the top of his head where his chestnut hair whirled, to his toes that tapped out music nobody else could hear.

Am I about to break his heart? So many deadlines reared up at Anna. The eleventh of November. The baby's due date. Telling Josh that his girlfriend and his therapist were making the beast with two backs.

'Santi, darling.' Neil thrust Paloma towards him. 'She's wriggling.'

Paloma's feet whirled as if she was cycling. Santi folded his arms. 'No.' He stuck his chin out. His silk shirt was dotted with teething drool and scabs of rusk. 'No, Neil, it's your go.'

'Yes, yes, very droll. Just take her.'

Santi ignored him, poured himself more wine.

Addressing the others, Neil said wryly, 'I thought he knew the deal. I bring in the big bucks while he looks pretty and wipes the baby's arse.'

There was muted laughter, a 'Don't say that!' from Josh, and Santi stood up, knocking over his chair. Throwing down his fork, he strode away. An embarrassed silence broke out as he battled with the sliding doors. Everybody looked down at the table as Santi gave up with the doors and turned around, his nose in the air, to stalk past them and make his escape through the front of the house.

Paloma burst into tears. Possibly because she wasn't accustomed to her papi showing such anger.

Neil looked dumbfounded.

'Go after him,' said Josh.

'Yeah, Neil, go!' Maeve widened her eyes, horrified by his inaction.

'I'll take Paloma.' Anna held out her arms.

Neil stood, saying, 'Sorry about him, folks.'

Josh said, 'Maybe you should apologise to him, not for him.'

Heads swivelled at Josh's unusual outspokenness.

The front door was left open. They could hear Neil's feet on the path. Paloma's cries redoubled.

'Shush, sweetheart, shush,' pleaded Anna, feeling helpless. *I need to get good at this before December.*

'She likes her blankie when she's distraught,' said Josh.

He'd noticed. He noticed small things other people overlooked. 'Thanks.' Anna crept out to the hall, where the three overflowing bags of gear stood beneath the coat stand. Finding the grubby chequered blanket, she swathed Paloma in it and sat on the bottom stair, rocking her gently. Blankie was the only dirty thing in the baby's life; she screamed for days if her parents dared to wash it.

The howls subsided into sleepy hiccups. Anna savoured the warm weight of the little girl. She'd missed out on countless moments like this with her own first child, but she'd been given a second chance. There were thousands of these moments ahead of her.

The baby inside her became startlingly real. It would draw breath on its own. Have likes and dislikes. Look like Anna, or look nothing like her. A ferocious sense of responsibility made Anna shake. They would be as close as the petals of a rosebud.

Neil and Santi brought their quarrel to the doorstep. Anna shrank back, out of sight, covering Paloma's ears.

Santi was angry. Anna had never known him to raise his voice before. His anger was volcanic, molten. 'Look me in the eye and tell me you think I am with you for this *lifestyle* of yours.'

'It was a joke, darling. A joke.' Neil sounded nervous.

As well he might, standing on the rim of a volcano, thought Anna.

'A joke?' Santi let out a short, irritated Spanish word Anna couldn't catch. 'Jokes are funny because they are true. No! No talking, Neil. I am talking for once and I do not stop until I say what I need to say. Deep down you believe that if you were not rich and if you didn't flash your platinum credit card I would not have agreed to go out with you back then.'

'The money doesn't hurt, Santi.'

'*Vete a la mierda!*'

'You enjoy spending it!'

'I warn you, Neil, do not insult a Spaniard. We are proud men. I am not a stereotype. I had a job when we met. I paid my rent. I held up my head. I was not some pretty boy on the lookout for a sugar daddy.'

'You were a *very* pretty boy, actually. I—'

'Stop it!'

Anna heard a slap.

'I am not a *type*. I am me. Santiago Cortes Quintana. I am flesh and blood and all of my flesh and blood loves you, you stupid stupid man!'

'Santi . . .'

That was not the Neil Anna knew. This Neil was . . . *crying*.

Anna wanted to creep away. This wasn't for her ears. Instead, she curled up even smaller around Paloma. Standing up would mean shattering the fragile moment.

'Santi, I thought we had a deal. I earn the money and you look after Paloma.'

'Like a macho straight man? You may not have noticed, but I am not a lady, and this is not a traditional marriage. We build the future, you and me. I don't want to be Doris Day, a nineteen fifties housewife in a pinny. I am your partner.'

'Life's better when we play to our strengths. I'm good at business and you're—'

'Nobody waved a magic wand over me and gave me the gift of being good with babies. I *learned* because I had to.' There was a pause. Anna could sense Santi's spirit sag. 'I learned because I *wanted* to. This is not about chores, Neil. This is about feelings. Why can't you see that?'

Neil said nothing. He sniffled instead.

Santi whispered, 'There is a reason why Paloma doesn't call you Daddy.'

When Neil spoke, it was with a heavy voice, as if he'd aged on the doorstep. 'I never thought I'd be a father. I never let the thought in.'

Anna closed her eyes. So much in common and they'd never discussed it.

'I hid my homosexuality. I didn't grow up like you. I grew up terrified that somebody would guess. That I'd get called a poofter. Get beaten up. Thrown out of home. So, I split in two. There was straight Neil, working hard, making a name for himself. Then there was gay Neil, clubbing, drinking, having one-night stands. Yes, some gay men were having children, but it was complicated, unusual – on the whole we were uncles and godfathers. It felt unfair, it felt like a tragedy, to be honest, but I cauterised those feelings. It wasn't going to happen for me. Then . . . *you*.'

Anna heard Santi's muted *Aww*. The man was a softie inside that gym-bunny bod.

'I thought we'd have a wild night or two, then you'd go back to your own kind. The slim kind. The good-looking kind. But something happened. We talked. You cared. Remember that morning when you ran after me with an umbrella so I wouldn't get wet on my way into the office? That's when I fell for you, Santi. Not in bed. Not in a bar. Under an umbrella.'

'I was already in love with you by then.'

'I know that now. But . . .' Neil couldn't seem to spit it out. 'Look, this is hard to say. None of this, this couple with a child thing, comes easily to me. Secretly – God, I hate saying this – deep down, part of me thinks it's wrong.'

Anna's gasp was cloaked by Santi's gasp.

'I know, *I know*, but you want the truth. It's conditioning, Santi. If you grew up in a house with my dad, you'd struggle with the concept too. He was hard-line. He thought men living together as lovers was unnatural. I can *hear* Dinkie thinking how can a baby have two fathers but no mum. I don't agree with my dad – goes without saying, I married you in front of a hundred people – but you have to allow me time to catch up.'

'These are the basics of our life together, Neil.'

'I know. But I didn't sign up for this fatherhood thing. You told me you'd always longed to be a father, that one day you knew it would happen. It was you who wanted to adopt, wasn't it?'

'You agreed!'

'I gave in.'

'No, no, no. That is not true.'

'It's more true than you want it to be, Santi.'

Anna looked down at Paloma, now asleep with her mouth open. *Thank goodness she doesn't understand language yet.*

Chapter Eleven

Lunch at Neil and Santiago's

CROQUETAS DE JAMÓN

SUQUET DE RAPE

CORDERO ASADO

The shed was quiet after a productive day. In the light of her desk lamp, Anna surfed the internet. Shoes. Then dogs. Then that day's *New Yorker* cartoon. A few feet away, Yeti – in a paisley headscarf – snored in the size-L dog bed that he'd already outgrown.

Sam had left some time ago to collect Isabel. They were going to a new restaurant. Or maybe a movie. *Somewhere sparkly and sexy*, thought Anna, knowing her own evening would involve rubbing salve into her aching back and staring at her feet, wondering if they'd ever deflate.

And waiting.

Waiting for the baby. Waiting for the right moment to tell Josh about Luca and Thea (he'd been elusive; *Is he ignoring my texts because he knows something is up?*). Waiting for a letter that might or might not arrive was worst of all; she'd taken matters into her own hands. She'd written to Carly, and was now waiting for a reply.

She wouldn't have done it if Luca was still around. He hadn't been around for two months now, ample time for her to pick holes in his professional advice.

In her defence, Anna argued – feebly – that by posting the third letter rather than hand-delivering it, Carly had left a trail of crumbs.

Come find me.

The internet made sleuthing easy. Sitting across from Sam in the shed, she'd searched furtively for a Carly in the postcode on the last envelope. She'd wondered if Carly was a nickname, or short for something, but no, it was a name in its own right. Luckily, it wasn't overused; there were only five women named Carly in roughly the right area.

One of these Carlys remained a mystery. Two of them, judging by their Facebook photos, were at least ten years too old. One was three years old, and was the proud owner of a new prosthetic leg, according to the local news site.

The fifth and final Carly was in the right age bracket, according to the electoral roll. She'd stared at the address until it blurred, and even as she'd thought, *No I mustn't*, Anna had ferreted out decent writing paper and her favourite pen. She'd written in haste, and dashed out with Yeti to post it, ignoring the October drizzle, forgetting even to pull on a cardigan.

Now, a fortnight later, she had to assume that Carly – *Bonnie, Carly, my daughter* – had read the letter.

> *Dear Carly*
>
> *I have tracked you down. I'm sorry if you don't want to hear from me but I dearly want to communicate. If we could meet we could talk and maybe we could heal some of our wounds.*
>
> *It's entirely up to you. I won't use your address again. You have my word on that.*
>
> *I send you only love,*
> *Anna*

Yeti turned over in his sleep, legs twitching as he chased a dream rabbit down a dream hole. Out in the garden, a pale bird flexed its wings in a bush. Anna leaned forward, glad of a speck of beauty in her evening.

It was a Lidl carrier bag. *Like Luca*, she thought, leaping on the unlikely metaphor. *It seemed to be a treasure, but when I looked closer, it was just a piece of rubbish.*

*

Peering into pots, stirring, tasting, Josh was in Santi's way when Anna arrived for lunch.

'Stop! Off!' Santi, wearing an apron as if it was haute couture, smacked Josh away from the cooker. 'Everything must be perfect.'

The Spanish feast was in honour of his parents, who were expected any minute. Anna helped herself to a cold drink and gave herself an afternoon off from worrying, waiting, wondering. 'Can't wait to see your mum again, Santi.'

Mari Carmen – noble-looking, conservatively well-dressed – had made an impression on Anna. She was the sort of contained, elegant but warm woman that Anna would like to be.

Santi wrapped his arms around himself, swooning. 'Oh my mama! She's a goddess.' He pushed Josh out of the way, backing him onto a high stool. 'Stay! You should have brought Thea today. I don't cook on this scale very often.'

'She's busy,' said Josh.

I bet she is. Anna said, 'You're letting your hair grow, Josh.'

'Yeah.' He pushed a lock behind his ear, self-consciously. 'D'you like it?'

'Suits you.'

'They're late.' Santi scowled at the kitchen clock. 'They're going to Oxfordshire after lunch. Is that how you say it?'

'Yes. Why Oxfordshire?' asked Anna, loitering by the tapas.

'To visit my Uncle Juan José.'

Neil, putting out wine glasses, said, 'How come this uncle wasn't at the wedding, darling?'

Anna was glad they'd patched up their rapport.

'Because he is a priest. More Catholic than the pope. He would not approve of us.'

'So,' said Neil, setting out bottles of a good red, 'there's at least one member of your family who doesn't know about your sexuality.'

Perhaps the rapport was still under strain – that comment sounded pointed to Anna.

The chink of glasses brought Sam in from the high-ceilinged living room where he'd been buried beneath the Sunday supplements with Isabel. 'I've had a funny pain in my leg all day,' he said.

'In future,' said Neil, 'how about you tell us what *doesn't* hurt?'

'Charming,' laughed Sam.

'Is that a car?' Santi was jumpy. He ran out to the hallway, wooden spoon in hand, and peered out through the dimpled glass of the front door. '*Joder!* No! How? Father Juan José is here with my parents.'

'Calm down,' said Neil, strolling out. 'It doesn't matter.'

'He cannot know! He'll make a scene!' Santi jumped from foot to foot. He seemed on the verge of tears.

'If he does, I'll throw him out,' said Neil.

Almost screaming, Santi said, 'He's a *priest*! Both my

grandmothers would rise out of their graves and kill me with their bare hands if I upset the priest of the family!'

Neil was grim-faced. 'We are what we are, Santi. You of all people don't need to be told that.' He pulled open the door.

Mari Carmen was first in, her eyes pleading for forgiveness. 'I called you many times,' she said in machine-gun Spanish as Santi kissed her. Then, in educated English, 'Father Juan José surprised us at the airport.'

'I did, I did!' Father Juan José, disconcertingly attractive in his inky black cassock, stood beaming on the doormat. 'You can fit one more at the table, can't you, Santiago?' He had the air of a man who expected a baroque welcome.

Santi did his duty, fawning, bowing, holding up Paloma to be blessed.

'I was so sorry to miss your wedding.' Father Juan José was holding court, beaming at everybody. 'It's time I met your wife, yes?'

Santi pushed Anna forward. 'This is Anna,' he said, his voice a squeak.

Uncle Juan José took Anna's hands in his. 'It is such a pleasure to welcome you to the family, Anna. The baby looks just like you!' He stood back and looked down at her stomach. 'Another one so soon!'

'Um, yes,' said Anna, stunned, trying to think quickly. 'We like to keep busy.'

'I see.' Father Juan José's smile reasserted itself. 'Congratulations.'

Introductions were made as Father Juan José was given a tour of the show-stopping house. Santi took Anna's hand, and demoted Neil to brother-in-law as they passed through room after exquisite room.

'*Precioso, precioso,*' murmured the priest, appreciating the artworks and the finishes and the come-sit-on-me soft furnishings. 'Oh,' he said, surprised, in the master bedroom, a cavernous loft painted dove grey.

They all followed his line of sight. Sam sniggered. Isabel gulped. Josh slipped away, shoulders shaking.

'Ah. Yes. The painting,' said Santi, swallowing hard.

Opposite the bed was a life-size, lifelike portrait of Santi, looking over his naked shoulder, arching his naked back, showing off his naked buttocks. It was one of the most homoerotic images imaginable.

'I painted it,' said Anna.

'Yes, she painted it,' garbled Santi.

'The male nude,' she said to Father Juan José, whose mouth hung open, 'is a classical subject. I was thinking of Michelangelo.' She swept her mind for other artists. 'And, um, Leonardo da Vinci.'

'Yes, Michelangelo painted lots of angels in their socks,' murmured Neil.

'Very nice brushwork.' Father Juan José put his nose

almost to Santi's watercolour bum. 'It is an arresting piece.'

They all needed the pre-lunch aperitivo. Santi's father kept mopping his brow, and Mari Carmen couldn't meet her son's eye. In the kitchen, Neil gave Anna a tray of delicious bites.

'This is your job, darling,' he said. 'You're the hostess. I'm only the bloody brother-in-law.'

Santi kept whispering apologies, with one eye on the vaulted sitting room. 'What else could I do?' he asked desperately.

'Tell the truth?' Neil was starchy; he retreated into his shell when hurt.

'Look, I came to London to be free, but Father Juan José represents centuries of conditioning. I can't come out to him.'

'Perhaps now you know how I felt telling my father.'

'Perhaps,' said Santi, stirring the monkfish stew, 'I do.'

Isabel was an asset over lunch. She knew Father Juan José's part of the country well, and she diverted him with talk of places and people they had in common.

'Papi!' yelled Paloma, having had enough of her strangely attentive Auntie Anna.

'Just as well,' said Santi to Neil under his breath, 'that Paloma doesn't call you daddy yet.'

Anna saw how Neil's face clouded. 'Yes, thank God,' he snapped.

'Ah, a wedding picture?' Father stood up, glass in hand, to examine a framed photograph on the white grand piano that nobody could play.

Anna leapt up. From a distance, the snap was recognisably of a happy couple, their heads close together as confetti rained down. Closer up, it was a happy kiss between Santi and Neil. She took in Father's *this doesn't compute* expression as Mari Carmen crossed herself back at the lunch table. 'Santi and my brother are very close,' said Anna, as Neil covered his face with his hand.

'Very,' said Father. 'It's, er, nice to see family getting along. Ah, here you are!' He leaned over and picked up a picture of Anna in a slightly less ornate frame. 'What a lovely simple gown.'

Anna had apparently walked down the aisle in a slip dress from Next. She had also got visibly pie-eyed at her own wedding reception. Neil had framed the photograph to tease her; her mascara was halfway down her cheeks and her hairdo was inexplicable.

The only person truly enjoying the elaborate Spanish banquet was the priest. Everybody else was tense, wondering what gay time bomb might detonate next. Josh sat folded into himself, alongside Sam, who no longer saw the funny side. Seeing Santi so anxious affected them all.

When Father excused himself to use the loo, panic-stricken twittering broke out.

'Why didn't you pick up the phone?' hissed Mari Carmen.

'I left it upstairs,' said Santi. 'How could you do this to me, Mama?'

Santi's father spoke for the first time. 'If I pretend to have a heart attack—' he began, before Santi shushed him.

'Is there anything incriminating in the downstairs loo?' asked Josh.

'Like what?' snapped Neil. 'Do you think we keep a giant dildo by the Molton Brown hand wash?'

Anna rubbed Josh's hand under the table. He smiled at her. He was buoyant these days, not so easily knocked down. *If that's Thea's doing, maybe it's wrong to tell him about her and Luca.*

Father was back, a secretive smile on his face, holding something behind his back. 'Santi and Anna,' he said, as if addressing two silly children in his Sunday school. 'You should be more careful. People might get the wrong idea!' He held up two monogrammed hand towels.

'His' and 'His' read the lunch guests. Laughter – too hard, manic even – ensued.

'My grandmother will be so sad to have missed you,' said Anna, handing out coffee like a good *esposa*. 'She's Catholic, very devout.' Dinkie was, indeed, nuts about priests. They could do no wrong in her biased eyes.

'Maybe I can call the dear lady?' Father Juan José didn't seem the sort to miss a chance to impress.

A phone was found. Dinkie's lined little face appeared, confused, on the screen. When Father said a suave, '*Hola, Dinkie!*' she screamed.

'Would y'ever say a quick Hail Mary with me, Father?' she asked, as star-struck as a Belieber.

Mercifully, it was time to disperse. *Marriage is exhausting*, thought Anna, her arms around Santi as they all gathered to pay homage to Father Juan José. He was making the rounds, clasping each of their hands, looking them in the eye.

'*Just go*,' whispered Santi as he and his 'wife' awaited their turn.

Mari Carmen held Paloma, smiling at the baby's musical burps and coughs. The noises changed. A horrible wheezing. Mari Carmen's face cracked with concern.

The air in the room changed. Paloma was silent. Her cherub mouth opened and closed but made no sound.

'Her face is bright red!' said Isabel.

'Paloma!' said Josh, as the baby's arms flailed.

They all moved towards her but all were irresolute. Nobody knew what to do, other than panic.

'Here.' Neil took the child from Mari Carmen. He sank into a low upholstered chair and laid Paloma along his arm, his fingers around her chin, keeping her mouth open. Face down, she struggled for breath as Neil tipped her gently. Her head was now lower than her bottom.

'Please,' said Santi to nobody in particular as Neil delivered one, two, three distinct blows between the little girl's shoulders with the heel of his hand.

'It's not working,' snapped Josh.

'One more, then CPR.' Neil hit the baby again. A tiny damp nugget shot out of Paloma's mouth. Her wails were welcome.

Anna had been holding her breath. Now she began to sob. As did Santi, falling on his mother.

'Neil, that was . . .' Sam was lost for words.

'My agency's producing a short health and safety training film for British Airways,' said Neil. He was calm, but he spoke robotically. 'It covers this. I literally watched it on my laptop before you all arrived.' He seemed to wonder at that, at the random nature of life. At the fine line between it and death. He stared at Paloma, who was recovering with the speed of a healthy child. Already looking around her, her face returning to its habitual strawberries and cream. 'Excuse me,' he said and hurried with her from the room.

The grown-ups took longer to recover. They migrated back to the seats, shocked, mulling it over. Praising Neil.

'Thank God her Uncle Neil was here,' said Father Juan José, shaking his head.

Santi flinched.

In the utility room, the soft hum of the dryer sang beneath Neil's words as he laid Paloma on a bale of fresh white towels. She wriggled and reached for him. He stared as if he'd just found her, as if she was new to him.

Paloma wanted to stand. She always wanted to stand these days, the little show-off. Neil helped her to her feet and held her by her hands. She stared at his tears. Neither of them noticed Anna through a slit in the door.

'I promise,' he said to the baby, 'I'll always look after you. I'll always be here. I'll always put you first. I'm your protector, your guide, your critic, your biggest fan. I'm your daddy.'

Neil pulled Paloma to him. She gave a yelp of surprise, then snuggled into him. He saw a stripe of his sister through the door and held out one hand to draw her in.

'Why did this take me so long?' asked Neil through his tears. 'What's wrong with me, Anna?'

'You got there in the end.' There was nothing really wrong with her bombastic, generous, bossy big brother. 'You've had to hide your feelings for much of your life.' An early love affair went catastrophically wrong, but Neil had simply kept to himself; it couldn't be talked about at home. 'Paloma's teaching you how to love, no matter who's watching.'

'She is,' blubbed Neil, his face pink. 'You are, darling, you are,' he said to the child. 'She's my daughter,' he said, as if surprised. 'She's mine and I'm hers. I'd give my life for her and I mean that literally, Anna.' All the cliché new parenthood emotions had hit him a few months late and very very hard. 'How did she creep into my heart when all she does is cry and poo?'

'Because your heart is where she belongs,' said Anna. Feeling rose in her throat. For Neil. For Bonnie. For the unnamed baby inside her.

'Paloma, I'm sorry it took me so long.' Neil held her at arm's length, talking seriously to her. 'I'm an old slowcoach, but from now on I'll be here to punch the baddies and throw your homework on the fire if it gets you down.'

Paloma laid a hand on each of Neil's damp cheeks. 'Ahhhh!' she trilled. 'Dada!'

Neil scooped her up and pushed past Anna.

The group in the sitting room got to their feet when he appeared.

'Is she OK?' asked Isabel.

'She gave us a hell of a fright,' said Sam.

'You were amazing, Neil,' said Josh.

'God bless you, Neil,' said Mari Carmen.

'Father Juan José,' said Neil, as Anna caught up with him. 'This lady isn't Santi's wife. She's my sister, yes, but Santi and I are married, and Paloma is our daughter.'

The priest frowned.

Mari Carmen pressed a handkerchief to her mouth.

Santi bounded across the room to kiss Neil on the mouth.

'I married Santi,' Neil went on, staggering slightly – when Santi kissed you, you stayed kissed – 'because I love him and respect him and I wanted to make a home with him.' He turned to Santi. 'And a family.'

'But ...' Father spread his hands in an appeal. 'How ... Mari Carmen? Is this all true?'

'Yes,' nodded Santi's mother. 'I'm sorry, Juan José.'

'I'm shocked. Truly shocked. So, young Santiago is a homosexual.' Father threw out his arms. 'We must start again. Why don't I bless your union, as I wasn't at the wedding?'

There was no fire, no brimstone. Father Juan José shrugged, later, as he was leaving. 'Look, I am a priest in the modern world, for all people. How can I love only some of them? You live your lives, boys, and be good to each other and to Paloma. That's all I ask.'

'Done,' beamed Neil. As the door closed, he said, 'I feel different now I've been blessed.'

'Oh shut up about it.' Santi, who'd been blessed countless times, was amused by his husband's new-found *penchant* for the Catholic Church.

'Saint Neil,' said Josh.

Anna snorted with laughter. 'Can I give you a lift, Joshy?'

'Yeah.' He looked at his watch. 'I need to get a move on.'

'Hot date with Thea?' asked Sam as he wound a scarf around Isabel.

'Yes, actually.' Josh stuck his nose in the air, as if deciding to be frank about it.

Anna caught his eye. Something about the defiance made her stare. Like a memory. No, not a memory, next door to a memory . . . She had to be nudged by Neil before she came to. Like a zombie, she walked to the front door.

Then, suddenly, she was all haste. Tooting the horn for Josh to hurry up. She had to dash home. She had to double-check. As he tore down the path, laughing, saying, 'All right, all right, keep your hair on!' a text arrived.

> OK let's meet. Sunday lunch 2 p.m. The
> Intrepid Fox SW6 8QA. Don't expect too
> much. I just want to look you in the eye.
>
> Carly.

'You OK?' Josh paused as he did up his seat belt. 'You look . . . spooked.'

'Yes. No.' Anna fumbled, dropped the car keys.

'We can take a minute. That was pretty hard-core,' said Josh.

You don't know the half of it. 'Let's get you home.' Anna checked her blind spot. 'Mustn't keep Thea waiting.'

*

Yeti barked as if Anna had been away for a month. He danced about her legs as she sprinted to the kitchen drawer where she'd stashed the hated Polaroid. She swept it up, brought it close to her eyes. She switched on the overhead light and studied it again.

She was right.

Chapter Twelve

Lunch at The Intrepid Fox

ROAST PORK/CRACKLING/
ROAST POTATOES/SEASONAL VEG

The eleventh of November is Armistice Day.

Anna kept the two-minute silence along with thousands of others, standing in her garden, looking up at a squally sky.

It was an anniversary of peace, a memorial to sacrifice, and her daughter's birthday. Today she'd be reunited with that baby after a gap of twenty-four years. Inside Anna, baby number two cartwheeled.

The third trimester was fulfilling all the pregnancy clichés. Anna was a weary, aching, egg on legs. Nothing fitted. Getting out of the bath was a white-knuckle affair. All day she couldn't wait to drag herself up the stairs to bed, only to spend half the night staring at the ceiling.

'Yeti!' She broke the silence when she turned to go back in and the dog almost tripped her up. 'Bad dog!' Anna imagined falling, and lying there like a turtle. Yeti got the brunt of her unease. 'In!' She pointed at the kennel Luca had built. It was warm, dry, but it wasn't a rug in front of the fire and was therefore spurned by the hedonistic Yeti.

In he slunk, fixing doleful eyes on his mistress as he folded himself up on the kennel floor.

'Stay!'

What to wear to meet the woman you gave away as a baby isn't covered in the style columns. Anna had bought two maternity dresses in sludgy colours. She hated them both.

The doorbell interrupted her as she flailed at the zip of the greeny grey one. *He's early.* She took the stairs sideways on, slowly, carefully.

'Josh. Hi.'

Her brother kept his head down. Waited until he had a mug in his hand. Leaning against the sink, he said, 'What's so urgent?'

The urgency of her call to Josh had come after a month of cowardly fretting. Anna didn't know where to start. *So I might as well jump in feet first.* 'Something's on my mind.'

'Yeah?'

He knows what I'm going to say. 'This picture.' She held up the polaroid of Thea and Luca.

'Yeah . . .' Josh's voice crawled to a halt.

'That's you with Luca, isn't it?' Anna ploughed on, even though it sounded insane when she said it aloud. 'Josh, you're Thea.'

Josh shifted, coughed, kept his gaze resolutely on his feet. 'Yup, that's me.'

Anna floundered. To hear it confirmed from Josh's own lips made it all real. She sensed that what she said next would have repercussions in their relationship for evermore, but clever psychological insight was beyond her. 'Josh, I don't . . . you're dressed as a . . .'

'As a woman.' He nodded vehemently. 'I'm transgender, Anna.'

'You're what?' The word was one of a slew of terms Anna had never picked apart. Transgender. Transvestite. Transsexual. 'What does that mean? Are you, like, a drag queen or something? Are you gay, Josh?'

'Of course I'm not a bloody drag queen!' Josh sounded exasperated.

'Be patient. This is all new to me.' Anna had to sit down. She crossed to the sofa. 'My back's in uproar,' she said.

Josh put a cushion behind her. 'That better?' he asked.

'Yes.' Anna was ludicrously grateful. Days went past

307

without anybody touching her. He was such a good guy, her brother. *My sister?*

'Transgender means that my gender and my sense of personal identity don't correspond with my birth sex.'

'And again in English?'

'Sorry.' Josh almost smiled, then seemed to collect himself and sighed. 'I looked it up before I left the house because it's hard to explain. I've never seen myself as a boy, Anna. I was born in the wrong body.'

'When did you—' Anna wasn't even sure which questions to ask.

'I always felt different. In a bad way.'

Their entire childhood, reassessed.

'You *are* different, Josh. You're spe—'

'Don't, please.' Josh winced. 'I don't want to be special. I want to be ordinary. I want to walk about and feel like I'm simply another person, nothing to see here. But I've always felt like a freak. And now you think I'm weird. You do. Be honest.'

'I'm always honest with you. I could never think of you as weird.'

'That's nice but—'

'No, hang on. No "but". You're being frank with me and I'm doing the same. Accept it, before we go any further. To me, you are just my beloved Josh. Even if you grow an extra head.'

It all came out.

'It was as if there'd been some terrible mistake made. As if God played a trick on me.' Josh had fought it and fought it. 'Imagine Dad knowing.' The understatement said it all.

'You could have told *me*.'

'No. You'd have looked at me differently. That was my worst fear. Still is. That people won't accept me as a person, but see me as a problem.'

Anna said nothing. To some extent, she'd always treated Josh that way. Luca had tried to tell her so; *I didn't listen.*

'I don't want sympathy.' Josh was almost angry. 'I don't want to be the pathetic baby brother. I want to be ...' He gathered himself. 'I want to be a woman. A strong woman. A woman who stands on her own two feet.'

'On her own two stilettos?'

'Exactly!' Josh laughed. 'But it's not about make-up and high heels, you know that, right?'

'Is it more about *here*?' Anna laid a hand over her heart.

'And here.' Josh tapped his head. 'The real me, the one that lives inside my head is female. That's that. Not a fad. Not a phase. It's the truth about me.'

'I believe you.'

Josh burst into tears. Hot, noisy sobs like he used to when he was little. 'Sorry, I don't know why ... sorry ...'

'Shush.' Anna beckoned him to sit beside her and they sat, their heads together, her arm around him, as Josh cried it out. 'You never cry,' she whispered. 'Perhaps you should do it more often.'

'It's relief more than anything. You believe me. You're touching me.'

'Of course I'm touching you.' Anna was close to tears herself. 'Your soul never changes, isn't that what our clever old Dinkie says? Your soul, Josh Patrick Piper, is exquisite.'

Tea was made. Cake was found. After years of silence, Josh couldn't stop talking. He mapped out the process to changing gender.

'First, you have to live as a woman. You have therapy. Loads and loads of therapy. Then you begin hormone replacement therapy. Then you legally change all your personal documents so you're a woman. And then, surgery.'

Ouch. 'Where are you up to in this process?'

'I forgot to say that it all starts with years of being too afraid to do anything about it. At least, it did with me. Then I got a therapist. Several of them. After a while you know what they expect to hear. That's how I was able to fool them that I was on step two, going out as a woman.'

'But you weren't?'

'Too scared. It's terrifying to go out dressed as a woman. It's not like when blokes do it for a laugh in the pub. I want to genuinely pass, to be accepted as female. I couldn't bring myself to do it, but I had to lie or they would have stopped my medication. After waiting so long I couldn't bear another setback. But then Luca started at my clinic. He saw right through me.'

'Did he take you off the medication?'

'He made a deal with me. I could continue if I joined a self-help group he'd set up, and if I promised to try to live as a woman part-time.' Josh digressed for a moment. 'It's really hard setting up those groups but Luca pulled it all together. He got funding, and premises, and volunteers. He's an amazing guy, Anna.'

'I know,' said Anna.

'So why did you . . .' Josh sat back, held up his hands. 'Sorry. Your business. Luca wouldn't tell me and he was right.'

Luca could have blamed Josh. Could have 'outed' him to Anna. But he chose not to. 'So, are you, Josh? Trying, I mean.'

'I'm taking it slowly. My heart thuds just popping out to the shops. I haven't turned up to see anybody I know yet. But then . . .' Josh looked shamefaced. 'I don't know many people. I've let my hair grow. When I'm Thea, I usually put a clip in the side, like this.' Josh pushed back a lock of hair.

'That suits you.' Anna was careful to stifle her discomfort. She accepted him – utterly, without question – but it would take a while for her reactions to catch up. 'What does hormone replacement therapy do?' She was fearful of the answer.

'It helps me be more womanly.' Josh eyed her, as if wondering how frank to be. 'Haven't you noticed I don't have stubble any more?'

Anna raised her eyebrows. She hadn't. *So much I didn't notice* – too busy worrying about him to really see him. She'd spotted the make-up in his flat, but not the medicine.

'And, um, well, under here . . .' Josh motioned to his loose shirt.

'Boobs?' blurted Anna.

'I love that word,' grinned Josh. 'Just the beginnings of them. Don't worry, I'm not going to come over all Katie Price.'

She laughed, guiltily, as if at some blasphemous joke. Josh was vaulting over taboos as if they weren't there. It was liberating. *I like this Josh.*

'There was a shake-up at the clinic, and Luca wasn't my therapist any more. I was devastated, but it freed us up to be friends. He's one in a million, that guy. I don't know whether I'd have come this far without him.'

'You would.'

Josh picked up the Polaroid from the coffee table. 'Do I pass, Anna?' he said quietly.

'It was a look in the eyes that told me it was you.'

'That was a great afternoon.' Josh looked at the snap as if it was from a dim and distant past. 'Nothing earth-shattering; lunch and a stroll. We mooched round an antiques place.

Luca gave me courage by being there. He accepted me. It matters, you know?'

Anna nodded. 'What's the next step?'

He said the word she dreaded.

'Are you sure, Josh? Surgery? It's a such a massive step.'

'Exactly! You've only had today to get used to the idea, but I've been turning it over in my mind since primary school. I'm ready. This is happening.'

'Right.' Anna slapped her knees. 'We have to tell the family.'

Josh groaned. 'Do we have to? I don't want Neil's advice or Maeve's pity or Dinkie's prayers.'

'Yes you do. Because the only reason they bother to give you advice or cry over you or light a candle at Mass for you is because they love you, Josh. They love you so much, they don't even know they love you. It flows, naturally, like a river, through your life. If you're going to *pass*, then you have to pass with the Pipers first.'

The Intrepid Fox was full.

Early and alone, at a corner table laid for two, Anna watched the door. She sipped a Coke she couldn't taste. She thought suddenly of Yeti, and regretted her bad temper. Today was a day of inclusiveness. *Hopefully.* She shouldn't have left the big daft thing outside. *I'll make it up to him.*

Every time the door opened, Anna sat up. An elderly

woman came in, then a cocky young man. A couple with a pushchair. A guy in a turban. Each time, she sat back disappointed.

Until ten to two when the door opened and she stood up, almost knocking over the table. 'You came!'

'Where else would I be?' Sam put down a bouquet of garage flowers. 'I'm sorry, Anna. I can be a right silly sod at times.'

'True dat.'

When Anna had faced him across their Artem desks and told him about the letters, Sam had gaped at her. He'd made her repeat it. He'd stood up and paced before sitting down and tapping his fingers on the wood until Anna begged him to stop.

'I can't – how . . .'

It was some time before he managed a sentence.

Sam had pushed the baby – he'd never referred to the child as Bonnie – into a corner of his mind so dusty and so rarely visited that being forced to confront the memory had unhinged him.

'I'm only telling you,' Anna had said, her head in her hands at his reaction, 'because I'm meeting her on Sunday and I'd like you, as her biological father, to be there too.'

'This is a hornet's nest.' Sam had found his tongue. 'It's madness, what's the point, after all these years!'

'Twenty-four. To the day.' Sam knew about Anna's ritual

314

with the newspapers each year, but he had never joined in. Except, she'd realised, for the very first one. Sam had brought in a copy of that day's newspaper when Anna gave birth, and folded it carefully into her hospital bag.

The physical pain of that day. The long stretches of suffering. Dipping down into reserves she didn't know she had. Time bending, unimportant. The endless bloody 'now' of childbirth.

Plus secrecy. Plus shame. Teenaged Anna had wondered what the nurses thought of her; adult Anna knew they were probably sympathetic.

'I don't know this woman,' Sam had said, his face distraught.

'Carly. Her name is Carly.' Anna remembered their marriage. The scrupulous use of contraception. The concerted effort to let sleeping dogs lie. Their first baby had overwhelmed them; another would remind them of the first.

'I didn't forget her, you know.' Sam had slumped at his desk. 'Trying not to remember is a strenuous thing. I couldn't forget her, but I did my best not to remember. Because she's not ours, Anna. The baby went on to have a new life. We're not part of it. This is dangerous.'

'Carly's our flesh and blood.' Anna could remember how her own flesh tore and her blood flowed. 'What if she's been mistreated? The letters don't read like they're from a happy woman.'

Sam had made a small noise. A meow of anguish. 'No. She's been fine. We did the right thing.'

'And what are you basing that on?' Anna had been incredulous.

'Nothing,' Sam had admitted. 'Hope, maybe.'

No matter how they tried to whitewash the space she'd left behind, Carly had been in every corner of their lives. They would never have married, Anna knew that now, if they hadn't been bound together by their tragic backstory.

We got married in order to heal each other.

Now, sitting opposite each other in The Intrepid Fox, Sam said, 'I'm sorry, Anna. What sort of man refuses to meet his own daughter?'

They'd never used that word. Too combustible.

'Ssh, it's fine, Sam. I had time to get used to the letters. The first one freaked me out, too. You're here now. It's fine.'

'What I said … about Isabel …' Sam swallowed. 'That was so selfish.' He had wondered aloud what Isabel would make of a child he had never mentioned. 'That wasn't your problem, and it certainly wasn't …' He smiled. 'I can't keep calling her the baby. She's twenty-four years old. It wasn't Carly's problem.'

'It was a knee-jerk response. Have you told Isabel?'

'Yeah.'

'And?'

'And she had a little cry. She's dying to know how today goes.'

'See?' Anna saw the landlady come out from behind the bar, notepad in hand, and head for their table.

'What can I get you?' she said. 'The beef's very good today.'

'Hello, Carly,' said Anna.

The tall woman had green eyes and freckles and a sleek head of dark hair she'd pulled back into a stubby ponytail.

'What?' Sam took a moment to catch up.

'I googled this pub and there you were, on the About Us page,' said Anna gently. She'd been surprised; Carly's home address was a couple of streets away. They evidently didn't live over the business. 'That's your husband, isn't it?'

The man at the bar, older than Carly, and bulky in an Argyll sweater, was keeping an eye on them.

Sam stood, gazing at Carly as if she was an apparition. 'Oh my God,' he said, and opened his arms.

Carly sat down abruptly.

Anna wanted to shout, *You're gorgeous!* She said nothing. At last, she took Luca's advice and let Carly lead.

Sam filled the silence that ensued. 'So, I'm Sam, and this is Anna. We got married, you know, after . . .'

Carly hung her head.

Anna flashed a look at Sam. *Too much!* She could practically read the young woman's thoughts: *So they could have kept me?* 'We wanted to salvage something from what happened.' This was not panning out as she'd imagined.

'From what happened.' Carly mimicked her. She was strong-looking, with solid limbs and clear features. Her clothes were plain. She had taste, restraint. And she was furious. 'I'm what happened, Anna Piper.'

'It's hard for us to talk about this. It's always been too painful to—'

'Whereas for me it's been lovely!' Carly pushed the edges of her mouth up with two forefingers. 'Thank you so much, Mummy and Daddy, for giving me away.' Her mouth dropped. 'Is that what you want to hear?'

'I don't want to hear anything in particular,' said Anna. 'I just want to see you. At last.' Something in her snapped. *I'm sitting here with my Bonnie.* Tears rolled of their own accord down Anna's face. 'I'm sorry,' she said, wiping at them with the back of her hand.

Carly said nothing.

Sam tried again. 'I wouldn't call it giving you away. It was more—'

'I would,' said Carly. 'It happened to me, so I get to name it.'

'There was terrible pressure,' said Sam. 'We didn't want to. We couldn't—'

'I have a baby,' said Carly abruptly. She battled for a moment to take charge of her emotions as Anna stared, gobsmacked. 'She's two. Yeah, you're a grandma,' she sneered. 'I would never ever let somebody take her away. So . . .' She shrugged. Wobbled her head.

'I'm sorry,' said Anna.

'I'm sorry,' said Sam.

Carly laughed. 'Oh, that's all OK then.'

'Your new family—' began Sam.

'They're not new,' snapped Carly.

'Sorry, yes, I didn't mean . . . were you happy with them?'

'I love my mum and my dad. They've given me everything. Spoiled me, even. Most of all, they were honest with me from the start. Told me I wasn't their natural child, but that never made a bit of difference. They're my heroes.'

Funny how Anna could feel intense relief and disabling jealousy at the same time. 'That's all I've ever wanted to know.' She turned to Sam, smiling, crying. 'You were right!' She turned back to Carly. 'He said you'd be loved, and you are.'

'Did you two have more kids?'

'God no,' said Sam.

'Isn't that his?' Carly nodded at Anna's bump.

'No, it's . . . well, it's complicated.' That comment about honesty had hit home: Anna wasn't up to confessing about Dylan, but she didn't want to fudge, either.

'Keeping this one, are you?' Carly's face was stone.

When she got her breath back, Anna asked 'Would you like us to explain? About how it was when I was pregnant with you. About why we gave you up for adoption.'

Carly's poise was crumbling. 'Your note told me everything I needed to know.'

'That note took me a long time to write.' Anna risked a smile.

'All I wanted from you,' said Carly, ignoring the smile, 'was a hug. I wanted the man and woman who brought me into this world to give me a hug and tell me ...' She was crying now, her words too damp to comprehend.

The man behind the bar abandoned his customers and hurried over.

'Carly, love,' he began, and she turned to him, burying her face in his jumper.

'Have all the hugs you want!' Anna put her hand on Carly's shoulder but was shaken off. 'We're here and we so want to hold you, Carly.'

Carly's husband, moustachioed, balding, an odd match for the vibrant young woman, whispered, 'I knew they'd upset you, love.' He snarled at Anna. 'Why'd you have to come here? And on her birthday, too.'

Forks were paused halfway to mouths all round the room. Anna reached out for Sam's hand, and he took hers gratefully.

'Best go, eh?' said the husband.

'If you say so.' Anna's feet were lead. So much had been

left unsaid. It was delicate, and now it was ruined. 'Carly,' she said, trying one last time.

'Here.' Carly rummaged in her sleeve and produced what Anna thought at first was a tissue. 'Take it.'

'It's my note to you!' Anna recognised the pale pink note-paper from the writing set she'd had as a teenager. 'But . . .'

'Take it, I said!' Carly broke away from her husband and hurtled towards the bar, disappearing through the back.

Anna felt more pregnant than ever. More pregnant than any woman had ever been. Sam had to help her to the car. She was heavy, ungainly, a dense planet balanced on insufficient legs.

She cried all the way home. Yes, Carly hated them, but that was the least of it. *She's so bitter.* Anna and Sam had messed up their own child.

'You never told me about a note,' said Sam, when they'd been parked at the end of Anna's road for ten minutes and the tears had ebbed.

Anna held the balled paper in her hand. 'It said, *Dear Bonnie, I want you to know that you are loved, and you'll be loved as long as I live. I'll think of you every day and never stop hoping that you are appreciated and happy and growing up just fine. You are special. You are beautiful. You are my one and only Bonnie. We must live apart. But we'll be OK, won't we? Because we love each other. Your first mummy, Anna Piper.*'

'Jesus, Anna,' whispered Sam.

'I put my heart into that note, and she gave it back.' Whatever Carly did, Anna would defend her to the end. *But it hurts.*

No Yeti at the door. Anna, sick and tired of her body and wishing she could take it off as easily as she peeled off her coat, padded out to the garden, unlocked the door, calling his name. Time to make it up to him.

She dragged herself upstairs, and pulled on her oldest, old lady-est nightdress. She needed comfort. Toast. Blanket. Yeti.

Crossing to the tin where she kept his treats, Anna noticed the absence of noise. No paws scrabbling on floorboards. No gruff barks. No dirty-phone-call panting. 'Yeti?' She poked her head out of the back door.

She knew he was gone. Just as Yeti could be emphatically there, he was now emphatically absent. She checked the kennel, her bare feet slithering on the damp slabs. Empty. She looked wildly about her. *Could he have jumped the fence?*

A soft bang made her turn. The narrow passage that ran between Anna's house and her neighbours was an unusual detail – a sort of tunnel, cut through the ground floors only. It was dank. The bins lived there. The door at the street end was always locked.

Except for today. It shivered open again.

Anna ran through the mucky slime of the neglected passage. 'Yeti!' she yelled, bursting into her front garden.

Through the front gate, her bump slowed her down. Anna bent over, panting, by a neighbour's wall.

'Is everything all right?' asked a voice from a doorway.

'My dog,' gulped Anna, setting off again. 'My dog.'

Three streets away, there was a shape against a skip. A dark mound, stained orange by the street lamp. *It's not him*, thought Anna. But she knew it was him.

'Yeti.' She fell to her knees, feeling her pelvis lurch. 'I'm sorry.'

Chapter Thirteen

Lunch at Maeve's

CRUDITÉS WITH HOME-MADE GARLIC DIP
RATATOUILLE
CHOCOLATE MOUSSE

Maeve's house had been tidied. The floor was visible. The windows were transparent.

Anna wasn't sure she liked it.

'Oh Christ, you're enormous,' laughed Maeve.

With only five weeks to go, Anna looked ready to pop. She pulled up a hard chair; *If I lower myself onto Maeve's kooky beanbag sofa, I may have to stay there until I give birth.*

'Terrible about poor Yeti,' said Maeve.

Anna was not at home to Mr Melodrama. 'Yes, yes, all very sad et cetera.' She looked down at Yeti, lying in his

XXL dog bed, one front leg stiff in a grubby cast. 'He's doing fine.'

More than fine, the dog lived like a medieval monarch. Travelling everywhere on a velvet litter, Yeti was never left at home. He was fed a steady stream of dog treats. His poor sore paw was kissed, often. Anna blamed herself for his broken leg, and had vowed to spoil him for the rest of his days.

Armchair psychologists the world over would recognise this as a pitiful attempt to try and make good all her mistakes. To assuage Carly. To win back Luca.

'Have you called him?' Maeve was half her old self, half the new model. The hair was tamed, but the dress was vintage (aka jumble sale) and a tad too low-cut.

'Who?' asked Anna innocently.

'Oh, shut up,' said Maeve, using the special permission that all sisters have to be just this side of horrid to their siblings. '*Luca*.' She held out her mobile. 'Do it. Call him. Tell him you want him back. Quick,' she added, with a glance at Anna's stomach. 'Before the big day.'

'He'll hardly want a woman who needs to be winched out of bed every morning.'

'Luca was bang into you, you silly cow.'

'Such poetry,' smiled Anna. Maeve was a dreamer; *Luca knows by now that Josh has told me all.* If he wanted to rekindle the affair he'd have been in touch. Anna allowed him the latitude he'd advocated for Carly. She was letting him take the lead.

Some nights it was tempting. His number was still in her 'favourites'. But then she thought of the disgust on his face as he left, of the limited time they would have together even if he did, crazily, come back.

'My focus is on the baby now,' she said to Maeve.

'You pompous bitch.' Maeve knelt to kiss Yeti's nose. 'What's good for you is good for the baby.'

Anna wanted to tell Maeve everything. About her first baby, the lost baby, the baby who'd grown up to hate her. She wanted to read her the note and yell, *Look! How could she loathe me when I wrote this!* But Maeve was still her little sis and must be protected.

'D'you miss him?' asked Maeve.

'All the time. I'm hoping it's my hormones.'

'You can't blame *everything*,' said Maeve, 'on your hormones.' She left woman and dog together as she went to stir things and chop things in the kitchen.

'I'll read the note to *you*, Yeti,' said Anna, groping for the pink notepaper in her bag. 'Are you listening?' Anna unfolded the wadded paper. The handwriting was wrong. She'd expected her own teenage careful loops. This handwriting was tiny, constipated. She read out the words to Yeti.

'*Do not contact us. You are nothing to do with this family now.*

*You were a sin and a mistake, but I don't blame you for that. I
sincerely hope you have a happy life. I wish you the best, but we are
going to forget you and I suggest you do the same for us. A. Piper.'*

The handwriting was recognisably Alan Piper's, as was
the sentiment.

Anna was too stunned to react. She went numb all over,
even her precious taut bump. It was difficult to believe, even
with the evidence in her hand. Her own father had found
her note, destroyed it, and substituted this cruel and sancti-
monious message.

At some point, but not just yet, Anna would allow herself to imagine how an adopted child would feel when they
read those words. She coughed, straightened her shoulders;
Maeve mustn't find her too changed when she emerged from
the kitchen.

'I'm popping out for a sec.' Anna was on the street before
Maeve could quibble. At the corner of the short, narrow
street, she put her phone to her ear. She could hear her
own pulse.

'Hello.' Luca was wary. Level. Giving nothing away until
she revealed her motives.

'Luca, hi, this is, um, this is strange, but, well, hello.' She
gathered herself. 'I need some advice.'

'About Josh? Listen, I don't want to—'

'Nope, About Carly.'

'OK.'

He remembered. Of course he did. He was that sort of man. 'We met up.'

'How did that go?'

She told him.

'Ah,' he said. 'Sorry. Sounds like an ordeal.'

'It was. But now there's something else.'

Luca was shocked out of his therapeutic tone by the enormity of her father's crime. 'What a monster,' he said, without thinking.

'I want to ring him and tell him to go to Hell.'

'Anna, don't. You need to reflect on this. Your relationship with your father is pretty distant, and it suits you that way. Why start a war you can't win? He won't apologise. He'll make you feel worse, if anything.'

Anna was melting with her need for Luca. His solidity. His wisdom. 'I suppose,' she said, like a petulant child.

'As for Carly, be careful. She's vulnerable. She's been through the mill, emotionally.'

'I want to apologise!'

'Did she want to hear your apology last time?'

'No, but that was different. This time I know where she's coming from.'

'This is such a tender subject for her. Possibly she's the only other person in the world as damaged by it as you are. Give her some space.'

'OK,' said Anna reluctantly. She wanted it to be like the

movies. All tied up neatly in an artfully lit final reel. 'How have you been?' she asked awkwardly.

'Fine.'

The word cut into Anna's skin. 'Good, good.'

'Busy, you know.'

'About Josh, and that picture—'

'Doesn't matter.' Luca was curt.

'No, it does. I jumped to conclusions.'

'Just a bit.'

'I'm sorry.' She said the word gravely, underlining it. 'I really am. I should have trusted you.'

'Yeah, you should have.'

She was leaving him an opening. An open goal. All he had to do was crook his little finger ... Anna held her breath.

'Anyway, I've got to be somewhere. Nice to hear from you.'

She closed her eyes as he said 'Goodbye'.

'Crudités?' Josh picked up a carrot baton. 'Aren't they carrots?'

'Not if you cut them up all posh,' said Maeve. 'I made the hummus.'

'I can tell,' said Neil darkly, before adding, 'It's delicious, darling.' He held Paloma casually, instead of flaunting her like a trophy. She was sleepy, cranky.

'Congratulations, you two!' Santi held up his glass at Sam and Isabel, who stood like Siamese twins.

'Why?' Maeve looked around at the others. 'What did I miss?'

'We moved in together,' said Sam, beaming at Isabel, who beamed back.

It's a good job I love them, thought Anna, *because they can be sickening.*

'So much,' said Neil, 'for taking it slow, eh?'

Isabel caught Anna's eye. She often did that now.

'No Paul?' asked Santi.

'He's joining us for dessert,' said Maeve. 'It's his turn to have his boys today. They're having a blowout at some café. I haven't met them yet. Paul thinks they're too young. It would confuse them. When they're a bit older, I'll get to know them. Gradually.'

'Sensitive guy,' said Josh approvingly.

'Here comes my favourite nephew,' said Anna, as Storm slouched into the room. 'Come for a walk with me.' She cut through his protests, propelling him in front of her. 'Come on. I need some fresh air before lunch.' *And if I don't do this now, I might lose my nerve.*

Storm's scowl was for show. He was chuffed, Anna could tell, at being singled out. 'Where'd you want to go?'

'The front?'

The narrow lanes of Maeve's patch of Brighton gave way

to the broad main road. Less charming, more brash, it carried them to the sea, which began as a grey stripe, growing as they walked downhill.

'It's so grey,' said Storm. 'Not like—' He stopped.

'Not like Boston.' Anna took an envelope from her pocket. 'Storm, use your young strong legs to run over to that postbox and post this for me.'

Anna watched him, her calves aching. The baby was making its presence felt that day. As Storm let go of the letter into the postbox's mouth, she had a sudden failure of confidence. *Too late!*

Trudging back upwards with Storm – 'Slower, matey, your auntie's got a bowling ball in her tummy!' – Anna refused to rethink her actions. Yes, it wasn't Luca's way of doing things, but Luca wasn't here. She couldn't let Carly go from day to day believing those callous words. Her father had misrepresented Anna, and done grievous damage to his granddaughter's emotional welfare.

She'd scribbled, while Maeve faffed in the kitchen, on a found scrap of lined paper.

Dear Carly

Please bear with me. I know you don't want to hear from me any more but this needs to be said.

The note that you kept all these years wasn't from me. My father wrote it without my knowledge and swapped it for the one I'd composed. I remember every word and please allow me to reproduce it for you. This is what I was feeling the day I let you go from my arms. This is what I have felt every single day since.

If you would like to try again, I will meet you. Anywhere. Any time. If you choose not to get in touch, I'll understand. But please do know that I love you. That can't change.

Anna

She'd controlled herself. There'd been no begging. No flowery language.

Anna realised Storm was talking. Something about school. She nodded, laughed.

'Oh look!' She caught him by the arm outside a seafront ice cream parlour. Inside, amongst the fondant colours and retro styling, she saw a familiar face. 'Isn't that—'

'Come on.' Storm strode on, pulling her with him. 'You said you were tired. Let's get home.'

'But . . .' Anna realised that Storm knew best. Meekly, she followed him.

The ratatouille was intriguing.

Maeve didn't like that compliment.

'It's intriguing like the occult is intriguing,' elucidated Neil. 'It draws you in, but becomes quite scary.'

'Bastard,' laughed Maeve.

Josh's mood had changed. He avoided making eye contact with Anna. She didn't blame him. She was anxious, too. They'd agreed that the Sunday Lunch Club was the perfect time to tell everybody his news, but now that the hour was almost upon them, it felt as if time had sped up, hurrying them towards dessert and Josh's big moment.

The main course was cleared away. Slowly, bit by bit, as was Maeve's way. She kept stopping to chat, or kiss Paloma, or ask Isabel where she got her hair done, with one hand on her hip and the other waving a dirty plate.

Anna winked at her little brother. Neil, who had the beady eye of a dowager duchess, intercepted the wink.

'What's going on?' he asked in a comedy voice, like a supercilious policeman.

A mobile phone propped against the flowers in the middle of the table let out a beep. 'That'll be my Paul.' Maeve snatched it up. 'He's on his way!' she said, as if being on his way was a major achievement. 'He treated the boys to an ice cream sundae at Del Monico's.'

'What a nice daddy,' said Isabel, high on the hair compliment and the proximity of Sam.

'Mum, we saw him,' said Storm. He was loud, abrupt, as if he'd had to steel himself to say it. He turned to Anna. 'Didn't we?'

'Y-e-s.' Anna drew out the word as long as it would

go. She locked eyes with Maeve. *You know,* she thought. 'Maeve, I—'

'You're happy now, aren't you?' Maeve slammed down the plate. Everybody jumped. Paloma stopped mid-hiccup, shocked. 'Yeah, Anna!' she yelled, leaning forward, knuckles on the table. 'You're proved right yet again! Maeve's a thicko! Maeve's the fool of the family! Congratulations on being so right.'

Neil half stood. 'Maeve, what the hell's—'

'Oh shut up, Neil!' shrieked Maeve. She took the stairs two at a time. They all heard her stumble on the top one, curse, and stagger on. Her bedroom door slammed.

All eyes turned to Anna.

She felt the baby lurch. As she opened her mouth, the doorbell rang.

'Go away!' yelled Maeve from upstairs.

Santi stood up, but Anna said, 'Let me get this.' She lumbered out to the hallway, shutting the sitting room door carefully behind her.

Paul didn't say hello. He said, 'You saw us, didn't you?'

'I'm not sure what I saw. You were in Del Monico's with a woman about your age. You had your arm around her. Her head was on your shoulder. You didn't look divorced, Paul.'

'Well, look, I can—'

'And were they your sons?'

Paul's nostrils flared. 'Yes.'

The strapping young men opposite Paul were not too young to meet Dad's new girlfriend. 'Maeve's upstairs. She's in a bad way.'

Paul's face fell. 'I was hoping to get here before you said anything.'

'I didn't. Look, Paul . . .' Anna spread her hands.

'Can you listen? Give me a chance?'

Anna had asked Carly for exactly that. 'Of course.' She folded her arms all the same.

'Right.' Paul swallowed. 'My wife, Pat, has chronic fatigue syndrome. Or CFS, as we call it.'

'I've heard of it.'

'Sometimes people say ME. It all means the same thing. Your life changes. Pat's always tired. Exhausted. Her joints ache. Some days there are headaches. Other days she has problems concentrating. She had to give up work. Before all this she was a teacher. A good one.'

He sounds proud of her.

'She rarely leaves the house. Actually, she rarely leaves her room. You might not have seen it, but today we took her out in a new wheelchair.'

'Poor woman,' said Anna.

'She's doing well.' Paul was uneasy with the sympathy. 'Pat's a fighter. But . . .'

'I thought I sensed a but hovering.'

'We were rocky before this happened. Talking about

separating. Then she fell ill. I couldn't leave. She needed me.' Paul's eyes appealed for understanding. But still those arms were crossed. 'We have help, but much of the time it's just me. I bathe her. I dress her. I take care of her medication. She gets very depressed, which can be ... difficult.'

Anna put her arms by her side. This wasn't black and white. This was the smudged grey she was familiar with. *Most of life is that colour.*

Paul, sensing perhaps that she was open to listening, unclenched. 'I need a life outside the sickroom. Something to cling to. That's your sister. I love Maeve. I want to take care of her. She's been dealt a poor hand.'

'Not that poor.' Anna didn't enjoy hearing her sister stigmatised. Yes, Maeve made crummy choices, but she had family around her and a son who loved her and a roof over her head.

'Maeve's always known about the situation with Pat, and she accepts it. It's not perfect, Anna, but is it wrong? Is it wrong to want love in my life again?'

'Always known?' Anna drilled down into that statement. 'When did you tell her?'

Maeve stood at the top of the stairs, shoulders rounded, dry-eyed but wild-looking. 'He told me the day of Sunday Lunch Club at Luca's. I told him not to come with me, let me think about the situation.' She took the steps one by one, plodding. 'You were suspicious, Anna.' Maeve half laughed. 'But then, you always are.'

'Maeve, please—' Paul was on the back foot, beseeching, no longer suave. His crisp shirt looked out of place among Maeve's mishmash of wall hangings and fairy lights and books.

'We'd made love by then. That's a contract, in a way, isn't it? I thought you might be . . .' Maeve looked tired, suddenly. Her bloom had fallen away. 'I thought you might be the real deal, Paul. I thought you might rescue me.' She turned, abruptly, and fled back upstairs.

'Should I . . .?' Paul dithered, distraught, one foot on the bottom step.

'Give her a minute.' Anna leaned on the bannister. *Maeve hates my meddling but it's in my job description.* 'My sister,' she began, 'is fearless, funny, forgiving.' As Anna spoke she thought of more and more positive things to say about Maeve; things she rarely thought. 'She lets people be themselves. She doesn't judge. She thinks animals shouldn't be eaten. She thinks everybody deserves to be happy and do what they want.' Anna put up an imperative hand when Paul tried to interrupt. 'You don't get to talk right now. You get to listen.'

Paul shrank against the wall as if Anna's words were actual weapons.

'Yes, Maeve's made mistakes. We all have.' Anna paused, repeating herself, heartfelt. 'We all have. You saw the chink in her armour. You saw that beneath the facade she was anxious about the future. That she was tired of keeping the show on the road all by herself. You knew, because she talks about it so freely, that the men in her life have been wasters. You wormed your way in by posing as a good guy. But if you were a good guy, Paul, you'd have told her straight away, before she gave herself to you, before she got in too deep. You played this very carefully.' Anna took a step towards him. 'I see right through you.'

Paul chewed the inside of his cheek. 'Put yourself in my shoes for a minute,' he said.

'Why should I? I'm putting myself in my sister's shoes. If you can only get something you want by lying and cheating, Paul, then don't expect any sympathy when you're rumbled.' She thought of his wife, oblivious, in pain. 'The truth is, you're not good enough for my sister. She doesn't just deserve *presents*.' Anna said it contemptuously, suddenly disgusted by this nauseating man. 'She deserves love. Honest and flawed and wonderful.'

'Nice speech.' Paul's backbone had rebuilt itself. 'I think it's up to Maeve, don't you?'

His confidence sickened Anna. 'What example are you to your sons? Have they grown up watching you move women around like chess pieces?'

Maeve bobbed over the bannisters. She'd been listening. 'Grown up? You showed me photographs, Paul. Two blond moppets,' said Maeve. 'You said they'd be devastated if Mummy and Daddy broke up.'

'They would,' said Paul.

'How old are they? The truth, now.'

Paul sighed, blowing out his cheeks, as if he was tired of being harried. 'I don't see how it matters, but they're twenty-one and twenty-three.'

'Out!' yelled Maeve, thundering down the stairs.

Paul backed against the hall door. 'Maeve, just because your family's found out, we don't have to—'

'Out! Out!' Maeve pushed at his chest. 'Out!' She was beyond words. Pummelling. Violent.

The sitting room door opened. The hall was suddenly full of bodies. Neil, shouldering to the front, was red in the face. 'Time you left, Paul.'

Santi tenderly smothered Maeve with his long arms, drawing her away from Paul, who was scrabbling for the handle. 'Come, *querida*, come away.'

'You've got this all wrong.' Paul made a last stand in the open doorway. 'Tell them, Maeve. Tell them how we feel about each other!'

Maeve kicked the door shut.

'Storm knew, didn't you?' Neil ruffled his hair as they all sat, shell-shocked, around the table.

'He didn't,' said Maeve, then, reflectively, 'Did you, Storm?'

'I didn't know about ... all *that*.' Storm fidgeted,

uncomfortable that the adults were staring at him. 'I only knew he was, like, horrible.'

Maeve rubbed her already red eyes. 'I know what you're all thinking, I should have—'

'With respect,' said Sam, laying a hand over hers. 'You *don't* know what we're all thinking. For example, I'm thinking that you were played by a player who's very good at the game. Somebody who lied to get close to you, and who only told you the truth when you'd come to rely on him.'

Maeve looked grateful enough to cry again. 'It's ironic,' she said. 'You know what I liked best about Paul when we met? The sincerity. The honesty.' She looked at the ceiling. 'Do you think he ever loved me? Even an incey-wincey bit?'

'He'd be a fool not to,' said Neil.

Anna's eyes widened. 'So *this* is what it takes to get a compliment out of you!'

Evening fell, creeping around the house. Nobody left. Maeve needed propping up, and ears to listen to her rambling confessions about what had really been going on. She'd consciously overlooked the fact that Paul had waited until they'd slept together to be frank with her. She'd batted away the suspicion that the gifts and the dinners were consolation prizes. 'If I'd known that he was lying about his children . . .'

'His poor wife,' said Isabel, with feeling.

'Don't.' Maeve was agonised. 'He painted our relationship as a good thing for their marriage. An escape valve.'

'At the same time,' Neil pointed out, 'as he was dangling a future in front of you. The man's a git.'

Yeti stirred in his bed, let out a yawning huff. Storm bent and tickled him. The boy could be forgiven for saying 'I told you so', but he'd said nothing.

'His wife,' said Anna, 'deserves some honesty, too. He's treating her like an ailment, not a person.'

'Did you mean what you said?' Maeve looked quizzically at Anna. 'About me?'

'Of course.' Anna could tell that Maeve doubted her. 'Every word, Maeve. Cross my heart.'

Maeve nodded, chock-full of emotion.

Anna was perturbed. *Doesn't she know how much I worry about her?* The trouble with worry is it can manifest as disapproval. She closed her eyes for a moment. Life had held up a mirror to her most unflattering angles lately.

She heard Josh say, 'Guys . . .' and Anna sat up, alert. He was doing it.

He faltered. All eyes were turned his way. Words stuck in his throat.

'Josh has something to tell you,' said Anna. 'It's important.'

'Should I open another bottle of wine?' Maeve stood up.

'Yes,' said Josh. 'And bring me an extra-large glass.'

Chapter Fourteen

Lunch at Josh's

SAUSAGE AND MASH
VIENNETTA

The park was wintry, bare. Yeti, a connoisseur of bins, stopped to savour one. Anna stood and waited, her tummy a hillock beneath a fake fur which no longer buttoned up.

Mid-December already. Christmas on the tip of everybody's tongue.

The weeks marched relentlessly on, dragging Anna through the calendar towards her due date. At first she hadn't registered that the twenty-fifth of December was Christmas Day. A day of turkey and arguments for most people, but a new beginning for Anna.

There had been nothing from Carly. It was over, their brief reunion. *But it can never be over. Love doesn't work like that.*

Yeti stuck close to his mistress. He'd lost confidence since his accident, but his need for Anna had escalated. She indulged him. Perhaps it was guilt at leaving him home alone with the side gate open, or perhaps it was maternal juices flooding her body. Whatever it was, the end result pleased both dog and woman enormously.

Loyal, faithful, always pleased to see her – he greeted her like a returning soldier every time she went to the loo – Yeti would sit up with her during night feeds.

The woman Anna visualised giving these night feeds, or bathing the baby, or pushing a buggy, didn't look anything like her. When she imagined the baby, out of her womb and in the real world, Anna imagined a self-assembly shelf unit with no manual.

Ankles puffy, legs begging for mercy, Anna turned for home. The sexy bloom of her first trimester had given way to a Soviet housewife look.

'Yeti,' she said to her companion, 'don't let me check my phone right away, OK?' She always checked it, and he'd never called.

After Anna had apologised to Luca she'd entertained a timid hope that she might have rattled his cage. That he might miss her. That he'd think, 'What the heck, might as well!' and turn up at her door.

That hadn't happened.

*

343

She checked her phone, swore at it, and plodded upstairs with a bag of diminutive clothes. Taking care, conscious that it felt like play-acting, Anna folded each tiny Babygro and placed it neatly in the new mint green chest of drawers in the spare room.

It was time to accept and move on. Luca wasn't a big love. He was a fling. Delicious. Fleeting. Like summer.

Time to focus on the birth. 'It's thee and me, pardner,' she said to her bump, closing a drawer with her hip.

Drawing on a socially acceptable face with the help of Mac and Bobbi Brown, Anna recalled a time when Luca had opened up about his work. He saw so much disruption and angst. 'There have been deaths,' he'd said, gravely. He'd told her he was fiercely protective of his own 'clean page'; 'It's so easy to mess up, to invite unhappiness in.' He wanted to live cleanly.

A super-pregnant woman amounted to a scribble on that page.

She was the last to arrive. A bombardment of 'hello's and 'at last's almost knocked her off her feet.

Paloma was walking. More of a totter, but she did a high-speed circuit of the room in soft new gold boots.

There was applause for the baby's virtuosity. Paloma fell over. Everybody applauded again.

It was exactly what Anna needed.

'I've mastered sausage and mash.' Josh was very proud of his new accomplishment.

'A sausage,' said Neil, poker-faced, 'is man's best friend.'

If Dinkie got the joke, she didn't let on. 'No, darlin', no.' She refused to take Paloma. 'She's too wriggly today.'

See? Neil's glare at Anna was eloquent. He retired to the other end of the studio flat. Which wasn't very far.

Sam searched out condiments. Maeve was on mash duty. Isabel rummaged for glasses. Santi went out to buy something to pour into the glasses. The Sunday Lunch Club was ticking over nicely, but something had changed.

They all knew about Josh.

Neil had been the most shocked. He'd kept repeating 'Bloody hell', in a contemplative way, while the others leaned in and asked questions.

'Josh, you're my little brother!' Maeve had whimpered. 'Not my little sister.'

'He'll still be him, Mum.' Storm hadn't understood the consternation. 'Or her, I mean. Still the same person. God, you old people, you're so prejudiced. There's a transgender boy in my class. He was a girl and now he's not.' He rubbed his nose. 'Still a dickhead, though.'

'I'm trying to get my head round it.' Maeve appealed to Josh for understanding, knowing she'd receive it.

'It's taken me my whole life to get my head around it.'

Josh had absolved her. He'd absolved all of them, freeing them up to say countless inappropriate things.

By the time the twittering ceased, they'd decided on three basics.

Firstly, it didn't matter. Well, it did matter, but it made no difference to how they felt about Josh.

Secondly, they'd support him. And find out all about transgender issues. (Josh had done his best to look pleased at that, but Anna could tell he foresaw an awful lot of explaining in his future.)

Lastly, Dinkie must never know.

Maeve, surprisingly, had started that particular ball rolling. 'Dinkie's too old to handle this,' she'd said.

'And too Catholic,' Santi had added.

'Look at how she treats poor Paloma.'

Anna had interrupted Neil to say there was nothing remotely poor about Paloma.

'Shut up, Anna. Dinkie can't accept an adopted child of two men so we can't expect her to get her head around Josh turning into a woman.'

Taken to its logical conclusion, this meant that after the surgery (which Neil insisted on paying for) Josh would have to stay away from his grandmother. Nobody wanted that.

'It's unthinkable,' Anna had said, firmly. She assumed that Dinkie would accept Josh. With some soul-searching, possibly, and certainly with a great deal of anxiety for her grandson's chances of getting into Heaven. She couldn't agree that the news would blight Dinkie's remaining years. 'You make it sound as if she's about to keel over!' That thought frightened Anna too much for her to allow it houseroom.

'So you brought Sheba?' said Anna to her grandmother as they sat, watching the others pull sausage and mash together. Sheba was setting out chairs, her face closed as ever.

'Yes.' Dinkie scrutinised Anna's expression. 'You don't like her.'

'I don't trust her. There's something going on between you two.' Anna put her mouth close to Dinkie's ear. 'I can get you out of Sunville. Just wink at me, and I'll take you home right now.'

Sheba stood over them. 'Come.' She held out her hand to Dinkie. 'Let me seat you at the table, Mrs Piper.'

The woman had impeccable timing.

Viennetta unites people in a way that nothing else can.

Storm had thirds. Anna, watching his elbow work as he cleared his plate, knew that soon he would stop attending Sunday Lunch Clubs. He'd be independent, making his own plans for Sundays. With *girls*. Anna gulped; she hoped life would be kind to him. That his heart would remain in one piece. Although her own battle-scarred heart wouldn't be half as useful if she'd led a sheltered, calm life.

Josh leaned over her, collecting dishes.

Anna scrutinised his face. Not a hint of stubble. He was morphing, transforming, into what he saw as his true self. She wondered what would be left of the 'old' Josh. *He can't wait to leave Josh behind, but I've always loved him just as he is.*

'I invited Luca,' he said.

'Did you?' Anna kept her expression ambiguous. Her heart hadn't got the memo, however, and began to sprint.

'He refused. Said it was too complicated. I kept on at him, but no dice.'

'S'fine.' Anna had to say something, and that was what she came up with.

A hand on her arm took her attention. 'I hear Dad called you,' said Neil in an undertone. With the others engrossed in noisy crosstalk, he and Anna could discuss their father without being overheard.

'He was ranting.'

'What a surprise.'

'It was terrible, Neil.' Anna recalled it verbatim. *First Neil's a nancy boy and now this? What's wrong with the men in this family?*

'I don't know, Dad,' Anna had answered. 'What is wrong with you?'

There'd been no answer. Alan Piper wasn't accustomed to being challenged.

'Don't forget,' Anna had added conversationally, 'that the girls let you down, too. We're such a disappointment.'

'I don't like your tone, young lady.'

'I'm not young, Dad. I'm forty. I have a child of twenty-four and another on the way. I don't need your approval, which is just as well as I'd never get it.' Into the shocked silence, Anna had said, 'You had no right to change my note to Bonnie, Dad. No right whatsoever.' She sent a heartfelt plea across the ocean. *Apologise, Dad!* If he said sorry it could kick-start the healing.

The line had gone dead.

'He rang me right after,' said Neil. 'Some choice vocabulary came out. I'm "bent", apparently. "Queer". Oh, and no son of his. Which, as you can imagine, comes as a relief.'

They laughed. Wearily. But they managed to laugh.

'How did you leave things with him?' asked Anna.

'I told him goodbye.' Neil seemed at a loss. 'I've had enough. Now that I'm a dad myself, I know how hard you have to work to make children feel wanted and appreciated. Dad set standards for us that had nothing to do with our happiness, or our fulfilment. He wanted us to live a life that wouldn't upset the neighbours. It's time I cut ties.'

They held hands, like they used to do when they were tiny. It was a bittersweet moment in the midst of an ordinary Sunday Lunch.

It wasn't the last one that day.

'I have an announcement.' Dinkie had to say it twice before the lunchers quietened down. 'Will youse whisht! I have a feckin' announcement.' She looked to Sheba, who nodded, and Dinkie said, 'I'm leaving Sunville.'

'But you said—' began Maeve.

'I know what I said, but the truth is I hate that place. Full of old people. I've never aquacised in me life and I don't intend to start. Don't get me started on the breakfasts. Sheba here is me only consolation.' She held out her hand and Sheba jumped up, took it. 'She comes in when she's supposed to be off duty to make sure I'm OK. She reads the paper to me when I lose me glasses. She's the best friend a person could hope to have.'

Sheba's impassive face cracked, and she smiled. It was a neon slice, transforming her face. She even spoke. 'It is my pleasure,' she said, in her ripe accent.

'So,' said Dinkie, silencing the mouths that opened, ready to question and gasp and add their two penn'orth. 'I'm moving in with Josh. I'm spending the money I would have wasted on Sunville on a nice two-bedroom flat for the two of us.'

'But—' Maeve made an urgent face at Josh.

'Dinkie knows all about my gender reassignment,' said Josh. He had a look of cheeky triumph; he'd trusted Dinkie and been proved right.

'Sure, I don't understand it,' said Dinkie, mildly. 'But

chopping off his bits is his business. If that's what it takes to make my grandson happy, then so be it. His soul won't change, will it? That has no gender.'

There was a stupefied hush, broken by Neil's best Head of the Family voice.

'Listen, let's not rush into—'

'Too late. Sit down.' Dinkie was imperious. 'Josh will need somebody to look after him while he recovers from surgery. Who better than his grandmother? And Sheba has agreed to help out. She's leaving Sunville, and working for me. She'll pop in, do her magic, but from now on she won't have to wear a horrible tunic.'

'I hate that tunic,' growled Sheba.

They all laughed. Relieved. Puzzled. But aware that something wonderful had happened.

'They know it's a fairy story, right?' Neil stood by Anna's car, leaning in to say goodbye. 'It's Dinkie who needs looking after, not Josh.'

'Dinkie won't admit to ageing, but by pretending this move is for Josh's sake, she gets to escape Sunville and Josh gets a permanent home. Win-win.'

'Except an old lady is now in the care of a man-child who forgets to pay his electricity bill.'

'It's time Josh had responsibility. I can tell he's looking forward to it. He's not a child, he's a man. Soon he'll be a woman. We have to allow our baby brother to grow up. We have to believe in him.'

'I sound like Dad, don't I?'

'You sound like you, Neil. But on a bad day.'

'We haven't sorted out Christmas yet.'

'All I know,' said Anna, buckling in, 'is that *no way* are we having lunch at my place.'

Giving birth is the perfect excuse to duck out of festive duties.

Chapter Fifteen

Lunch at Anna's

SMOKED SALMON TAPAS
ROAST TURKEY, WITH ROAST POTATOES,
BACON-WRAPPED CHIPOLATAS, STUFFING,
CARROTS, PEAS/MUSHROOM AND
TARRAGON STRUDELS WITH MADEIRA SAUCE
CHRISTMAS PUDDING WITH BRANDY BUTTER

T'was the season of glitter and snow and enormous fowl. The turkey was 'resting' – the quaint term always made Anna imagine it with a cocktail and a Jackie Collins novel – and the hostess was wilting.

She couldn't even blame anybody else. It had been her decision to host Christmas. Anna knew, just knew, that the baby wasn't ready to show its face, due date or no due date. Sitting around waiting made the minutes tick by like sludge, so, one group email later and she'd been knee-deep in red napkins and paper hats. It was a reaffirmation of Piper togetherness in the face of her father's frostiness. He'd turned away from his grown children, and her mother, loyal as ever, stood shoulder to petty shoulder with him.

One day, Anna hoped, her mum would challenge the tyrant, and be frank with them all about what her blind allegiance had cost her. But Christmas Day was not that day.

Somewhere among the cards hanging like bunting was a cartoon of Santa getting stuck in a chimney with the message 'From Mum and Dad' neatly written inside. No kisses. No asking after the baby. Thanks to Storm, there was a card from Yeti, with an inky paw print. But nothing from Carly.

I should have sent a card to Carly. Anna flip-flopped on this thrice a day. Luca would approve of her original decision not to reach out. It was scant comfort. Here she was on Christmas Day with neither of them near.

It was, felt Anna, her duty to respect Carly's silence. Robbed of the chance to show maternal love in more usual ways, she did her best with this opportunity. It wasn't easy, but then it wasn't supposed to be.

Potatoes ticked over in the oven. Peas and carrots waited their turn on the worktop. Yeti prowled, now the size of a deer, and with a distinctive mince since his accident. Anna lumbered around the table, tweaking the crackers and rotating the mini poinsettia at each chair. Her physicality seeped into everything she did; her size had altered the way she walked, sat, *thought*.

An oversized teddy, the size of a toddler, stood drunkenly against the fridge. Dylan had delivered it yesterday, en route to the airport. Peru, this time.

'So you won't be here for the birth?'

'Is that a problem?' Dylan looked apologetic. The level of apology more suited to forgetting to return a borrowed book. 'I mean, it's not like I could do anything.' He'd assumed a look of horror. 'Unless you want me to be with you when it comes out?'

Anna had valiantly managed not to laugh. *Dylan in the delivery room!* 'My sister's my birth partner. We've been practising the breathing and stuff. I just thought you might . . . well, I'll email you afterwards.'

'Tell me if it's a dude or a girl.'

'Er, yeah.'

Beyond the kitchen window, the shed was wreathed in fairy lights. They flickered, disco-fast, which might induce a fit in one of her guests, but it was too drizzly and grim for Anna to venture out and change them. No cleansing, festive snow had fallen on Anna's suburb, only persistent chilly rain.

The to-do list stuck to the fridge accused her. Anna wouldn't admit she'd taken on too much. Instead, she ploughed through her chores, an apron over her 'best' maternity dress, feeling like a spangly marquee. Usually she pranced around in high heels on Christmas Day, relying on the anaesthetic qualities of Prosecco to see her through, but today her feet were in slippers.

Not long to go before she met the baby. Anna already knew the child intimately; the togetherness is absolute when you share a body. *I can't wait to see what you look like*, she told her bump as she reached for the platter with the ivy pattern.

Almost there. The house was warm, the table was laid, Yeti was wearing a red ruff edged with white fake fur. Presents sat, wrapped, beneath the tree Sam had put up for her. All was as it should be.

Almost.

There was a lull in the action. So much turkey had been eaten that Storm had burst into tears at the word 'afters'. The visitors were dispersed around the house, all recovering from the Christmas Lunch Club.

'Now you all know how I feel every day.' Anna stepped over outstretched legs, carrying a tray of empties from the sitting room back to the kitchen.

Sheba popped out to the hall. She wore a traditional headdress, a twisted affair of printed cotton that made her neck look slender and long. 'Let me,' she said, reaching for the tray.

'Absolutely not. You're a guest, Sheba, and it's my turn to look after you.'

A week ago, Josh and Dinkie had moved into a halfway house, a small rented maisonette. A cat had been procured. Sheba, working her notice at Sunville, had appeared most evenings, helping Dinkie settle in.

'Sheba's amazing,' Josh had told Anna. 'She and Dinkie have a telepathic thing going on. They, like, love each other.'

I was wrong about Sheba. Anna was happy to make it up to the woman, pamper her. She wasn't easy to pamper; 'Seriously, Sheba, sit down,' had been heard a dozen times that afternoon.

Perhaps it was because Anna was so very tired, or because being hostess strips away the glamour of an occasion, but there seemed to be very little that was magical about Christmas this year.

Even with Paloma to spoil and cuddle, even with Neil and Santi sharing the load, with Maeve bright-eyed again after mourning Paul, with Dinkie and Sheba and Josh, there were still personnel to miss.

Sam had taken Isabel skiing. Rosy-cheeked in the snow, goggles pushed back, they'd woken her with a bawdy carol via Skype.

'How's your sore throat?' Anna had indulgently expected a barrage of symptoms, but Sam had answered, 'What sore throat?' The love of a good woman had cured his hypochondria.

They were all moving on. All being pulled into their futures. Distances were opening up, and in a couple of cases, doors had slammed. If Carly was ever going to get in touch, then the season of goodwill was the ideal opportunity. And Luca . . .

'I asked him to come.' Josh had been shamefaced, confessing over the gravy.

'Oh. And . . .?' Anna attempted coolness; *I can blame my pink face on the steam from the carrots.*

'He's spending the day with his mum.'

'I see.'

'I told him you want him back.'

'You did what, Josh?' Anna thought she'd been enigmatic. Apparently, she'd been transparent. 'Why? What good can that do, other than to make me look like a schmuck?'

'You can't look like a schmuck to the people who love you.'

'Exactly. If Luca loved me, he'd be here. And he's not, therefore . . .' Anna didn't like to dwell on whether or not Luca had been serious about her before she stomped her feet and pulled down their Wendy house. 'We could hardly rekindle an affair with me like *this.*' She pointed down at the vast region south of her head. 'If he was the father, it'd be different.'

'I think he should be here.' Josh's eyes had misted over. 'Love doesn't happen every day. We should take care of it when it shows its face.'

'I know about Dinkie's fall.' Anna had chosen that

moment to mark her brother's card. 'Don't keep that sort of thing from me, Josh.'

'Who told—' Josh realised. 'Sheba.'

'She did the right thing. Sheba doesn't want to be stuck in the middle of family fibs.'

Josh had nodded. 'I didn't want you to worry. It wasn't a bad fall.'

'Worry's my middle name. Every fall is potentially dangerous at Dinkie's time of life. Look, I know I've been overprotective of you in the past. I get it. You're not a kid any more. But don't shut me out.'

Now, the revellers came back to life, one by one. Like a festive zombie apocalypse, they staggered to their feet, appetites magically renewed.

Waving away offers of help, Anna found a sprig of holly for the Christmas pudding as she put the kettle on to boil, as she looked out the brandy butter, as she fetched plates, as she suddenly felt a lightning bolt zip through her core.

Shocked, she clutched the edge of the sink.

Storm jumped back. 'Urgh, you've wet yourself, Auntie Anna!'

He was disgusted. Anna was disoriented. 'Is that my waters breaking?' She harboured a hope that somebody would explain it away. Nobody did.

'Jesus, right, bloody hell, shit shit shit.' Maeve went in all directions at once. 'Where's your hospital bag?'

'It's not packed.' Anna clung on to the sink. She'd been so sure. 'Not now, this can't be happening now.' Her body disagreed. It knew something was coming, and wouldn't let her move.

As Yeti, sensitive to Anna's feelings, began to whine, Neil and Santi put their arms around Anna. Maeve opened and shut kitchen drawers.

'Car keys, car keys,' she muttered.

'You can't drive, Maeve,' said Josh. 'You've had tons of wine.'

'I'm her part birthner! I mean, her birth partner.' Maeve scratched her head. 'Maybe you're right,' she said, and dropped like a felled oak to the sofa.

'We came by Uber so we could drink,' said Neil.

'And we did drink,' said Santi.

'I'll take you, if you want me to, Sis.' Josh looked so scared that Anna almost laughed.

'No, darling, this isn't a job for *yoooooooooooou.*' Something ripped through her, then left. Her knees buckled and she was helped to a chair.

Sheba offered to take her, but she could only drive manual cars and Anna's was automatic.

'I know.' Neil plucked Paloma off the floor. 'I'll call an Uber minibus and we'll all come with you.'

'No, please, stay and enjoy the *ooooooooh.*' Anna was hot with pain. She didn't know if she was up to this. Panic swarmed through her. Sweat stood out on her forehead. 'I'm scared,' she said.

'We're all with you,' said Santi, as behind them Neil could be heard yelling into a phone, 'Forty minutes' waiting time?'

Christmas Day isn't the best time to call a cab.

'I don't want *aaaaaargh*.' Anna was crushed again. White lights behind her eyes. She didn't want them all to go to hospital with her. She didn't want to go to hospital at all. She wanted to rewind the past forty weeks and ignore Dylan. She wanted life to be dull again. This technicolor suffering was too much.

Shuffling together, the entire family moved as one towards the front door. Anna, at their centre, was a bulky queen bee, her fringe plastered to her forehead, her feet wringing wet. She felt both untethered and claustrophobic; hot and cold and heading for something that promised to get much worse before it got better.

The doorbell rang.

'The cab!' said many voices at once. The shuffling sped up. The door was flung open. Luca stood on the step.

'It's happening!' Neil shouted in his face.

'The baby!' shouted Josh.

Anna, crucified on her family, her enormous stomach leading the way, locked eyes with Luca. He was the only calm person present. A still point in the whirling chaos of her house.

Rescue me, she begged mutely.

He rescued her.

Luca reached out and extricated her from her gaggle of helpers. 'My car's here,' he said. His voice was soothing. As if he chauffeured women in labour all the time. 'I've got you, Anna.'

'Nobody else,' she managed to whisper.

'Folks, my back seat's full of stuff. I'll take her to hospital and call you, OK?'

Dinkie emerged from the scrum. 'Look after her!'

'I promise.' Luca lowered Anna into the passenger seat. The belt wouldn't reach over her tummy. 'Does it hurt?'

'Only when the contractions come.' Anna lived in fear of them. She was breathless with it.

Luca drove steadily through empty streets.

'Your hair's grown,' said Anna, in one of the lovely valleys between crests of agony.

'You've put on weight.'

'Don't make me laugh,' smiled Anna. She crawled backwards up the seat as a wave hit. 'I'm so frightened,' she whispered.

'No need. Happens every day.' Luca put his foot down. The car sped up. 'Nearly there.'

'Why are you here, Luca?'

'I was invited.'

'You were going to your mother's, I heard.'

'I ate lunch with her. Family turned up.'

'I can't quite believe this is happening.'

'You're not the only one, Anna. I only came round to give you a Christmas card.'

Her laugh segued into a howl. Delirious, she wondered if she was hallucinating. *Maybe I'm flirting with an elderly ambulance driver.* 'I'm glad,' she panted, 'you're here.'

She leaned over and clutched his arm. She held on until he pulled up like a bank robber outside the hospital.

Luca dealt with the reception staff. Smiled encouragingly as she was folded into a wheelchair. Stood waving as a hospital porter turned her expertly and began to roll her away down a long dishwater-coloured corridor.

The nurse walking beside her turned. 'Aren't you coming with us, Daddy?'

'Oh, I'm not—'

Anna turned. Her face was hot, red and helpless.

'Yes, I'm coming.' Luca caught up with them and took Anna's hand.

Life looks different flat on your back.

Anna saw circular lights, as if this was an elaborate photo shoot. She saw masked faces. The midwife's clever gaze. The anaesthetist's glasses. Luca's anxious eyes.

'OK, Anna, this is your first, oh hang on, no.' The midwife scanned her clipboard. 'Your *second* baby. Bit of a gap, eh?'

Anna nodded. Words had slipped away, along with her sense of time or place. She held Luca's eyes. Him, she recognised. He made sense in a world gone mad with pain.

'Hold on a mo'.' The midwife disappeared.

Anna entertained dayglo fantasies of twins, breech births, record-breaking birth weight.

'It's all OK,' said Luca, manfully allowing her to grip his hand as another contraction rolled over her like a lorry.

A man, also masked, bent over her most private parts. 'Yes, absolutely,' he said, and began to give orders.

The room went up a gear. Professionals doing their thing. Anna found another level of panic to descend to. 'Is something wrong? Please, is something wrong?'

'We need to get Baby out,' said the midwife, busy amassing mysterious items on a steel tray.

'Why?' Anna wrung Luca's hand. She was the focus of the room yet nobody made eye contact. 'Luca, why, why?'

'Why a C-section?' He repeated her question, but louder, with force.

An explanation didn't help. Anna had suffered a prolapse of the umbilical cord.

'Is that dangerous?' she squeaked.

'It means the cord has popped out ahead of Baby.' The midwife scribbled something on a clipboard. 'The cord is how Baby gets oxygen, so we have to act fast.'

'Oh no, oh no.' Anna heard somebody – *Me,*

apparently – mouth those words over and over. Memories she'd held at bay, of being in strangers' hands, of losing control of her body, of white-hot suffering, crashed over her.

'Don't you worry,' said the midwife, with the calm of an expert in her element. 'Mr Dooley here has delivered more babies by caesarean than you or I have had hot dinners.'

Bonnie's birth had been slow, arduous, with troughs and highs. This was a sprint. Anna was rolled onto her side, and a cold hard sensation began in her lower back. As if somebody was pressing with all their might.

'Epidural,' said the midwife briskly.

'Man, the size of that needle,' gasped Luca.

Anna held his hand in her fist. He seemed to be urging strength into her, even though his face kept changing colour behind the mask, as blood ran into then rushed out of it. A couple of times he swayed. His blinks became a language. She chose to believe they were saying this would all be over soon. There'd be no oxygen deprivation. She'd have a healthy baby in her arms.

A small curtain was strung across Anna's middle, turning her body into a puppet theatre. A particularly gory puppet theatre; she had no desire to see what was going on beyond the green cotton.

Neither did Luca, if his posture was anything to go by. He cold-shouldered the action, leaning over Anna.

'I feel cold,' said Anna.

'That's good,' said the midwife. 'Can you feel this?'

Anna could indeed feel the touch on her toes. A minute ticked by. All the medical staff in the room were powered down, on standby.

'How about now?'

'I can feel it.'

That was the wrong answer. Twice more Anna was rolled like a rug. Twice more she felt the bite of the needle.

Luca seemed to be suffering with her. She had time to feel for him. 'One second you're knocking on my front door with a Christmas card,' gulped Anna, wondering how awful she must look with her hair smarmed back and her mascara sweated off. 'The next you're in a delivery room witnessing the miracle of birth.'

'Usually at this time on Christmas Day I'm watching an old movie with a Baileys in my hand.'

Anna realised that the pain was absent. She didn't own her body any more, but at least it wasn't hurting. 'I can't imagine you with a Baileys.'

'That bit wasn't true.'

'Really, though, I'm sorry.' Anna was woozy. She had to remind herself where she was. Luca's presence didn't stop being surprising. She'd trapped him into this high-drama event.

He was not immune, it seemed, to the emotion of the moment. Luca's eyes crinkled above the white of the mask. 'Anna, you're making a new life. You clever, clever girl.'

'It was easy,' smiled Anna. *God, I love you*, she thought. Maybe, after all, he could be an uncle for the little Piper about to make an entrance. That wasn't quite enough, but it would keep him near.

'How's it going?' Luca asked over the curtain. 'The oxygen situation . . .?'

'We're waiting for Ms Piper to numb up.' The consultant implied the delay was Anna's fault.

'Can you feel that?' asked the midwife.

Anna was no longer a whole person. From the chest down she was vapour. 'No!' She was triumphant. This was all she could do for her baby right now – be numb. *But I did it!*

Everybody powered up. Purposeful. Bustling.

'Keep Mummy amused.' It was an order, the way the midwife said it.

Luca bent down. 'This is it,' he said. Anna felt him tremble.

A whirring noise suggested a blade of some sort.

Anna hung on harder. 'Amuse me, you bastard, amuse me!'

'I love you,' said Luca. 'That's why I'm here.'

'Am I hallucinating?' asked Anna.

'Josh invited me to Christmas Lunch, said you missed me, and I thought "no way". I didn't want the fuss. The trouble. The complication. But I woke up this morning and realised all I want for Christmas is fuss and trouble and complication.'

'Luca, you don't have to say this stuff.' The bottom half of Anna, if it still existed, was being sawn open. The top half was hearing the man she loved read from a script her heart wouldn't dare to write.

There were clattering noises. Mr Dooley said, 'This may feel a little odd. As if I'm doing the washing-up in your uterus is how some ladies describe it.'

Not this lady. Anna couldn't feel a thing. She heard squelching, muffled slops. 'Luca,' she said, salty tears sliding down her face and into her mouth. 'I love you and I'm sorry and I love you.'

'*I'm* sorry. It's me who's sorry.' Luca the cool, Luca the self-possessed, was no more. This was Luca the gibbering mess. The delivery room had broken him wide open. 'I've tried, but I can't seem to miss you any less, Annie.'

'You have a daughter.' Mr Dooley held up a tiny person. Jazz hands waggling, scrawny legs cycling, this daughter was a pinky blue colour. 'And she's perfect.'

'She's perfect!' Anna was sobbing. 'Did you hear, Luca?'

'I heard, I heard.' Luca's mask was wet.

'Would Daddy like to cut the cord?' asked Mr Dooley.

'He's not—' said Anna.

'I'd love to,' said Luca.

*

The small hospital room, although decorated like a mid-level B&B, was blissful after the theatre. It was the centre of the universe. Anna and her new baby were on a complicated bed with a guard rail and levers and an alarm pull-cord dangling beside it. The baby was across Anna's still numb chest. Keeping her arms around the child was exhausting, but it would have taken the proverbial wild horses to persuade her to let go.

It was evening. The lamplight lit them like an old master, despite the ugly functional furniture. Luca sat by the bed, slumped on a padded chair, staring at the ceiling. 'Have you thought of a name?'

'I thought of loads, but none of them seem right now she's here.' Anna snorted. 'She! She's a she.' She leaned into the swaddled baby. 'You're a she.'

Her daughter looked slightly annoyed. Her eyes barely opened, but when they did they were a muddy blue. She was disgruntled, her movements underwater-slow. She was fascinating. Whether she was ugly or pretty, Anna couldn't tell; she was emphatically herself.

'My second daughter,' said Anna.

'Your second chance,' suggested Luca.

'No. Nothing can be that.' Bonnie, or Carly, was firmly in her own special niche in Anna's mind. 'This girl has no job to do other than be herself.' Thinking of Carly turned all the fuzzy feelings on their heads. 'Luca, you should get home. You look shattered.'

'Do you want me to go?' He sat up, with a hurt look on his face. Luca was vulnerable, as if he'd opened up another layer of himself in the quiet room.

'I want you to do what you want to do.' This was double-talk. Anna carried on. She had a pin to prick her own bubble. 'It was very emotional in there. I won't hold you to anything you said.' She controlled her voice. Sacrifice was nothing new. 'It's not just me now, Luca, it's me and my baby. I can't do casual. So thank you a million times over for getting me across the finishing line, but I don't expect anything more from you.'

'Phew,' said Luca. He stood up, leaned over the bed, spoke slowly and clearly. 'That, by the way, was sarcasm, mama bear. When have you ever heard me say anything I didn't mean? I love you and how could I not love this little one?' He sped up. 'Annie, don't answer now, it's madness talking like this right after you've given birth, but why don't we give it a try? You, me and what's-her-name. I know I'm not her biological father, but who cares? Let's write our own story. Let's plonk a happy ending on it.'

'You don't like children,' said Anna. She had more than one pin.

'I know!' Luca threw up his hands, giggling. 'Except for this one. This one I love.'

Anna gave herself permission to believe him. To lie back on the pillows his love provided. It was too much. She was crying again. 'You came back,' she said. And then she said it again, because she liked the sound of it so much. 'You came back.'

Sleep came. Softly, on tiptoes, it spirited Anna away. Time receded. Night and day didn't matter, they were silly affectations. It was constant dusk in the room. She slept soundly, only beckoned out of her dreams by a peculiar noise.

Was it a dog snuffling? Was it Yeti?

It was her daughter, wriggling and rolling in her transparent plastic crib.

Anna surfaced. The room took shape. Luca, looking decidedly second-hand, reached in and picked up the baby in its white waffled blanket.

'Ouch.' She sat up too quickly, forgetting the neat embroidery on her pubic line.

'Careful,' said a voice.

Anna looked to the other side of the bed, as she stretched out her arms for the baby.

'I had a caesarean and you have to take it easy for a while.' Carly sat on another of those uncomfortable plastic chairs.

Anna stared. She felt a weight in her hands and took the child to her. She looked at Luca, who beamed back.

'I went to the house,' said Carly. 'They told me. Your sister, I think it was.'

'Your aunt.' Anna said it without thinking. 'I mean, sorry.'

'And this,' said Carly, jiggling her knees so that the small sleepy girl on her lap laughed, 'is Holly. She's my daughter.' Carly wavered. Then, as if stepping off a high ledge, she took a deep breath and said, 'Your granddaughter.'

It was a magical Christmas Day after all.

Chapter Sixteen

Lunch at Thea's

Vol-au-vents
Cod baked in foil
Sticky toffee pudding

Everything – but everything – had changed.

The cutlery Thea laid out was old and well handled. Mellowed by years of lunches and dinners, it enhanced the flat's eccentric blend of old-fashioned cosiness and hipster style. She picked up a dessert spoon, felt its weight as it balanced on her finger, then set it down again, just so.

The table looked perfect, even if she did say so herself. Not showy, not styled, yet welcoming and beautiful and thought about. She thought deeply about things, this slender woman with the carefully done nails and the well-cut dress in cornflower blue. She bent down to tweak the clean blanket she'd laid over the cat bed, amused at herself for such Mad Housewife attention to detail. This was not her usual style.

The doorbell rang.

Thea froze. Had she bitten off more than she could chew? Inside these walls she was safe. When that door opened, the world would flood in, dabbing its fingerprints all over her safe place.

An old fear was exhumed; she could lose everything.

Thea looked at the door to the garden. She could open it, race out, hurdle the low fence, leave the bell ringing and the cod in the fridge and the wine unopened. Each guest was a friend, but what would they make of her? Would they find her odd, exotic, alien? Or would they recognise her for what she was?

A quote from a wise old woman popped into her head. 'Your soul never changes,' murmured Thea, taking one last appraising look around as the doorbell repeated itself, churlish this time.

If she'd forgotten anything, it was too late to do a damn thing about it. Thea pushed a strand of hair behind her ear, cleared her throat, gave herself a last searching look in the hall mirror and opened the door.

It was time.

*

Anna brushed her teeth, her sleepy eyes still full of grit. Ivy disagreed with the whole notion of sleeping through the night.

She forgave her. Readily. But she also looked forward, with an almost physical yearning, to the days when Ivy would get with the programme.

Ivy had her father's nose. Small, snub. Her mother's eyes. Expressive, greenish. Yeti's love of snacks.

Yeti regarded Ivy as his. He sat with her. Occasionally *on* her. He licked her cheeks clean. He growled if a stranger dared to approach his ward. The size of a Shetland pony, Yeti was hard on Anna's soft furnishings but gentle with the baby.

A year of Sunday Lunch Clubs had passed since Ivy's theatrical arrival. Anna heard her chuckling to herself in her cot. *If anybody else had cut a crescent-shaped scar across my tummy, I'd hate them forever.* Anna's wound was a badge of love. It was still numb; feeling had never returned to that line on her body. The rest of her, however, was overloaded with feeling. Having a baby had turned her skin inside out. She cried at news bulletins. Felt for the whole world and wanted to heal it.

A year of Sunday Lunch Clubs had meant a total of eighteen get-togethers. High points had included a renewal of Neil and Santi's vows on a yacht in the South of France. The lowest of low points had been a 'special' meal for Anna's parents in a local pub. Her mother had arrived alone, mouthing an excuse about 'Dad's ulcer flaring up again'. They all knew Dad didn't have an ulcer.

Today's New Year's Lunch Club was a fresh start. She thought of Josh, preparing for them all to arrive. She corrected herself. *Thea*. It would be her debut. *Careful with my pronouns!*

The surgery had been harrowing. *Thank God for Sheba*, thought Anna for the hundredth time. She'd moved in temporarily with Josh— *no!* Thea and Dinkie, and had stayed. Her healing touch, her solidity, her high good humour once you got to know her, had made Sheba the essential third member of the trinity.

'We're going to be late.' Anna whisked into her bedroom. 'And it's all your fault,' she said to Ivy, who had, with the sarcastic timing of all babies, fallen fast asleep.

A bird's-eye view of the tree-lined roads around Dinkie's new flat would show various cars trundling towards lunch.

Neil and Santi were in their new minibus. Apparently, two-year-old Paloma merited a minibus. Listening to 'The Wheels on the Bus Go Round and Round' for the thirteenth time that morning, they were ready to let down their hair and hand their daughter over to other, less tired, arms.

In the back of a cab, Maeve dabbed on lipstick. 'Did you like him, Storm?' she asked.

'He's all right.' Storm, head shaved, had shot up in the past year. He looked like a man but spoke like the fourteen-year-old he was. The man Maeve had brought home the night before had not impressed him.

'He's a very very good kisser.'

'Shut. Up. Mother.'

Sam was still running-in the Saab Isabel had picked out for them. She rubbed at a smudge on the dashboard. She asked Sam to remind her to buy 'two little mats to go under our feet'. Life with his new wife involved a lot more cleaning and tidying than Sam had expected. He said things like 'She keeps me on my toes!' and 'No such thing as downtime in our house!' all the while secretly wishing she'd relax and let him eat Pop-Tarts in his pyjamas.

None of that really mattered. Sam loved Isabel's face. He looked forward to watching it grow older. He realised she was talking, said, 'Sorry, darling, what?' and nodded, agreeing that, yes, he really must unblock the waste disposal as soon as they got home.

The camper van had seen better days. It coughed, belching out sooty exhaust as Dylan peered out at the street names, directing his mate at the wheel. He knew it was somewhere around here. 'Who,' he murmured, 'has a *lunch* party the day after New Year's Eve?' Possibly he was still drunk. Tequila tastes better drunk from the navel of an actress/model/whatever, but the hangover is the same. Ivy would cheer him up. Ivy always cheered him up. If the Australia idea came together, he'd miss the next few years of Ivy's development, but she wouldn't mind. He hoped.

'Nearly there!' sang Carly over her shoulder.

Holly fidgeted in her car seat. 'Said that afore.'

Carly smiled to herself. 'Yes, I did, but this time Mummy means it!'

Luca, accepting the cup of excellent coffee his mother handed him, was nowhere near the flat. He was looking out at the river from the big wide window and wondering where Anna and Ivy were right now.

They were on Thea's doorstep. Anna was anxious. Of course she'd seen her brother – *my sister, remember, my sister!* – since the surgeries, but this first day of a new year was to be Thea's real debut. No more androgynous clothes, hair. No more Josh.

The door opened. 'Hi,' said Thea. 'Happy new thingymabob.'

'Oh dear God, you're gorgeous!' said Anna without thinking. She barged in, stood close to Thea, examining her so hard that Thea laughed. 'Your make-up is . . .' Anna was lost for words. 'And your hair is . . .'

'What were you expecting? Ringlets and clown lipstick?'

'No. Yes. I don't know.' Anna, usually so careful to say the right, sensitive thing, was gabbling. 'You look . . .' She found the word. 'You look *right*, Thea.'

'I feel right.' Her big brown doll's eyes wet, Thea swallowed hard. 'Thanks for sticking by me.'

'Quite literally,' said Anna, 'the least I could do.'

Dylan's friend was called Rizzo, and he was staying for lunch. Ivy was kidnapped and cooed over. Dinkie was hugged. A glass of something. A soft seat. Anna breathed out.

The garden flat was roomy, with good 'flow'; a term Anna had learned from the afternoon TV property programmes she watched, Ivy at her breast. Like that day's menu, the differing tastes of the flatmates met and mingled without ever clashing. Josh supplied the ironic twentieth-century furniture and Dinkie supplied the crocheted table mats.

Anna let the spirited conversation splash all around her. She watched Josh. *Thea*. He, *she*, was elegant in the blue dress. Anna had dreaded high heels, or a décolletage. She saw that fear as silly now: Thea had dressed for her core values. They hadn't changed. Whether male or female, Thea's preference was for the stylish, the low-key.

The atmosphere was heightened. Sharpened. Thea unsettled them all. Remembering that this was not simply Josh in a dress, that their brother was now their sister, had disrupted the status quo. Terrified of saying the wrong thing, they elected to say very little about Thea's appearance. As if people changing gender was neither here nor there.

There had been no deeply personal grilling, no questions

about exactly what the operation entailed. Maeve had almost 'gone there', but the others held her back. Josh was a human being, they said, not public property.

It was newbie Rizzo who broke the spell. 'She's a *dude*?' he yelped to a whispered comment from Dylan.

Conversation stopped abruptly.

Thea, on the threshold of the room with a platter in her hands, stood stock-still. She looked lost, as if deciding whether to turn and run.

'She was a dude,' said Neil, stepping over to take a vol-au-vent from the platter. 'Now she's a dudess.'

'No such word,' said Anna, her tone playful.

Rizzo looked at the floor.

The conversation staggered back to its feet, and Thea made a round of the room with the hors d'oeuvres. 'Dinkie made them,' he said encouragingly.

'You OK?' whispered Anna as she bent down to let her take a vol-au-vent.

Thea looked her straight in the eye. 'I can handle it,' she said.

There had been a period of something close to mourning after Josh announced his plans to change gender. As if they all separately grieved for the loss of their brother. Neil had struggled with the concept, admitting his confusion to Anna in late-night calls.

She'd advised and encouraged; that came easily to her.

Taking her own advice had been harder. Particularly when Josh had dropped out of sight, avoiding family, ducking out of every Sunday Lunch Club.

It had been Dinkie's job to give them updates. She witnessed his anxiety before the operations, the long hours in the bathroom staring at his reflection. Dinkie had been brisk, reminding everybody that to make an omelette you needed to break eggs.

That image – of Josh as a fragile, cracked egg – had almost undone Anna.

She'd visited him as he recuperated in his new bedroom. Dinkie had warned that he was in almost constant pain as nerve endings reconnected. There were setbacks – an infection, exhaustion caused by the super-strong medication – but Thea had emerged, as if from a chrysalis.

Watching her now, as she made the rounds of the room, Anna papered over memories of the melancholia that had swamped Thea as she recovered. The past was done with; there were new battles to fight. And today Thea was fighting them with humour and elegance and heart.

On the rug, Dylan squatted to say 'All right?' to Ivy. When she replied with 'Dada?' he sprang up as if scalded.

'Don't panic,' laughed Anna. 'She says that to all men. And even some inanimate objects.'

'She's a crazy one, isn't she?' Dylan seemed wary of touching his offspring. *There's time*, thought Anna to herself. If

Dylan ever came back from Australia, he had the rest of his life to bond with Ivy. 'Come here, you,' said Anna, as Holly dashed past.

The little girl, a guarded child, stopped and stuck her thumb in her mouth. 'Granna,' she said. 'You sewed Mummy's handbag.'

Carly, bringing up the rear, said, 'Clever Granna made everybody's handbag.' There had been an Artem gift under the tree for everybody that year; Carly's bold fuchsia bag was slung across her body. 'Do you want me to bring you some nibbles, Anna?'

'You're an angel.' Anna settled back. She wasn't 'Mum'. That title belonged to the mild, canny woman who had adopted Bonnie, renamed her Carly, and brought her up with scant money but great tenderness. A tentative friendship of sorts had been struck between Anna and Carly's adoptive parents, but it was flimsy.

'Uncle Thea,' said Holly, eliciting a guffaw from Neil, and nervous laughter from the others. 'What?' demanded Holly, fuming. She was a precocious child; teasing her was dangerous.

Santi swept her up, twirled her around until, annoyance forgotten, she began to cackle. Holly was still entranced with her new uncles and aunts and cousins.

As Anna made room on the sofa for Carly to sit beside her – they tended to stick together at Sunday Lunch

Clubs – she covertly watched 'Uncle Thea'. She hadn't quite got the hang of standing like a woman; there was something subtly male about her posture. *It'll come*, thought Anna.

Thea found her eye and made her way over. Perching on the arm of the sofa, she bent down to whisper, 'Anna, tell me, do I pass?'

'As a woman?'

'Yes.'

'You do.' Close up, Thea was beautiful in much the same way Josh had been handsome. Ethereal. Fine. 'We're all a bit stunned. It's such a big change.'

'I'm still me.'

'And we're still us. We'll catch up with you.' A few months ago, Anna had passed on an old swimsuit to Thea. She'd changed her mind a dozen times, then stuffed it into a carrier bag and handed it over. The tears in response had astounded her; it wasn't just an M&S swimsuit – it was acceptance.

Carly leaned over. 'Love the dress. I couldn't wear something like that. But you carry it off.'

Thea stuttered her thanks. 'Where's your other half today?'

'Manning the bar. He sends his best.'

There had been relief when Carly's husband didn't arrive. He was a trifle Neanderthal about gender reassignment; Anna wondered if Carly had engineered his absence. *She's a sensitive soul, my daughter.* Anna still felt a swell around her heart when she described Carly in that way. Pride. Poignancy. A deep gratitude for second chances.

The pile of newspapers had been lugged over to The Intrepid Fox. As a form of proof. The front pages – all twenty-five of them – were framed and hung in formation in the main bar. It was a new tradition; Anna would continue to buy a newspaper on the eleventh of November every year. No more plodding up to the attic with them; she'd put them into Carly's hands.

Her older daughter was no longer a stranger, but there were aspects of Carly that felt foreign, *other*. They were building an emotional shorthand, the best ways to navigate around each other. Their relationship was like no other – it gave Anna intense joy to be near Carly, and disquiet when Carly said or did something that dismayed her. It was complicated. Disappointing. Joyful. It was beyond precious.

'Do you think,' whispered Carly, as Thea moved away, 'that she'll ever have, you know, a *relationship*?'

'Not sure.' Anna had given it a great deal of thought. 'But she's changed gender not personality, and Josh never talked about his sex life, so Thea probably won't either.'

'I'll geddit!' shouted Holly when the doorbell sounded.

'No you don't!' Sam hoisted her into his arms as he opened the door. He didn't look old enough to be the child's grandfather; he grew younger as he grew happier. 'Luca, in you come, mate,' he said.

'I'm late, I know, I'm sorry, Mum sends her love.' Luca did the rounds, double-kissing everybody, even Storm, who mimed throwing up. 'For you, your highness,' he said, flourishing a bunch of white roses for Dinkie.

'He's a charmer,' said Dinkie.

Yes, he is. Anna watched him spread warmth, bundled up in his chunky cardigan, hair wild, three days of stubble carpeting his chin. He winked at her, and she felt a tickle of lust dignified by the intimacy of co-parenting.

In every way that mattered, Luca was father to Ivy.

The emergency C-section had kept Anna in hospital for three days. Luca had lain on her bed like a Labrador for most of that time, holding Ivy, feeding Ivy, gazing at Ivy and seeing things in her face that delighted him.

Dylan had visited, white as a sheet, inspecting the baby from a safe distance as if she might explode. Luca had shown off, nonchalantly changing Ivy's nappy and chatting knowingly about her birth weight.

He had been proprietorial about Ivy. About Anna, for that matter; chiding her if she picked up anything heavier than a tray. And when Anna and Ivy went home, he went with them.

And kind of stayed, thought Anna. There'd been no formal powwow about the future. They didn't need one. It seemed obvious. His lack of doubt about fatherhood had counter-balanced Anna's misgivings about being a mother.

She hadn't felt like a natural. There had been panic when Ivy cried, something like despair when the child didn't take to her breast. Slowly, she gained confidence. She mimicked Carly's insouciance with Holly, and Luca's ease with Ivy. Eventually it clicked. She felt at peace, as if the last piece of her jigsaw was Ivy-shaped.

'So, Rizzo,' Anna heard Maeve say behind her. 'What do you do exactly?'

It was her flirting voice. Anna saw Neil throw his hands in the air, but she silently applauded her sister. Maeve kept her choppy craft afloat; Anna criticised less these days. There was more to life than being sensible. *I learned so many lessons while Ivy was in my tummy.*

'Come on, everybody, to the table,' said Thea. She'd added an apron to her outfit; a Stepford Wives touch which amused Anna. 'To the actual real proper dining table,' she added.

The mahogany table had been extended, but still wasn't quite big enough. Maeve helped out by sitting on Rizzo's lap.

'Is Ivy all right over on the sofa?' asked Dinkie, utilising her great-grandmotherly right to poke her flat little nose in everywhere.

The baby slept against Yeti, who would not move a muscle until Ivy woke up. He was too thick to understand the word 'dinner' but he knew all about love and loyalty. Anna wondered how she'd ever got along without him. Dinkie's cat had taken a short sabbatical; she'd reappear when Yeti went home.

As cutlery was taken up, and lips were smacked, and appreciative noises made about the cod, Dinkie continued to gaze at Ivy. 'Would you look at her hair, the way it curls over her forehead. That's like mine. She gets that from me, the little dote. Takes after her great-grandma, she does, bless her.'

Anna smiled. 'She does,' she agreed. She saw Neil purse his lips and stab his fish with his fork.

'Doesn't she, Sheba?' Dinkie turned to her. 'Doesn't Ivy take after me?'

'She don't talk as much,' said Sheba.

'Ha!' barked Luca.

Sheba had been absorbed into the family, and now they loved her not only for the quiet kindness with which she cared for Dinkie, but for her utter lack of patience with pretension. She had famously told Josh to save his money and stuff socks down his bra.

'Paloma, no,' said Sheba, as the two-year-old raced around the table, whooping. 'Sit down. Be a good girl.' Sheba was strict; Paloma was obstinate. There was a face-off.

'Paloma has my stubbornness.' Dinkie preened herself. 'I see a lot of meself in her.'

'Only the good bits, presumably,' said Maeve, feed-ing Rizzo.

'She'll show youse all, one day.' Dinkie narrowed her eyes at the child. 'Paloma has spirit.'

Anna checked on Neil. His mouth hung open. It opened even more when Dinkie told Dylan's friend, 'We're a very modern family, Rizzo. Oh yes. Sure, one of me granddaugh-ters used to be me grandson – look at him, doesn't he make a pretty woman, puts me in mind of Audrey Hepburn – and me other grandson is married to a fella. I can imagine the nuns who educated me whirring round in their graves, but Pipers don't follow the rules. We'd rather be happy.' She squealed as Neil rushed round to her seat and bear-hugged her. 'Jaysus, Neil, have you gone doolally tap, love?'

Neil's own prejudices had been blown to pieces; Dinkie's mind wasn't closed. It was as open as her heart.

Over dessert, after copious compliments for Thea's cooking, Neil asked Storm that standard question adults ask children.

'So, Storm, you're fourteen now. Time to knuckle down and study. What do you want to be when you grow up?'

'Normal.'

Carly hooted. 'Good luck with that in this family!'

The casual reference to 'this family' thrilled Anna. For the first time she understood the expression 'warm the cock-les of your heart'; she didn't know what cockles were, but her own were glowing. There had been so many potholes on Anna and Carly's road to this special Sunday Lunch Club (the others didn't yet know just how special it was). If Carly hadn't kept Alan Piper's vile note. If she hadn't returned it to Anna. If Anna hadn't read it. If Carly hadn't found the courage to swallow her bitterness and sit quietly with Anna in the hospital room and hear the story of her conception and birth from the only woman qualified to tell it.

We got through it all, thought Anna, Ivy on her lap, and Carly and Holly opposite. She fancied she saw similarities between the two little girls, but there was no need for such proofs. Their bond was one of love, not mere blood. Anna would never stop being grateful that Carly had believed her, given her a chance, and found the bravery to step into a tight circle such as this. *My Bonnie is home*, she thought.

Luca raised his glass to her. He could still read her mind. A commitment had been made in the hospital, when Anna had become a mother and a grandmother all at once, and Luca had declared that 'for some reason', he found that incredibly sexy.

'Actually,' he had added, 'everything you do is incredibly sexy.'

He wasn't to know that Anna, like most brand-new mothers, was lying there, aching, vowing never to have sex again. She'd jettisoned that resolution.

They fought a lot. This surprised them both. During

the pre-Ivy portion of their affair they'd got along like the proverbial house on fire. Luca suggested that their lack of experience in shouting insults at each other had helped them break up after their first real row.

Anna had asked him, secure one night in his arms, why he had stayed away.

'Your delivery date got nearer and nearer. I couldn't get involved with the pregnancy because you were so adamant about the baby being yours, and yours alone.'

'That was because I didn't want to scare you.' Anna had twisted to see his face in the dark. 'I didn't want to burden you when we were still such a new thing.'

'So I didn't get involved because I thought you didn't want me to get involved.'

'And I didn't involve you because I thought you wouldn't want to be involved.'

They had looked back at their slightly younger selves with affectionate pity.

'All I wanted,' Luca said, 'was to be as involved as possible. Roll up my sleeves. Get my hands dirty.'

Now, at lunch, they regarded each other across the table. No words were needed. They were in sync. No matter how much Anna and Luca argued about who'd forgotten to buy teabags, or whose turn it was to get up in the middle of the night with Ivy.

Storm had a question, as he scraped the last of the sticky

toffee pudding from his bowl. 'Auntie Anna, did you decide on Ivy as a name because she was born on Christmas Day?'

'Yes,' said Anna. 'And because it goes so well with Holly.'

'Oh yeah.' Storm, who aced his maths exams, was slow on the uptake with family facts. 'Isn't . . .' He frowned. 'Hang on. Ivy is Holly's aunt? And she's Carly's sister?'

'Half-sister.' It was Carly who corrected him. She added, 'But we don't do anything by halves here, do we?'

All could agree on that.

Thea sank into her chair with such a huff of relief that they all turned to look at her. Many of them saw her still as a him. Thea said, 'You've all been polite. Nobody's sniggered. I know this isn't easy for you to get your heads around, but I have to ask: Do I make a halfway decent woman?'

'Yes.' They all said it in unison. It was true. Thea was no caricature.

'Although . . .' said Maeve.

'Yeah . . .' Thea shrank in her skin.

'Lose the earrings, babe. Hoops are not you.'

Coffees were handed out. Bottoms moved from table to easy chairs. Holly counted Ivy's fingers over and over. Sheba handed round chin chins, a Nigerian cookie flavoured with nutmeg.

'Don't take them all!' Anna was wise to Maeve.

'So many calories,' said Isabel.

'And every one of them is delicious.' Sam took two.

Hearing praise for the food Sheba cooked from her mother's recipes turned her luminous. 'Take another,' she said to Santi, her most vocal fan.

'I shouldn't . . .' Santi took another, and wandered off to check on Paloma, who was napping in Thea's bedroom.

Neil nudged Anna. 'My old man's filled out a bit,' he said.

It was true. Santi was heavier around the middle. 'Do you still love him despite that?'

'Don't be ridiculous.' Neil was insulted. 'It doesn't make a bit of difference.'

'Now you know how it feels to be accused of that. You needed convincing that Santi wasn't with you for your money.'

'Hoist by my own petard.'

'Sounds painful.'

'Me and Santi, we're in it for the long haul. Like you and Luca. With some people, you know. They come together and it works.'

'That's . . . that's verging on mushy, Neil.'

Neil patted the cushion beside him as Sheba passed again with a fresh plate of chin chins. 'Sit, darling,' he said. 'Tell us how things *really* are.'

Sheba sat, darting looks at the kitchen door, beyond which Dinkie could be heard overseeing Storm's reluctant washing of the dishes. 'A little better,' she said, in her liquid accent. 'She has been sleeping well. The new medicine helps with the nausea.'

'Any more of those light-headed spells?' Anna was anxious. Dinkie's health was a low-level constant, like a car alarm going off in another street. At some point, she knew, it would become too loud to ignore. The doctors had given her less than a year. Dinkie was on borrowed time. *We all are*, thought Anna. 'How's her appetite?'

Sheba whispered a precis of the last few days. 'She was tired after Christmas Day with the family, of course, but she has been in great spirits.'

'And she has no idea?' pressed Neil.

'As far as your grandmother is concerned, she will live to a hundred and twenty,' said Sheba. She sighed. A throaty sound, filled with sadness. 'I wish to God she could.'

The decision not to let Dinkie know had been unanimous. It had been a mistake to keep her in the dark about Josh's transition, but this felt right. They would act normal until it was no longer possible; until then Dinkie would believe that the treatment had zapped the misbehaving cells in her body.

Anna put her hand over Sheba's. Her gratitude to this unassuming, sterling woman was boundless. 'I don't know what we'd do without you,' she said.

'Whisht.' Sheba had caught Dinkie's Irish slang. 'Joshthea is doing as much as me.' She had such trouble remembering to use Josh's new name that she had coined a hybrid. 'He is strong. Made of iron.'

'We used to treat him like a delicate flower.' Anna had reappraised her brother just as he transformed into her sister. There was no special treatment, no excuses.

'Come on.' Luca slapped his thighs. 'No long faces, ladies, or the old girl'll guess.'

Anna stretched her lips into a smile. The notion of a Dinkie-less world was too enormous to grasp at once. She kept catching sight of its bulk from different angles. So much would change. So much would be lost. *But she's still here!* Anna reminded herself. Better to make the most of Dinkie in the here and now than to fret about the future.

Holly was yawning. Carly began to make noises about getting back to her husband. She was reluctant; Anna smelled trouble there but would wait for Carly to bring it up. She didn't have the right to prod and pry, not yet.

Anna winked at Luca. He returned the wink – rather more skilfully; Anna's winks were very lopsided – and bent to take Ivy from her nest against Yeti's side. 'Are we all here?' He looked around. 'Yup, it seems so. We have an announcement to make.'

'You're getting married!' shrieked Maeve.

'No, no,' laughed Luca. 'White doesn't really suit Anna, so that's not happening. I'll let her tell you.'

He reached out his hand to pull Anna up from the sofa. They stood together, a solid unit, a happy trio.

'We waited until we were all together to let you know that ...' Anna looked over at Dylan, smiled at him. 'With the approval of Ivy's biological father, Luca has now formally adopted Ivy.' Anna gulped out her new favourite words. 'We're now officially Mummy and Daddy.'

Nobody wanted to leave. It was the start of a new year, three hundred and sixty-five days for them all to ruin or enhance. The dusk was a cocoon, a haven for them all where problems were on hold.

'I knew,' said Maeve, smug, 'Luca was going to adopt Ivy. I *knew*.'

'For the last time, you are *not* psychic, darling,' said Neil.

Or is she? Anna recalled the day Maeve had 'seen' a handwritten letter in a dream.

'I'm a daddy,' Luca kept saying. He jiggled Ivy in the 100% acrylic hoodie Dinkie had knitted for her. 'To be precise, I'm *your* daddy.'

'Best job in the world,' said Neil, who seemed to have received all his backdated sentimentality at once.

'Give her here to me,' said Dinkie, in that tone that demanded immediate and complete obedience. 'And Paloma. I want a snap of me with the little ones.' She turned her head, found Holly over by the window, and called her over. 'Come here, darlin'. You're the chick that was born outside the henhouse, but you're here now, and you're safe. Like your mammy, there.'

Anna saw Carly's secret smile.

A Polaroid was taken. Dinkie showed it to the children, who clung to her, enjoying her smell of face powder and lily-of-the-valley perfume.

A posse was formed to check out and comment on the paint colours that Sheba had tested out on her bedroom wall. Dinkie was left in her chair with the three small girls around her. She craned her neck to see Maeve kissing Rizzo in the kitchen. 'Ahem!' she called, and Maeve reached out to shut the door with a clunk. 'Good. It's just us girls.'

Holly had fallen asleep across Dinkie's lap. Her mouth hung open. Paloma, in the crook of her great-grandmother's arm, stared up at her with guileless eyes. At her feet, Ivy wiggled on the rug.

Dinkie's voice was low, the voice she used for fairy tales. 'None of youse will take this in, but I want to tell youse anyway. I spoil you, don't I? Why d'you think that is? Partly 'cos I love you all, obviously. Partly 'cos I won't always be here to spoil you. The grown-ups can't cope with me knowing. They think I'm a frail old lady when really I'm tough as old boots. Somebody has to look after that crew, so I'm passing the baton on to you ladies. When you know the end is near, you grab at everything good. Holding youse like this, or smelling Anna's hair, or hearing J— *Thea* sing along to the radio first thing in the morning. You grab on and you try to keep hold of it, 'cos as you get nearer and nearer to the end it all happens too fast. This moment is like a gold bar. It's a five-course meal. A trip to Venice. You're asleep, Holly, and youse other two are too tiny to understand, but you'll remember what I'm saying without realising. It's a seed that'll grow inside you. You know you're loved, girls, and you can do anything when you're loved. No crying over me, now. Leave that to the silly adults. You and I know a soul isn't perishable. You can't squash it or hurt it, or fold it up. My soul will carry on loving you, and as long as you three remember me, I won't die. I'll live for as long as I matter.'

At the sitting room door, having crept back to get her handbag, Anna hung her head.

Dinkie knows.

Anna crept back to the stairs, and stamped her feet. Giving Dinkie notice, so the old lady was composed when she joined her.

The others tumbled in, disagreeing about whether Desert Peony or Morning Sun was the better shade for Sheba's boudoir. Anna watched them settle, fidget, chatter. She saw Maeve coming out of the kitchen with her top on back to front. She saw Luca drawn to Ivy as if the baby were a magnet.

My premonition was right about the big love in store for me.

Anna had been wrong that it was just about Luca. She'd been wrong that it was just for Ivy.

The big love had been under her nose all along, around the table of the Sunday Lunch Club.

Acknowledgements

If it takes a village to raise a child, then it takes a small town to make a book.

In my town I'm lucky enough to have Jo Dickinson, an editor of infinite patience and delicacy, whose friendship I value almost as much as her expertise. Nothing happens in my professional life without the powerhouse Sara-Jade Virtue; she's just as important and appreciated in my private life. Emma Capron surely keeps a little padded room to scream in, but she shows me nothing but good cheer and understanding when I am late with, well, this page for example. Thank you Emma. And thank you Justine Gold, and thank you Gemma Conley-Smith.

The usual cheerleaders, who buck me up no end when I'm writing and remind me to believe, must all be thanked again and again. In no particular order, but jumbled up cosily together are Kate Haldane, Janet Cosier, Kate Furnivall, Penny Killick, Chris Manby, Katia Gregor, James Little, Victoria Routledge, Jane Allan and Jen Strachan.

Particular thanks to Sonia Lopez-Freire, for her help with the Spanish character in this book.

Lastly, my daughter Niamh, who should be at 'that difficult age' but who gives me time and space to write. Thank you, sweetiepie.

THESE DAYS OF OURS

JULIET ASHTON

Kate and Becca aren't just cousins, they're best friends. Growing up together, they've shared all the milestones – childhood parties, eighteenth birthdays and now a double wedding day.

Kate and Charlie were meant to be. That's what everybody said. So why have things turned out so differently?

Best friends are forever, and true love always finds a way ... Doesn't it?

'Warm, witty and surprising'
Louise Candlish

'A delicious story of love and loss that had me utterly entranced'
Kate Furnivall

AVAILABLE NOW IN
PAPERBACK AND EBOOK

THE WOMAN AT NUMBER 24

JULIET ASHTON

Welcome to number 24, a Georgian villa in West London that is home to five separate families and five very different lives.

Up in the eaves, Sarah finds that recovering from a nasty divorce is even more heartbreaking when your ex-husband lives one floor beneath you with his new wife. Their happiness floats up through the floorboards, taunting her. A child psychologist, Sarah has picked up great sadness from the little girl, Una, who lives with her careworn mother three floors below, but is Sarah emotionally equipped to reach out?

Spring brings a new couple to number 24. Jane and Tom's zest for life revives the flagging house, and Sarah can't deny the instant attraction to handsome Tom. Having seen at first-hand what infidelity does to people, she'll never act on it... but the air fizzes with potential.

The sunshine doesn't reach every corner of number 24, however. Elderly Mavis, tucked away in the basement, has kept the world at bay for decades. She's about to find out that she can't hide forever...

Love, rivalry and secrets ... all under one roof.

AVAILABLE NOW IN
PAPERBACK AND EBOOK